I0744426

Duchess' Throne

(Book 2 of the Ashridge Duology)

Kimberly M. Ringer

Kimberly M. Ringer

Copyright © 2021

KIMBERLY M. RINGER

All rights reserved. Printed in the United States of America. Copyrighted property of the author. No part of this book may be used or reproduced, distributed or transmitted in any form in any manner whatsoever without the written permission of author except in the case of brief quotations embodied in critical articles and reviews. The characters, names, businesses, organizations, places, events and incidents portrayed in this book are fictitious and of the author's imagination. Any similarity to real events or persons, living or dead, is coincidental and not intended by the author.

Dedication and Thank You

Tara (T.S. Tappin): TARTA! That is really all that needs to be said, but you are the essence of what is the Hype Girl Squad. Thank you for always being there and pulling my head from the back end so many times I have lost count.

Elisabeth (Elisabeth Garner): You know what you did. Thank you for helping me make "that scene" so much more painful and rewarding at the end.

Tara & Elisabeth: I don't know what I would have done without you two over the last year. Your aggressive love and encouragement has been priceless. I appreciate you two more than I can ever express. All I can say is "Yeah, and?" and "I'm not sorry." Hype Girls forever. I love you so freaking much.

Kate (K. Elle Morrison): Thank you for helping me better describe 'eye juice.' Thank you for all the late night chit chats, the encouragements, and being such an amazing person.

Auntie Hen (Mama Hen): Your love and support mean the world to me. Your enthusiasm for my books brings a smile to my face every time. You are a shining light in the book community. We love you so freaking much.

Kel and Bean: Thank you for letting me hide in my office and get things done. I appreciate all the years you have supported me through living in the Nalrin World. **BOOP SNOOT!**

Content Considerations

Murder

Blood

Homophobia
(not within main cast)

Graphic Violence

Coercion

Threats

BDSM

Hostage Situation

Explicit Sex Scenes

Adoption

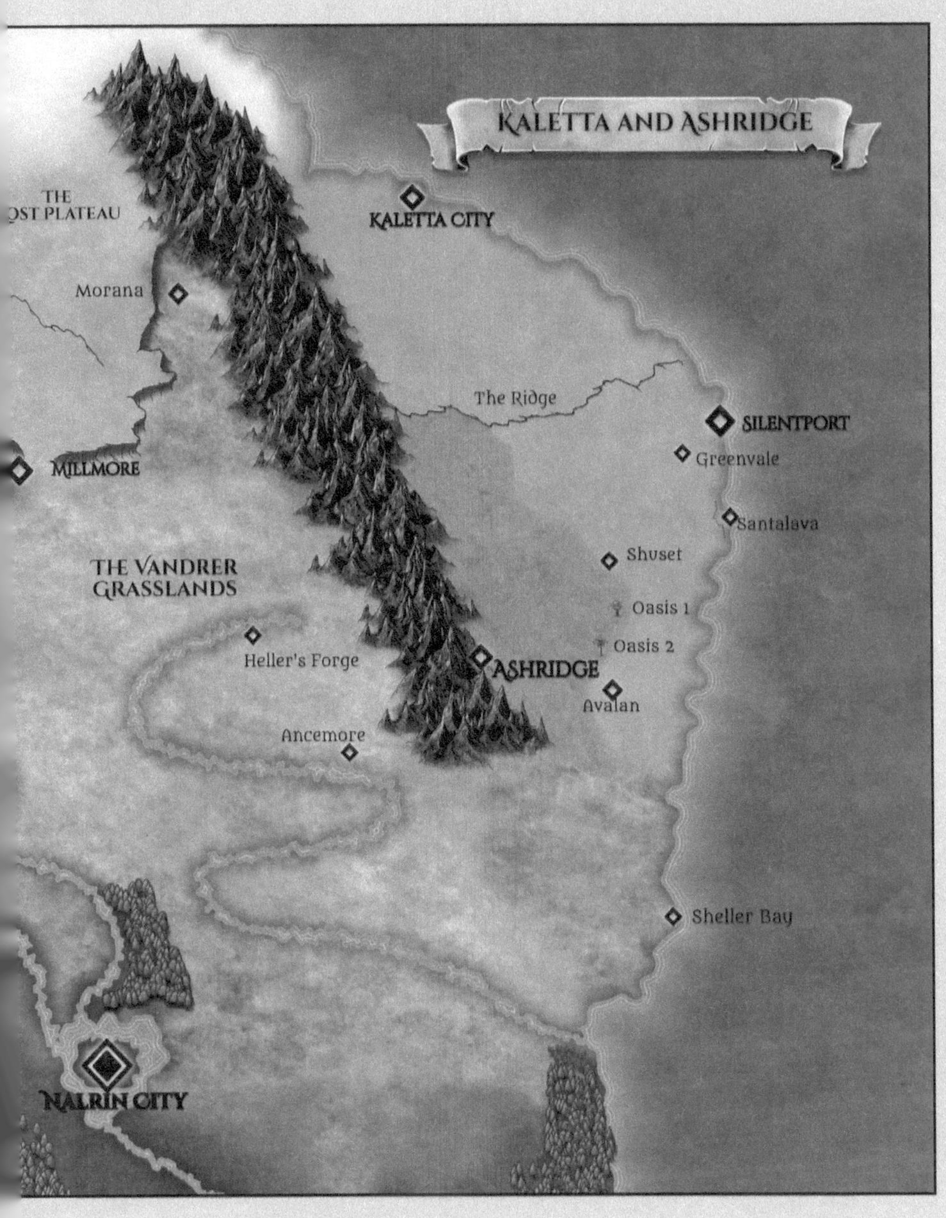

KALETTA AND ASHRIDGE
THE
OST PLATEAU
KALETTA CITY
Morana
The Ridge
SILENTPORT
Greenvale
MILLMORE
Santalava
Shuset
THE VANDRER
GRASSLANDS
Oasis 1
Oasis 2
Heller's Forge
ASHRIDGE
Avalan
Ancemore
Sheller Bay
NALRIN CITY

CONTENTS

Ashridge – Kaletta Territory Agreement	1
1. Aiden	11
2. Jessika	20
3. Jessika	27
4. Aiden	36
5. Jessika	41
6. Aiden	51
7. Aiden	55
8. Jessika	60
9. Jessika	68
10. Jessika	72
11. Jessika	76
12. Aiden	83
13. Jessika	90
14. Aiden	95
15. Aiden	100
16. Jayden	109

17. Aiden ... 121

18. Aiden ... 128

19. Jayden ... 136

20. Jayden ... 143

21. Jessika ... 147

22. Aiden ... 155

23. Jessika ... 163

24. Jessika ... 172

25. Aiden ... 179

26. Jessika ... 191

27. Jessika ... 204

28. Aiden ... 213

29. Aiden ... 223

30. Jessika ... 230

31. Jessika ... 237

32. Jessika ... 246

33. Jayden ... 251

34. Jayden ... 260

35. Jayden ... 266

36. Aiden ... 271

37. Jessika ... 279

38. Jessika ... 284

39.	Aiden	291
40.	Aiden	295
41.	Jessika	302
42.	Jayden	307
43.	Aiden	315
44.	Jessika	319
45.	Jessika	323
46.	Aiden	329
47.	Jessika	340
48.	Jessika	349
49.	Aiden	354
50.	Jessika	357
51.	Jayden	362
About the Author		371
Books Also By Kimberly M. Ringer		373

THE ASHRIDGE - KALETTA TERRITORY AGREEMENT

SIGNATORIES:

Grand Duchess Bonita Chantel Valenti

Grand Lord of Kaletta

Duchess Jessica Petra Valenti

Lord Jayden Parahov

Ashridge - Kaletta Territory Agreement

We, Lord Jayden Panahov, Lord of Kaletta, and Jessika Petra Valenti, Duchess of Ashridge, under the command of the Crown of Ashridge and Lord of Kaletta, agree to take each other as marriage partners on the understanding that this contract shall regulate our relationship and duties to their respective territories.

Marriage is a contract or agreement between two territories for the hand of Duchess Jessika Petra Valenti to be given to Lord Jayden Panahov, in exchange for certain services and commitments. We commit ourselves to constantly striving to ensure that the well-being of both territories will always come before ourselves, as is the duty of rulers.

This contract is for the betterment of the Ashridge Kingdom and Kaletta Realm.

We acknowledge the basic equality of all people, in accordance with the laws of Ashridge and Kaletta territories, and to each other insofar as our respective rights and responsibilities in our marriage are concerned. We commit ourselves to striving for a marriage characterized by mutual respect, appreciation, support, cooperation, and loyalty between the territories.

Marriage will involve the joining of two individuals with the purpose of forming a partnership with interdependence and a mutually beneficial relationship where each retain individual control over their respective territory. Any heirs will be governed by the below positions in regard to territory status.

We commit ourselves to a relationship which contains openness, trust, strong communication, and mutual consultation. We will discuss personal matters by taking into consideration, among others, the personal, social, and economic consequences.

We understand marriage as being a relationship that should be free from abuse of an emotional, physical, or verbal nature. We therefore undertake to refrain totally from abusive behavior and speech toward each other, and to create an environment within which all members of our family will feel safe. We agree to identify goals and priorities and strive toward achieving these. Vicars of The Five Angels shall be retrieved to solve any interrelationship issues. Any assigned Vernadali to either Duchess or Lord will be required to attend and help facilitate correction of behaviors.

Our daily interactions with each other will be guided in the spirit of fairness, dignity, and justice as deemed by The Five Angels. We will strive to ensure that our interactions with each other are full of compassion, mutual respect, and courtesy, with free and clear communication at all times, and with the humility and the courage to admit mistakes and learn from them.

RIGHTS AND RESPONSIBILITIES

Financial responsibilities will be determined and shared in a way that is mutually agreeable and equitable for the territories.

RULING RESPONSIBILITIES

All overseeing of the territories will be split between the Ashridge Kingdom and the Kaletta Realm. Duchess and Lord may oversee separately, but when overseeing together, weighted ruling decision will be given to the home territory.

RESPECT

We will endeavor to respect each other's humanity, intelligence, and family. We will thus give due and serious consideration to the words and actions of each other and other members of our family. Neither of us will have any right—nor will resort—to physically, mentally, or psychologically abusing the other, no matter what justification or rationalization could be given for such action.

SEXUAL RELATIONS

Sexual relations will be consensual at all times and will, like all other relations in the marriage, be based on mutual trust and respect. Lord Jayden Pavahov and Duchess Jessika Petra Valenti agree that heirs will be provided within the first five years of the marriage. If no heir is produced, medical intervention may be petitioned for assistance in the production of an heir.

If no male heir is produced within the first ten years, Ashridge will allow Kaletta to have sexual relations outside of the marriage for the production of a male heir.

Consorts

Consorts must be agreed upon by the other. Lord Jayden Pavahov will be permitted no more than five (5) consorts. Duchess Jessika Petra Valenti shall not exceed one (1) consort. Should either decide to have a consort without the express written approval of the other, it shall be grounds for divorce.

Any being produced by Ashridge or Kaletta consorts, will be deemed heirs to the throne should no heir be produced within the first thirty (30) years of marriage or after all full-blooded heirs have been exhausted.

Family obligations

As a result of our marriage, the betterment of both territories will be a priority. All relations and oversight of the other's family will not be dictated by the non-ruling territory.

Heirs

Duchess Jessika Petra Valenti accepts the responsibility for feeding of any produced heirs. During this period, Lord Jayden Panahov will solely be responsible for the material maintenance of the family and household. Delegation to a nanny or other house staff may be given for the daily well-being of any heirs, should either be required to handle matters of the kingdom or realm.

Heirs will, and may, inherit both territories upon the deaths of Lord Jayden Pavahov and Duchess Jessika Petra Valenti. Said heir may take the crown one year after obtaining their respective Maltal. Shall the heir not be of crowning age, all ruling and oversight will be given to the Empress Clarice of the House of Heros, or the Empress' designee.

Territory Requirements

The Ashridge Kingdom agrees to the following:

- Provide heirs to the Kaletta Realm; and

- Provide fuel resources for medical advancements within the Kaletta Realm.

The Kaletta Realm agrees to the following:

- Providing military support in time of war;

- Provision of goods and resources for the betterment of the people of Ashridge:

  - Goods: Include but are not limited to, fish, cotton, water, meats, vegetables, grain, minerals, lumber;

  - Resources: Include, but are not limited to, personnel for the rebuilding of cities, personnel for transportation of goods across the two territories;

- Provide financial assistance in the rebuilding of Ashridge; and

- Provide material assistance in the preservation of the natural lands.

MARRIAGE CEREMONY

- Marriage ceremony must occur in Ashridge Capital;

- Marriage ceremony cannot occur within ninety (90) days of the death of either the Grand Duchess or the Grand Lord;

- Marriage ceremony cannot occur within forty-five (45) days of an immediate family member's death;

- No stand-ins or substitutions. If either the Lord Jayden Panhov or Duchess Jessika Petra Valenti are sent to The Five Angels, or lie in state to be sent to The Five Angels, or their heart ceases to beat for more than sixty-one (61) seconds of time, this contract becomes null and void;

- If either party deserts or abandons with four months of no contact, this contract becomes null and void. No contact will be determined by the absence of written correspondence, in person discussions, or discussions via LightCall system; and

- If war is declared by either territory, all time frames are declared null and void.

PERMANENT SEPARATION

DISPUTE RESOLUTION PROCEDURES AND THE INITIATION OF SEPARATION PROCEEDINGS

Before the termination of the marriage, counseling must be completed for a minimum of three (3) months. Should counseling not help to resolve the dispute, before either decide to initiate permanent separation proceedings, there shall be a final effort to save the marriage by undergoing a trial separation for a period of three months, with zero communication for the first 30 days. If, however, after this time, the marriage still cannot be healed, then either may submit a declaration for divorce to the head of the dimension.

Either shall have an equal right to submit divorce declarations and these will be governed in accordance with the terms stipulated in this contract.

GROUNDS FOR IMMEDIATE SEPARATION

- Desertion of family life inexcusably or absence without contact with the family for four continuous months would be grounds for seeking a separation. Head of the dimension shall immediately sign documents upon arrival of a declaration;

- Relationship, either with consent or not, with a being that would not produce heirs to Kaletta;

- Relationship without the consent of the other,

in accordance with the consort portion of this agreement; and

- An act that would have war declared on one of the two territories, without the express approval of both Ashridge and Kaletta.

Custody of heirs that might result from this marriage shall be determined according to the heir's best interests. Should the custody of heirs be contested, the matter shall be referred for dispute resolution as set out in this contract. If an agreement is reached, it will be incorporated into the agreement which will be attached to the application for separation.

Regardless of who gets custody, there shall be no denial of reasonable visitation rights to the parent that is not granted custody.

If the marriage ends in separation and heir(s) have resulted from the marriage, both parents will be responsible for the financial maintenance of the heir(s).

Territory Financial Support Upon Separation

Territory maintenance and the maintenance of the heirs will be determined in a fair and equitable manner at the time of separation. All requirements for support by the territory who left the marriage must continue in full force and effect of this agreement.

CONCLUSION

We undertake to inspire each other to achieve the best that we are capable of.

May the Five Angels grant Ashridge and Kaletta *Love*, *Beauty*, *Remembrance*, *Healing*, and a peaceful *Death* to make this marriage a successful one.

Grand Duchess Bonita Chantal Valenti

Duchess Jessica Petra Valenti

Grand Lord of Kaletta

Lord Jayden Panahov

CHAPTER 1

AIDEN

JESS AND I HAD met with the Grand Lord every other day for the last two weeks. He kept pushing for her to marry Jayden, but the both of them had made it very clear that while they cared for each other, they didn't want the marriage. We had fought over land rights, citizen rights, and he even had the audacity to claim that Ashridge needed Kaletta to help fix the moral wrongs of the territory. I could still hear Jess screaming at him that people would be allowed to love who they wished, regardless if that pairing resulted in biological offspring. Then she gloriously kicked him out of the meeting and was hesitant to meet up with him this morning.

I had just finished the morning debrief with the guards, and when I got back to our quarters, the whole place was quiet as a mouse. I sighed when I got to the bedroom, leaned against the door jamb, and looked at her lying in bed.

"Jess, you gotta get up."

"I don't want to. I'm so tired of having to justify my position with everyone. Can't I just have a me day? Take a damn day off?" She pulled the blankets up over her head, and I couldn't help but chuckle, but if she wanted to play, I would give it to her. I couldn't refuse my mate anything. That being said, she did have responsibilities and was going to be late if she didn't get her beautiful ass out of bed.

"No." My tone was final, but she pulled the blanket back just enough to glare at me.

"I wish your parents were still here. I'd send them in there, and I could stay in bed!" She stuck her tongue out at me as I chuckled. With a flick of my wrists, I used my power to pull the blankets off her and throw them against the wall.

"Aiden!" she exclaimed, sitting straight up, and I couldn't help but let my eyes roam down the length of her and back up. I may have fucked her to exhaustion last night, but damn if my cock didn't twitch at the sight of her in that nightgown pooling around her hips.

Smirking, she sat up and spread her legs wide, reminding me that she had nothing on underneath. It took everything I had to stay where I was as she pushed her breasts out. The growl that came from me pulled on the Claiming, and she just lifted the corner of her lips and said, "Too bad you were being mean and stole the blankets."

I launched for her, kneeling between those parted legs and running my hands up those thick thighs, squeezing her hips. *Fuck!* I drank in the sight of her.

Reaching up, I looped a finger into the heart of her necklace and pulled her in for a soft kiss. Anything more, and this was going to be over long before it started. She knew it too, because there was a smirk on her lips as she brushed them against mine.

"Kotě," I warned as I slid my other hand into her hair, cradling her head.

"You said I was running late and needed to get up."

"Now, you are going to be really late." I pushed her down onto the bed, taking in the sight of her. Releasing my finger out of her necklace, I slid her nightgown up her hips and ran my tongue along my bottom lip. "Looks like I missed breakfast."

Kissing down her neck and laying open-mouthed kisses along her collarbone, I felt her purr against me. I palmed her pussy and slid a single finger up and down the center of her. She purred much louder this time, and I couldn't help the satisfied chuckle that came from me.

BANG! BANG! BANG!

I was instantly down the hall and to the door.

The guard was panting and pale as he bowed before me. The entire hallway was lined with the Ashridge Guard, and if that wasn't enough to put me on edge, the tone of the guard's voice did it. "Vernadali Aiden."

"What is it?" I threw my charge out, creating a barrier between the two of us.

"There are hostages being held in the main hall. They are requiring the Grand Duchess' presence immediately."

"She won't negotiate with them."

"Sir, it's the Grand Lord and Lord Jayden…" His eyes were wide, and I turned and ran down the hall, throwing my charge to wrap around Jess.

When I made it halfway down the hall, she was standing in her doorway. "Jess, get dressed now!"

She didn't hesitate and turned and threw on a pair of pants, a bra, and a shirt. "Aiden, get me a hair tie out of the bathroom so I can throw my hair up!" she commanded and started buckling her syth belt as we strode for the door.

I felt the other Vernadali's Charge in the air and realized I wasn't the only one who was on edge. We were halfway to the main hall when the other four Vernadali stationed here in Ashridge City fell in behind us.

"What the Underworld is going on?" Jess demanded as we hurried down the hall.

"The rest of the Kaletta Army from the ridge showed up this morning." There had been a quick mention of it in the daily meeting, but not much else.

"Aiden, you are not telling me everything. No lies. No half-truths." I didn't know enough. I couldn't answer her. Fuck. I needed to get better at getting all the information. We were going in blind. Jess pulled me to a stop and made me face her before we got to the end of the hallway. "Aiden, tell me."

"The Grand Lord is in the main hall with… hostages."

"What do you mean, *hostages*?" Her face was a mix of horror, and she was bringing up the mask that was the

Grand Duchess. When it was in place, she asked, "As in, he is holding hostages or he is being held hostage?"

Turning the corner, I felt the rage, fear, and disbelief that flowed through Jess. My stomach turned inside out at the fierceness of it. I felt the vibration of her power along the Claiming before I felt it in the world and grabbed her hand, sending what calm I could. It was hard to bring up as my eyes flicked around the room, taking in the location of where each and every Kaletta soldier was standing. I wanted to dispatch them all.

The ones standing behind Jayden, Killy, and Ilris, swords at their necks, had to be dispatched first. Killy had a cut along his jaw, and Jayden's left eye was already turning colors and was half swollen shut.

Somehow, Jess ground through her teeth, "Release them now."

The Grand Lord, however, rolled his eyes. "No. This time you are going to listen to me, child."

"Why would I do that?" I felt the weight of her words in the bond. I couldn't look at her but continued to study the room. The doors were closed, and I felt the four Vernadali take position behind me. Signaling to them to protect the Grand Duchess at all costs, I twitched my fingers three times and clenched my fists, and I heard the responding three-foot tap. The restraint I felt along the bond and Claiming coming from Jess was impressive, so I sent more of that calming feeling, hoping it would even her out.

"You will marry Jayden in a fortnight or I will slit each of their throats."

Yeah, so much for that idea. This was going to go so, so *bad.*

My eyes met each of theirs, and they all reflected back their acceptance of death. When my gaze met Jayden's, I held it. We had talked about this. We knew the Grand Lord was going to use them as bait, as a tool to manhandle Jess into caving to what he wanted.

Fuck. Jayden and I had fought over it for hours last week. He had already told me he would sacrifice himself if it came to it. Jayden had asked that if something happened to him, to let the people of Ashridge and Kaletta know that he had been willing to die to keep Ashridge out of Kaletta's hands and to stand up for what he believed in. Then he demanded I let the dimension know of he and Ilris, and that he died for their love. Ilris had come over, kissed Jayden stupid, tears running down his face, and agreed to die for Ashridge as well. He turned to me, and with Killy stepping up beside him, swore allegiance to Ashridge, but we all knew he would sacrifice himself to protect Jayden.

Looking at the three of them on their knees at the command of the Grand Lord, I saw them each mouthing their silent goodbyes. Not everyone was leaving this room, and if the Grand Lord did, it would be only because the Grand Duchess allowed it.

I knew when Jess understood what was happening. She screamed through the Claiming, "*You knew this was a possibility?! You talked to Jayden about this.*"

I winced and then nodded. My eyes flicked to her, and there was pain but also understanding in her eyes.

"I'll repeat, in case you didn't clearly understand me the first time," The Grand Lord said. "Agree to marry Jayden in a fortnight or I will kill all three of them."

I felt the paralyzing fear that ran through her and flicked my fingers and fisted my hand behind me again. Simple orders to the Vernadali behind me to get the Grand Duchess to safety, no matter what happened next. I wrapped my Charge around Jess tight and willed it into a solid being. Nothing would get through it. *Protect her at all costs.*

Then I let my eyes cross over each of our friends, knowing that one of them wouldn't make it through today. I met the Grand Lord's eyes and caressed down the Claiming, tugging it gently. She needed to say the words that would kill one of them, if not all of them. She knew it, I knew it, and they did as well.

Dread filled her again, as she found the strength to say, "No. I have made it clear I will not be bullied into decisions."

The command wasn't visible, but blood was in the air, splattering everything in its path, and Killy's head rolled toward Jess.

My syths were out and twisting in my hands. Whirling around Jess, I moved, slicing through the throats of the two that were holding Ilris and Jayden. Jess' screaming still echoed in the hall as the Kaletta guards I killed crashed to the ground.

I lunged at the guard nearest the Grand Lord just as I heard him say, "Keep stalling, Grand Duchess, and Jayden and Ilris will be next to die."

The guard swung, but when my leg swiped out, he fell to the floor and I slit his throat on his way down. Twisting, I threw the syth in my hand at the guard on the other side of the Grand Lord, where it embedded in his eye and he fell to the floor.

Leaning backwards to miss the syth thrown toward me, I maneuvered until I had my other syth at the Grand Lord's neck. He froze as I jabbed another just under his ribs and held him there.

Moments had barely passed as I looked to where Jess stood, staring at Killy's head at her feet. It took entirely too long for her to raise her head and look at us. But when she did, I saw the Grand Duchess' body outlined in purple.

The empty hollowness that came from her moments ago was now a fiery storm that the Underworld would not be able to control. The Grand Lord stiffened for a moment, and I felt when Jess' power pressed upon him. I would be lying if I didn't want her to end him here, it was her decision. Jayden should have that honor, that privilege. It was my job to help make sure she didn't regret her decisions.

I pulled on the Claiming and she blinked. I tugged again and her eyes met mine. The Vernadali stood on either side of her, syths out, and she took a deep breath through her nose as I caressed down that Claiming again.

"How do you want the Grand Lord dealt with, Grand Duchess?" I asked loud enough that it was heard throughout the room. If she wanted to vibrate him to goo right here, I would let her. If she wanted me to slice his throat, I would do it. Whatever she wanted, I would give to her.

"Take him—"

"Maybe next time, Grand Duchess. You have a fortnight to agree or I will declare the agreement broken and war declared." Then he disappeared out of my grasp in a swirl of grey-blue smoke.

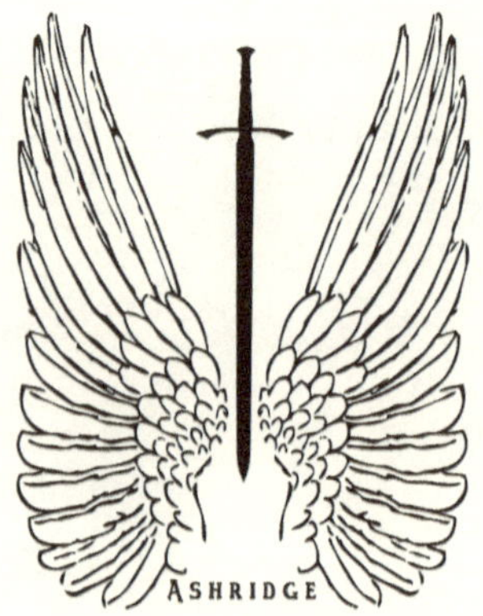

CHAPTER 2

JESSIKA

I BLINKED, AND THEN Aiden had my head in his hands. "Are you okay?"

"Where in the fuck is he?" My power burst through the room, and Aiden's quickly followed, finding no trace of the Grand Lord. I turned my head to look at where Jayden and Ilris were holding each other. Jayden's arms were so tight around Ilris, I wondered if he could breathe. There were a few muttered words between them before Jayden gave him a kiss on his temple and his gaze went to Killy's body.

"We will find him, Jess," Aiden tried to reassure me. Without taking his eyes from mine, he ordered the

20

Vernadali, "Secure the main hall and residence buildings. Search the whole fucking city."

"Vernadali Aiden, where in the fuck is the Grand Lord?" I growled. My power pulsed and begged to be let loose. There was nothing but Aiden's face, and it was the only thing keeping me remotely grounded. "He killed Killy. He will pay for this. I will..." My voice caught in my throat, and I felt Aiden pull on the Claiming again as he rubbed his thumbs along my cheeks, pushing his power through me to settle my anger.

Aiden swallowed and removed his hands from my face, taking a step back. Our gazes held for a long moment as he stood at attention. This wasn't my mate at the forefront. No, this was my Vernadali. "We will find him. Let's get you secure in your residence first."

Oh, the Underworld can burn before that happens. As I felt my lips thin, I bit out, "No, call the council. I need to meet with them immediately." I turned and looked at Jayden. "Jayden, Ilris?"

Slowly, they pulled their gazes toward me and stood. "Yes, Grand Duchess."

"You are hereby under Ashridge protection. You will have Ashridge Guards with you at all times. Your rooms must be secured before you can return to them, but..."

"Grand Duchess, I hereby request full asylum for Ilris Aavana within Ashridge," Jayden asked in a rush as he took Ilris' hand and squeezed it. There was a muffled, "*Jade*" from Ilris, but he didn't say anything more.

"What of yourself, Lord Jayden?" I pulled on all my years of training and forced myself to be the monarch I had to be. "Do you ask for asylum for yourself?"

"I do not. I hereby formally ask for asylum for Ilris Aavana, Personal Guard of the Lord of Kaletta."

"Granted." I confirmed his request without hesitation, and Jayden's shoulders dropped in relief. He turned to Ilris, placed his hand on his cheek, and gave him a sweet kiss that had me refocusing on Aiden. I could feel his worry through the Claiming, so I envisioned a hand running across it and concentrated on saying, "*I'm under control. I'm okay.*" I saw the smallest of nods before I turned back to Jayden and Ilris. "I'll have the paperwork drafted and a copy provided to you, Ilris, before the end of the day. Lord Jayden."

When Jayden nodded, I asked, "Why did you not ask for it for yourself?"

Jayden released Ilris' face, turned toward me, and, in a tone I had only heard from him once, said, "Because I will need to rule Kaletta when either you or I remove his head for threatening my life or at the very least for slaying Killy. He didn't deserve that."

A single nod was all the response I gave him as I leaned into Aiden and looked around the room. The Vernadali who had taken position behind me in the chaos were now gone, and there were only a handful of guards left in the room after Aiden's orders to find the Grand Lord.

I felt the tears rolling down my cheeks as I told Jayden, "I'm sorry that my denial to marry you caused his death." Jayden's eyes flicked to Aiden's, and I glared up at him too. "You knew that this was a possibility?"

He ran his hand through his hair and nodded. "The three of us met a couple weeks ago, and Ilris and Killy swore their lives to Ashridge. They all knew that the Grand Lord would likely use them as bartering chips. They also knew you wouldn't be able to agree to any of it. I'm sorry we didn't tell you, but we didn't want to burden you with something that would have just been another thing you couldn't change. This was my responsibility to make sure you were safe, and *they* chose this."

I looked between them, and they nodded. "Grand Duchess, what your Vernadali and mate says is true. We made the decision and knelt there ready to die to help you protect Ashridge. I heard Killy; he was ready as well. He had no regrets. He loved the people of Kaletta, yes, but he had fallen in love with the people and fierceness of the Court of Ashridge."

There was a warmth of love and respect that balled up in my throat. "Thank you."

"We need to get you two secured. I don't want you unguarded," Aiden said beside me.

"And I need to meet with the council. I have questions that need answers, and they cannot wait."

Aiden smiled at me but, still in that tone that was all Vernadali, said, "Grand Duchess, would you like to change before you meet with the council?"

I looked down, noted the blood splattered all over the front of my shirt, and closed my eyes a moment, taking a deep breath. "No. Let them see that I won't shy away from the situation." I looked at my two friends still clutching hands like their lives depended on it. Turning to look at the

Vernadali behind me, their horror was barely contained, and before I could order them to protect Lord Jayden and Ilris, Aiden commanded, "Please put Lord Jayden and Ilris in the residence down the hall from the Grand Duchess and stand guard. There will be three twelve-hour shifts. I want Grandle and Shilmar to relieve you."

Three more guards came rushing in from the hall, and as the two Vernadali nodded, I jerked my head for Jayden and Ilris to go. "I'll talk to you after the meeting with the council."

"Jessika…"

"Jayden, you just lost one of your best friends," I pressed.

"I should be there in the meeting with the council. Show a united front with you."

"Lord Jayden," I commanded, becoming the Grand Duchess, "find comfort with Ilris and he with you. A friend and trusted companion died and you need the appropriate time and space to process and mourn that loss. You will be brought up to speed later. You need to rest and have your injuries tended to. That is an order."

His eyes narrowed at me, and I let a small smirk lift the side of my lips. He couldn't stop me on this one. I said he was under my protection, and that included the fact he needed to go and process, break down, or do whatever he needed to do to grieve for a few hours, if nothing else.

"Jayden, please," Aiden said softly next to me as he put a hand on my back.

"Very well. I want a report in a few hours, though, okay?" he finally conceded.

I nodded and turned to one of the guards. "Have the council await us in the meeting room."

"Yes, Grand Duchess."

I looked around the main hall. Blood and bodies were littered everywhere, and I opened my mouth to order for it to be cleared, but a knot formed in my throat. Aiden pushed some of that calm through me again, and I looked up at him, meeting his warm eyes. "Thank you," I whispered before turning to the rest of the guards and saying, "Please gather the bodies of our Ashridge brothers. Take Killy to the state holding room. We will prepare for the pyre. We will keep it small. I want the main halls on lockdown."

"Yes, Grand Duchess." Then they all turned to leave.

I looked down at Killy's head, still only feet from me. Kneeling down, I ran my finger over his cheek. "I'm sorry, Killy. Thank you for your love and dedication to Ashridge."

"It wasn't just for Ashridge," Ilris muttered just loud enough that I could hear him. "He had dedicated himself to you. You had proved yourself a rightful and just ruler, and while he loved and respected Ashridge, he admired *you*. He would have given his life for you just as quickly as Aiden or Jayden would. As quickly as I would. Jessika, we consider you part of our family. You've proven yourself as a being with good morals and a kind heart. Don't let the Grand Lord take that from you."

Then Ilris and Jayden strode away, and my eyes fell back to Killy's vacant ones.

Aiden let me kneel like that until I was ready, and when another guard came to stand at the doorway to the enchanted meeting rooms, Aiden went to him. I heard hushed whispers, and when he returned, his voice was soft. "Grand Duchess, the council is waiting for you."

I sniffed, not even realizing the tears had started, and stood. Wiping my tears, I barely flicked my eyes to Aiden before saying, "Let's go."

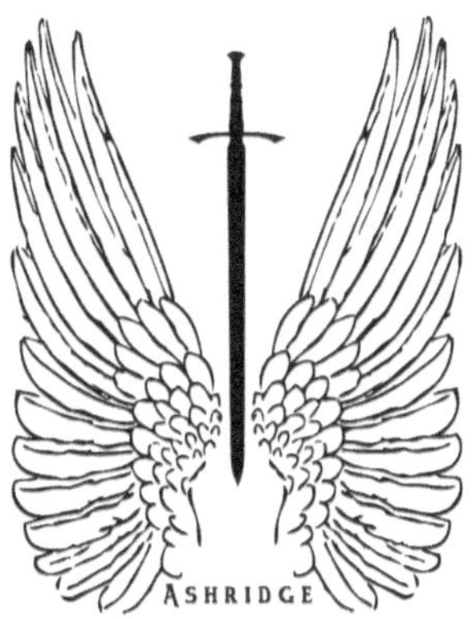

CHAPTER 3

JESSIKA

STARING AT THE DOOR, determination set in. I focused on standing tall, reached over, and took Aiden's hand. Aiden squeezed it, and when he went to drop it, I tightened my fingers around his.

Using my power, I opened the door and strode for the head of the table. I felt the gaze of each of the nine of my personal council and advisers follow us to the front.

"Grand Duchess—" Gerald, one of the council members, started to say, but I held my free hand up.

"How many of you know what occurred in the Grand Hall less than an hour ago?" Aiden, still holding my hand, came to stand just behind me. Reaching around, I gripped his hand between the two of mine, feeling him push calm through me. I took a deep breath as I met each of my council members' eyes. All of them were blank, but when my gaze met Noah's, his eyes narrowed in confusion as he scanned the blood on my shirt.

"From the looks on your faces, it appears you don't know much. Well, here is the breakdown. The Grand Lord of Kaletta, as you all know, wishes for me to uphold the terms of the agreement made between Ashridge and Kaletta. My mother had been trying to get out of the contract for years."

"He has failed to provide what is required for Ashridge, even though we have upheld all of the provisions required by Kaletta, except for the marriage," Lady Georgina said from the middle of the table.

"That is true. When Vernadali Aiden, Lady Amala, and I were in Shuset, we were attacked by Kaletta Guards. Lady Amala died at the hands of Kaletta soldiers while protecting me, and I will not forgive the Grand Lord for that. He has now..." The knot in my throat was back, and I squeezed on Aiden's hands and pulled on the Claiming. He leaned into me slightly, and I took a deep breath. "This morning, I was summoned from my residence to the Grand Hall to find the Grand Lord of Kaletta holding three hostages. Lord Jayden and his two personal guards."

I waited and let that fact sit in the air. There was nothing but stunned silence from all but Declan. He ran his fingers through his long black beard, his matching long hair tied behind his head as he met my gaze. "He's been playing games since he got here. It was a matter of time, Grand Duchess, before he showed his hand. He did once the power players of the dimension had gone and you were left with only one of the Mathewsons. One to deal with is better than the entire family."

"Careful, Declan," I warned. Aiden bent down and whispered in my ear, "But he isn't wrong."

"Not the point, Aiden," I grumbled.

"Back to the matter at hand." I took a deep breath and shoved away the hurt and images that threatened to engulf me. "The Grand Lord of Kaletta had Lord Jayden and his two guards, Killy and Ilris, beaten, bruised, and on their knees at sword point. He demanded that I marry Jayden immediately, but when I refused, he killed Killy."

When I blinked, I saw blood spraying in the room as Killy's head rolled toward my feet. I heard the commotion that was happening in the room, but all I saw was the blood flying... Killy on his knees as he said his final goodbye... Him looking at me and telling me it had been a pleasure to serve.

"Kotě, look at me."

Aiden.

Aiden's voice went through the fog, and I realized he had his forehead to mine and my head in his hands. Reaching up, I rested my hand on one of his and nodded. "I'm okay."

"No, you are not. I feel the turmoil rolling through you. I can feel your panic. Which are both justified."

I squeezed his hand and nodded, but when I tried to face the council again, he held me in place. I met his gaze and held it, watching his focus bounce between my eyes. When he found what he needed, he nodded and released my face.

The voices of my council had started as a muffled background sound, but now that I had pulled myself from my own internal panic, they were becoming louder. I couldn't make out exactly what was being said, but they needed to stop and listen to me. Turning to face them, Noah and Gerald, who were standing next to me, were studying us carefully. I gave them a small smile, and there was a small nod.

"Silence." My voice wasn't loud, but it wasn't a whisper either, yet everyone in that room froze and turned to me.

"Vernadali Aiden and Ashridge Guards secured Lord Jayden and Ilris. Both are under Ashridge protection, and Ilris has been given sanctuary and asylum."

"Grand Duchess, where is the Grand Lord now?" Gerald's eyes met mine, and they were hard with barely contained anger and fury as his fists shook with the force of it.

"Vernadali Aiden had him secured, but he teleported out." I glared across the room. "Anyone want to tell me why he was able to do that? Even Empress Clarice shouldn't be able to teleport from the Grand Hall." When no one answered, I looked back to Gerald, the defense coordinator who had the good sense to look a little scared. "Why in the hell was he able to magically teleport out of the Grand Hall, Gerald?"

"I don't know, Grand Duchess, but as soon as this meeting is adjourned, I will set to finding out." His voice was strong, but I could see his mind working a dozen different solutions.

"You do that," I spat.

Noah, Secretary of Territorial Relations, cleared his throat and asked, "Grand Duchess, have you declared war on Kaletta?"

I took a deep breath and realized as much as I wanted to make that formal declaration, there was more to consider than just my anger and grief. "As much as I would like to do so, at the time that Killy was slain, he was technically a citizen of Kaletta. I have no legal standing to make such a declaration. However, when I find proof that the Grand Lord was behind the death of my mother, *that* will be another story. Until then, I do not want to start my rule with a war."

It was Vincent this time who asked. "Do we know that Kaletta was behind the death of the Grand Duchess?"

"Looking to invoke some of your own justice there, Vincent?" I asked, letting a little smile come to my lips. I had named him as Chief of Justice because he was as deadly as a Vernadali, even without the bloodline. He would enjoy tearing down Kaletta's forces. There was a long history there.

"Only on your orders, Grand Duchess. However, my question stands. Do we know that the Grand Lord is responsible for her death?"

"While Lord Jayden was stationed at the ridge, there were rumors and boasting of how successful Kaletta's assassination was, so it sounds as if that is the case. However, we need more than hearsay and speculation. We need to directly tie the Grand Lord and Kaletta to the purchase of the black chicklory snake.

"What of the Ashridge – Kaletta Territory Agreement?" Noah asked carefully.

"The Grand Lord of Kaletta has given us two weeks to agree to my marriage to Jayden and set a firm date. That obviously isn't going to happen."

Strangely enough, it was the quiet Head of Finance, Braxten, that said, "I don't understand, Grand Duchess."

I reached over, took Aiden's hand, and threaded my fingers with his, letting a small smile cross my lips as I met their gazes. "Did no one listen to what I said during the pyre or my coronation?"

"You have no intention of marrying the Lord of Kaletta." Noah groaned. I actually laughed at his tone. Looking over to Aiden, his eyes sparkled with guarded humor.

"That I do not. There is only one person who will be crowned Duke of Ashridge." I hadn't let my eyes leave Aiden's, and there was just the slightest widening of his eyes.

"Jess, what are you doing?"

"I am telling my most trusted advisors that you are the future Duke of Ashridge." I reached up, kissed his cheek, and then turned to the table, where I was met with nine very stunned faces.

"Grand Duchess?" Noah asked in disbelief.

"I will not marry Jayden Panahov, Lord of Kaletta. Jayden, my mom, and I have been trying for years to convince his father that we do not want to go forward with the marriage. At the time that decision had been made, I was not involved with Vernadali Aiden. However, there is a long history between us, which will not be discussed." I heard Aiden sigh next to me. I knew what was going through his head, and I was sure he would yell at me later for not discussing this with him first. He never wanted our relationship out in the open because so much of his life was in the spotlight. He would just have to understand that being bound to me, being my mate, meant that there was going to be very little sacred about our lives.

"I believe it goes without saying that this information does not leave this room. Other than my family, you are the only beings to know. Though I would have rather waited to disclose that." He gave me an even look at that last part, confirming my thoughts.

I shrugged and continued, "Regardless, Noah, Lady Megan is studying the contract. Please speak to her via Lark Messenger or secure LightCall only regarding the strategy to be able to nullify the agreement."

"Yes, Grand Duchess."

Aiden looked to Gerald and then to Vincent before saying, "I have ordered the Ashridge Guard to find the Grand Lord. They will hopefully do so discreetly, but there may be some concerned rumors floating around the city. You may want to get ahead of that. I'll be meeting with the Vernadali when we get closer. I have already set four guards to be on rotation to guard Lord Jayden and Ilris. Should one of them not report, I want the Vernadali to cover their position. I don't want it getting out too loudly that we are protecting them. We want it to look as if they are here freely."

"Yes, Vernadali Aiden."

An older portly man at the end of the table asked, "Will the Mathewson family be returning to Ashridge to help us?"

"Charles, I will not use the family or his name to further Ashridge. I will rule without their influence."

"But you have to see the benefits, and once the information gets out, whether or not you want it, the fact is, you will be a Mathewson. It will open doors for Ashridge that were not necessarily open before, or at least open them wider."

I took a deep breath. "I realize that. However, none of that is a today problem. As Grand Duchess, I will do what I can to mitigate that very situation."

"But aren't you using Lady Megan to find a way out of the contract?" Vincent asked with a raised eyebrow.

"My mom is helping me find a way to marry the woman I love," Aiden said beside me, and while he had told me he loved me many times, for him to say it in front of my council made my chest swell with pride.

"I will work on the contract and speak to Lady Megan outside of usual hours," Noah said, rubbing his temple. "It will all be volunteer time."

"That isn't what I meant," Vincent said. "We've all been here for the Grand Duchess and her mother for years. We all want you to succeed and be happy." I met his warm gaze. "But Jessika, you can see how this does look of favoritism."

I did, so I nodded.

"Doesn't matter. Mom is already working on it, and I have no doubt that if we can work out some of the other hurdles, she will at least free Jess' hand for me to marry." Aiden's voice was strained, and yet there was something about it that was comforting.

"Outside of the issue of my hand in marriage, there are other issues to build a case for nullification. The destruction of our crop supplies and the re-routing of the water supplies by Kaletta being two of the most pressing." I sighed, pulling the chair out from the table and taking a seat. "Now, Charles, where do we stand? How hungry are our people?"

CHAPTER 4

AIDEN

FUCK, I WAS PROUD of that woman. The Grand Lord of Kaletta had crossed a line so wholly today that she was throwing it all to the wind. I stood there while she told her council exactly the way it was going to go and then dove into working out the solutions for the missing and ruined supplies.

When she finally sat down, I backed up and stood against the wall, at attention, as I waited for her. She had been at it for about three hours when there was a knock on the door. Striding across the room, I opened it, and it was Vernadali Dadan, one of the Vernadalis I had charged with finding the Grand Lord.

"He's with the army outside the gates," she whispered, but her eyes flicked to the room where I could practically feel Jess' eyes boring into my back.

"Tell the guards to line the hall and protect this room." When she nodded, I turned and went and bent down to whisper in Jess' ear, "He's with the armies. I'll be back. The guards will be standing outside. You are not to leave this room without me or a Vernadali. Is that understood?"

I leaned back as she turned her head, and I raised an eyebrow at her. Her eyes narrowed as I took a step back and made a fist in front of me. *Behave.* Jess took a deep breath before she nodded once and turned back to the table.

When I closed the door behind me, muttering the Vernadali incantation so that no one could leave unless under death, I looked down the hall and commanded, "No one enters or leaves this room unless accompanied by a Vernadali."

"Yes, sir," they said in unison and thumped their fists to their chests. I met Vernadali Dadan's eyes and headed out to find the Grand Lord.

At the gates to Ashridge, horses awaited us, along with a note from the Grand Lord himself.

VERNADALI AIDEN,

SHE HAS TWO WEEKS TO RATIFY THE AGREEMENT BEFORE I CONTACT HEAD JULIAN AND DEMAND COMPLIANCE. MY ARMY WILL AWAIT YOUR CONFIRMATION EACH DAY AT NOON AT THE MIDWAY POINT BETWEEN

ASHRIDGE'S GATES AND MY FRONT LINES.

I EXPECT A COMPLIANT ANSWER TOMORROW.

GRAND LORD OF KALETTA

Looking out toward the expanse, I only knew that the Kaletta camp was there from the wisps of smoke and the occasional guard running the length of the rise in the black sands.

Vernadali Dadan was standing next to me, and I sighed. "What are your orders, Vernadali Aiden? Do we gather the troops and go in after him?"

I shook my head. "No. He has a whole army at the helm and ready to go. Any troops we throw at him now, we would be signing their death clauses. Besides, the Grand Duchess hasn't declared war, and I don't want to tip our hand while we work this out."

"Three pyres and a wedding. She hasn't been back for a week yet," Vernadali Dadan muttered as quietly as she could.

"Careful." I didn't correct her on the wedding part, because there would be no fucking wedding this week or next, not unless the Grand Lord's head was delivered to me on a literal silver platter. I breathed in deeply through my nose to calm myself, but it was difficult. I felt my Charge and power rolling beneath my skin.

Vernadali Dadan's head popped up, and when I saw her eyes, I knew she hadn't meant anything malicious by it. "I only mean... Well, there is no real way for me to explain without it sounding bad. The timing is horrible, that's all."

"I agree. She doesn't want to start out her reign like this." I'd been her Vernadali for less than six months, and we were already being tested. With a heavy sigh, I instructed, "Don't start full war prep, but start taking inventory. Let's see where our numbers stand. How many do we have within the walls? What are our weapons like? Any special powers I should be made aware of?"

"I know we have a light fire elemental on the Ashridge Guard. He can't do what your sister can, but he can ignite arrows, if needed."

I huffed a laugh and shook my head. "There are not many in history who can do what LJ can." I ran my hand through my hair again and looked out to the rise in the sands. "Let them cook out there. Let's see how long we can wait them out. It's the heat of the summer, and they are going to be baking on the black sands. Do we know what their supply stores are like? How long will they be able to hold out if the weather isn't an issue?"

"We don't. I can't expect what water they have will last long. We are pulling some of our guys inside soon. Temps are already rising."

"Noted. You have your orders."

She nodded. "I'll start pulling accurate numbers for you. I have rough ones, but give me a few hours."

I was still staring out over the sands as she strode off. Guards acted on Vernadali Dadan's orders, and I heard citizens starting to move farther inside the walls of the city. While we wouldn't be evacuating anyone from the edges, the front row would not be in use until the situation with Kaletta was resolved. Taking a deep breath, I turned and started making my way back to the main hall and to Jess.

Walking down the smooth gravel road, I couldn't help but smile at the sight of children playing on the townhome stoops and out in the streets. Balls were being kicked around as their parents sat and watched them. I couldn't help the smile that crossed my face at the normality of it all. Ashridge was my home now. This was where I was going to build a life with Jess. To help her shape the future of the territory. It was now my job to protect the people. To protect Jess.

Angels, I finally had Jess, both in duty and love.

My eyes met a woman watching a couple of children as she sat in front of her black, white, and grey brick building. I smiled at her, and she lifted a fist and put it over her heart as she bent her head in mutual respect. Smiling at her acceptance, I returned the gesture and headed back to Jess.

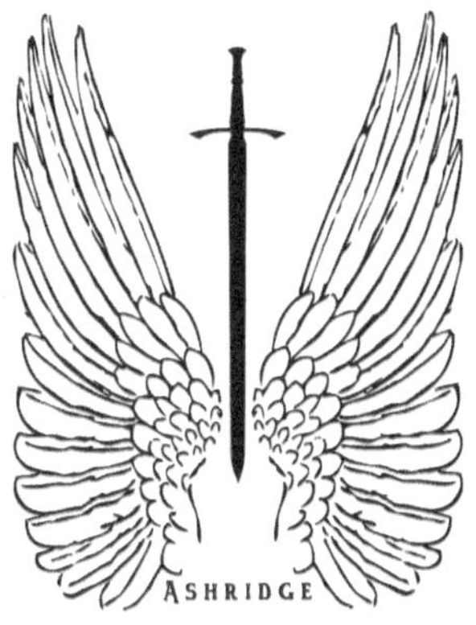

CHAPTER 5

JESSIKA

AIDEN CAME BACK THROUGH the doors to the council room just as we were finishing up and handed me a note. Reading it quickly, I tried to hide my reaction to his father's words. CJ was giving me an update on his progress in convincing Vernadali Samuel to sign off on my and Aiden's marriage when the time came. Taking a calming breath, I refolded it and slipped it into my pocket.

"Report, Vernadali Aiden," I commanded.

"The Grand Lord is with the army outside the city. He is still demanding that you marry Jayden within two weeks. He will have someone meet us at the halfway point between the city and the army for your agreement tomorrow and every day thereafter at noon."

"He can continue to wait out there. He can sit there and bake in the hot sun for those two weeks if he wants," I scoffed.

His lip twitched. "Agreed, Grand Duchess. I have asked Vernadali Dadan to obtain firm numbers and skill set profiles for the guards currently stationed in Ashridge City." Turning to Gerald, who raised an eyebrow at Aiden in question, Aiden continued, "Get me firm numbers on anyone who could trickle in through the back door in the next two weeks."

"As you wish, Vernadali Aiden."

"I want each of you guarded at all times. I don't trust the Grand Lord, and we can't afford to make mistakes. The Grand Duchess is newly crowned, and there will be those who test her. I will assume that none of you will be testing or questioning her rule, so we need to keep a united front."

I didn't know what to feel for Aiden at that moment. Love, admiration, pride? They all seemed to apply. He was leading the council and giving orders just like a duke, and I couldn't help but smile.

"You are all dismissed." Aiden's focus met mine and held me as my council stood and left the room. Gerald was the last one to leave, and I saw him nod before shutting the door behind him. "Jess..."

"Aid?" There was something different about how he said my name this time. I rushed over to him, and he wrapped me tight in his arms. "What is wrong?"

"When you are in my arms? Nothing." He pulled back and gave me a soft, lingering kiss. "I love you, my kotě."

"I love you, too, Aid." I let him hold me for another long minute before I asked again, "What is wrong?"

He huffed a laugh and said, "Do I really need to answer that? Since I was assigned to you, so much has happened. I find out the man I've been jealous of for the last few years doesn't really want to marry you for reasons that were totally not on the radar. Momma Grand Duchess was assassinated, then while en route, we were attacked by Kaletta soldiers, where those fuckers killed Amala. Fuck, it didn't even slow down once we got here. No, we had to send Momma Grand Duchess and Amala to the Angels, and then, when the Grand Lord didn't get what he wanted, he killed one of our friends."

She smiled at me and said, "That is all true, but in the midst of that, we were able to mend our hearts by finding each other again. We found that we are meant to be together. And I transformed." I winced, and he shook his head.

"You say that like it's a bad thing. I love those fangs, and the ears are freaking adorable."

"You like the fangs running against your cock," I whispered as I kissed him.

"Yes. Yes, I do." He took a shuddering breath, but it didn't hide the hard-on I felt pressed against me.

"Look, I know that it's been a crazy five months." I kissed him again to make my point. "I have you, Aiden. That is what is going to get me through all of this. We *will* get married, and while you don't think you can command a room and be a duke, what you just did in here said otherwise. You came in here, head held high, and gave them all orders, which they will follow."

"That's just because I'm Vernadali."

"No. It's because it's *you*. After you left, they all said that I made a good choice in Ashridge's Duke. They care not that you have no lands, no armies, or no territory to join with ours. They realize the old antiquated rules won't work with our modern view set. They also said it shouldn't. The world isn't in the Middle Ages anymore. I've known these men and women for most of my life. They are almost family. Many of them care for me as such."

There was a soft knock on the door, and Aiden kissed my forehead before answering it and retrieving a message.

"It's from Mom." He opened it and just smiled. "She wants an update."

"Let's do this via LightCall. I don't want a written manifestation of the shit show we have dealt with out there."

"In that case, let's get you changed. You still have Killy's blood on you." I blinked and looked down, and I was indeed covered in blood splatter. I knew it wasn't only Killy's, but I nodded, and we headed for our residence.

AIDEN SLID INTO THE chair he placed next to me, wrapped his arm around me, and kissed my temple as I put in the code for Lady Megan, and then the backup code to ensure it was secure.

"Hello." Head Julian's face appeared before me, and I blinked.

"Popa, can we talk to Mom?" Aiden asked without missing a beat.

"Yeah. She got your message. Give her just a moment," Head Julian said before another voice came through in the background, and I chuckled.

"Hi, Uncle Mickey." Then Mickel's face was in view, and Julian was rolling his eyes.

"Jess." Mickel was beaming, and then he narrowed his eyes at Aiden. "You better take care of her, mister, or I'll whoop your ass."

"You can try. You've slowed down, old man," Aiden teased.

"Will you all get out of here so I can talk to the Grand Duchess?" Megan was yelling at everyone. "Damn, can't even have a few minutes with my son and daughter-in-law without everyone sticking their damn nose in my shit."

"Mom," Aiden said admonishingly, but there was no real bite to it.

Once Megan was settled in front of the screen and everyone had left, I asked, "How are you now that you're back in Nalrin City?"

"Fine. Lots of stupid paperwork for Julian to fill out from my time there, but I'm fine. Now stop deflecting. What's going on up there that you couldn't just send a message back? Must be big if we are having this conversation via secure LightCall."

I looked at Aiden, who tipped his head to the side and drew his lips into a thin line. The shit was going to make me tell her everything. Megan opened her mouth, and I saw the concern grow in her eyes, so I interrupted her, "Don't panic, the two of us are fine."

"Jessika Valenti! You don't start a conversation like that." She glared at me.

"Aiden and I are okay, physically." Then I took a deep breath and thought through the day's events. Angels, was it only today? *Goodness.* "Since you left, we have continued to meet with the Grand Lord, who has been pressing us to rectify the contract. Obviously, we have no intention of doing that because Aiden will be the only male to stand at my side in the Duke's chair."

Her eyebrows raised, and I felt Aiden pull on the Claiming. I stopped and took a deep breath. Aiden took pity on me for a moment and said, "What she means is that we have made our stance crystal clear that she won't be marrying Jayden."

"So, what happened?" Her head turned slightly in confusion, and when I didn't say anything, she gave me the "mom" look.

I let out another long breath and said, "Shortly after we woke up this morning, a guard arrived to tell us that there were hostages being held in the Grand Hall. When we arrived, Jayden, Killy, and Ilris were all beaten, bruised, and being held at crossed-sword point by the Grand Lord."

"I'm sorry, what?" Megan's voice was hard and cold. I could see the waves of seething anger and death rolling off her. I nodded, and then her electricity was crawling over her hands and arms… CJ was there in a blink, working to calm her down.

Once he had, he asked, "What in the Underworld happened?" His eyes flicked between Aiden and me, a cross between the Vernadali protecting his Charge, a husband caring for his wife, and a concerned parent worrying about their children.

"We are physically fine, Dad."

"Okay, thank you for that bit of clarification, but can you please explain what just set off your mother like that? Shit. I haven't had to move that fast since the fucking war."

I flinched, but then I became the Grand Duchess. "Lady Megan, do you have yourself together?"

"Don't you fucking *Lady Megan* me, Jessika Petra Valenti." Then she saw the look on my face.

"Angels." The horror on her face was not unjustified. "Who?"

"Killy. The Grand Lord killed Killy," I croaked out.

Aiden's arm tightened around me as he said, "I was able to disarm the two who were over Jayden and Ilris, disarmed two others and had the Grand Lord at syth point, but he teleported out."

CJ and Megan looked between us, blinking. I knew what they were thinking, and we didn't have an answer for it either. "No, we don't know how he was able to teleport from the Grand Hall."

"Not even Clarice can…" Megan looked at CJ, and they both looked as confused as we felt. After a moment, she turned to me and asked, "When?"

"This morning. I have spent most of the day with the council working out ways that we can provide for Ashridge. I won't cave, and hopefully, even though it came with the price of Killy's life, he knows he can't bully me into complying. I'm not holding my breath, but I can hope."

"What did he ask for before he slaughtered Killy?" CJ asked carefully.

"He demanded I marry Jayden within two weeks. I declined." I looked at Aiden and then back to the orb floating in front of me with Megan's and CJ's concerned faces. "I also told my council that Aiden would be Duke."

They both blinked and looked at Aiden. "Yeah, I'm not wild about that at all. Can I even be Duke? I'm her Vernadali. I will also be Jess' Vernadali and mate first. And before either of you ask, she didn't talk to me before telling them."

I smiled brightly at him. "No, I did not. I'm Grand Duchess and will do what I want."

He bent down and whispered in my ear, "That's one, Kotě."

I rolled my eyes and looked back at my in-laws, but Megan had a strange look on her face. "What is it?"

"The Grand Lord is demanding you marry Jayden within two weeks?" I nodded. She waved her hand and a document appeared. She scanned it quickly, looked up to the ceiling like she was thinking about something, and then smiled. "You can't marry him within two weeks. It goes against the very agreement that he is so fond of."

"What?"

"Jess, when was the last time you actually read the thing?" She crossed her arms and leaned back.

"Years. I mean, I know the sections pretty well where they are supposed to help us with supplies and military because that's what we have been trying to nullify the contract with."

"In the section regarding the marriage ceremony, it states, and I quote, '*Marriage ceremony cannot occur within ninety (90) days of the death of either the Grand Duchess or the Grand Lord.*' So, you can't abide by the terms of the agreement if you marry him within two weeks. It would nullify the entire thing, which means he wouldn't be required to supply any of the help required under the agreement or any of the other terms."

Doing some quick math in my head, I said, "I can't marry him for like another month and a half at least. Time's a little fuzzy right now, but that's at least another six weeks."

I took a deep breath and leaned back. Aiden was concentrating on something, but when I looked up at him to ask what he was thinking, he shook his head.

"I've found a couple possible loopholes, but I need to look into it first."

"Like what, Mom?" Aiden asked before I could.

"I... Let me read them over some more and I'll get back to you, okay?" Megan reached over and, whether she realized it or not, ran her fingers over CJ's Vernadali herald. His shoulders lowered a bit, and I saw the small smile that crossed his lips, regardless of the conversation we were having.

"Talk to Gerald when you have. He's going to be looking it over as well."

She nodded and asked, "Do you want us to come back?"

"No, we have just bought a little time. Thank you. I stand firm on wanting to do this on Ashridge's own. I'll pull in the family if I feel like I have no other choice."

She looked off to the side. "Sure. Looks like Julian wants his desk back. We will be in contact soon. Love you both."

"Love you, too, Mom," Aiden said at the same time as I muttered, "You too." The light faded from the room as the call ended.

We sat in silence for a couple of minutes before Aiden reached over and put his finger through the heart of my necklace. As I looked up at him, I saw his eyes were full of worry. "You okay?"

I nodded, but he pulled me closer so that his lips were only a hair's breadth away. "You sure?"

I leaned forward and kissed him. "Yeah, I'm sure. I'm tired. Are there any more meetings I have to attend to?"

"Not to my knowledge. When was the last time you ate? Had any water?"

"They brought in some sandwiches and water while you were out, but I didn't eat much." I couldn't help it. I had taken a few bites, and the vision of Killy's head rolling toward me and Amala's face as that soldier slit her throat kept going through my mind, and I just couldn't eat without my stomach rolling.

Aiden simply nodded in understanding. "Let's get you something, and then you need to rest."

CHAPTER 6

AIDEN

I WOKE UP AND couldn't help but snuggle into the crook of her neck and breathe her in. There was a soft rumble in her chest as my hand splayed across her stomach and I ran my thumb back and forth on her soft skin.

It was still an unworldly experience to be able to wake up with this woman in my arms. Kissing the back of her neck, I reveled in the feel of her, in body and Claiming. I was her mate and Vernadali. I couldn't imagine a better fate than to be bound to her forever. Bound to the one that my heart and body knew belonged to her long before the Angels deemed me her Vernadali. Did it complicate shit? Yes. It did. What was I going to do when she gave me those wide onyx eyes filled with total and complete trust?

Protect it at all costs. That was what I was going to do. And if that meant my own life, I had no qualms with doing just that.

Her small snores were so damn adorable. Slowly, I ran my fingers up her side, letting them trail across the curve of her hips, down her thighs to her knee, and then back up. Fuck, she was the most beautiful being in any dimension. I repeated the movement, relishing how her skin felt under my fingers.

When I reached her hip on the way back up for the fourth time, she muttered, "Aid, if you don't stop, I'm going to scream in frustration."

Chuckling, I flattened my hand on the section between her hip and thighs and squeezed. "But you are so beautiful. I was just taking in what is mine."

"Humm," she muttered and wiggled her hips against me, causing a groan to come from me. "Only enjoying the view, huh? I feel something else enjoying it as well."

"Kotě, there is nothing wrong with me enjoying the view of you, the touch of you, and getting a raging hard-on."

My hand wrapped around her waist again. I pulled her tighter against me and kissed the spot where her neck met her shoulder. I felt her entire body heat and melt into me.

"Not fair, Aiden."

"I don't know why not? If you don't want me to touch you, all you have to do is say so, Kotě. I will never force you to do anything."

"I know that, asshole." She swatted my arm at her stomach. "What isn't fair is that delicious cock of yours isn't in my mouth or pussy."

I chuckled against her skin, laying soft kisses along her shoulder. Letting my hand slowly trail down to the center of her, I purposefully avoided her clit to run my fingers to her opening, where I plunged two fingers into her.

She moaned but said, "That isn't what I asked for."

"I don't recall you asking for anything, Kotě." I nipped at her shoulder and felt her tighten slightly against my fingers as they worked in and out of her. She moved her hips, trying to get the heel of my hand to rub against her, but I pulled my hand back and took my sleep pants off.

Pressing my cock against her, she shifted her hips so it slid along the length of her, but I pulled back just before I reached that spot. The whimper out of her was delicious, and I nipped at her ear as I thrust into her. There was an entirely different kind of whimper from her this time.

I worked in slow steady strokes as I moved my hand to her breasts and tweaked her nipples. Her hips moved with me, and I relished the feel of her under me. More than that, I could feel her caressing that Claiming bond. I bit down on her shoulder when she gripped it like a cock and stroked in short movements to match the rhythm of my hips.

"I don't know how you are fucking doing that, Kotě, but fuuckk." I was trying very hard not to lose it with each mirrored movement.

She chuckled and turned her head toward me. "You like that, Aiden?" She did it again as I started pounding into her.

"Fuck yes."

Her moans and breaths were getting shorter, and as her hips ground against me, she continued pumping me along the Claiming. I felt that tingling at the base of my back and my balls tightened, but there was no way I was going alone. Reaching down, I flicked her clit, and she let out a yip, and then I was circling and pressing against it.

"Cum for me, Kotě."

"Yes, sir."

Two more thrusts and she was clamping down around me, her mental hand against the Claiming tugging one more time as I released deep inside her.

CHAPTER 7

AIDEN

WE LAY THERE COVERED in sweat, trying to catch our breath and see straight again. I turned her to face me as I let myself retreat from her. She rolled over onto her back and lifted a hand to hold my cheek.

"Morning, Sir."

"Morning, Kotě." I leaned down and kissed her. Her hand slid around to the back of my neck as her fingers threaded through my hair and gripped tight. I nipped at her bottom lip, and she chuckled. "Be right back."

She kissed me again, released me, and as I crawled out of bed, the sheets were at our feet. She was anyone's wet dream lying there, and she was mine.

I blinked and remembered why I got out of bed. Grabbing a washcloth from the hallway and turning the faucet to let the water warm, I looked at myself in the mirror. I looked tired. It had been weeks since the stress level was reasonable. Hell, the time on the boat when I had to restrain myself from kissing her at every moment had worn me out, even if all the meetings hadn't.

I was so lost in my thoughts that I hadn't noticed that the sink now had steam coming from it until Jess' hand ran across my back and she pushed a little bit of her power into where my Maltal was. I closed my eyes as the vibrations soothed the muscles in my back, and I rolled my neck as the tension released.

"Thank you." My response was more breathy than I anticipated, but I took a long breath in through my nose and met her gaze in the mirror. Reaching over and grabbing the washcloth, I wet it and turned to face her. "You are supposed to still be in bed."

"You were taking too long." Jess laid her hands on my chest, and I reached down to clean her up but laid a kiss at her collarbone. She wiggled, and I tossed the washcloth into the laundry basket in the alcove next to the bathroom. "What were you thinking about?"

"Everything that has happened since I was assigned to you." I wrapped my arms around her waist, and she leaned into me.

"What was your first thought when you found out you were going to be assigned?" Jess was running her fingers along my necklace, and I picked her up and carried her to the living room, where I grabbed a blanket and tossed it over the two of us. We had nothing on, and it was still early enough there was a chill in the air.

"I had mixed feelings. It was the moment I had been training for my whole life. It was the main reason I had walked away from you..." I turned to look at her face. "Then I saw you in that room, and it was like that day all over again. It was everything I could do to stand there and wait to have my name called. At first, when they called Reka's name, I tried not to laugh at the hilarity of if I had been assigned to her, but thankfully, I was not. Then Vernadali Samuel called out to the room Duchess Jessika Valenti..." I took a deep breath before saying, "It shredded me. I was the one who should be protecting you for life. I've known since the day we met I would give my life for you. I ran through a hundred scenarios of what I would do if you were assigned to one of the other Vernadali. Then you weren't. He called my name and said that I was the Angels' determined Vernadali signed to protect you for the rest of your life. It was as if every fiber of me had finally clicked into place."

She chuckled under me. "When I saw you walk through that room with your Vernadali brothers and sisters, I was certain the Angels were fucking with me. How cruel could they be to have me there and watch you go be bound to someone else when you still held my heart. So, when Vernadali Samuel called my name, I decided to show you what you walked away from."

I leaned down and kissed her hard, gripping her tight against me. "I knew what I walked away from, and watching you strut your sexy swaying hips up to that podium..." I bit my bottom lip, and I felt myself get hard for her at the memory of it. That satin green dress had shown her off to me with perfection. She wiggled and smirked. "It took a lot of control not to grab you and fuck you against the wall."

Jess smiled at me and said, "Well, you didn't show it. I wasn't sure you even noticed."

"Trust me, my kotě, I noticed."

She shifted and straddled me. My cock was at full attention, and when her eyes flicked to it, she licked her lips.

"Do you think you've been good enough to earn that reward?" I asked her in that voice that instantly had her clenching against my thighs. When she stuck a finger in her mouth and nodded, I had to take a deep breath but gave her what she wanted and tapped my chin. "Well then, get to it."

She dropped to the floor and only a moment later, her lips were tight around the head of my cock. Her tongue snaked out and gave me a lick from balls to head, and I leaned my head back and moaned, letting a hand thread through her hair and cradle her head. She found a rhythm, licking and sucking me in quick, hard succession.

Before I knew it, both of my hands were on her head and I was trying not to thrust my hips too hard. After she swallowed me whole three times, she released me and whispered, "Fuck me," before swallowing me again. I felt her against the Claiming, and I knew what she was going to do.

I lifted my hips as I slid down her throat. She gripped me against the Claiming again, just like she had in bed. "Fuck, Kotě. I'm not gonna last if you do that."

With another thrust, she repeated the motions and chuckled. "Nope, not at all." I felt my balls tightening again, then her fangs scraped along the length of me, and I said,

"Jess, if you want me to fuck that pussy of yours, you better stop. Otherwise, I'm gonna cum down that pretty little throat of yours."

I lifted my hips and fucked her mouth. Each thrust was accompanied with the grip and pull on the Claiming. Fuck, it was amazing. I had felt nothing like it. I gripped her hair tight, and with one more final thrust, I spilled down her throat.

Once she swallowed every ounce, she ran her tongue through the slit of me, making me twitch. Jess climbed back into my lap, and I pulled her close, wrapping my arms around her waist.

"Seriously, how did you figure out how to do that?" I was still panting and a little breathless.

"I had been wondering if I could, so when you were teasing me in bed, I figured I would try." Then there was a mischievous grin on her face. "Now, I know how to really make you squirm in a meeting."

Oh, fuck. I was in so much trouble.

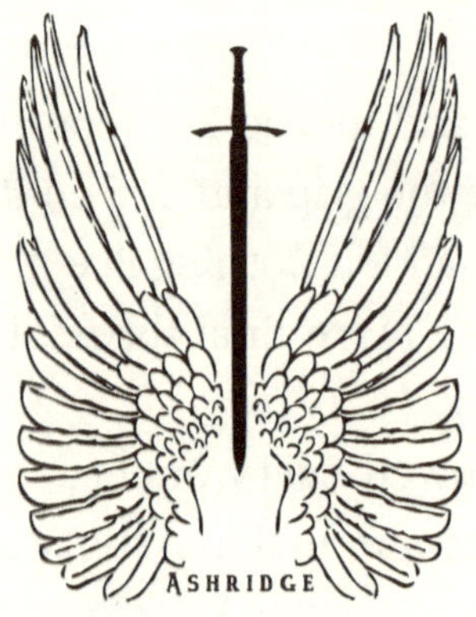

CHAPTER 8

JESSIKA

THE LOOK ON AIDEN'S face when I told him I knew how to tease him during a meeting was hilarious. I kissed him and swayed my hips on the way out the door. I heard his growl behind me, and he chased me down the hallway.

When he caught me, he just pushed me against the wall and kissed me until my lungs were burning with the need to breathe. He pulled back, my head cradled in his hands, and said, "I love you."

I smiled at him and sent my power into his hip, making him jump away and growl at me. "Growl all you want, Aiden Mathewson, but there is something I need to do before we meet back with the council this afternoon."

"Ilris and Jayden." He sighed as I nodded. "Alright, but that little push of power earned you a one."

Smiling, I rolled my eyes because while they were meant as threats, I always enjoyed what happened when I got to three. Well, eventually I would enjoy it. He would edge me, spank me, and tease me until I was on the brink of sanity, but at the core, I loved every moment.

I pulled out some panties and put a bra on, then a pair of black jeans and a white top, with my favorite over-the-top faux corset. As I got dressed, I heard him doing the same behind me.

"The guards last night said they were fine and were not planning on leaving the residence." Aiden pulled a shirt on over his head, and I bit my lip and squeezed my legs together at the sight before me. He was mine, and I had to be the luckiest person in Nalsar. "They ate dinner, too, so that's a good thing."

Blinking and bringing my mind back around to what I wanted to talk to Jayden about, I asked, "They put them in a two-bedroom residence, right? I mean, we know they will be sharing a bed, but if he plans to ever go back to Kaletta, under current rule..."

"They are in a two-bedroom, Kotě." His eyes roamed the length of me, and I felt him pull on the Claiming and then run a single finger along it. I smiled at him and huffed a laugh. "Come on, let's get something to eat, then you can go and talk to him."

"JESSIKA, WE ARE OKAY," Jayden tried to tell her, but she knew that haunted look in his eyes.

"Bullshit you are. You and I both know that you are not okay," I spat at him.

"I'm just as okay as you are about losing Amala," he said, gripping Ilris' hand.

I flinched but volleyed back, "I've had a few weeks to process Amala. Sure, it hurts like the fucking Underworld to think about how she's not here anymore, but she didn't die yesterday, Jayden. You lost one of your most trusted beings in the world. Your best friend."

His eyes flicked to Ilris, who had tears running down his face. I realized he was faking it to be strong for Ilris, and I felt like the most stupid and shittiest friend ever. Sighing, I ate my own words. "I realize you are trying to be there for Ilris, and you should be, but you can be there for each other."

Jayden's eyes met mine again, and I held them. We were two rulers not budging. "What did you come here to talk about, Jessika?"

"To see how you were doing and what I could do to help." He narrowed his eyes at me, calling me out on my bullshit. "First and foremost, I came here to check on my friends." I sighed, though. "But I also wanted to talk more about why you aren't asking for asylum for yourself as well."

"It really is as simple as I said yesterday, Jessika." His hand tightened in Ilris' again, who was looking at him with worry and respect.

A quick sniff, and Ilris said, "We fought over it last night. He doesn't want to abandon others like us in Kaletta. Jade will be in a position to be able to change things. I told him I want to do that by his side, but we all know we aren't safe there together. I am his guard and can't be seen as anything else until the day he is Grand Lord."

Jayden took a deep breath. "There is too much change that needs to happen in Kaletta. Not everyone is a homophobic bigot like my father. In fact, I have to believe most people in Kaletta will set aside the past and allow people like us to live freely. I know it will not be an overnight change." He took another long breath. "Maybe we can allow anyone who cannot and will not accept it to head to the tip of Savanora to be with those like-minded people."

I studied him for a long moment as he fidgeted a bit. "Do you want his head?"

"I do, but I think you have a better right to it," Jayden said without hesitation. "He killed your mother and your best friend."

"If I take his head right now, without physical proof of our accusations, it would be an act of war, Jayden. You and your council would be in the right to declare war against Ashridge." I met his stare because this was important. I felt the shock from Aiden down the Claiming, and I refused to look at him. "If you take it, you are taking your rightful place. If you take his head, you can take it in the name of all of those like you who he persecuted and murdered. The council won't be able to do anything. You'll be the Grand Lord upon his last heartbeat. Under Kaletta law, they have to obey your commands. You are the next Grand Lord by blood and right."

Jayden blinked. Then blinked again.

Aiden, however, finally tugged hard on the Claiming, demanding my attention, and I slowly turned my head toward him, but I didn't release the hardness of my face. "Jess?"

"I'm serious about this, Aiden. I have thought about it a lot in the last thirty-eight hours. Jayden has every right to take the Grand Lord's head."

"Jessika, you have just as much right to as well," Jayden finally said, and when I turned back toward him, his eyes flicked to Aiden. "Aiden and I discussed it back in Silentport. When we first found out about your mom, we knew it was likely The Grand Lord who arranged it. We also decided that we would stand aside to allow you to kill him."

I let the hard look on my face drop as I looked to the floor and played with my fingers. My voice turned hard, but I kept my focus on the floorboards. "On an emotional level, I want to vibrate his body slowly, so much so that he feels as each of his organs turn to liquid before he dies. I want to watch his eyes as he realizes I'm the one ending him and then let him all just fall to the floor in a pile of liquid goo."

"Then you shall have that oppor—" Jayden said, but I interrupted him.

"As Grand Duchess of Ashridge, I have to think of my people first. I have to put them before any want I have for revenge. And if I take his head, I have to be able to live with the fact that it will be an act of war. You could stand there all day and tell your council you will not sign off on it, but you and I both know if they are unanimous, that gives them the right to overrule you. War *will* come down on my people. I won't do that. I *can't* do that."

Jayden and Ilris shared a long look before Jayden turned to me and released his hand from Ilris'. He leaned forward with his elbows on his knees and looked at me carefully.

"What?" I felt that knot in my stomach and knew that whatever was going to come from Jayden's mouth, I wasn't going to like.

"I have to look into the logistics of it, and it may not happen immediately, but when I take over the territory, I will change many laws. I will bring them to be more in line with Ashridge law. I'll wait six months to a year to let my citizens get used to a new norm and then sign over the entire territory to Ashridge rule and command. I would be willing to continue to watch over it and report to the kingdom as a duke or any other title, but it will be ruled by an Ashridge monarch and become a sub-territory of the Ashridge Kingdom."

"What?" I whispered in complete shock; every nerve in my body had gone numb.

"I will sign over Kaletta to the Ashridge Kingdom." He held my stare, and I saw the conviction and determination in his eyes.

"A territory hasn't been turned over to another in..."

"Almost since the 1,000 Years War," Aiden muttered behind me.

Jayden still hadn't broken my gaze and nodded. "Once I hold the title of Grand Lord of Kaletta, I will be contacting Head Julian to ratify my decision."

"Jayden…" I blinked and looked off to the side. "To assimilate that many people into… well, everything is not going to be a small feat."

"Which is why I want to do it in stages." Jayden's stare was firmly on me as he continued, "Like I said, first I'll change the laws to be in line with those governing Ashridge. It will give the people time to adjust and become comfortable with the way of life there. Then when everything is ironed out, it's done. While we are doing that, we will work together on how to adjust the economics, defense, healthcare, resources… Angels, that is going to be—"

"It will be an undertaking, but we can do it," Aiden interrupted. I looked at the both of them and groaned. Great. Both of the men in my life were trying to put me through the deepest depths of the Underworld, weren't they?

Jayden leaned back in his chair and then looked at Aiden. "I couldn't make your job as Duke be easy now, could I?"

I couldn't help the snort of a laugh as Aiden said, "Asshole." There was no animosity in it, and I couldn't help the chuckle that came from me this time.

"Well, this whole conversation took a turn I didn't expect it to take." My eyes swung back to Jayden, and I shook my head. "We don't make *anything* easy, do we?"

"Ahh, where would be the fun in that?"

As the room burst into laughter, I looked at Aiden. "Well, that's one down. Ready to head to the city walls?"

He looked over at the clock, and I knew he was wondering how we had spent all morning as well, but then I pulled on the Claiming in the way he enjoyed earlier. I saw his eyes widen just slightly before slowly moving over to meet mine and narrow. I sat there and smiled brightly.

"Let's go, Kotě."

CHAPTER 9

JESSIKA

AIDEN AND I WERE the only two standing in the small room at the top of the Ashridge City wall. I was staring out the little window as he wrapped the ends of my long white hair around his fingers, staring at it.

"You have an obsession with my hair, Aiden."

"This is true." He leaned forward and kissed my neck just below my ear. "To be fair, though, I'm obsessed with every part of you."

I elbowed him. "Be serious, Aiden. We can play later."

"Yes, Grand Duchess."

"Asshole."

"You know, that isn't the first time I've been called that today." He chuckled but straightened and looked out the window at our delivery person, a volunteer because we didn't know if they would be allowed to live after delivering this particular message.

Aiden wasn't especially fond of the way I told the Grand Lord to shove off and come talk to us in six weeks, but that was a him problem. I also told them to inform the Grand Lord that if he and his army did not leave the black sands and the Black Mountains immediately, then I would declare war upon him and his territory for the sizeable military presence without prior authority. It was only a mild, empty threat. If they didn't leave, I would be more than a mild annoyance. I would declare war.

I watched as the horses met in the middle and my message was delivered. A minute later, our delivery person was rushing back to the gates. Aiden stepped outside onto the landing, and when the rider lifted the message up, Aiden used his power to float it to him.

He handed it to me and raised an eyebrow. "I'll let you have the pleasure."

I unfolded it and looked down at the scrawled writing:

GRAND DUCHESS,

MY ARMIES AND I WILL NOT MOVE. YOU HAVE THIRTEEN DAYS, GRAND DUCHESS, TO AGREE TO OUR TERMS. WE WOULDN'T WANT YOU AND ASHRIDGE TO FALL AS YOUR MOTHER DID, WOULD WE?

PS: I KNOW JAYDEN'S LITTLE SECRET. IT'S WHY KILLY WAS THE ONE TO DIE. ILRIS WILL BE NEXT IF MY DEMANDS ARE NOT MET.

Anger rolled through me, but Aiden had expected that. Without looking up, I commanded, "I want triple guards on Jayden and Ilris. The Grand Lord knows. I won't have their blood on my hands."

I read through the note again, and I saw purple. "Jess…" Aiden's voice was a warning, but I looked at him, and he knew I was seeing everything through my power. I shoved the note into his hand, and he pocketed it without looking at it, following me as I turned, strode out to the walkway at the top of the wall, and pushed my hands out and pulled them back in. After a few rounds, the rise in the blank sands the Kaletta army had been hiding behind flattened out to span out toward the Ashridge City gates.

There were shouts in the distance, and I smirked as I spoke to the wind. "You will leave."

Waiting, I saw a line of defense form between the Kaletta encampment and the city. Through the purple haze that had formed, I mentally reread the note from the Grand Lord, my mind focusing on two sentences. *We wouldn't want you and Ashridge to fall as your mother did, would we?* and, *I know Jayden's little secret.*

Loss and anger fueled my power as it came to my fingertips and they started sending out waves of vibrations under some of the clusters of the Kaletta soldiers.

"Jess, be careful." Aiden came to stand behind me, and after putting his hands on my waist, he bent down to my ear. "What are you doing?"

"If they won't leave peacefully, then they can be buried in my sands." He was muttering something in my ear, but the hatred, anger, and heat that I felt inside of me threw the entire conversation I had with Jayden out the window.

Throwing waves of my power out toward the sands, I sent it vibrating. Commanding shouts and horrified screams were heard over the plain, and I smiled widely. Aiden was pulling then caressing and pulling on the Claiming as I shot more and more of that power toward those edges.

All I saw was purple, then flashes of Amala's throat being slit, my mom lying in state in a stone bowl, the flames licking their bodies and me watching as they turned to ash before me, as Jayden, Ilris, and Killy were beaten and bloody, and the Grand Lord's arrogant face told me what he wanted me to do and I denied him. I screamed, releasing more of my power toward the Kaletta camp, as I saw Killy's blood spray into the air and his head roll toward me again... but my power snapped and stopped.

I saw Aiden's face just before there was a whispered, "Sleep, Jess."

Strong arms caught me as I collapsed and I saw nothing but darkness.

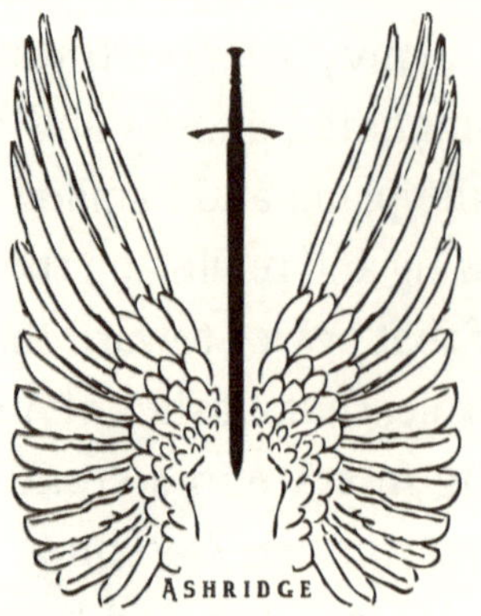

CHAPTER 10

JESSIKA

STRONG ARMS WERE WRAPPED around me, and I heard the steady beat of his heart. Inhaling, I smiled and curled into Aiden. His grip tightened around me, and then I felt the compulsion to open my eyes.

His Charge. He was using his Charge on me. I jerked up, but he still held me tight. "Let me go, Aiden."

"No."

"Let me go, Vernadali Aiden Mathewson."

"Again, I say no." This time he looked down at me, and his face was hard.

"Jessika, what were you thinking?" Jayden's voice was to the other side of me, and I flipped my head to him.

"What are you doing here?" I blinked as I remembered what happened before I blacked out... not blacked out... "Aiden, did you stop me?"

"I did, Grand Duchess."

I sighed as he pulled me back against him. He held me tight, and I remembered what I was starting to do. Did I really blame him for stopping me from slaughtering the entire army staged outside of Ashridge? I hadn't fully processed that thought when Jayden started laying into me.

"Damn it, Jessika. You said that if you did it, it would be an act of war." Jayden was pacing. Ilris was standing at attention, observing him.

"Did I?"

"No. He sent a follow-up message and said he would forgive this treasonous act because you are new and still grieving over the loss of your mother." He rolled his eyes. "Which is a full-blown piece of shit. The army is in the process of moving out, though. I replied with a message that the agreement still says nothing can happen for six weeks and to give you that. He agreed but said he would return then. I'm not happy with what you almost did, but I can't argue with the results."

"How did he feel about you still being within the walls?"

Jayden let out an annoyed huff. "He demanded that I accompany him back to Kaletta, but I told him he could shove it up his ass and that I was staying in Ashridge for now. I would like to spend additional time with my betrothed." He smirked at me. "I don't think he liked that much, but when you beat the shit out of me and kill one of my guards, do you really think I'm going back to the Kaletta capitol with you? The man has really lost any sense of rationality."

"He knows about you and Ilris," I whispered. He froze and stared at me. My gaze flicked to Ilris, who was staring at Jayden. His face had gone to stone. There was no emotion on it, but his eyes betrayed all those conflicting feelings that were going through him. I looked back to Jayden. "Said that was why Killy died and not Ilris."

There was a long moment of quiet, and it hadn't failed my notice that Aiden hadn't let up on his vice grip on me. I ran my hand along his arm, letting him know I was okay, but his muscles just tensed more against me. I wasn't sure how he did it, but he did.

"Aiden, have you read his initial response?"

"I haven't. I have been a little preoccupied with keeping an exquisite and powerful grand duchess from turning all of the black sands into quicksand." He let out a long sigh. "I know you told me you are okay, but are you under control?"

"I'm still... well... I'm not going to turn the black sands to quicksand anymore." There was a tight knot in my chest, and I felt it rising to my throat, but I swallowed it back down. Aiden gave me a quick kiss on the temple before allowing me to get up and stretch. I was a bit more stiff than I thought I would be. "How long have I been out?"

"About six hours," Jayden said carefully. "Now, what exactly happened out there?"

I took a deep breath and held Aiden's gaze as he pulled the note from his pocket and looked down to read it. There was a long blink, and then he looked at me and read it again. "Well, that would be a good reason, but you said—"

"I know what I said this morning. I have every right, but politically it's the wrong move."

Jayden was looking between us, his brain sorting through the possibilities, but at our continued silence, he nailed it down. "Oh, fuck the Underworld. Did my father confirm he killed Momma Grand Duchess?"

I nodded my head. That knot burst in my chest, and I couldn't hold it in anymore. Tears started falling and before I knew it, Aiden's arms were back around me. I let myself collapse into him. Regardless of everything else, he was my safe space. The sobs caught me by surprise, but he just held me as I gripped his shirt and cried.

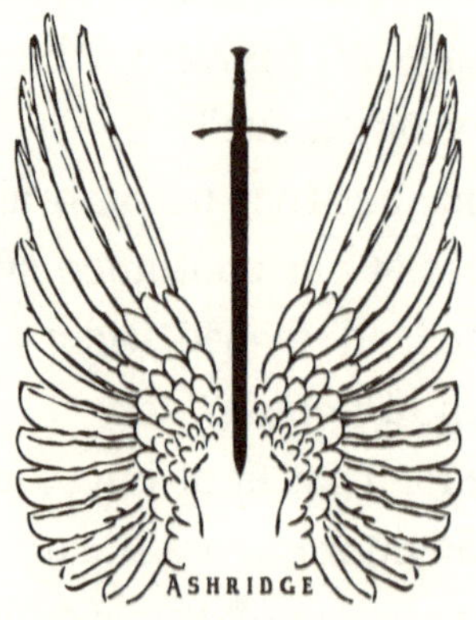

CHAPTER 11

JESSIKA

"GRAND DUCHESS?" GERALD ASKED from the doorway. A moment later, I looked up from the reports I had been working on and saw him stop short for a moment before saying, "Lady Megan would like to speak to us and is awaiting your LightCall."

I looked down at myself, realizing that I had only thrown on a pair of leggings and a T-shirt. My hair was up in a messy bun, had fallen out a little at my temples, and little pieces were starting to stick out in all directions. I let out a long breath as I lifted my tired eyes to meet his, and he gave me a small smile.

"Grand Duchess, you look like you haven't slept over the last three weeks."

"I've had some. Aiden has been working late meeting with the guards and Vincent. Meanwhile, Braxten is sending me the financials of the kingdom, and I have to attempt to make sense of them. Bethany is having concerns over the conservation of the fissure trees that are infected with beetle bark disease, while Charles is sending report after report on the lack of food getting to the citizens from Kaletta. It's so much worse than I knew. Mom was hiding a lot from me."

The little blue light by the bookshelf lit up, and Gerald and I stared at it. "She supposedly has information on the contract."

I raised my eyebrows at him. "Well, why didn't you start with that?"

"I was asking how you were doing because you look like you haven't slept in three weeks, Jess." He chuckled and tipped his head toward the room, and his voice was a little mocking as he said, "Let's not keep *Lady Megan* waiting."

Rolling my eyes, I stood and went to the bookcase, pulled the fifth book, and then laid my hand on the screen when it popped out. After another moment, the door to the LightCall room cracked open. Stepping inside, I took a seat and clicked the button as Gerald came in, closed the door, and stood behind me.

Megan's face appeared on the projected circle over the table, and I crossed my arms. "Hey."

Her eyebrows raised slightly, but there was a small smile on her face. "Hey yourself, missy."

I huffed a laugh. "Let's get to the point. Gerald said you might have some info on the contract?"

"I do." She watched me though the LightCall, and I leaned back and gestured for her to continue by waiving a hand in front of me before tucking it back under my other arm. "I would think you would be a little more excited, Jess."

"I have had a lot of ups and downs over the last couple of months, Megan. I'm trying not to get my hopes up until it looks like we really have something viable. I will marry Aiden. I just want it legal so that he can be Duke of Ashridge, whether he likes it or fucking not."

Megan laughed, and I waited patiently. When she wiped a tear from her laughter from her left eye, I couldn't help the smile that crossed my face.

"Well, while I have found a couple of things, none of them are great solutions." She paused, but when I didn't say anything, she continued, "The first loophole is that either you or Jayden have to die for at least sixty-one seconds. Your heart has to stop."

"Well, that's not preferable, for obvious reasons," I muttered.

Gerald's voice was low, but Megan could hear him all the same. "We could be standing by after either of your hearts stop with a timer and bring you back. Have the medical staff from Nalrin come—"

I shook my head. "Last resort, and it will be me, regardless of what Aiden would say because I'm not taking a chance with that shit on Jayden. What else?"

"You and Jayden would need to separate for a minimum of four months. You couldn't talk at all during that time."

My heartbeat picked up. That was a much more feasible possibility. "I would have to find a way to keep Jayden and Ilris safe. They couldn't be compromised at all, and if people could get to Mom, they would definitely be able to get to them." I chewed on my thumb for a moment before asking, "What does the provision actually say?"

She flipped over some papers before her on the desk and read, "*If either party deserts or abandons with four months of no contact, this contract becomes null and void. No contact will be determined by the absence of written correspondence, in person discussions, or discussions via LightCall system.*"

Just as I thought. *Thank you, Mom.* I let a slow smile cross my face. "Nothing about Lark Messengers?"

"Brilliant." Gerald's voice was in awe behind me.

Megan's lip lifted on the right side, but I saw the sparkle in her eye. "Nope."

"I had to ask. Anything else?"

"Just that you and Jayden could marry." When I narrowed my eyes at her, she sighed. "Marry, wait six months, proceed with the separation provisions."

"What would that really accomplish?"

"Angels, Jess." Megan shook her head. "I would have thought you would have read the thing since you took the crown."

"I've been a bit busy."

With a dramatic sigh, she continued, "If Jayden were the one to file the separation, then Kaletta would be bound to continue to supply Ashridge per the contract."

"Why would that make any difference? They aren't abiding by the contract now. We've called him on it in the past, and it gets a little better, but then it stops." I took a long, deep breath and let it out slowly. "Anything else?"

"No, those are all we can think of. Gerald, Dad, and I have spent hours going over it."

"I'll talk it over with Aiden, Jayden, and Ilris."

"You are including his partner in decisions?" Megan's voice sounded almost impressed.

"Anything that Jayden and I do will affect our partners," I said evenly. "I won't make any decisions that drastically change their life without their input."

"Okay. I'm sorry we haven't found more, but it's something."

Gerald asked from behind me, "The second option. There would have to be zero contact between them?" A nod from Megan. "Jess, what's the longest you and Jayden have gone without talking to each other since the signing of the contract?"

My eyebrows pinched together as I thought about it. He had been in Cinder for months before he stepped on the boat in Kaletta with us. "About three months?"

"Could you go four months without talking?"

I half turned in my chair to look at Gerald. "It's fine. Besides, if the Lark Messenger is the loophole, then we can still talk and continue looking into other options in case it doesn't work. Besides, I don't have a concern about the no contact order. Are there provisions whereby the time would be restarted or negated?"

"If you do have contact in accordance with the agreement, or if war is declared, or if the Grand Lord dies."

I nodded. "If the Grand Lord died, Jayden and I would just burn the contract anyways. Fuck it all to the Underworld. I'm more concerned about where in the dimension he's going to go that the Grand Lord can't find him."

"Let me talk to a couple of people. Go talk to Jayden and Aiden."

"Okay. Keep me updated. Thanks, Megan." I stared off at the wall, leaning my elbows on the edge of the table, and chewed on my thumb again.

Megan hung up, and the light faded from the room. Gerald didn't move, but I sat there staring at the opposite wall. He let me sit there for a few minutes before he cleared his throat, and I looked at him. "Grand Duchess?"

"Well, I knew it was highly locked down, but the fact that Megan... Megan Mathewson, couldn't find anything but one remotely viable option?" I rubbed my face, and when I looked at him again, he just gave me a sad smile. "You and Megan have been working endless hours on options. I can't tell you how much I appreciate it."

"We have been here for you your entire life. The Ashridge Council wants you happy, and your mother was trying to find a way out of it. I'm just continuing to try."

"Why didn't you tell me the options?"

He shifted uncomfortably on his feet. His voice was low and tentative. "Because they would be better received from Lady Megan. She's your family."

"And you have known me your entire life. There should be nothing that you hold back from me, Gerald." He only tipped his head to the side and shrugged. Smiling at him, I stood and walked out. "It's been a long day. I'm gonna head to my residence and talk to them tomorrow. I'll update you later."

I barely heard the whispered, "Yes, Grand Duchess."

CHAPTER 12

AIDEN

SITTING IN MY OFFICE, I was going through the most recent reports of our numbers from Vincent. We had increased our numbers within Ashridge City by a few thousand, but that meant that we also had to figure out how to feed them since supplies were starting to run short.

There was a knock on the door and Ryder, the Grand Duchess' chief of health and human services, popped his head in. "Vernadali Aiden, you asked for me?"

"Come on in." I waved him inside, leaning back in my black leather chair. It squeaked under the pressure and after taking a long breath, I leaned toward my desk. I waited for him to take a seat and asked, "Is there any way to get the supply lines from Silentport running again?"

Silentport's caravans across the black sands were out of commission after the last two had been slaughtered. Jess had lost her shit when the report came in, and the only caravan left was taking the long way around, delaying the much-needed supplies.

Ryder sighed and shook his head. "I'm sorry, sir—"

"Please call me Aiden."

"I'm sorry, Aiden, but there is no one else. We already have some Ashridge guards accompanying them." Nodding at him, I let out a long breath through my nose. "Are we trying to see if Sheller Bay can help supplement?"

"We are. They are sending grain, Choklar meat, and seafood. Will take some time though. It's a long trek. I'm sure Georgina is talking to all her number crunchers to make sure the kilns we have last." He sighed. "Have you and Gerald found anything to stop the destruction in Silentport?"

Shaking my head, I leaned back in my chair again. "Nah. We see it arriving. It's still getting signed off, but then it is destroyed or disappears."

"So, almost nothing is getting to the people, Vern... I mean, Aiden."

I nodded, rubbed my face, and shook my head to try to wake up. I really needed to just curl up with my kotě. "Thank you. You can head out. I'm gonna go and try to sleep."

CLOSING THE DOOR AT our residence, the room was fairly dark, with only enough light to make sure I didn't run into furniture. I had stopped by Jess' office, and Noah said she had headed back early.

When I got to the main living area, there was just enough light through the floor-to-ceiling window to illuminate the couch, where Jess sat holding a pillow close to her chest and chewing on her thumb. I leaned against the wall and, as I watched her, my confusion grew. I had been so distracted by what I was doing today that I hadn't checked in with her emotionally. Now, her feelings were a mess of concern and confusion. Her eyes narrowed as she thought through whatever was on her mind.

Caressing the Claiming, I felt her do the same, and I smiled. "What's wrong, Kotě?" Her head popped up, and a small smile crossed her lips. My heart swelled as I smiled back at her, feeling the rush of love and admiration flow through that bond, but I repeated, "What's wrong?"

"I talked to your mom a few hours ago." I raised an eyebrow and pushed off the wall to go sit with her. Once I was next to her with her legs straightened over my lap, she continued, "She has three suggestions for getting out of the contract."

"Three? I'm surprised she found that many. What are they?"

"Two aren't really options at all. There is one viable one, like *really* viable if we can work a few things out."

I waited for her to continue, but when she didn't, I narrowed my eyes and asked, "What are the two nonviable?"

"Well, it isn't that they aren't viable. We could do them, but I would have to be pretty desperate." She was looking at her fingers, playing with them, and I felt her anxiety ratchet up.

"Jess, you gotta give me a little more than that." She shook her head. Reaching over and taking her chin in between my thumb and finger, I made her look at me. "No secrets, remember?"

"It's not a secret. It's just..." She took a deep breath, obviously to steel herself, and launched into it. "The first is to marry Jayden then have him file the separation paperwork after a few months. The second is that I die for sixty-one seconds and *hope* that you can bring me back." My whole body went taut, and I felt my Charge fly through the room. She didn't even wince or blink. Her gaze held firm to mine. My fingers, however, tightened on her chin. "I'm assuming neither of those are your first choice."

I felt every protective instinct to pull her close and carry her far, far away. My voice came out much calmer than I was, but I said, "You could say that."

"Good because they aren't exactly at the top of my list either." She smiled at me, trying to lighten the mood, but I kept her chin firm. "Finally, the only viable option." She took my hand from her chin and slid her fingers through mine. I took a long breath and let it out through my nose, centering myself and making my world focus on the woman who was indeed safe and alive in my lap.

"Relax, Aid. I promise, this is actually viable if we can work some things out."

"That's what you were thinking so hard on?"

Nodding, she swung her legs off my lap and stood before she began to pace back and forth. "Jayden and I separate for a minimum of four months with no contact. No written, physical, or LightCall communications." Then she stopped pacing and crossed her arms, smiling at me. There was a sliver of hope that went through me, and I was smiling back at her. I could tell by the look on her face and the clever feeling that I was getting from her, that she had a plan, so I waited. "What do you hear in that statement, Aid?"

"Jayden and Ilris go on vacation somewhere and you two don't talk for four months." I cocked my head to the side and studied her. "What am I missing?"

"What other method of communication wasn't listed?" I thought through it, and when I finally realized what she meant, I laughed. "Did he seriously think that a Lark Messenger wouldn't be available to you?"

"I don't know, but if needed, we could still get messages to each other that way. There is one problem." I waited for her to continue as she returned to her pacing. "I put Jayden and Ilris under my protection. Ilris is now part of my kingdom, so wherever they go, they have to be safe and far enough away that the Grand Lord can't get him."

"And you don't think this can happen here in Ashridge?" She shook her head and started pacing again. "Nalrin City, even under Popa, Mom, and Dad would be a risk."

She was chewing her thumb again, and I stood up and took her hand out of her mouth. She huffed a small laugh and said, "I don't know where to have them go. Lemi is on his way here, so I can't send them to Cinder either."

My mind was racing through a bunch of ideas, and I narrowed my eyes at her as I thought of one place she could send them, and there wasn't a single person in this or any dimension that would mess with them. I started chuckling.

Jess turned to face me, narrowing her eyes. "What are you thinking?"

I strode to her and put my hands on her hips, pulling her close to me. Taking my finger and lifting her chin, I bent down and gave her a soft kiss. Her whole body leaned into me, and I felt a satisfied moan come from her. Pulling back, I smiled against her lips.

"If I were not so exhausted, I would take you up on that moan, Kotě." She gave me a little bit of a pouty lip, and I kissed her forehead before saying, "I have an idea. I can reach out to Auntie Clarice and see if we can take them there."

"They can't teleport though, and I can't ask them to travel that far. There is too much opportunity for them to be discovered and for Kaletta to make an attempt on their lives." She leaned forward, wrapping her arms around me, and rested her head on my chest.

I laid my cheek on the top of her head and just said, "I have an idea. Let me worry about it and talk to a couple people in the morning."

"Okay." She was exhausted. Kissing the top of her head, I bent down, picked her up, and carried her to bed. "First, we both need sleep."

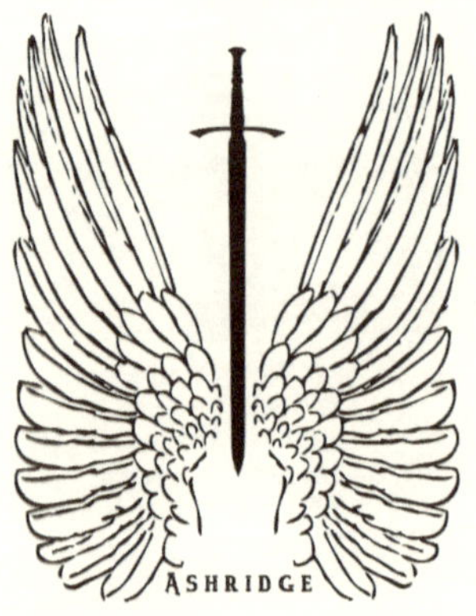

CHAPTER 13

JESSIKA

SITTING IN THE LIGHTCALL room for the second time in so many days, I rubbed my face and tried to settle my thoughts. Aiden filled me in on what he was thinking this morning over breakfast, and we sent word to Therth that we needed to speak to the Empress as soon as she was available.

I took Aiden's hand, and when he leaned over to kiss me, I couldn't help but lean into it. Of course, that was when Clarice clicked in and her face showed in the bright orb.

"Angels, Aiden Chatwell and Jessika Petra. I realize you are in a private room, but I did not need to see that first thing."

"Auntie Clarice, I don't really care." He quickly kissed me again and then turned toward her, smiling brightly. "How are you, Auntie?"

"Oh, Angels in Nalrin. What do you want?" Her eye roll was so dramatic that I felt it from here. I chuckled and smiled at Aiden, who was putting on the ultimate little good boy act. It was sort of adorable.

"Aid...," I whispered, and he chuckled.

Clarice gave him an even look before turning toward me and asking, "Jess, what does Aiden want?"

"Well..." I looked at him, and he took over.

"I have a major favor to ask." I hated this. It was using the Mathewsons to further my personal agenda, and as much as I preached not wanting to do that to everyone, I just didn't see another option.

"I'm listening."

"Mom found a loophole." Then he leaned forward on the desk to steel himself as Clarice's eyebrow rose. "If Jess and Jayden don't have contact for four months, the agreement will be considered null and void."

"Okay?" Her eyes flicked between us, then she tipped her head to the left, and I saw her eyes go smokey. Aiden looked at me, and we waited for her to finish whatever it was she was doing. When she did, a tear slipped out of the corner of her eye. "You need somewhere safe for them to go and you were thinking of Therth?"

"How?" I asked.

Smiling, she said, "Your mom. She says she's so proud of you and that she did the best she could in putting last ditch loopholes in that agreement. She also said it was about damn time that you and Aiden committed to each other, but she warned to be careful with the Grand Lord. He's slippery, and if we aren't really careful, Ashridge could fall."

"My... mom?" My voice was broken.

Aiden kissed my temple as he whispered, "Gatekeeper secrets, remember?"

"Right. I forget you could talk to the dead. Next time she shows up, tell her I love her."

"I will. Now, back to your situation. Your mom mentioned something about having Jayden lie low for a bit and keeping him safe."

Nodding, I told her how the biggest concern was his safety, even admitting how the Grand Lord was able to get to Mom under all the protections afforded here. When I told her that there was no provision for messages to be given through Lark Messenger, she laughed so hard, she had tears leaking from her eyes.

"How did the Grand Lord miss that? Is he really that arrogant that he missed that in the contract?"

"Apparently."

"I'm assuming that you will want us to pick them up since you don't want to take the chance of anything happening en route."

Aiden's chipper, "Yes, please," had me chuckling.

Clarice looked at him, shaking her head. "I swear, if you were not so damn adorable... Underworld's being... that's exactly why you get what you want."

The red that crept up in his face was adorable, but then he looked at me and said, "I just had to get out of my own way and have a little intervention from the Angels."

"There is a problem, though, Aiden. The loophole for Alexei, Reka, and I only works because we have the Underworld's darkness in our blood."

I narrowed my eyes for a moment in concentration. Seeing that, Aiden asked, "What are you thinking about, Jess?"

"Jayden and Ilris are completely committed to each other." I gave Clarice a meaningful look.

"Just say it."

"Could you make them Silnaree and put darkness in their blood? With their consent, of course. Would that make it so you could teleport them?"

Clarice shook her head and smiled. "Only if they consent to it. I won't force the Underworld's darkness onto someone. It's not a decision made lightly. We've told you about Alexei and me."

Nodding at Clarice, I toyed with my bottom lip with my teeth. "I haven't talked over any of this with Jayden and Ilris yet. I wanted to make sure that you would even be open to the idea of them coming down. No reason to get hopes up if you weren't going to be able to help. Now there is the consideration of whether to make them Silnaree or not. I do appreciate you helping, Empress Clar—"

"Don't make me full name you again, Grand Duchess." I winced but kept her gaze. "You are family, ma'am. We protect and help family. I'm not sure why I have to keep reminding you of that."

"Because she forgets she is a Mathewson," Aiden gloated.

"THIS. This is why," I tried to combat, but there was no real bite to it, and they both knew it.

"Alright, alright. Let me know when you want us to collect the package and we will make it happen."

"Thank you, Clarice," I said as Aiden's, "Thanks, Auntie," came through.

"Love you both." Then she clicked the LightCall off and the orb disappeared.

I leaned back in the chair and huffed. "Now, to talk to Ilris and Jayden."

My words may have been almost calm and resigned, but... Mom. Clarice had just freaking spoken to Mom. All that pain and loss came rushing back, and as Aiden stood to open the door, I caught the look he gave me and I shook it off. My chest was too tight, and my stomach suddenly felt like I needed to throw up.

You got this, Jess. You can pull yourself together and be the Grand Duchess. You got this.

But did I? Was I sure I wasn't drunk half passed out on my couch in my room right now? I felt like I was stuck in a nightmare that wouldn't relent. The only thing that brought me peace was being in Aiden's arms and feeling him against me, reminding me that he really was here and I was not all alone. His touch brought me comfort like it did all those years ago, as if time hadn't moved. He was the only thing that could pull my mind away from my responsibilities and duty. The only thing that pulled me from my grief, even if only for a moment.

Chapter 14

Aiden

Jess and I were halfway to Jayden's residence when a wave of anxiousness, sadness, and a sense of being overwhelmed came over her. I caressed down the Claiming, and she stopped to take a deep breath. The fact she stopped to do it wasn't what had me taking her hand and pulling her into the small room. It was the hitch in it and the despair she felt. It was how I could feel it in the very core of me.

Once I had the door shut and locked, I turned around and caged her against the wall. "What was the trigger?"

Jess didn't look at me, but she ran her hand along the buttons on my shirt before resting them on my chest. I felt a whole new sensation flood through her, but I needed to know what set her off. She wouldn't look at me, so I leaned down, kissed her neck, and ran my jaw along hers. "Please, tell me what was the trigger for you to fall into that despair you are feeling?"

"Clarice." She stared at me a long moment. Studied my eyes, as kept mine took a shaky breath, and her hand grabbed a hold of my shirt.

"There was a lot in that conversation. Can you be a little more specific?" I leaned my forehead against hers and let her take her time. There was so much going through her, I didn't know where to start. She went from brief flashes of rage, to horny, to that sadness that would have her breath hitching again.

"I forgot that Clarice would be able to talk to Mom. Why didn't I think about that? Why wouldn't I have already asked her to find out if Mom knew how to do this? If there were any loopholes in the contract we could use."

"Stop." I was stern, but I was very careful not to push any of my Charge into it. "Gatekeeper secrets. Okay?" She nodded. "The Gatekeeper can't initiate contact without major preparation. It means that Momma Grand Duchess went to Auntie Clarice."

"But she could have checked with Mom. Why didn't I think about it? Why didn't I—"

"Stop."

When her head snapped up and her gaze met mine, I had to restrain myself from raging against the world and letting it burn for making her feel like this. Tears were falling down her cheeks, and her eyes were red. "Kotě, what do you need from me?"

Her gaze didn't leave mine, but I saw a little of that despair leave, and then she caressed down the Claiming.

Fear crossed her eyes and when I felt it, it was like a punch to the gut. I kissed her forehead, and her fingers gripped my shirt tight as she hiccupped. "What do you need from me?"

"I... need..." Another shudder of her chest and she reached up and kissed me. It was hard and meaningful, so I let her guide it. I threaded my hand through her hair and when she moaned, I tightened the grip of it.

She pulled back, just enough so that we could catch our breath. Her hands trailed down, and she undid the buckle and top button in one fluid movement.

"Kotě."

"You asked me what I need, Aiden. I need you. I need you to remind me that I am yours and you are mine. That we will be together. That we have a future. That I'm not drunk in my residence, having a fevered dream you are here. That in the end, everything will be fine." Every word came out urgent, but there was a fear that was laced in that broke my heart.

"If you doubt my love for you, if you doubt that I'm here," I said as I stripped her of her boots and pants, "then I haven't done my job as your Vernadali—"

"My Vernadali wouldn't have to love me, Aiden. Anyone can fill that position." She whispered as I growled, knelt before her, and kissed just above her clit. I lifted a leg and threw it over my shoulder.

"If you doubt my love for you as your Dom or mate, Jessika Petra, then I am not doing my job." I spread her wide and with a flat tongue ran the length of her before flicking over her clit. "I'm truly sorry for that and vow to do a better job."

Her hands dove into my hair as I latched onto her and sucked. Her hips moved, and I snaked my tongue across every inch of her. Dipping in and tasting her was like ambrosia. Jess was my mate, and I would never again make her guess whether I was here. I felt her getting close and pulled back as I stood, freeing my cock from my pants.

"Aiden," she pleaded, but I kissed her hard, pushing her against the wall, and when she wrapped her legs around my hips, I caught her, lining myself up. I lifted Jess slightly so that I could run up and down her center and as she moaned, and I felt her chest rattle against me. She nipped at my lip, and I smiled against those little fangs.

When she did it again, I thrust into her in one hard stroke. She pulled back with a sharp intake of breath. "Look at me." When she did, I pulled out and thrust back in. "I am here. Feel me. I am going nowhere. I am yours. I am your Vernadali. I am your mate." Each sentence was emphasized with a long drag out and a hard thrust back in. "I love you, Kotě."

Her nails dug into my shoulders and sent pleasure down my spine. I pounded into her, not letting up until I felt my balls tighten. Lowering my head, I licked and kissed the spot where her neck met her shoulders. Her pussy clamped down on me as I fell over the edge, and she bit down on the mating spot to muffle her own sounds.

We stood there wrapped up with each other, trying to get our breathing under better control. She lowered her legs as I retreated from her. I let my hands run up her sides and cradle her head, making her look at me. "I am here, Jess. I am here for you always. You are mine. We will live long, happy lives together. I will always be here to protect you. I vow that as your mate."

"I know. I'm sorry that I made you think I doubted you. I—"

"Spiraled."

She nodded and then said, "Since we vowed ourselves to each other, I have never doubted you. I just keep thinking that everything is a fevered dream. My mom, Amala, the Grand Lord, and if that is all a dream, then that means you are too, and I can't lose you again, Aiden. I don't think I could live through that." Lifting her hands to cover mine, she smiled. "Thank you for reminding me, though."

I smirked. "Anything for you. Anything at all."

We righted our clothes, and she stared at the door. "Can we wait until tomorrow to talk to them about this plan? I want to go back to our residence."

"If that is what you really want. Just remember that we can't avoid it forever. It's a solution. Now, whether he will be willing to go to Therth for four months or not is a wholly different matter."

She turned to face me, and I felt that dread filter through her and saw tears fill her eyes. "Tomorrow morning. First thing."

Pulling her in tight against me, I whispered, "No problem. I'll get a hold of Noah as well and have him cancel anything else you had scheduled for the day."

There was a wet sniff before she nodded.

CHAPTER 15

AIDEN

I GOT JESS CURLED up in bed, and once she was asleep, I stepped out into the hall and gave orders that no one go in or out. Heading to her secretary's office, I passed someone in the main hall who kept their head down and tightened a pouch on the right side. He turned down one of the guest halls, and so I let it go.

I stopped and talked to a couple of the guards before I made it to Noah's door. When I knocked, he hollered for me to come in. "What can I do for you, Vernadali Aiden?"

"I just wanted to let you know that the Grand Duchess will not be available this afternoon."

He raised his eyebrow. "Of course, Vernadali Aiden. I'll reschedule her appointments. Is she unwell?"

"She had a difficult morning and will be recovering. Tomorrow morning, she will be meeting with Lord Jayden. Please let him know to expect us right after breakfast."

"Yes, sir." His head tilted to the side. He looked worried, but he still tried to stay formal. "Anything else?"

"She will be fine, Noah." His shoulders relaxed, and he nodded. "I'm heading back. If someone is looking for me, I'll be at the residence."

"Thank you."

As I headed back to Jess, the guy who was walking to the guest rooms turned down her hall. I caught the eye of one of the Vernadali and gave him the silent signal to protect the Grand Duchess, and he instantly started giving orders to the other guards in the main hall.

I picked up speed and before long, I was about twenty feet behind him. As he moved, his shirt rose just enough that I could see the emblem etched on the black leather that curved and moved on its own. A golden lion. *Kaletta.*

Sending my power out toward him, he lunged to the side and then bolted for Jess' door. There was a wave of power that he had thrown out in front of him, hurling all of the Ashridge Guard back onto their asses. His hand shot out, creating a wall between me and him. I pulled hard on the Claiming as I grabbed a syth from my thigh and threw it.

I felt Jess tug on the Claiming, and I jerked it hard and focused for a moment to tell her, "*Stay inside.*" As he turned toward me, I threw my power back at him and his shield fell. My Charge rolled down the hall, but just as it would have hit him, he kicked the door to our residence along with a concentrated blast of his power, shattering it.

He went to take a step into the room, but my Charge reached him, wrapping around him tightly. Launching myself forward, I flicked my wrists, pushing him against the wall. His hand reached for something on his right side, and when he unbuckled the pouch, I saw a black chicklory snake slither out.

I threw my other hand out, pushing my power around it, willing my Charge to encase it. Opening its mouth wide, fangs fully extended, it tried to strike out at me but hit the wall instead.

Taking my syth and pressing it to the neck of the man I had pinned against the wall, I asked, "Who sent you?"

His eyes lit with amusement as his mouth started to foam. When he went limp against my power, I let him drop and opened his mouth. "Fucking suicide teeth," I muttered.

"Aid?" I heard Jess behind me, and when I turned to face her, her focus was set on the snake coiling and hissing, striking the wall again. "What in the fuck is that?"

"The same kind of snake that killed Momma Grand Duchess."

Fear coursed through her, but she kept her composure in a sheer force of will that came from years of court training. She lifted her hand and looked at me as if to ask if she could destroy it. I nodded, and her wide eyes went contemplative. Sending her power toward the snake, it flowed over my Charge. I let a small pinhole open for it to flow into, and I felt it slide through the small opening.

The snake froze with its mouth opened wide, and I felt my Charge heat against her vibrations. I focused on thinking of ice between the Charge and her power but watched as the heat cooked the snake in its place. When it was nothing but charcoal, I released it, sending it crashing to the floor.

My eyes snapped to Jess', and I saw the terror in them. "Guards, find out how he gained entrance and why he even had access to the Grand Duchess' residence hall. He's been wandering around for a while. Why did no one stop him? I saw him on my way to see the secretary of the kingdom over an hour ago. Yet, he was still here and had gained access to this hall?"

I reached out my hand to Jess, who took it, but hers was ice cold. My back was to our residence and that ensured she was behind me. She curled up to my back and pressed her forehead to the area between my shoulder blades. Her breathing came in long, deep breaths as she squeezed hard on my hand. Slowly, as she continued to breathe, the tension and adrenaline in her released. Once the last suffocating bit released her, I felt her breathing hitch behind me.

"Find Vernadali Dadan and have her head the investigation. Get this door fixed immediately."

There were affirmatives, and then I took her back into the residence. Once inside, I turned and secured the doorway with every incantation I could muster. Turning, I found Jess standing right behind me with her hand to her throat. Her breathing quickened, and I took her hand, pushing calm into her. Wrapping her arms around my waist, she held me tight as I tried to calm her down.

It took a few minutes, but her breathing evened out. I reached down, carried her back to bed, and when I put her down, she grabbed a hold of my shirt in a death grip.

"Don't leave me alone." Her voice was so quiet I hardly heard it, but I felt the plea from her.

"I won't leave the residence, but I need to keep the entrance secure. I promise I will be close. Just tug for me, okay?"

Her eyes were wide, and I felt my heart in my stomach. "Don't leave me."

"Kotě, I promise I won't leave the residence." I pushed against the Claiming and held her gaze until the fear and terror lessened her eyes. "Three minutes."

She nodded, and I felt her hand on the Claiming. She held tight, so I bent down and kissed her forehead. Her fingers slowly loosened.

When I got to the entryway, Vernadali Dadan was standing at the other side of the incantations, looking a bit put out. I chuckled and with a wave of my hand, they disappeared, and Dadan threw her hands up and sighed. "Really, Aiden?"

"What? We don't have a door, and there was just an attempt on my Charge's life."

"Did you have to go full war mode? That shit hurt to walk into."

I smiled at her, and she tucked a lock of hair that had fallen out of her low bun behind her ear. "That was sort of the point, Vernadali Dadan. Again, there was an attempt on my Charge's life."

Sighing, Vernadali Dadan nodded in understanding. "There was no identifying information on the attacker. We don't know how he was able to get past the wards of the main hall."

"That's two that have circumvented them. We gotta get a hold of this." I ran my hand through my hair and tipped my head back. "What else have you found?"

"Not much else. Only that this snake was registered. Had a chip in it. It was damaged when the Grand Duchess cooked it, though." She tried not to chuckle, but even I let a smile cross my face.

"How are the guards that got knocked back?" I jerked my head to where six of them sat with their head in their hands.

"All of them have concussions and will be pulled from duty until the physicians clear them. Probably out for a couple of days. I'll update you in the morning."

"We are meeting with Lord Jayden and Sir Ilris tomorrow." I looked back over my shoulder and had a thought. They were going to be pissed, but Jess... I had to protect Jess. "Actually, I want all four Vernadali to move Jayden and Ilris to the Grand Duchess' residence. We will work out the accommodations. I want an enchanted door installed here by the time they arrive."

Vernadali Dadan's eyes barely widened at the order. She put a fist on her heart, bent, and took off down the hall. I stood guard at the door, and I felt Jess run a finger over the Claiming that she still had gripped tight. "*I love you, Aiden.*"

"*I love you, my kotě.*" I felt the grip loosen a little bit but continued to stand guard.

It was another ten minutes before the door arrived, and another eight before the Vernadali escorted Jayden and Ilris in. Jayden gave me a look, clearly telling me he was highly unhappy with my orders.

I waited for the door to be completed, added a few of my personal Vernadali incantations, and then turned and walked into the main living area.

"What the fuck, Aiden?"

"Don't move. I'll be right back. I need to check on Jess." I walked past them, down the hall, and back into the bedroom. She opened her eyes, stretching out a hand toward me. Taking it, I rested my other hand on her cheek. "Go to sleep, Kotě. I've got Jayden and Ilris moving into the guest room. I'll talk to you more about it later."

She nodded, and I kissed her temple quickly before returning to the main room. When I turned the corner, Ilris was sitting on the couch, but Jayden jumped up and asked again, "What the fuck?"

Looking around the corner, I saw that the new door was installed and turned back to the Lord of Kaletta and his partner.

"There was an assassination attempt on Jess. I need the Vernadali to guard you *and* her. If you are in the same residence, then it will be easier." I ran my fingers through my hair and then put both hands on my hips. "I realize that there are appearances to be kept, and you can still have them. We will handle it."

"Someone tried to assassinate Jessika?" Jayden's face had drained of color as he looked to Ilris, whose eyes were wide. "Is she okay?"

"She's had a rough day. Luckily, I was able to stop him before he actually got full access. He blew the door apart, hence the new one. She did have the pleasure of killing the snake they brought."

Jayden's face turned into cold fury at that statement. "They tried to kill Jessika the same way as they did her mom?" When I nodded, Jayden looked to Ilris and then back to me before he said, "I will have his head the next time I see him."

"We will have to talk about this more in the morning. You two are staying in the guest room. Jess is trying to sleep. There is a lot to cover."

Ilris' head tipped to the side as he noted how I deflected Jayden's statement, and I sighed when he opened his mouth and said, "What aren't you telling us, Aiden?"

I looked between them and groaned. "Jess wants to talk to you about her discussion with my mom earlier today. It's a bit to unpack, and we may have a plan, but we all need to get some sleep first. I promise we will talk in the morning."

"Is that an order from her Vernadali or a request from the future Duke?" There was a small lift of Jayden's lips and I shook my head.

"It's a personal request from your friend, asking you to let it sit until morning."

"As a friend, can you give me any more than that?" He took a step toward me and crossed his arms.

"There is a viable option, Jayden. She wants to discuss it with you. That's all you are getting from me." I flicked my eyes to her through the wall as I felt a wave of anxiousness and fear wash over me. "I need to get back to her. Please go and get some sleep."

"Okay." He reached over and gripped my shoulder quickly, and then he reached out for Ilris, who took his hand. I followed them down the hall, waiving all the lights out as we went. They filtered into the guest room, and Jayden nodded quickly as he shut the door and locked it. I ran my hand over the wood, giving it a little more protection from anyone with intent or desire to cause harm to them.

When I got to our room, I did the same thing and stripped to my boxer briefs. As hard as I tried to not bother her when I climbed into bed, she rolled over and full-on sprawled on top of me.

I didn't have the heart to try to move her, so I just wrapped my arm around her and ensured the blankets were over us before falling into an exhausted sleep.

CHAPTER 16

JAYDEN

I WOKE UP SMELLING the rich scent of clove and cinnamon. My eyes fluttered open, and I found myself nestled into the crook of Ilris' neck. I pulled him closer to me, where he let out a small satisfied sound that warmed my heart.

I lay there taking in the feel of him against me. It had been a couple months since I almost lost him. For ten years, Ilris had been mine, and over the last couple months, I'd actually been able to have him as *mine*. Been able to truly have nights where we didn't have to hold back. We could just be us without the worry of who was going to bust through the door and find us in bed together.

I let my hand spread across his defined abs and slowly along the scar that almost ended us both. I took a deep breath and wrapped my fingers tight around his waist before there was a rough whisper, "You keep doing that, *liefde*, and Jessika is going to be mad we dirtied the sheets so quickly."

Jessika. I kissed his shoulder and let out a sigh. "I know. I'm not going to push it."

He rolled over to face me and gave me a quick kiss. When the sleep had pulled from his eyes, though, his gaze flicked over my face. "You didn't sleep much, did you?"

"No. Was thinking about what Aiden said."

"He mentioned a viable solution. Any ideas?" he asked as he ran a thumb over my cheekbone. I shook my head as I looked to the door. I thought I heard Jessika and Aiden moving around, and... I smelled breakfast cooking. "Well, *liefde*, you know what you need to do then, right?"

"What's that?" I let a small smile lift the left side of my lips.

"Get your sexy ass out of bed, get dressed, and go find out. I'll be right there with you."

I narrowed my eyes at him as I studied him. He always took point for me, letting me release that control and fierceness in private without having to jeopardize anything in the public eye. He was everything I would ever need, and I would endeavor to be the same for him.

The pain of losing Killy was still raw for both of us. But I was the Lord of Kaletta, and as soon as I could, I would relieve the world of my father's existence. As Grand Lord, I would change the fucking laws and hand it over to Jessika.

I would protect him. I had to protect him. He was the most important thing in my world. "I love you, Ilris. Whatever happens out there today, please just remember that."

His eyes were bright as he leaned down and kissed me hard. His tongue swept across my lips, and I opened for him, swallowing the ball of emotion that was coming up my throat. He threaded his hands around the back of my head and held me as his tongue stroked every inch of my mouth. When we were struggling for breath, he pulled back and leaned his forehead to mine. "I love you, too, Jade. I know that you won't agree to anything that will hurt either of us. So, let's go out there and find out what we are being asked to do."

"But I don't want to get up. I want to stay here in bed with you today." I stuck my lower lip out and let my fingers play with the hair along his happy trail. I lost the pouty lip when his stomach contracted against my touch, and I smiled.

He groaned, and when I licked his neck, he ordered, "Alright, *liefde*. In the shower now."

"Yes, sir."

Forty minutes later, after a thorough, loving shower, we strode into the main room and around the corner to the kitchen where Aiden and Jessika were cooking.

"Oh, good. I was hoping the smell of food would lure you out of the bedroom, or should I say, the shower?" Jessika smiled brightly and winked at me quickly as she turned from the pan of what looked like falish links. Aiden wasn't taking his eyes off the childer eggs.

"When it smells so good, did you expect us to lie in bed all day?" I chuckled, and Ilris poked my side, giving me an even look. Yeah, I would have liked to stay in bed with him for a long while, but he was right. The shower was a compromise.

"Go sit down." Aiden flicked his eyes toward us and gave me a nod. He knew I was still upset about last night. The fact he pulled rank and just ordered us to move without asking rubbed me the wrong way. Once we were in the guest room, though, Ilris walked me through the process from a guard's perspective and I realized it was just my ego slightly bruised.

While Ilris turned to sit in the main room, I stood at the entrance to the kitchen and leaned against the wall. Jessika seemed chipper, but I noticed how Aiden kept looking at her and the way she would stop and take a breath before plastering a smile on her face and continuing with preparing breakfast.

I stood there for a good five minutes before Aiden removed the eggs from the stove and met my gaze. I raised my eyebrows in question to him, and he shook his head. Rolling my eyes, he said quietly, "After we eat."

Jessika froze, and when she looked at me, I was taken aback by how drawn in her eyes were. She jerked her head and repeated what Aiden said, "After we eat."

Sighing, I turned and sat down at the table. Whatever they were going to suggest was big. Aiden had mentioned that there was a viable option, but with the look in her eyes, I had to wonder what it was that had her so tied up.

"What is it?" Ilris bent down and whispered in my ear, and then he gave me a small kiss on the top of my head before sitting down.

"It isn't like Jessika to put off a discussion. It's got me a bit... scared."

Aiden and Jessika came in with plates of food, and they sat in awkward silence for a minute, taking bites.

"How did you sleep, Jayden?" Jessika asked. There was a tremble to her voice that I hadn't heard from her since the day I almost killed myself. I put another piece of the link in my mouth and chewed slowly before saying, "After we got settled, it was okay."

I didn't look at her, but I felt her eyes on me. Ilris' hand slid to my thigh under the table and squeezed it. I sighed heavily and, while still not looking up at her, asked, "Are we really going to sit here and make small talk?"

"I..." She stopped, and I put my fork down on the plate where it clanked loudly.

"Jessika, we have known each other for too long. You are literally one of two people who are the reason I am still breathing. You are one of the most important people in my life, and last night your mate ordered Ilris and me to relocate to your private residence, where we find out there was an assassination attempt on your life. And *then* he hints there might be an option for nullifying the marriage contract, but you've been stonewalling me with the information?"

Her eyes filled with tears, and then she pulled them back.

It was Aiden, though, who laid into me. "Jayden, yesterday was a lot. Jess had a particularly emotional LightCall in the morning, and then when I told her to take the afternoon off, she was attacked where, if they had been successful, she would have died in the same manner as her mother. So yes, she did slow roll the information to you, because while it is highly important, she wanted to make sure she could think clearly and have the conversation with you. Is that sufficient for you?"

I still hadn't broken my gaze with Jessika but took a deep breath to reel in the hurt and impatience. I nodded to him and said quietly, "I'm sorry." Ilris squeezed my thigh again, and I looked back at Jessika. "I'm sorry. I didn't think... Angels, I'm a right asshole sometimes."

Jessika nodded and put her fork down carefully. "I spoke to Lady Megan yesterday morning. She said there are three options. One of them is completely off the table for the foreseeable future for a lot of reasons. The third option she gave me is less than ideal, but the second, while also not ideal, is the least of the evils. I think we can make it work, but I need you to keep an open mind because you likely aren't going to like it."

My heart raced, and I took a calming breath. Ilris' fingers intertwined with mine, and he tightened the grip to reassure me. "Does this have to do with the fact that Ilris and I have been brought to your residence?"

"No, that is purely because I don't want the Vernadali and guards to be stretched too thin until we know what we are doing. I needed the Vernadali here to protect Jess, but we also need them to protect you. So, here you are." Aiden's smirk was one where he knew he was playing the system, but it got what he wanted.

There was a knock on the door, and Aiden went to get it. I vaguely heard the tearing of paper, and then Aiden thanked whomever had brought the message. When he returned, everyone was watching him as he sat down, picked up a piece of bread, and took a bite.

He looked at us as we all stared at him. "What?"

"What was that?" Jessika asked.

"Vernadali business," he said, but there was something about it that didn't sit right.

"Aiden, what are you hiding from us?"

He looked at each of us, and I thought Ilris was the only one looking at him with curiosity in his eyes, where Jessika and I were staring him down as monarchs of our territories.

His lips thinned before he said, "The Grand Lord has increased the troop count at the ridge."

"How many?" I asked without thinking.

"Fifteen thousand."

I swallowed and felt Ilris go stiff against me, but as I watched Aiden, there was a small twitch in his jaw, and considering my mood this morning, I wasn't going to let him get away with that.

"What else?"

Aiden looked over to Jessika, and there appeared to be a silent conversation going on between them. When Aiden scratched his temple and she winked in return, I was sure of it.

Looking at Ilris, he was studying me. He mouthed, "*Are you okay?*" I nodded and he gave me a small smile.

Jessika stood and took Aiden's plate as she said, "This is going to be a difficult conversation, and Jayden, I don't think either of us are going to like what Aiden has to say."

"For the Underworld," I growled. "Will you guys just say what the fuck is going on? I feel like we are about to be told Mom and Dad are divorcing. I mean, we know that you two aren't, but what in the fuck is happening?"

Aiden sighed as we dropped dishes into the sink and went to sit in the main room. Once we were all settled, Aiden turned to Jessika and said, "Not only has the Grand Lord increased his troops by fifteen thousand at the ridge, but there was also a large group spotted heading east."

I narrowed my eyes. "Do we know how far east? Like to the coast? There isn't anything out there except for..."

Ilris let out a heavy sigh and leaned back. "He's making a move on Silentport, isn't he?"

Jessika was staring off at the opposite wall. "I need to talk to Gerald and Ryder when we are done."

"I'll have the meeting set for lunch," Aiden muttered as she stood and paced for a moment. "The marriage contract. As I said, I spoke to Lady Megan yesterday morning."

"There are two not-so-great options, but one that might be acceptable?"

"Yeah." She looked at me, and I narrowed my eyes at her. "Basically, we can't talk to each other for four months. No in-person, written, or LightCall communications."

I narrowed my eyes in confusion and looked at Ilris, who was thinking hard. I opened my mouth, but Ilris said, "But nothing about Larks?"

"Nope," Jessika said with a pop. "You picked that up quicker than Aiden."

"I don't understand why this has you tied up in knots."

"Well, the problem isn't that you and I don't communicate other than by Lark, but more about you being somewhere safe. So, while Aiden and I have a plan about that, I will ask you first. Where do you think you could go where you would be 99% safe?"

I blinked and thought about the retreat in North Kaletta, but that would put us back in Kaletta, and that wasn't such a good idea. Jessika had hideaways in Savanora and the Black Mountains, but both were close to the Kaletta border. "I guess that Nalrin City—"

"Kaletta has too many agents in the Nalrin City, Jade," Ilris muttered beside me. He was thinking of different places that we could go, but I could see now why she had been so concerned.

I blinked and flicked my gaze between the two of them, but when there was a smug smile growing on Aiden's face, I sighed in defeat. "What are you thinking?"

"Therth," Jessika muttered.

"What?" My eyes nearly bugged out of my head in shock.

"You and Ilris go to Therth." Aiden's voice had taken on the tone of the Vernadali, and I narrowed my eyes at him. "Empress Clarice can protect you there. Even if the Grand Lord were to have someone travel that far, there is no way they could get access."

"So, you want us to go there because it's the safest place in all of the Nalsar dimension, but you want us to travel that far, where we could be attacked at any point?" Their logic was so fucking flawed for two of the smartest people I knew.

"That is your response to being told that we want to send you to my auntie's house? To the Gatekeeper of the Underworld's residence?" Aiden was trying not to laugh as he said it, but some of the words sputtered out.

"I've been to visit Janreka before, Aiden. I know what it's like at Therth Castle and all the rules that are tied to the gate. Ilris, too."

"There is more." Jessika's voice was tentative, and when she took a deep breath, I felt my chest tighten. She looked up at me and there was fear, concern, and something that looked like regret in her onyx eyes. I raised my eyebrows, encouraging her to continue. "The reason that Clarice and Reka can teleport is because they have the Underworld's darkness in their veins."

"But Grand Duke Alexei can as well," I stated, not fully understanding what she was getting at.

"That is true," Aiden said carefully and met my gaze, "because he is Auntie Clarice's Silnaree."

"So just how are Jayden and I supposed to be able to get to Therth with Princess Janreka?"

"First, you may want to get used to calling her just Janreka, if you are going to go through with all this, Ilris. Second, she has offered to make you Silnaree."

Both Ilris' and my eyeballs nearly popped out of our heads as we looked at Jessika and Aiden, who looked very smug sitting there. "You are kidding."

Ilris' grip tightened in mine, and I looked at him. There was a question there, and I leaned my forehead on his before kissing him softly and turning back to them when Aiden said, "You two need to talk about this. We don't doubt your commitment to each other, but it is a serious commitment, stronger than marriage, and just as binding as my Vernadali and mating bond to Jess."

I had no hesitations but needed to know what was going through Ilris' mind.

Jessika smiled then, and I noticed her shoulders drop a little. "So, you don't hate the idea of it, then?"

I took a deep breath and said, "Jessika, we have been trying for a long time to find a way out of this marriage agreement. You and I care for each other, but we obviously have other people in our lives who are our forever." I reached over and took Ilris' hand.

"Jade...," Ilris whispered, and I looked over at him to see tears in his eyes. I looked at him in confusion. "Forever?"

I reached up with my other hand, rested it on his cheek, and wiped a tear that fell. "Of course. I'd marry you right now if I could. I have no hesitation in creating the Silnaree bond with you, hun."

Ilris' lips crashed onto mine, and he reached around to pull me closer to him. When he pulled away, he rested his forehead on mine and said, "I am yours, forever, *liefde*."

"We should still talk this through in private, though," I whispered, and he nodded before I leaned forward and kissed him quickly. Looking back at Jessika and Aiden, who were both smiling, I asked, "Alright. We need to talk about the Silnaree bond, but when do you think we should leave?"

CHAPTER 17

AIDEN

NOAH SET UP THE call to Therth so that I could talk to Auntie Clarice. Hopefully as Gatekeeper, she would be able to help out her favorite nephew. To my surprise, Reka's face popped up on the LightCall. "Reka?"

"Hi, Aiden. Mom's a little busy right now. She asked me to talk to you. What's going on?"

"How much has auntie told you about the contract?" I asked carefully.

The smile she gave me was bright and mischievous. "That we will be having a specific lord and his partner staying with us for a while and the background regarding those circumstances."

"You are looking forward to having Jayden around, aren't you?"

"Little bit." She chuckled. "You can't blame me. He's hilarious, and I can bounce ideas on how to take care of things here. When do I get my friend?"

"That's why I'm calling, Reka. When can auntie be here?"

"If Mom is coming, a few days, but I can be there tonight," she said after thinking for a moment.

"The sooner the better."

"She mentioned the Silnaree provision. Have they agreed to it?"

"They are discussing it as we speak."

Nodding, I could see the wheels turning in her head before she let out a long breath and said, "Where do you want me to meet them? I can't just come into the middle of the main courtyard. Not to mention that if this is gonna work, he needs to disappear in the night. I can't just whisk him away where everyone can see. They will know something is up. This has to look like Jayden is abandoning Jess in order for it to work at all."

I thought about that for a long moment and then remembered the secret tunnels that exited at the edge of the Black Mountains. Reka had been there with Jess and me a hundred times so would know where it was too.

"Remember that time when we were all here in Ashridge and we found the cabin at the base of the mountains?"

"You mean when my girlfriend at the time and I walked in on you and Jess mid-act?" She was chuckling, and I couldn't help but huff a laugh at the memory.

"Yeah, that one." She nodded. "How about I meet you there around 26:00 tonight? It will be getting darker, then we can come back here and work on securing the cabin so that it will be a safe place to teleport in and out for you."

Reka let out a long breath, looking off to the side before looking back at me. "Aid, tell me the truth. How much danger are Jayden and Ilris in?"

"Considering that his father killed Killy just to make a point? I don't think it's that far of a jump to assume he would kill Ilris thinking it would make Jayden comply."

"He kills Ilris and Jayden will never forgive him. He's been in love with that man almost since the day he met him. If it weren't for Jess…" Something dark crossed over Reka's eyes, and I remembered what she had told me about how Jess and Jayden's relationship changed.

"When he tried to kill himself, what else happened that day?"

"That's not my story to tell. I know bits and pieces, but not the whole story, and please don't ask Jayden." Her eyes were pleading and full of pain. It bothered her still to this day that Jayden thought the only way out was suicide. "All I will say is that if something happens to Ilris, we won't be able to stop him from following almost immediately. He will make sure of it."

"Okay." I ran my hand through my hair and leaned back in the chair. "I'll see you tonight."

"Love you, Aid."

"You too, Reka."

She smiled and nodded before I reached over and turned off the LightCall. Taking a deep breath, I rested my head on the edge of the chair. I sat there for a long time before I finally stood and stepped into Jess' office.

She was sitting there, hair up in a bun, and chewing on the end of a pen as she studied the documents in front of her. Reaching behind me, I shut the door and just watched her.

"Please don't drool on my floor. If you need a bucket, I'm sure I can ask my Vernadali to get one." She hadn't raised her head but instead kept looking at one of the documents, pinching her eyebrows together.

Walking over to her, I kissed the top of her head, glancing at what she was working on. It was a report on the caravans coming from Silentport. "Confirmation of the caravans getting attacked?" A quick nod from her. I ran my hands down her biceps and asked, "Kaletta?"

"That's the assumption, but those who have survived said there were no identifying markers to see where exactly they came from." Leaning back, she looked up at me and sighed. "Now I know why Mom was so exhausted at the end of the day. If it isn't ambushed caravans, it's financial reports, or repairs that need to be made, or wildlife preservation issues, or... a whole list of things. Sure, I have a council to help filter the mass of information, but even after they have condensed it down to ask for the approvals or considerations—" She let out another heavy sigh and looked up at me. "Angels, it's a lot."

"She taught you how to manage it, though. You are doing great." As I kissed her forehead, she looked back at the stack of papers on her desk. "You are never going to get through everything, Kotě. No matter how much you want to, you can't do it all."

"What am I going to do when Jayden hands over Kaletta? *Can* he hand over Kaletta without the council's approval?"

I took a deep breath and let it out slowly. "Good question. I guess Popa is the only one who can answer that. I really don't know."

"The social dynamics of that integration... The economics of that alone is going to be horrendous." She leaned forward and put her head in her hands. "Maybe I can convince Jayden to not hand over Kaletta."

"They have a lot of resources that would be useful to Ashridge, though. The lumber and minerals alone will help."

"I realize that. I'm not saying that the resources wouldn't be a benefit. I'm not saying it can't be done. I'm not saying that..." Her voice was so weary. "It's just an overwhelming thought."

"And you have people to help carry that load." I turned her chair to face me and knelt down so I was eye to eye with her. "You don't have to do this alone. You have Noah, Gerald, Georgina, Declan, Vincent, Bethany, Ryder, Braxten, and Charles all here to help. They will do most of the heavy lifting and only give you what you need to really concentrate on. I'm not saying that it won't still be a lot, but you don't have to carry the entire thing on your shoulders, Jess. It's literally what your council is for."

Nodding, she changed the subject. "You can tell me what Clarice said over lunch."

"You haven't eaten yet?" She shook her head, and I sighed at her. "You gotta remember to eat, Kotě."

"I know. I just got wrapped up in the pile on my desk."

I took her hand and slipped my fingers through hers as I led her out of her office and down to our residence so we could eat. Once inside, I made a simple meal of basktull sandwiches. It wasn't her favorite, but we hadn't gotten much in the way of fresh meat in over a week. Filling a couple glasses of water, I took it to the table and sat down across from her.

"So, what did Clarice say? Can they help with getting Jayden out?"

"I didn't talk to Clarice. I spoke with Reka, who will be here tonight."

She was mid-bite and froze. She chewed quickly before she asked, "Why did Janreka take the call? Is Clarice okay?"

I shrugged. "Yeah, just busy, and since she had briefed Reka on what was going on, it wasn't a big deal. She'll be here this evening."

"What about her Vernadali?"

"Since Vernadali Natasha doesn't have the Underworld's darkness in her blood, I'm going to assume she's staying home. I don't know how either of them are going to feel about that. Reka's... probably ecstatic not to have a shadow."

Jess took another bite of her sandwich, nodded, and chewed slowly as she thought over a few things. Her emotions were a fluttering mess. Worry, regret, fear, anxiety, sadness, and when there was rage, I narrowed my eyes at her.

"Jess?"

Her eyes popped up to mine, and she gave me a questioning look. "Humm?"

"What's with the rage? Did I say something? Would you rather it be Auntie Clarice that gets them instead of Reka? Why *wouldn't* you want to have Reka do it?"

"No. No. I want to see Janreka. I'm fine with her coming to transport them." Tossing the crust of the bread onto the plate, she leaned back and took a large drink of water. "I'm pissed that it has come to us having to be deceitful. I never wanted to do anything closed-door. I don't want anyone other than Clarice, Alexei, and Gerald to know that Jayden hasn't abandoned us and he's just in Therth hanging out."

"You know Mom and Dad are going to know. There is no way for that not to happen." She tipped her head to the side in agreement. "I agree it needs to be tight. So don't let the other council members know."

"I'll talk to Gerald this afternoon and make sure he knows to stay tight-lipped."

I watched her as she got up, put the dishes away, and went to flop on the couch. "You gotta stop thinking so hard, Kotě."

She gave me an even look, then a smug smile came across her lips as she tugged on the Claiming in that way that made me instantly hard. Then the little kitten did it again. Slowly, I stood from the chair and let out a small growl at her as she yipped and took off running.

"You better run, Kotě," I muttered as I took off after her.

CHAPTER 18

AIDEN

I WAS ALMOST TO the end of the tunnel when I thought I heard voices, only no one should know that the cabin even existed. I softly leaned against the doorway that opened into the closet of the cabin and listened.

Nothing.

Not a thing.

Shaking my head, I slowly opened the door and stepped inside the closet. I waited another moment, just to be sure, before stepping into the main room.

The old cabin was a bit more worn than I remembered, but as I walked around, it was pretty much how we left it all those years ago. It was supposed to be spelled to only royal attendance, but as I sent my power out, I could feel that limitation weakening with every moment. I doubted it would really do anything.

Jess' parents had used it as a way to get out of the city and just escape on numerous occasions, and when Jess and I found it, we used it every chance we could when I was in Ashridge. I scanned the room and saw the door to the bedroom cracked open. I thought I saw a shadow and slowly pulled my syth out from my thigh sheath.

The shadow was increasing in density, and when I got to the door, I saw a form start to shape out of it. "Fucking, Reka. Scared the crap out of me."

Then she was standing there, arms crossed and looking very put out. "Why did it take so long for me to get through the ether here?"

I narrowed my eyes at her and then felt her power flow through the space. She was muttering a series of incantations that I suspected were extraordinarily specific to the Underworld.

"Reka?"

She held up a finger, and I was left to lean on the door jamb and wait for her to finish. After another five minutes, she turned to me and said, "Unless it is Mom, Dad, me, Aunt Megan, you, or Jess, no one will be able to teleport in here."

"What if they come in on foot?" I smirked.

"You're the big bad Vernadali, Aiden. Figured you could handle something that simple." The crooked smile she gave me had me rolling my eyes at her.

"Fucking sisters, I swear. Between you and LJ... who needs more?" Then I went about casting several Vernadali specific incantations to protect the cabin and shy people away from the area. I gave Reka a long look, and when she nodded, I started on one that was going to take just about everything out of me. If someone was able to gain entry into the cabin but were not part of our circle of beings, they would be killed instantly. As I finished the incantation, I felt my strength drain and sat on the bed.

"It's a necessity. I know you're exhausted now, but give it a few minutes."

An hour later, we were back in the main hall when she stopped dead in her tracks. When I didn't, she reached out and took my arm. "Aiden."

Turning, I looked at her as she stared at the ceiling. Her eyebrows knitted together and her head tipped to the side. I saw dark whips of her power flow up into the open rafters of the room before coming back down to her.

"What is it?"

"I could have teleported directly here." Her eyes met mine. "Anyone can. The blocker was removed."

I turned and ran down the hall, Reka on my heels. When I got to our door, I flung it open with my power as I ran in, and when I got in the main room, Jess was sitting there with a bowl of ice cream and a book.

"Janreka!" She jumped up and ran toward her, and I let out a long breath.

Reka looked at me over Jess' shoulder and nodded. Going back to the door, I called for Vernadali Dadan, who was there in just a few minutes.

"Yes, Vernadali Aiden."

"Get Gerald. Now." She nodded and turned down the hall. Closing the door, I went back to where Jess and Reka were. "Jess, are you okay?"

Looking completely confused, she laughed and said, "Yeah, why?"

It was Reka who looked at her and said, "I know why the Grand Lord was able to teleport out of the main hall. Someone fully removed the blocker. There wasn't anything left but the shell. On a cursory sweep, anyone who isn't one of the family wouldn't have even noticed it was gone."

"So, basically, you are saying that someone has some serious skill and was able to remove it."

She nodded but then sat down in the oversized grey chair that was next to the couch and put her feet up on the oversized ottoman. "Had to be after we all left, though, including Aunt Megan and Uncle CJ. They would have noticed."

"So, when you say one of the family, you really mean a Mathewson, Heros, or Popa Julian." I sighed heavily. I pulled Jess into my lap on the couch, wrapping my arms around her tight as Reka nodded.

"Shit. More to deal with," I muttered as the door to the guest room opened and Jayden came out.

"Janreka." He swallowed hard before looking over to Jess and saying, "I take it time starts tonight?"

"We told you she was coming tonight."

"I know." He looked over his shoulder as Ilris came out and stood behind him. "Guess the reality of the situation is just crashing down. Four months, huh?"

She nodded, and there was a wave of sadness that flowed through her. "Yeah, Larks though, if you really need to talk to her. But if we want to be *really* careful, we don't mention your name during LightCalls or even use that many Lark Messengers."

He nodded, but I could see how hard it was for him. "Jessika, the only reason I didn't talk to you while in Cinder was because I was out in the middle of nowhere and couldn't. I hated every minute of it. I missed you like crazy."

She smiled brightly. "Jayden, it isn't forever. Just a few months then you and Ilris will be able to live a long and happy life together."

Ilris put his hand on Jayden's back, but Jayden looked between me and Jess. "Knowing that I couldn't get in contact with my best friend because of location is wholly different from not being able to contact her and her mate because of... what we are doing."

Reka looked at Ilris for a moment and then back to Jayden. "I'm assuming that these two have advised you of why I can teleport even though it's still locked down after Momma Grand Duchess' death?"

They both nodded, and Ilris took Jayden's hand before he said, "They have, and Jayden and I have talked about it at length. I have no doubts and frankly feel honored that you and Empress Clarice would even consider making us Silnaree and protecting us for the next four months."

"We take care of family, and we have known each other for a very long time. I know that you two are completely committed. There is no way you could have done and gone through everything you have for the last ten years if you were not." She stood and gave a meaningful look to Jayden who had tears in his eyes as he looked to Ilris.

"*Liefde*, I know we have talked this into the ground, but—" Jayden kissed Ilris, and when he pulled back, Ilris was smiling. "Just wanted to make sure."

Janreka chuckled, but then she composed herself before she said, "Do you consent to tying yourselves to each other for life and beyond? To having the Underworld's darkness flowing through your veins and becoming Silnaree?"

"We do," they said in unison.

"It is not reversible. There is no separation in this. My parents tried for many years, for Mom's sanity, and they still found their way back to each other. When the first of you travels to the Underworld, you will stand there at the other side of the gate waiting, however long it takes, for the other."

Ilris smirked at Jayden and looked at him. "You are literally never getting rid of me."

Jayden shook his head and kissed Ilris' forehead, chuckling.

"Before we do this, there are a few rules for you both while in Therth," Reka explained.

Ilris' eyebrow lifted, but he was listening. However, Jayden scoffed, "We've been to Therth. We know the rules."

"Yes, you know all about staying out of court and away from the Gate. I wasn't even going to mention that." She met his gaze. "We are basically locking down the castle so that you can have free rein around the grounds. However, there are a few events that couldn't be rescheduled. There also may be random situations that would require you to stay in the residential area so that you aren't seen. While we doubt your father will think you are all the way in Obsecuritan, we still have to be careful. We have bound all staff by the darkness, so they will be unable to speak a word to anyone."

"What if they do?" Jayden asked.

Reka huffed a laugh. "Jayden, they literally won't be able to. Anything that is said about you, your staff, or territory is unable to be spoken."

I blinked and looked at her. I went to ask how she was able to manage that, but she just gave me a look that had me shaking my head. "Gatekeeper secrets."

"I'm beginning to hate that phrase," Jess said from my lap.

There was a sequenced knock at the door, and I slid Jess from my lap and went to answer it.

"Come in, Gerald." I opened the door wider to allow him in, and when Vernadali Dadan turned her back on the door, she stood in front of it. "Relieve the guard, Vernadali Dadan. When Gerald leaves, you will need to escort him back to his residence and then go to the armory to check on *something*. Understood?"

She looked back over her shoulder with a questioning look but nodded. "Of course, Vernadali Aiden. Once I've accompanied Master Gerald, I will look into it in the armory."

I let a small smile sit on my lips, shut the door, and heard her command the Ashridge Guard to break for dinner. I huffed a hard breath and when I returned to the main room, Jess was giving Gerald a rundown of what was happening and ordering that fresh incantations be secured upon the main hall building. When she smiled at me, I felt that mischievous playfulness within her.

"Jess…," I drew out her name in a warning.

"Am I not Grand Duchess?" She smiled brightly before turning to Gerald and saying, "But I want the teleport incantation to have a hole in it for Princess Janreka and Empress Clarice only."

Gerald blinked, looked to Reka, who looked just as shocked as the rest of us felt, and then looked back to her. "Yes, Grand Duchess."

"Look, they are the only ones that can circumvent Head Julian's lockdown. There are reasons for that, which won't be explained."

"Yes, Grand Duchess. It will be completed by morning." Then he bowed and left.

CHAPTER 19

JAYDEN

TAKING A DEEP BREATH, I looked to Janreka and asked, "So, what does this entail?"

"I need a small bowl." Jessika went to the kitchen and got a small sauce dipping bowl and a bowl the size of her palm.

"How big?"

Smiling at me and Ilris, she said, "The smaller is fine."

Anticipation and nervousness filled the pit of my stomach. "What are the bowls for?"

Janreka smiled as she took the small bowl from her and unsheathed a syth. "Hands out." My eyes widened, but I held my hand out at the same time that Ilris did. "Perfect. You were even in sync."

"Can we have an explanation, please? I mean, it's obvious you want our blood for this, but... a little information would be nice, Janreka." I tried to keep my voice playful, but I heard the nervous waver in it.

"I need enough. More than a couple drops, but not buckets." She was deliberately fucking with us, but I let her run the syth over my hand and tip it until the bowl was just under halfway full. She did the same to Ilris, her eyes on me the entire time. When Janreka had enough, she waved her hand, and I watched as the blood swirled in the small bowl. "Keep your palms up and don't let the wounds close up yet."

Placing the small bowl on the counter, she then took the syth to her palm as well. As the blood pooled, she muttered incomprehensible words. When she tipped her hand over, allowing the blood to pour into the bowl with ours, it shifted to something that was reminiscent of wispy shadows.

With her finger, she circled about it, muttering again, mixing the shadows and our blood. It sizzled, and she gritted her teeth at the mixture. "Yeah, yeah, yeah, I know. I don't care."

She continued her muttering. It sizzled again, and when it stopped, she lifted the small bowl. Cradling it in her hands, she turned to face us both. She raised an eyebrow, and we nodded.

She pressed our hands so they were side by side, palms still facing up. "This may sting a bit, since it was being mouthy with me." Again, in unison, we nodded.

Muttering more incomprehensible words, she slowly poured the mixture of our bloods over the open wounds on our palms. It stung slightly, but otherwise, it just felt ice cold. As the last bit dropped into the edge of the wound on Ilris' palm, she didn't remove her eyes from the wounds and muttered another long string of words before taking our hands in hers and slapping them together.

A rush of ice went through my veins that then turned fiery hot. Smoke filled my vision, and then there was nothing. Slowly, Janreka separated our palms, and grey wisps were stitching the wounds together.

Once it was done, I saw her shoulders relax. Then she took a deep breath and let it out slowly. When her eyes met mine, they were bright. "Well, now you are stuck with each other."

"That's it?" Ilris asked carefully.

Janreka shook her head, chuckling. "That's it? I just bound your souls in the Underworld's darkness and you ask if that's it?"

"Well, it was pretty quick and rather painless."

Shrugging, she smiled at them. "Not everything has to be a huge grand event."

Jessika and Aiden were chuckling but had their hands around each other's waists. Jessika had tears in her eyes, and I crunched my eyebrows together and asked, "Why are you crying?"

"I'm happy for you, Jayden. You basically just married Ilris by binding yourself to him."

Ilris' arm wrapped around my waist, and then his finger was on my chin, making me face him. "Married."

His whisper was a soft caress against my soul. Looking into his deep amber eyes, I saw everything I wanted in life: love, admiration, security. This man gave me everything. He loved me, regardless of all the hardships. He had stayed with me for years, even though our relationship could get us killed.

My power sang under my skin, and when his cheeks heated, I heard Janreka say, "*There* it is. Aiden, Jess, how about we go for a long walk? Maybe take some time to walk the outer walls."

My lips tipped up as Ilris' arms wrapped tight around my waist and picked me up. He took long, determined strides to the room that we had been sharing in the residence.

As he tossed me on the bed, I vaguely heard the door close and felt a sealing incantation sizzle across the walls. His lips were on mine a moment later. My hands pulled at his shirt, and then my hands were running over his back. The moan from him had me lifting my hips. Grinding against me, I pulled his shirt off and ran my tongue down his neck as I undid his belt and slid it off his hips.

Rolling him over, Ilris had my shirt up and over my head as I pulled his pants off. He bent to get up and with a single look, he lay there, cock twitching. I licked my lips slowly and then kissed my way up his legs. As I positioned myself before him, I stripped my pants off quickly.

My eyes met his, and his hand met my jaw, running his fingers through the scruff. Then, in that voice that had me doing anything for him, he commanded, "Suck it."

I snaked my tongue out and slowly took his balls into my mouth, sucking carefully with just enough pressure, causing him to hiss in pleasure. I had taken very good care not to touch his shaft, as it hardened even more before me.

When I dipped my tongue lower and circled the puckered skin, Ilris' breath hitched, but he relaxed, spreading his legs wider for me. "Fuck, Jade."

Taking his balls back into my mouth, I chuckled as I reached up and ran a single finger through the slit of him. His moan of pleasure undid me. Releasing him with a pop, I licked my finger and circled his ass at the same time I ran my tongue up the length of him.

His whispered, "Oh, Angels," brought a smile to my face as he bowed his back off the bed. His breathing was becoming more erratic, and when I reached the head of him, I let that bit of pre-cum hang between us.

Pressing against him again, his body relaxed slightly as I took the head of him into my mouth, working farther and farther down his shaft. When he hit the back of my throat, I licked my way back up him and spit on my finger and circled my tongue around his hard length again as I swallowed him. His hands landed on my head, but he didn't try to control me. No, he simply threaded his hands through the longer pieces on top, letting me take him as I sucked and swallowed.

When I did, I pressed my finger in and out of his ass, I shifted slightly so that I could swallow him down my throat. With his breathing becoming more and more erratic, he was fully down my throat when I hummed and I held him there as I looked up at him. The look of complete lust and love that met me in his eyes had me pulsing three times before coming back up.

My finger did not stop hitting that spot within him he loved so much as I swallowed him over and over again. The pleasure he was taking had me rock hard, and I wrapped my free hand around my own cock and started stroking.

Ilris panted, "Fuck, Jade. Yes. Just..."

I stroked myself faster and matched those movements as I fingered his ass. Swallowing him over and over again, I felt Ilris' fingers tighten.

"Suck my cock," he whispered, but then his voice was more demanding. "Are you jerking off?"

I popped off his cock and lifted to stroke myself before him.

"Good." I moved my finger against that spot inside of him, his whole body stiffened, and I saw his cock twitch before me. "Now swallow me and drink it all."

"Yes, sir," I growled as heat flooded me, and I pumped myself a couple more times for him to see. I was so close to finishing myself just listening to him mewling under me.

I licked the head of him again, letting my tongue run through the slit of him, and when he growled, "Jade, swallow me now," I smiled as I took him again. His hands pushed me down, holding me. "Yes, hold it there, baby."

He released me a moment later, but then his hips thrust up as he slid in and down my throat. Every time he went deeper, I moved within him as well.

"Every bit. You understand?" he demanded, and I hummed an acknowledgment before he thrust one more time and spilled himself. I held him there a moment, making sure that there wasn't one drop that was missed.

I was still pumping myself faster and faster. He lifted me off of him and brought me to him to kiss me. His tongue swirled with mine as his hand replaced mine, pumping me. His thumb circled the bulbous tip as he swallowed my groan.

Dropping to his knees, he took the head of me into his mouth and stroked the smooth skin just below my balls. "Angels, I am not lasting long."

"Fuck my mouth, *liefde*," he said when he released me. I smirked and did as he commanded. It took moments. I couldn't deny this man. When he hummed as I was down his throat, I pulled back and thrust one more time, spilling myself.

Slowly, he licked me clean. As he stood, he held my waist and kissed his way up my torso. When he got to my neck, I stretched it to the side to give him better access. "Angels, *liefde*."

I hummed against the feel of his lips sliding up my neck and along my jaw before he kissed me softly on the lips. Forehead to forehead, I whispered, "I love you, Ilris."

He took my hand, pulling me onto the bed, lifting the sheet for me to slide in next to him before he said, "I love you, too, Jade."

CHAPTER 20

JAYDEN

"JADE, LIEFDE, YOU GOTTA wake up." Ilris' voice came through the fog and I opened my eyes. "Aiden just knocked on the door and said that we need to finish packing up."

I groaned and wrapped an arm around his waist, trying to pull him to me, but noticed he was already dressed. "I don't wanna."

He huffed a laugh and reached down to kiss my temple. "I know, but after we get to Therth, we can have lots of just us time." I whimpered like a child, and Ilris just chuckled, pulling back the blankets.

There was a groan that came from him, and I rolled over onto my back and grabbed my semi-hard cock, pumping twice. When my eyes met his, he lifted an eyebrow. "*Liefde*, if you get that anymore worked up, you are going to be uncomfortable for a while, and it will be no one's fault but your own."

I narrowed my eyes at him. "Fine."

Hauling myself out of the bed, I got dressed and finished packing. Once it was all put back into my duffle bag, I threw the strap over my shoulder.

Ilris just chuckled and then put my chin between his knuckle and thumb, kissing me softly before saying, "Good boy."

I felt that go through my entire body, and I did harden at that. I took a deep breath as I met his heated gaze. The left side of his lip turned up. "I promise to make it up to you once we are settled in Therth."

"Yes, sir." Then I leaned forward and kissed him.

When he turned, I took another deep breath to calm myself before heading for the door.

When we got to the main room, Jessika's head was lying in Aiden's lap as he played with her hair. They each looked up at us and smiled. "Where is Janreka?"

"Behind you." I jumped.

"What the Underworld?"

She laughed. "I was putting my glass away in the kitchen. Damn, jumpy much?"

I rolled my eyes at her. She turned her attention to Aiden and Jessika and smiled at them. "I'm so happy that you guys have all found your people."

"It will happen for you, too."

"I didn't mean that as a personal pity party, as Aunt Megan would say, Jayden. I'm just saying that I'm happy that you all are happy."

"Thank you, and in case we don't say it enough, thank you for all you are doing for Ilris and me."

Nodding, she smiled softly. "Are you ready?"

"Ilris, how do you feel about taking a walk in the mountains?" I asked, and he chuckled.

"Actually, we don't need to. We can go from here since the barriers are down."

She reached out, and I took her hand. Threading my fingers through Ilris', I looked at where Jessika and Aiden were on the couch. Her eyes were filled with tears, and I saw one fall as I said, "I love you. Stay safe, and I'll see you soon."

Then everything was disappearing in black smoke and the world fell out beneath us.

A moment later, we were standing in a courtyard with a giant sculpture of the Five Angels with a swirling black and red orb. It had always fascinated me whenever I saw it.

"Welcome to your temporary home," Janreka said, and then there was a clearing of a throat behind us.

Turning, I saw the Grand Duke Alexei standing there. I put my fist to my heart and bowed as he scoffed. "You are family. Family doesn't bow to each other."

Lifting my head, I gave him a questioning look. "What?"

He rolled his eyes. "You have been around Janreka for over eight years. I think that qualifies you for family status until you fuck up so royally that she disowns you. And something tells me that would have to be one major fuckup considering everything that is happening in the dimension right now. Clarice, Janreka, and I wouldn't be doing this for anyone."

"Thank you, sir," Ilris said carefully.

Alexei just smiled and nodded. "Reka has you set up in the far south wing. That way, you can roam as needed, but for those times when you need to stay hidden, you have access to places other than just the southern suite."

"What?" Ilris was right at my side as we strode inside.

Janreka looked over her shoulder, shook her head as her Vernadali quietly appeared, and said, "There are passages to other levels, including the library, kitchens, and workout rooms. Guests and dignitaries who visit obviously can't know you are here, and they won't have access to those areas. So, by putting you in the southern suite, you will have direct access to those areas and not be caged in while they are here."

I blinked at her and shook my head. They had really gone all out in trying to make this the most nonintrusive thing possible. "I don't know what to say."

Her shoulder lifted. "Like Dad said, you are family, Jayden. Ilris too, by extension. Now come on, let's get you two settled and I'll show you how to get into those passages."

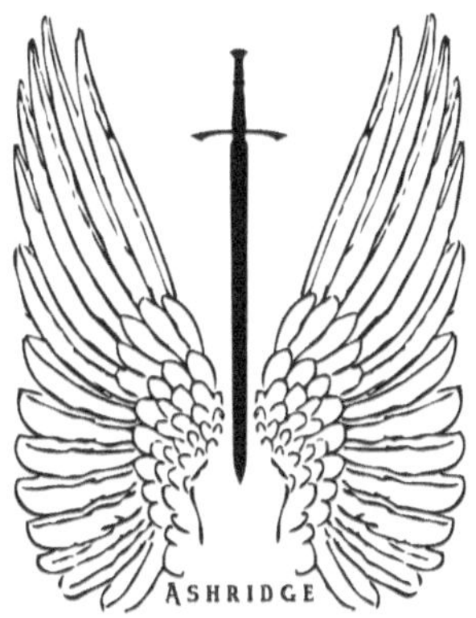

CHAPTER 21

JESSIKA

As I was slowly pulled from my sleep, I felt Aiden curled along the length of me. I let out a long, contented breath and smiled, snuggling up closer to him. As I did so, his arm tightened, and he kissed my shoulder. I would never get used to waking up next to him or the fact that he was really mine for the rest of our lives, both of which I would always treasure.

"Morning," I whispered, and there was nothing but a grunt and his arm became an iron vice around my waist. I couldn't help the chuckle that escaped me, but I just accepted it and closed my eyes again. We lay there for a few minutes while my mind started thinking about Jayden, wondering if he got there okay. I knew he *did*, but sleepy brain. Was he mad that we shipped him off? I mean, we kind of sprung it on him.

"What has you thinking so hard this early in the fucking morning, Kotě?"

"Jayden," I mumbled.

He nuzzled in through my hair and sat up a little on his elbow, kissing along my shoulder before looking at me and saying, "I don't know if I should be jealous or not that you are thinking about another man, a man who is technically your betrothed, while in bed with me."

Rolling my eyes, I said, "Except, while technically I'm engaged to two males, only one of them gets to share my bed and have my heart."

"It's Jayden, isn't it?" He sat up and threw his hands in the air dramatically. "I knew it. You prefer him over me. I'm just a placeholder. I see how it is."

I laughed. He was being so ridiculous that I couldn't help it. "Yes, Aiden. That is exactly it. I mean, maybe if you satisfied me more in bed, then there might actually be a chance for you to win out over Jayden's stunning good looks."

His eyes flashed, and there was a devious smile that crossed his face. "Is that so, Kotě?"

My eyes widened as he looked down my body and licked his lips. Then his fingers spread into a V. I rolled over and spread my legs as instructed, but the only thought going through my head was, *Oh, I fucked up.*

I felt him run a caressing hand along the Claiming, and I bowed my back, shut my eyes, and shuddered. "Aid…"

"You think I can't satisfy you, Kotě? You think I need to try harder?" I felt a phantom hand run up the center of me as a moan crept out. I bit my bottom lip as he continued, "Look at me."

My eyes popped open as he removed his sleep pants, gripped himself at the base, and stroked. Fuck, it was a beautifully sexy sight, and I just wanted to have him down my throat.

"You think you deserve this after what you just said?"

My gaze popped back up to meet his, and there was a playful smirk on his lips.

"Please." It was a desperate plea on my lips, and he made me wait way too long before he winked with a chuckle.

I was instantly rolling over and tipping my head off the side of the bed. I heard his throaty chuckle as he stepped closer but was careful to stay just out of reach. I didn't dare remove my gaze from his.

I squeezed my legs together. I saw how his gaze flicked to it and heard his moan as he licked his lips and continued to pump his cock in front of my face. Finally, he shifted forward and tapped the head of him on the fleshy portion of my bottom lip. "Open."

I did, and he slowly pushed himself into my mouth. I licked up every delectable inch of him until he reached my throat. When I tried to shift to swallow him, his other hand gripped my chin and kept me from moving. He moved in and out of my mouth, allowing me enough movement to lick and suck him but not to give me what I wanted.

When he was pushing against my throat and still denied me, I whined. His cock twitched, and I ran my fangs along him as he dragged out.

"Fuck." He growled, but then he released my chin and gripped his hand around my throat slightly. "You want me to fuck your beautiful mouth?" I winked at him in answer and waited for him to slide down my throat. "Anything my mate wants, she gets."

Then he was sliding in and down my throat. He set the pace, watching me the entire time. After a few minutes, he pushed in and held me close to him for a long moment before pulling away, allowing me to breathe. He repeated it over and over again, his hand still on my throat, feeling himself sliding in and out. When he pulled himself from my mouth, my saliva hung from the head of him to my lips. My eyes were on his cock as it bounced in front of me.

He wiped the saliva from my chin and then caressed my cheek. "I'm not too proud to say that if I didn't stop, I wasn't gonna make another round."

Crawling back up onto the bed, he pulled me back so that I was all the way on the bed again. There was a long look down between us before his lips crashed onto mine, and I wrapped my legs around his waist. Rolling my hips, I felt him slide against me. When he got to my entrance, he didn't hesitate to thrust into me in one quick movement.

I ripped my head back and gasped at the pure pleasure of it. His lips were running down my neck, and then his hand was there, pressing against the sides, putting just enough pressure against it to make me roll my hips and moan.

"That's my mate." He growled at me as his other hand reached down and pinched my clit. "Now tell me how I don't satisfy you in bed?"

"FUCK." I was so close to orgasming, and he fucking knew it. "Please let me cum, sir."

With a thrust to accentuate every word, he asked, "Do I satisfy you in bed?"

"Yes, sir."

There was a chuckle, and then he was pounding into me hard and fast. "Then cum for me, Kotě."

He pinched my clit hard as he increased the pressure at my neck, and with another thrust, I was gripping his cock as my mind went blank, and I screamed his name.

"That's my good girl," he growled and spilled himself deep inside me.

Collapsing on top of me, we tried to catch our breath. When we could breathe again, he kissed my shoulder and said, "I love you, Jess."

Smiling, I pumped him along the Claiming, and I felt him twitch inside me. "I love you too, sir."

"Angels, woman. Do you have any idea what that does to me?"

Rolling my hips and doing it again, I cooed, "I have an idea."

Then he was slowly drawing from me and pushing back in. In slow even strokes, he made love to me without letting his gaze leave mine. It was slow, sensual, and hot in a whole different way than his domination over me.

When he kissed me, letting his lips linger there, I scraped my nails along his back. There was a hiss, but I bent down and licked over the mating mark, and I heard him moan in pleasure.

I already felt my release building, but just when I would be ready to go over that edge, he would drag out incredibly slowly and then, with the restraint of the Angels themselves, push back in. When he did it for the fifth time, his moan was more guttural than anything. There was no stopping the steady pace he set, and when I felt his ass tighten as my hand gripped it tight, his lips slammed to mine as he gave one final thrust and fell over that cliff again. It sparked my release, and I let him swallow my moaned pleasure.

An hour later, after we had both showered, dressed, and ate, we prepared for the performance that we would have to give outside of this residence.

Opening the door, I asked Aiden, "Do you know where Jayden is? He was planning on having breakfast with me this morning."

"I'm sorry, Grand Duchess. I do not. He must have gotten up and left before you rose. I'm sure one of the guards will be able to locate him."

When we reached the end of the hall, I turned to one of the Ashridge Guard and asked, "Do you know where I can find Lord Jayden?"

"No, Grand Duchess. I haven't seen him this morning." He looked at the other guards who shook their heads that they hadn't seen Jayden either.

One of the Vernadali who were supposed to be staying outside my residence said, "I'm sorry, Grand Duchess, Vernadali Aiden. The shift got messed up. I apologize for us not being there this morning."

"It is fine, Vernadali Keith. However, have you seen Lord Jayden or his guard Ilris anywhere this morning? They were to have breakfast with us, but they weren't in the residence when we arose." His voice had turned worried toward the end.

"We haven't."

Then his whole demeanor changed to that of a Vernadali charged up and on the defensive. "We need to find them. If the Grand Lord has them, then that would be a very large problem."

His eyes flicked to mine, and I deliberately let my eyes go wide before I said, "Vernadali Aiden, what if someone got to them and they are..."

"We will find them, Grand Duchess," Vernadali Keith said.

"I want a report by lunch," Aiden said before the one named Keith bowed and took off down the hall.

"Grand Duchess, I will be staying with you all day or until we are able to locate Lord Jayden and his guard," Aiden said to me, but I felt the humor through the Claiming, and I blinked because that was new. While he could read my emotions through the Vernadali bond, I had rarely been able to feel an emotion from him. Unless it was a specific action, I shouldn't be able to feel that.

"Of course. I will be meeting with the council this morning but then working in my office. It will be boring guard duty, essentially."

He half bowed and said, "Lead the way, Grand Duchess."

It took everything in me not to roll my eyes at that, but there were appearances that needed to be kept, and there they were. So, I turned and headed for the council chamber.

When there was no else in the hall, I whispered, "You realize that there could be questions as to how they were both able to get out of my residence without you hearing them, right? Where were they sleeping, and where were you sleeping that they were able to sneak out without Vernadali Aiden Mathewson noticing?"

He ran his hand through his hair and huffed, "Yeah, I guess there are a lot of holes in that story, huh? I'll deal with it."

We reached the council doors, and he reached over and pinched my hip. Returning it, I reached for the doors and headed inside.

Chapter 22

Aiden

After standing guard all day, I felt restless, and while Jess was working on a mountain of paperwork in her office, I snuck out to check on the cabin. I wanted to make sure the incantations were holding, and if I needed to get Jess out quickly, I already had a safe place to do it from.

It had even been a topic in the council meeting this morning. They wanted to know if I had an exit plan to get the Grand Duchess out of the city if something were to happen. I told them I did but that I wouldn't be sharing that information with anyone. Of course, they pushed, and it was one of the few times I had ever pulled rank of my own accord in my life.

"Vernadali Aiden, we need to know so that if you are unavailable, we will get her out of the city," Vincent, the chief of justice, had demanded.

I felt Jess' anxiousness over it, and I took three steps up to stand next to her, placed my hand on her shoulder, and said, "As an A class Vernadali, I am not required to give you that information."

There was a stunned silence that fell about the room, and I felt the shock from Jess. While she didn't show it, I felt it through the bond.

"Vernadali Aiden, we only ask to help ensure the Grand Duchess' safety."

I had let a small smile cross my lips before I looked down at Jess and said, "I can assure you that if I were incapacitated, you would have a very hard time getting her to leave my side."

Every eye shifted to her, and she said, "I don't know why you are looking at me. Vernadali Aiden hasn't said a single falsehood. If Aiden is hurt, I won't be leaving his side, and Angels help anyone who tries to force me."

Pride filled me at her words.

Charles, the secretary for business and agricultural affairs, shook his head and rubbed his forehead. "Grand Duchess, you are really continuing to move forward with nullifying the Ashridge-Kaletta Territory Agreement, not marrying Lord Jayden, and plan on making Vernadali Aiden Mathewson Duke of Ashridge."

"I don't know why you seem surprised. I thought I had made that abundantly clear. What else do I need to say for you to accept that? Lord Jayden and I have not been quiet with the council about our attempts to nullify the contract, and neither did my mother while she held this position. It has always been the Grand Lord who rejected that reality. While he may not have known about Vernadali Aiden, he certainly knows that Lord Jayden and I have no intention of marrying."

"It's not that, Grand Duchess—"

"Then what is it, Charles, because I tire of having the same fucking discussion over and over again. I made it abundantly clear during the pyre *and* my coronation that I will not let Ashridge be bullied, nor will I marry for political reasons and that the person who takes the throne as Duke by my side will have my heart. I also entrusted my council with the knowledge that the person is none other than Vernadali Aiden. If you are unable to perform your duties to not only Ashridge but to me in that right, then what are you still doing in this room?"

We watched as a few of the council's eyes flicked between the two of us. Charles swallowed, and when I narrowed my eyes at him, he said, "You are certain that person is Vernadali Aiden Mathewson?"

"I know that you are not calling my Charge, no, *my mate*, a liar, are you?" There was a lethal calm that raced through me, and I felt my power sitting on the edge. Aiden's hand tightened on my shoulder slightly.

"No, sir. I would never."

"Really? Because it seems that not only are you challenging my mate's decisions, you are also challenging your Grand Duchess.'"

"Aiden will be Duke of Ashridge as soon as we nullify the agreement with Kaletta. The decision is final and this conversation will not be brought up again." Then she stood and met everyone's gaze before saying, "Charles, since you seem to question my logic, reasoning, and ability to make decisions for myself and my territory, why don't you start looking into ways that we can increase our ag resources."

"Yes, Grand Duchess."

"Oh, and Vernadali Aiden?"

"Yes, Grand Duchess?"

I met Charles' gaze and watched as he swallowed, and I let all amusement fall from my face. "Ensure that Councilman Charles has a permanent shadow for the foreseeable future. If he is going to question me while he has confidential knowledge, then we can question his loyalty to both me and the entirety of Ashridge."

"As you wish, Grand Duchess."

"Now, I'm heading to my office to go over the various proposals you have given me. I don't want to be disturbed the rest of the day."

IT HAD BEEN A couple hours since she so gallantly shut her own council down, and I was walking down a tunnel with just a small orb of light power illuminating the way. It didn't take much longer before I opened the door and stepped into the closet. Listening carefully, I sent my power out and felt something near the front entrance. Pulling a syth out, I made my way to the entrance to see a Kaletta soldier on the ground, his body crisscrossed with burned and charred flesh.

"Well, now I guess I know how the assassin got in," I muttered. Not to mention, I knew the incantations I put on the place worked. I let my Charge flitter out and double-checked for any holes.

I closed my eyes and concentrated on it, and when I found nothing, I stood, relieved. This was the only way out for Jess, and I couldn't have it compromised.

I searched the man on the floor and found a few vials of poison stuffed in a sack. At least it wasn't a snake this time. I couldn't help the shiver that went down my spine at the thought. I really hated the things. When the other assassin had come in with one, I had pushed that fear aside for the sake of protecting Jess, but... I shuddered again at the thought.

That woman. That woman was everything.

After double-checking a few more things around the cabin, I headed back to her.

WHEN I OPENED THE door to her office, she wasn't at her desk. Looking around, I saw the little blue light on, showing that the LightCall system was in use. I narrowed my eyes and pinched my eyebrows together, wondering who she could be talking to, and sat down, leaning my head back in the oversized grey chair. It was exactly like the one in our residence, and if you weren't careful, you could become one with it. It just swallowed you whole in comfort, and you wouldn't ever want to move.

I thought I had dozed off for a few minutes because I woke to Jess standing in front of me, chuckling. "I think I'm a little jealous of the chair. It ate you up."

I smiled at her and just responded with, "Well, you ate your fill this morning, figured I'd share."

She rolled her eyes, huffing another laugh before turning back to her desk and sitting down. I waited patiently for her to tell me who she was on the call with, but instead, she flopped in her chair, muttering, "This is so mentally exhausting."

"Who was that on the call?"

"Lord of Sheller Bay. He's sending more supplies." She let out a long sigh, but when her gaze met mine, they were full of worry. "The problem is that once they hit the black sands, they will have a hard time keeping any of the meat fresh. So, they are going to send dried stuff this time around and water." I raised an eyebrow, but she waved it off. "Don't ask me how. My brain glazed over when he was telling me how they were going to get that much water across without losing it in the heat."

"It's getting late in the summer. The sands are only going to get harder to trek. Can we get supplies from Nalrin City or Heller's Forge?"

"But then they have to—"

"Come over the mountains," she interrupted. "I know. It's a no-win situation. They either cook in the sands or they spend twice as long getting over the mountains."

"Have you contacted Ancemore? They are on the southern edge of the mountains, wouldn't have to go quite as far, and the pass is reasonably close," I suggested, and she tipped her head to the side, thinking about it.

"We haven't had great relations with them in the past, though." She rubbed her face and sat up, trying to bring back some brain power. "I'll ask Gerald to reach out to the Lady of Ancemore. He has history with her. She's a feisty one, but maybe he can get some results if they have anything to spare. They've been plagued with flooding the last year."

Her head tipped to the side as her face contorted in thought.

"What is it?"

"They have been having issues with their farmlands flooding..." Jess' head popped up and her gaze met mine in realization. "Kaletta soldiers have been in the Black Mountains, and there have been rumors that they are redirecting our water supplies, which we thought was just from low snow levels... But if they were redirecting the water to the west side of the mountains... it would be a major undertaking, but the Grand Lord is determined to make us dependent on Kaletta..." She chewed her thumb as she stood and began to pace across the grey carpet.

"Kaletta would have had to install some sort of major water redirection lines, though. Not everything on the east side of the mountains could be redirected."

"Right. We've been getting about a quarter of the water we normally do for the last two winters. He couldn't completely cut us off. If he is redirecting, then that would explain our lack of water and Ancemore's abundance of it." Her breath hitched on a large intake, and as she breathed out, she said, "I'll talk to Gerald."

I nodded and let her sit there for a few minutes, working on some other documents. When her eyes started to get heavy, I walked over, took the pen from her hand, and picked her up. "You are exhausted. Let's go home. I'll make you some dinner and then you can sleep."

"Is this my Dom or my Vernadali talking?" She mumbled as she curled into my chest.

I let the chuckle rumble through me and down the Claiming. "Both. Remember, our duties overlap."

I used my power to open and seal the office door as we left. We got a few side eyes as we walked down the hall, but I really didn't care. As her Vernadali, I could explain just about anything away. Besides, the world would know I was hers before the end of the year. When we got to our residence, I put her on the edge of the bed and said, "Get undressed and ready for bed. I'll make you something quick."

I kissed her on the forehead, and she grabbed my shirt, pulling me down for a soft, sweet kiss. "Thank you."

I just smiled and got to work taking care of my girl.

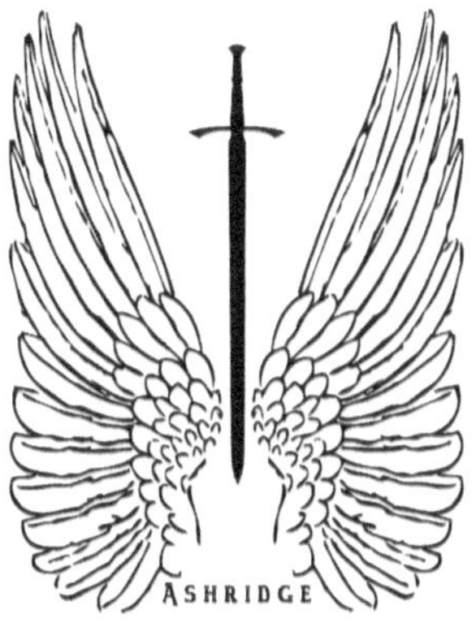

CHAPTER 23

JESSIKA

GERALD HAD INDEED TALKED to the Lady of Ancemore, and it set off weeks of council meetings and communication back and forth. The stress was getting to me, and I was short tempered to boot. Charles had been all but kissing my ass since his little outburst a couple weeks ago, but I hadn't let his shadows fade away. They were going to stick around for a long while.

Today's meeting had been intense, and when they brought in lunch, I hardly ate any of it, and was currently on my third glass of wine, when Aiden came in and eyed my plate with narrowed eyes.

"Now that we know that Ancemore is sending aid, I have another concern, Grand Duchess," Gerald said carefully.

I stared at him for a long moment, and he gulped. "I'm waiting, Gerald."

He fidgeted for a moment in his chair, and it was putting me on edge. "We have confirmed military movement toward Silentport. I am formally requesting we send forces from Greenvale to help secure the city."

I closed my eyes and took a deep breath. "Granted. We need to hold the city. If we lose it, we are cut off from Savanora and the support we need from them. Their grain alone is supplying that region of the territory."

Ryder was thumbing through a stack of papers in front of him and then finally said, "There are a lot of people to protect there."

"And there is no rise or walls around the city," Noah muttered.

"What about the financial district? With Silentport on the coast, it —" I cut Georgina off with a raised hand.

"I know how important Silentport is. No one needs to convince me that we can't afford to lose it. Between the supplies, finances, and communications, it *is* critical we keep the city." I reached over and downed the rest of my wine, and Aiden came over, took the tumbler, and replaced it with a tall glass of water.

I looked at him, and he raised an eyebrow. After narrowing my eyes at him, I took a sip and continued to listen to my council strategize what would happen if we lost the city for a few more minutes before I bit out, "Gerald, send a sizable force to help protect them."

"Of course, Grand Duchess, but we have to have contingency plans."

I reached for the bottle of wine and got up to get a new tumbler, filled it, and just before I sat back down at my seat, I saw Aiden's mouth tighten slightly and him give me a fist. *Behave.* I gave him a side-eyed look. He was not pulling this shit on me right now.

I took a pointed sip of my wine and sat down, turning back to my council. He came to stand behind me, where I heard the sigh he gave me and could almost feel the irritation flowing off of him.

"Contingency plans are fine, but you are talking like the city is lost. Did we not just have the discussion about how important it was that we keep it out of Kaletta's hands?" I took a long drink of my wine, and when I sat it down, Aiden reached over to take it.

I tugged hard on the Claiming, and he bent down to whisper in my ear, "You need water."

"The fuck I do, Vernadali Aiden." He fisted his hand, and I whispered, "I heard you the first time."

Aiden stood behind me and stood at attention. *Seriously?* Right now was not the time for my Dom to show up. Right now, he was to stand there and protect me.

"I'm sorry, Grand Duchess. What was that?" Gerald asked.

Sitting up straight, I met his gaze. "I said that we should always have a contingency, but I don't plan on losing the city to start." I slowly met everyone's gaze and then finally asked, "So, what are we doing to stop Kaletta?"

Gerald looked at Aiden, and when I looked toward him, his mouth was tight, but he finally sighed and said, "We need to keep Ashridge City protected, first and foremost, but the Grand Duchess isn't wrong. We can move troops, but we need to do something to save the citizens as well." Running a hand through his hair, he flicked his eyes to me before he ran a calming hand down the Claiming. He brought the water closer to me and then looked back at Gerald.

My irritation grew at the gesture. Had he completely forgotten our agreement?

"We can send help, but it would take time for them to reach Silentport. Most of our forces are in the southern region. Ashridge has long thought of Kaletta as an ally. We have to be careful. Sending enough of a force to protect Silentport would tip off the rest of the Nalrin continent that there is a problem there."

"How many are stationed in Silentport?" I asked.

Gerald's gaze slowly slid toward me before flicking back to Aiden. "About eight thousand."

I swallowed. "And how many do we believe are on their way from Kaletta? Do we know how many are physically being sent that direction or if there are any special forces?"

"Kaletta doesn't hold any registered elementals. Likely, your standard issue Sangra. As for a count, well, more than what is stationed at Silentport."

"And how many can we get there in short order?" Aiden's voice had taken on every ounce of the Vernadali he was.

Fuck. We needed to protect the city, and I leaned on the table, putting my head in my hands. There had to be something we could do. "Dimension is still locked down, right, Aiden?"

"It is, Grand Duchess."

I turned my head toward him and took a deep breath. He was so going to hate me for asking this question. "Do we know where the twins are?"

He blinked at me, and then he realized why I was asking. "I don't know." He leaned in closer to my ear. "Separation?"

"I know. It's just a thought. Last resort." He nodded at my instruction.

"Why is it a last resort, Grand Duchess? If we can utilize the Mathewson elementals, then why wouldn't we?"

"The Grand Duchess has made it clear that she wishes to rule Ashridge on her own," Noah said carefully.

I reached over and drank the rest of my wine, feeling Aiden stiffen next to me. His hand landed on my shoulder, and I felt his fingers tighten. There was a harsh tug on the Claiming, and I mentally slapped it. We were so going to be having a talk when we were back home.

"You are correct, Noah." My voice was low but firm. I had asked more because of that last resort, but there was also the knowledge that they were somewhere in Kaletta. I opened my mouth to ask what else we could do to prepare Silentport when there was a knock.

Aiden went to the door, took the note, read it, and then came back down the table, handing it to me. After reading it, I looked at Aiden and raised an eyebrow.

"Well, you wanted to know where they were." His voice had something to it that I couldn't place.

"Are we sure it's them, though?" It had Owen and LJ written all over it, but the general public wouldn't know it.

It was Noah who interrupted our little side discussion. "Care to enlighten your council, Grand Duchess?"

"I'm having a conversation with my Vernadali, secretary." I smirked at him, but he just shook his head. I chuckled before I turned back to everyone and said, "It appears Kaletta has had a bit of trouble with the Shilrick Dam. The engines overheated and part of the dam wall broke, almost emptying the reservoir down the river."

Ryder's eyes widened and he looked at Bethany. As the heads of health and being services and natural preservation, they knew the impact that was going to have down river. Ryder asked, his voice barely-contained horror, "What of the people of Shilrick?"

"It appears there was an anonymous call through the town to get everyone out. Not a single life was harmed. Even all the livestock was spared," I told them.

Aiden was reaching for the water again, and I latched onto the Claiming and squeezed. His arm froze halfway to the glass, and when his gaze slid to mine, I knew he could see the anger in my eyes. He blinked, gave me a quick nod, and stood back at attention. I heard a whisper along the Claiming that sounded something like, "Kotě," but I gave a quick shake of my head.

There was a collective release of breath around the table. "You were thinking it could be the Mathewson twins?" Declan asked.

"We can neither confirm nor deny. We do not know of their whereabouts." I shrugged.

Vincent looked to Aiden and almost growled the words, "As their brother, you don't know where your own brother and sister are?"

"You will find, Chief Justice, that I have a strained relationship with the elemental Mathewson twins." Aiden's voice was riding a thin edge. "I will not be compared to them, and while they will defer to me while in Ashridge, you will find that outside of my Charge's territory, I am their little brother and they take full advantage of that."

Eyebrows were raised all over the room, but I kept my face even. This had always been a point of contention for Aiden. "The spotlight on the family has been strong, and I want to keep the family dynamics out of this discussion. We, meaning both Vernadali Aiden and I, do not know where the twins are. End of discussion."

There was a collective, "Yes, Grand Duchess," throughout the room. Leaning back in my chair, I looked at the note, knowing it was very likely Owen and LJ's work. It would be just like them to make sure that the town down river and anyone else in the water's path would be safe.

"Now, where were we in the planning for saving Silentport?"

Hours later, we were nowhere closer to a real solution. We would send about a thousand troops from Greenvale as discreetly as possible. Aiden was pretty upset at that and argued that the city should be turned into nothing short of a fortress, but I overruled him.

When the last of my council walked out of the room and Aiden shut the door and locked it, he sighed and turned toward me.

"Kotě."

"Don't you fucking dare," I growled at him. He crossed his arms and raised an eyebrow at me. "We have rules and boundaries in place for a reason."

When Aiden blinked, I realized he was just now putting together why my irritation had been so high all afternoon. "You need to drink water. You'd had multiple glasses of wine and you needed to hydrate and stay focused. It's my job to make sure you are healthy."

"There are boundaries. You have to abide by them. I appreciate you having my well-being in mind, I really do. When we were on that bed in Avalan, I told you there would be times that you couldn't Dom me into compliance. Today was one of those days, Aiden."

"You are going to call me out on your drink choice?" He took a step toward me, and I stepped back from him.

"Yes."

"So, all that irritation today was because you were mad that I wanted you to be healthy and not dehydrated?" He took another step toward me, and I realized when I took another step back that I was against the wall at this point.

I lifted my chin and said, "Aiden, whether it was over the water versus wine or if it was whether we send troops to Silentport from Ashridge to protect our people there, you tried to Dom me in *my* council meeting. Both happened."

His hands flattened against the wall on either side of my head as he took a step closer, but he didn't touch me. "Is this about the water then, or the troops?"

His voice was getting husky, and I narrowed my eyes at him. "Both. Don't gaslight me. Rules and boundaries, Aid."

He studied me for a long moment, and I slowly saw the Dom in him step back. He let out a long breath before saying, "Okay."

"Okay?"

He nodded and leaned forward to kiss my forehead before saying against my skin, "You are right. I pushed it and you held your ground as Grand Duchess, not as my kotě. I respect that."

I felt myself settle at him, relenting. "Thank you." I reached out and wrapped my arms around him. He encased me in his and pulled me close.

He rested his cheek on the top of my head, and I could feel his heart beating fast. I caressed down the Claiming and at first felt his heart skip, but then it slowly returned to a normal beat.

"Can we go home now?" My voice was soft against his chest but still felt too loud for the room. His head nodded against mine, and he pulled back to look at me. I pushed up on my toes and gave him a soft kiss. His hand reached up to cradle my cheek, and then he leaned his forehead against mine before he kissed the tip of my nose and pulled back.

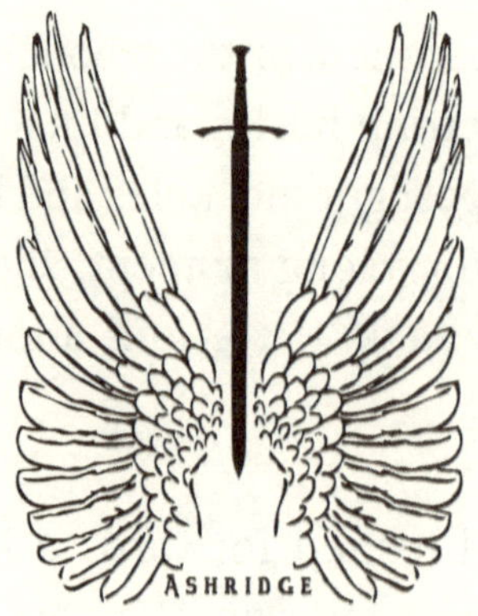

CHAPTER 24

JESSIKA

AIDEN HAD MADE MY favorite dinner last night, fire-grilled moss affenpinscher, a seared tender meat with mashed yinkar. His mom had always said that yinkars were a lot like potatoes in the Manusia, but I wouldn't know. Aiden was trying to kiss my ass. It wasn't like he needed to. He apologized, and I let it slide. He had promised again that he would be more careful when and where he Domed me, and I just nodded to him. Then he proceeded to hold me all night. It was so strange. I wasn't mad at him anymore. He just had overstepped, and once we had talked it out, I had released that energy.

When I woke up this morning, I slowly slid out of bed and went to make breakfast. When he came out, he blinked and asked, "What is this? Chilnar eggs and toast with cloud mint jam?"

"If you can make my favorite dinner, I can make your favorite breakfast." I smiled at him and handed him a plate.

"But—"

"No buts, Aiden. I know you were kissing my ass last night. That was completely apparent, but there was no need to. I'm doing this because I want to, okay?" I kissed his cheek and walked around him to sit at the table.

"I don't deserve you."

"You do. Now eat. I want to go for a run this morning." He blinked at me and cocked his head to the side. As we ate, I could see him assessing my emotions, and they were all over the place. I was worried, scared, and anxious. There was also something making my power move under my skin.

"What's wrong?" He reached out and took hold of my hand when I finished my food.

"I don't know."

"Don't know, or don't want to say?"

Huffing a laugh, I met his gaze and repeated, "I don't know. I feel like something is coming, and my power is on edge."

"Mine too. Is that weird, or is it that it's feeding off yours?"

"You are the Vernadali. You are supposed to know more about how all that emotion-share thing works than I," I teased.

He threw a piece of crust at me. "Brat."

I shrugged, grabbed our plates, and went to wash them in the sink. I was just finishing up the last piece when his arms wrapped around my waist, and he kissed my shoulder.

Drying my hands on the towel, I turned in his arms and tossed the towel on the counter. "What's going through your mind?"

He shook his head, leaned forward, and just as he was a hair's breadth from kissing me, there was a knock on the door. He kissed me quickly and groaned.

"I'll get it," I said and tried to move toward the door, and he eyed me carefully. "What? I can't answer my own door?"

"When there have been attempts on your life? Underworld, no." I gave him a look, and he smirked, knowing what I was thinking. "As your Vernadali, I am answering that door."

"Okay, okay."

I followed him out of the kitchen but waited around the corner when he walked down the hall to the door. He was back a moment later and said, "Our presence is required in the main hall. The run is going to have to wait."

I humpfed, and he shook his head as I turned to head back to the bedroom to change. I stopped as I got to my closet and asked, "Who am I meeting? It makes a difference how I present myself."

"You are the Grand Duchess of Ashridge. You can wear what you want."

"You know that isn't true."

"Nothing formal. You can be casual." When I narrowed my eyes at him, they sparkled with mischief, "Yes, I know who it is. No, I won't tell you. They haven't arrived yet."

"It's not Jayden and Ilris, right? They are still—"

"I've been assured that they are still just fine where they are." He chuckled.

I grabbed a pair of blue jeans, a loose-fitting top, and the black faux corset, snapping it on, much to Aiden's enjoyment. His eyes heated, and I smiled at him. "There is no time for that look you just gave me, sir."

"Fuck, don't I know it, Kotě."

I strode past him, swaying my hips a little more than was necessary until I was at the front door, where I grabbed my boots and zipped them up. Just as I was reaching for the door, Aiden took my hand and pulled me around against him. His hands threaded through my long white hair and gripped tight.

I couldn't help but melt against him. Then his lips were on mine and he was kissing the Underworld out of me. There was nothing but love and want in that kiss, and I basked in it. When he pulled back, he took a deep breath and slowly opened his eyes.

"Come on."

He led me out the door and down the hall. When we reached the main hall, one of the guards came up and said, "They will arrive in just a moment."

I strode for the main doors and walked outside but heard Aiden grumble behind me. I ignored it.

Standing on the landing before the entry doors, I heard the clopping of horses down the road to the left. I stood tall, and when the horses came around the corner and I saw who it was, I turned to look at Aiden quickly, who smiled, and then I instantly burst into tears.

Vaguely, I remembered hearing Aiden's voice hollering after me as I raced down the stairs. The new arrival had just barely gotten off his horse before I leapt and he caught me in his arms.

"JessieBessie."

"Lems," I muttered against his neck as we held each other close.

When he put me down, I laughed. "You smell like shit."

"Been on horseback and haven't been in a town for a few days."

I stood back, and then Dakota, captain of Lemi's personal guard, said, "Permission to come home, Grand Duchess."

I gave Dakota a look, and he smirked. A throat cleared behind me, and I saw my entire council standing on the upper platform. I sighed at the same time as all of Lemi's party, my brother included, fell to one knee, punching an arm out. It was Lemi this time that said, "Grand Duchess."

"For Underworld's sake." I muttered, and I heard Aiden attempting to cover a chuckle. I looked at Lemi, whose eyes had just barely lifted enough to meet my gaze. There was amusement and weight to that stare.

"You may rise, and welcome home, Duke Lemi Valenti." He rose to his feet, and then slowly, the rest of his guard did. I turned to head back up the stairs, where Aiden was smiling. I looked over my shoulder and said, "Now, come on."

"Is that a command from the Grand Duchess?"

I whirled back around and put my hands on my hips. "You are my brother first, you smart ass. Don't make me be the Grand Duchess right now."

"Brat."

I shrugged and looked at Dakota. "What? I don't get a hello from you?"

"Grand Duchess—"

"You and I have known each other for over twenty years and you are going to sit here and go by fucking titles? I don't call you Captain Dakota, do I?"

He looked at Aiden, who I saw smiling and shaking his head. "Seriously, don't fight her on this one. It's not worth it."

"Jessika...," Dakota finally said tentatively, "You are Grand Duchess now, not just my best friend's bratty sister."

My heart skipped a beat at the emotions that burst to the forefront. He was holding them back as well. "Yeah, well..."

He stepped forward and wrapped me up in a tight hug. I held him tight, and I felt his chest hitch before he leaned back. Tears were in his eyes, but he blinked them back. "Welcome home, Dakota."

There was a quick nod of the head before Lemi said, "Please tell me you haven't turned my residence into a sparring room yet."

Stepping back, I looked at him and said, "No, not yet. Go get settled and then meet me in my residence."

"Yeah, okay." His voice held everything that I was now trying to hold back.

I turned, and with Lemi, Dakota, and Aiden right behind me, we walked up the stairs. When we got to the landing, each of my council fell to a knee before us. It was protocol when the royal family returned home, but damn, it hurt.

My breath hitched as I strode through them because all that pain of Mom and Amala came rushing back when I saw Lemi. Now he was here. Aiden's single finger down the Claiming had me taking a relieved breath as we went back inside.

CHAPTER 25

AIDEN

WHEN LEMI ARRIVED AT the residence, I excused myself to give them some space to process together. I knew she needed this time with him, and it gave me a moment to head down to the rise to check things out.

I felt the wave of despair, loss, and grief that rolled through Jess, and it was hard not to run back to her. It was what she needed, what they *both* needed. They needed to grieve as siblings and to process their new roles together.

She had been doing so well on her own and had found her stride, but it would be easier with the support of her brother. Dakota and I had talked for about an hour afterward so I could bring him up to speed on what had happened since Momma Grand Duchess' death. Once that was done, he went to set a protection schedule with Lemi's personal guard. There were eight of them, and it was going to be an adjustment having two royals in the main buildings again. And I was in charge of them all. *Angels be.*

I was almost to the rise when a messenger found me and said, "Vernadali Aiden, secure message for you." The kid couldn't be more than Maltal age.

"Thank you." I took the message, and I felt the familiar threads of LJ's power through it. I sighed and found a corner where no one else could read over my shoulder.

AIDEN,

FORCES ARE HEADING TO THE EAST. THEY WISH TO TAKE SILENTPORT BY THE END OF THE MONTH. THEY AREN'T EVEN TRYING TO KEEP IT UNDER WRAPS HERE. WE PASSED A FORCE OF ABOUT TEN THOUSAND YESTERDAY. OWEN SUSPECTS THEY WILL BE THERE WITHIN A WEEK.

THERE IS RUMOR THERE MIGHT BE RAGING FOREST FIRES BLOCKING SOME OF THE ACCESS ALONG THE RIDGE IN A FEW DAYS. MAYBE IT WILL SLOW THEM DOWN AND GIVE ASHRIDGE MORE TIME.

OWEN IS ALSO UPSET ABOUT THE SITUATION AT THE DAM. THANK GOODNESS ALL THOSE LIVES WERE SAVED. WE'VE BEEN TRYING TO SORT OUT HOW THOSE ENGINES OVERHEATED. MAYBE KALETTA SHOULD TAKE BETTER CARE OF THEIR RESOURCES.

WE HAVE AN EXTRA WITH US.

I'LL EXPLAIN MORE WHEN WE GET TO SILENTPORT.

GIVE JESS OUR LOVE.

-OWEN AND LJ-

I shook my head and tried not to laugh at the blatant statements she just made. One of these days someone was going to know how to break the protections. I guessed there were perks to being who we were, but Angels, she was going to get herself in trouble again.

There was a tug on the Claiming and I tugged back, caressing it as I released it. My shoulders relaxed when the wave of relief came from her.

"Vernadali Aiden."

I turned and saw Vernadali Keith striding toward me. I pocketed the note from LJ and kept my hands in my pockets for a moment. "What can I do for you?"

"I wanted to make you aware of a couple of breaches we've had along the south side of the wall."

"Okay."

"Permission to speak freely?" I nodded, and he leaned against the wall. "We don't know much, unfortunately. There have been extra wards installed along the wall and rise since the Grand Duchess arrived, but someone has poked a hole in it on the south end on the mountainside. It's got some strange tang to it."

"What do you mean, *strange tang*?"

"It's laced with something."

"What is laced with something? The wards, the power breaking through?"

"Whoever is breaking through the wall. Their power is different than a standard Sangra's," Vernadali Keith said carefully.

"Show me."

Nodding, he pushed off the wall. We headed down the rise, and fifteen minutes later, we were looking at the exterior wall. I laid my hand flat against it and pushed my power into the wards.

There was something there, but I couldn't quite place it. I took a deep breath and slipped my boots off and shifted my feet to be sitting a little into the sand.

"When I'm done, if I'm incapacitated, get the Grand Duchess and Vernadali Dadan. They will know what to do."

Vernadali Keith jerked his head back slightly and blinked at me but nodded, saying, "Understood."

I took a deep breath, centering my power, pressing both hands against the wall, and pushing my power in again. Warmth flowed back through to me, and I felt like I was lying in the sun, soaking up the heat of the day in the most blissful way.

It took a few minutes of running my power through, but then just where the wall met the rocky mountain face, there was an outline of grey. Pulling my power back and taking my hands from the wall, I walked over to where the outline was and recentered myself before sinking my feet fully into the sand and pressing my hands back against the wall.

Ice cold washed through me and I shivered, feeling bumps erupt across my skin. I winced, as it felt like an iced-over syth was being pressed into the base of my skull. Obviously, there wasn't, but fuck, it hurt. Distantly, I heard Vernadali Keith's voice, but it was muffled through the thumping in my ears.

I concentrated on the power itself and, after a moment, realized why it felt so familiar. For years, Auntie Clarice had worked with all of us on how to recognize and control it when we found its threads in the world. But what was the Underworld's darkness doing here?

I reached for it, pulling on those years of training from Auntie Clarice, and when it stopped avoiding me, I latched on. Whispers reached me, and I heard them searching for Lord Jayden. Heard them willing the wards to release to allow passage through. Then there were sharp jabs piercing through it all, demanding entry through the wards meant to protect from ill intent, demanding entry to allow death upon the royal house.

Who do you belong to? I demanded.

Whispers of names I didn't know. Over and over again, I demanded who it belonged to, until it said its wielder demanded their name stay hidden. Concentrating, I pried into the darkness, willing the release of their name. I wasn't sure how long I pried, but I weaved my way through the consciousness that was the Underworld's darkness, demanding the name of the one who commanded it. When it finally relented, shock ran through me because it shouldn't be possible. I pressed again into that darkness, and it just kept chanting Grand Witch Bethezda.

Thank you, I whispered against it before slowly and carefully dragging all my power back. Once it rested within me again, I collapsed onto the sand. The grainy granules stuck to the sweat that had been running down my back, but I focused on letting them ground me for a few minutes.

Vernadali Keith rushed over and knelt beside me. Before he could say anything, I whispered, "I'm good. Just need a minute.

"What just happened?"

"I used my power to get answers."

"How in the hell did you do that?" He was crouching before me and studying me closely.

"There are things from my childhood that most don't know. I used one of those things to help me find out the source of this. There are very few in this dimension who would have been able to do what I just did." I took a long calming breath and stood, but I waited to remove my feet from the ground for a moment. Wiggling my toes, I concentrated on the grains of sand rubbing along the soles of my feet, filtering through my toes, and soothing away the aftereffects of what I had just done.

The sun had moved significantly in the sky, and I realized I had spent hours talking to the darkness. Focusing in on Jess, I felt her calm and a little giddy. I inwardly smiled, and when I felt somewhat normal again and my head wasn't all ice, I reached for my boots. "I need a LightCall to Therth."

As I waited for either Auntie Clarice or Reka to appear, I centered on Jess and tapped my fingers on the desk. There were waves of sadness occasionally, but there was also giddiness, silliness, and of course those flirtations down the Claiming that had me shifting in my seat. When the light came on, I was met with an exhausted-looking Reka.

"Shit. Have you slept?"

"I was sleeping when Vernadali Natasha woke my ass up, telling me my fucking Vernadali brother was requiring an immediate LightCall and Mom is tied up." She rubbed her face and pushed her microbraids back out of her face and up into a bun at the top of her head. "So, what is so important, Aiden?"

"Is Witch Dorith around?" I asked.

She blinked at me, nodded, and got up. I saw the door open and heard her talking to someone. "She'll be here soon. Can you explain, please?"

"There has been someone working the wards on the walls of Ashridge City."

"And this has to do with Witch Dorith how?"

"Remember all those years that Auntie taught us how to latch onto the Underworld's darkness and demand info from it?" She nodded but tilted her head to the side. "The power that was working through the wards was laced with it. So, I demanded to know who it belonged to."

There was a knock at the door behind me, and I got up, opening it to see Vernadali Keith. "The Grand Duchess is asking for you, sir."

"Please let her know that I am in a LightCall and will be with her as soon as I am done?" He nodded. "Is Duke Lemi still with her?"

"He is, sir. Vernadali Dadan is working with Capitan Dakota in overseeing his protection."

"Good." I ran my hand through my hair as his eyes flicked behind me to see Reka.

"Princess Janreka?"

"As I said, I needed a LightCall to Therth. She was available, and the Empress was not. Discretion, please, Vernadali Keith."

He nodded. "As always."

"Thank you. Please advise the Grand Duchess that I'll be there soon." Closing the door, I tapped my fingers on the Claiming. She soothed her hand down it, and I turned back to Reka, who now had Witch Dorith with her.

"Witch Dorith." I bowed slightly and then smiled at her. The deepening lines on her face were starting to show her age, but her eyes were warm, even through the milkiness in the left one.

"Aiden, you look good. Happy."

I couldn't help but smile. "I am. Thank you."

"What can this old woman do for you?"

"I was investigating a hole in the wards at the wall and found the Underworld's darkness. When I spoke to it..." I swallowed and then met her gaze. "When I demanded who it belonged to, it finally told me Grand Witch Bethezda."

She blinked at me and whispered, "Impossible."

"Exactly my thought. She died a few years ago. Her coven was taken over by Grand Witch Emerelda. The Witches of Udish wouldn't allow this, would they?"

"I can't imagine they would, but I'm more concerned with how Bethezda's power is still being used in the world." She looked off past the orb where my likeness was and, after a moment, huffed out a breath. "I'll contact Grand Witch Emerelda. See what she might know."

"Thank you. When you have something, please let me know."

"We will, Aiden," Reka said carefully. Then she asked, "Has Lemi arrived yet?"

"This morning. He's been with Jess all day. I'm headed back to them once we are done here."

"They are unguarded?"

I feigned hurt. "You think I would leave my mate unprotected? And her brother?"

She rolled her eyes dramatically. "Jerk."

I shrugged. "Vernadali Dadan is watching over them. She's going to be stationed with Duke Lemi."

"Did Dakota make the trip back?" I nodded. "Let him know we said hi. I haven't seen him in like four, maybe five years. Yeah, almost five years because it was just after you and Jess broke up."

I twitched at the statement, and she gave me an even look. "I know. Facts are facts. I fucked up, but I won't leave her again."

"We know, Aiden. I'll message you when we have something. Love you."

"Love you, too, brat."

I pushed the button to turn off the call and stood, raking my hands through my hair. What was I going to do? This whole thing just got more and more complicated. Sure, we knew there was a witch involved with the Grand Lord in Kaletta, but now a supposedly dead witch was helping get through the wards?

After stepping through the LightCall room door, closing, and locking it, I looked at the pile of papers on Jess' desk. It was littered with financial and supply issues. Ashridge wasn't in danger of becoming bankrupt, but we would be real hurt if we lost Silentport.

Jess pulled on the Claiming again, and I tapped it quickly, letting her know I was on my way. Closing the door behind me, I turned to see Noah standing there, leaning against his desk, arms across his chest. I held his gaze, and when he raised his eyebrows to ask what was going on, I sighed.

"I need to get back to the Grand Duchess."

"Vernadali Aiden, the LightCall system hasn't gotten this much use in years. What is going on?"

"You've been in on the council meetings. You know exactly what is going on."

He waved his hand in the air, dismissing that before saying, "Outside of that. Not all those calls are because you are trying to get out of the contract with Kaletta or help Silentport. What else is going on?"

"Security. There are still those attempting to get in to harm the royal family. As that information is obtained, it requires more answers from outside of Ashridge. It's too privileged to be put out into the world where it can be intercepted. This is easier than always sending Larks." He nodded in understanding. "I'm not giving anymore than that, Noah."

"Alright." He dropped his arms from across his chest. "Let her know I've rescheduled her meetings for today and tomorrow. If she wants to stay and spend time with Duke Lemi, that is. If there is anything that can't wait, we will find you."

"Thank you." I slapped my hand on his shoulder.

"Anything for Jess. I've watched that girl grow up, become a woman, and grow into the determined, powerful, stubborn as hell Grand Duchess she is. Most of us on the council have. Gerald has only been around for about eight years, but he's proud of her. Even Ryder and Bethany, who usually feel a little offset because everything is so military—and finance-based—know that Jess wants to have happy citizens. She wants them to go and see nature, and not just the city. Bethany came in here once and cried at Jess' desk over it. All because Jess had signed her petition to protect a section of the Black Mountains."

"Jess loves the outdoors. The Black Mountains hold a special place in her. There are a lot of very good memories up there." I looked out in that direction and smiled. "A lot of *really great* memories."

Memory after memory flashed through my mind, and when I was thinking of us back at the cabin, I knew my smile grew even more. I shook my head and looked back at Noah, who had turned to start cleaning up his desk.

"Have a good night, Noah, and thank you for everything you have done to help Jess through this."

"Of course, Aiden."

I strode out and down the hall. There were people calling out for me, but having those memories of her and me up in the mountains had lit a fire under me to have her in my arms again. When I got back to our residence, I had to take a deep breath and force myself not to throw the door open and just take her wherever she was inside. Lemi was in there, and I doubted he wanted to witness that. I nodded to Vernadali Dadan and opened the door.

I toed off my boots, and when I walked around the corner, I saw her sitting across the chair and Lemi half lying on the couch. When she turned her head to look at me and smiled,

I rushed for her and pulled her up into my arms. I buried my head in the crook of her neck as her white hair surrounded me. The smell of her conditioner enveloped me wholly. I kissed her neck, and she held me tighter.

"You okay? What's wrong?" she whispered in my ear.

I just shook my head. She was in my arms. How could anything possibly be wrong in this very moment.

After a long moment, I leaned back to kiss her softly before saying, "Yeah, I'm fine. Sorry."

She chuckled and held my cheek in her hand. I reached down and ran my finger across the heart at the base of her neck. Her smile widened, and I just shook my head. I picked her up, stepping back into the chair, and set her down across my lap.

"So, Lemi, how are Kat and the kids?"

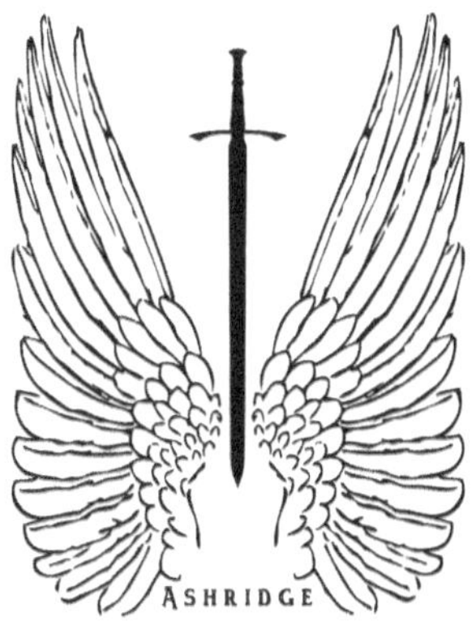

CHAPTER 26

JESSIKA

LEMI HAD BEEN BACK a week, and Aiden seemed to be more and more stressed. He had only said there were security breaches and things he needed to deal with. A message came for him a couple days ago from Janreka, but it was spelled against me, and I couldn't read it. Again, he only told me it was regarding breaches in security and he was getting some assistance from Reka.

"Not from Jayden, right? No communication from him?"

He had kissed my forehead and said, "No. I'm not talking with Jayden. I won't jeopardize what we are doing by having any communication with him."

"Okay." I leaned back, resting my head on the back of the couch. Aiden, however, came to stand in front of me, crossed his arms across his chest, and narrowed his eyes at me. "What?"

My voice was too tired even to my own ears, but he asked, "What are you planning on today? Noah said that you had cleared your schedule."

"When did you talk to Noah?"

He huffed a laugh, relaxing a bit and sitting down before pulling me onto his lap. "There is a reason I'm up before you and am usually the one to wake you, Kotě. I met up with him after the meeting with the guard, and he asked if you were okay. I told him you were fine and just tired. He wanted me to let you know you need to rest at least one day a week." He went contemplative. "Seems like there was someone else who said that just a few days ago."

I lightly smacked his chest and curled up into him, resting my head on his shoulder as his arms encircled me. "There was, and I decided to take his brilliant advice." I sat there a moment before telling him my plan. I knew he wasn't going to be thrilled about it. "Was thinking of going for a walk through the city with Lemi."

His arms indeed tensed up. "Kotě."

"We brought Lemi up to date on everything that has happened with Kaletta since Momma Grand Duchess died. He wondered where Jayden was, and I told him he left the city. Of course, we didn't give him any specifics. He's not stupid, he knows that there is more going on, but he's letting it be." I took a deep breath. "I'll have Vernadali Dadan as a second shadow, on top of Dakota. Not to mention the rest of his guards."

"You'll be exposed."

"I'll be more than protected."

I looked up at him and he studied me for a long moment. "I'll reschedule my meetings—"

"Oh, hell no. I'm perfectly capable of going out in town without you, Aiden." His lips thinned. "Is this my mate or my Vernadali right now? Because while I can sort of see it from the Vernadali side, as my mate you need to trust me, and Lemi, and the litany of guards that will be with us."

I held his stare, and then he finally let out a long breath through his nose. "There are breaches in the security, and I don't want you outside of my reach."

"But it's okay if I just sit here in the residence all day, reading a book, or in my office, without you, but going with Lemi, the Duke of Ashridge is off the table?" I looked at him like he was crazy. "Come on, Aiden, you have to understand how ridiculous that sounds."

I climbed off his lap and started pacing. He let me, and I saw him take a deep breath.

"Aiden, this is my city. Is there the potential for danger? Yes, yes there is, but I won't live in fear. I've decided that what will happen will happen. I'm Grand Duchess, and there isn't a head of a territory that hasn't had attempts on their life. I've been living in that fear. Fear for you, for me, for Ashridge, and fear of losing what future we might have together. And yes, all of that is still a concern, but I can't let it control me anymore."

He sat there, listening to me, elbows on his knees, hands laced together, and when I was done, he held my gaze. I didn't relent. I stood there, hands on my hips, until the left side of his lip lifted and he stood. When he reached me, his hands lay over mine, and he pulled me to him.

"That was sexy as fucking hell." He kissed my forehead and then leaned back, taking a deep breath. "In all seriousness though, if Lemi, Dakota, Vernadali Dadan, and as you so put it, the whole litany of guards are going with, then alright."

"Aiden, I'm not fourteen years old asking to go out on a date with a boy."

"No, you are not." He looked at me brazenly but shook his head.

"I'm going."

His jaw twitched, but he said, "Okay."

"I'M SURPRISED YOU AREN'T going with us, Aiden," Lemi said, but I rolled my eyes.

"As the Grand Duchess so eloquently reminded me this morning when she enlightened me about your plans for today..." He gave me an even look, but I just smiled at him and poked him along the Claiming. "She refuses to live in a world ruled by fear, and as her Vernadali, I also need to trust the other guards in Ashridge."

"And you have meetings you need to attend to work out the issues we are having with security. It is also why Vernadali Dadan is going with us even though we have Dakota and the other four of your personal guard."

Aiden looked over the six of them meant to protect Lemi and me, and I laughed when Dakota rolled his eyes at him. "We've got them, Aiden. I promise they will come back in one piece."

I felt the echo of a growl down the Claiming and reached out and took his hand. "I promise, Vernadali Aiden, we will be careful."

He took a very large breath and said, "Yes, Grand Duchess."

With that we turned and strode down the stairs, Lemi and me walking ahead of everyone else. I felt Vernadali Dadan's Charge snap against us, and Lemi froze for a moment.

"It's just the Vernadali Charge. You'll get used to it." I turned and smiled at Vernadali Dadan. "Surprised she hasn't used it before."

It was Dakota who said, "She hasn't really let Lemi out of the main resident and hall buildings. We had to sneak off in the middle of the night to go out to the hills."

"You what?" she bit out, and I couldn't help but laugh.

"Vernadali Dadan, our parents couldn't keep these two within the city walls. You have no chance of doing it unless you bind them to their beds, and Dakota would only take that as an invitation."

"What the fuck, Jess!" He pushed my shoulder, and I laughed harder. It was such a freeing moment.

Lemi threw his arm around my shoulder and Dakota's. "I've missed this."

"You are the one who had to go and get married, to a wonderful woman by the way, and then give me the most adorable nieces and nephews."

"I did." His steps slowed. "I was able to get on a LightCall with them this morning. I miss their hugs and kisses. Those kids are amazing. Kat... well..." His face was pure bliss. "I don't deserve her, yet she chose me."

"You gave up the throne for her." I smiled. "That was enough right there to convince Mom and Dad that you loved her more than anything."

"She's everything. I know I chose her over Ashridge, and I envy that you are strong enough to choose Ashridge over Aiden—"

"Yet, he is still here."

It was Dakota that said, "It's not like he had a choice."

"He had a choice, Dakota. He made it five years ago. The Angels deemed him my Vernadali, and then he made the choice to..." He looked over his shoulder and then back at us. "Well, you know."

I couldn't help but blush and nod.

Lemi leaned close and said, "At least you are happy. He is, too. I can see it in his ey—" Then he was cussing and pulling me down to the ground. As I twisted to try and catch myself, there was a burn and burst of pain in my left forearm. I looked down at the same time I heard Vernadali Dadan and Dakota giving orders to the guards.

The "fuck" that came out of me was more of a growl as Lemi looked down and saw the needle-like throwing dagger sticking out through the fleshy part of my forearm. "By the Angels." He cursed before saying, "We have to get you out of the middle of the street."

I looked up and saw Dakota jab his hand up into his opponent's nose, but there was an orange glow to the force. I knew by the way his head had snapped back and he crumpled to the ground that he wasn't getting back up. No sooner did that one fall then there was another that threw their power at him in a faded blue wave. Dakota stumbled back and tripped over my feet. I threw my power out to help right him, and his head whirled to me. He nodded, but then he saw my arm.

"Lemi, get her out of here," he ordered.

"And just where do you expect us to go, *the fucking bakery?*" Lemi growled.

I turned toward Vernadali Dadan, who was busy enough with two assailants.

"JessieBessie—"

"I'll be fine." Then someone was grabbing my ankle. I rolled, and when my arm hit the ground, I screamed, throwing my power at the hooded and masked figure dragging me off. Lemi had my other hand, and I concentrated on sending my power down through my legs to where the person had their hand around my ankle.

There was a shriek and they froze. I sent my power into the air, hearing shrieks and howls of pain coming from all around us. Then Dakota was there and slicing through the throat of the one with their hand on my ankle.

"JessieBessie..." I was seeing purple and ignored them. Lemi let go of my hand, and I stood, pulling the needle throwing dagger out of my forearm. As a figure lunged for me, I struck up with the dagger and twisted, instantly stabbing them through the heart. I felt the warmth of the blood seeping onto my hand.

I sensed a presence behind me, and I whirled around to see Lemi's wide-eyed face. I froze, stopping mid-swing so as to not kill my brother, and then he said, "Duck." Doing as he asked, I ducked under his arm and circled behind him. We dispatched a few more back-to-back. Vernadali Dadan and Captain Dakota worked with us to end anyone who got through the rest of Lemi's guard.

When one of the last came through, I kicked them in the balls, and when they bent over, my hand sprawled across their forehead as I sent my power into their head full force. Liquified brains and other things leaked from his nose and ears as the eyes popped under the force of my vibrations. I only winced slightly when thick, oily eye juice splattered all over my face and chest.

The body fell to the cobblestones, and our guard tightened up the circle. Dakota's voice was all command as he said, "Into the walls."

"I want three in front and three in back. Captain Dakota, you want front or back?"

"I am at your command, Vernadali Dadan." She scanned the area in the same way that I had seen Aiden do, and I started to chuckle. "Why are you laughing?"

"You and Aiden..." I kept chuckling but winced as I realized I still had the throwing dagger in my hand. Aiden pulled on the Claiming, and I tugged back. That bond had for sure told him there had been some excitement but didn't tell him everything. Vernadali Dadan came over and ran her hand over my arm, muttering the healing incantations. I winced, and she cursed.

"This is going to take a minute. Let's get you secure in the walls first, then we can get this healed up. Maybe Vernadali Aiden won't completely lose his shit."

My eyes snapped to Dakota, whose eyes went wide as he cursed loudly, "Fuck! He's gonna kill me."

"No, he won't," Lemi said, but even he had a worried look on his face.

"He won't kill anyone," I tried to reassure everyone, but when they gave me disbelieving looks, I shook my head. "He may not let me out of his sight for the foreseeable future, but just patch me up before we get back to the main residence hall and it will be fine. Most of the blood on me isn't mine, anyway."

"You sure about that?" Dakota asked as we stepped inside the walls of the city, and Vernadali Dadan sent her power thrumming through the passageways, sealing all doors in or out. I sighed. Protocols. I knew it was only a protocol, but still.

I rolled my shoulders and felt Aiden tug on the Claiming. I caressed it, and there were three distinct taps on it before a whispered, "*What happened?*"

I took a deep breath and heard the guard surround us. Vernadali Dadan took my arm and started the healing incantations again.

"*I'm fine.*"

"*That isn't what I asked. Where are you?*"

Irritation flooded through me, and I sighed. *"In the wall passage near the baker shop. Will be back in the main hall soon."*

There was a wave of fear that flowed through that Claiming, and I blinked. Shit. "Ummm, we may want to get moving before one very pissed off Angels Blessed Vernadali comes down this hall ranting and ready to level the world."

"What?" Dakota asked, his head whipping toward the main halls.

Vernadali Dadan nodded, and then her eyes narrowed. "The bond wouldn't tell him everything."

"It told him enough." My eyes met Lemi's, and he nodded. He knew exactly what had been happening. "Seriously, I suspect at Vernadali speed he'll be here in—"

"Jess..."

"Now," Vernadali Dadan, Lemi, and Dakota said in unison, just as his Charge hit and wrapped tight around me.

"I'm fine, Aiden."

"If you are fine, then why is Vernadali Dadan healing your arm?" When he came to stand next to her, she gently handed over my arm, and he resumed the healing incantations. "If I don't have a report being rattled off in short order, someone is going to be on gate duty for a month."

Vernadali Dadan and Dakota looked at each other and the other guards stood at attention. Their eyes bounced between the two of them, and I muttered, "Wimps."

Aiden huffed, and I gave him a quick rundown of what happened.

"That doesn't explain why I'm standing here healing a pretty good-size wound in your left forearm and you are hiding the slices on your right hand behind your back." I slowly raised my eyes to his and narrowed them. There was a victorious glint in his eye, and I stuck my tongue out at him. Dakota chuckled, and Lemi kicked him, effectively cutting him off.

"Don't you dare take this out on them. They did everything right. What you are healing right now is the worst of it, and the dagger only hit me while Lemi dragged me down. The hand is because I pulled the throwing dagger out of my arm and used it as a weapon. It's my fault I didn't bring my syths. Lesson learned. You don't have to say shit."

His jaw was tight, but when he was done with my arm, he took my hand and healed it as well. When he was finished, he ordered, "Vernadali Dadan and Captain Dakota, please secure the Duke in his rooms. I will be there to speak to you when I am done ensuring the Grand Duchess' safety."

"Aiden, I said don't."

"As Vernadali to the Grand Duchess, they will obey my commands to ensure the royal house's safety."

"Vernadali Aiden Mathewson, as your Charge and Grand Duchess—" I felt him and Vernadali Dadan stiffen and Lemi and Dakota whisper their astonishment. "I command you to not reprimand them for today. Each of them protected me as well as if you were standing there. We are all whole. We are fine. We would all be standing here like this whether or not you were there."

I waited for him to meet my gaze. "As you command, Grand Duchess."

He wrapped his hand in mine and let out a slow breath and closed his eyes. Caressing down the Claiming, he tapped three times. I repeated it but kept my eyes on him. When his opened, he said, much calmer this time, "Guard, please move ahead and sweep the passage and the main halls to the Grand Duchess' and Duke Lemi's residences."

"Yes, Vernadali Aiden."

When it was just Vernadali Dadan, Dakota, Lemi, Aiden, and me, he threaded his fingers through mine and pulled me close. "I'm okay, Aiden. I'm safe because I *was* well-protected."

He kissed the top of my head and said, "Vernadali Dadan, I'm sure you have realized that the Grand Duchess' and my relationship is more than her being my Charge."

She visibly swallowed but nodded. "Yes, sir. However, it is not my place to—"

"She is my mate."

Vernadali Dadan's eyes flicked over my features, and then a small smile crossed her face. "Well, then I really don't see how it is any of the Vernadali Council's business what happens between mates."

"Thank fuck," Lemi muttered. "Only my sister would be lucky enough to be surrounded by so many people who are willing to keep her secrets."

"It's a Valenti trait to be a pain in the ass though." I smiled at him as I pulled Aiden closer to me.

"Ain't that the truth? Angels, help Kat if I ever transform."

My whole body went cold at that statement, and Aiden's voice was icy when he warned, "Lemi, we hope you never experience that kind of loss."

"Me either, and I'm sorry JessieBessie. I didn't mean... well, anyways... yeah." He turned to Dakota. "Let's get back."

I was still wrapped up in Aiden as the three of them moved down the passage. He stood there for a long moment before we made our way behind them.

Silence. There was nothing but the sound of our boots hitting the stone floor as we walked. When we finally made it back to the residence, he pulled me inside, turned, sealed the door with who knew how many incantations, and then pushed me against the wall, his lips crashing on mine.

It was need. It was fear. It was every ounce of his control slipping. I let him feed it all to me. I knew what I had been going through, but to feel it from his end, and then for me to just say I was fine... yeah, I could see how he needed this.

"You scared the fuck out of me."

I threaded my hands through his hair and whispered, "I know, but you can't let it take control. You know why I had to pull rank."

He nodded but picked me up, pressing me between him and the wall. Then his lips were on mine again, slow, sensual, and then they lingered a long moment before he broke it.

"I do, but security is going to be tighter after today. I won't jeopardize your safety. What happened is something I can't allow again. So, you are going to feel a bit suffocated, but get over it." One more quick kiss and he said, "And good luck being beyond one arm's length from me for the foreseeable future."

"I figured." As long as he didn't go full alpha-mode, then it would be fine. It would be fine, right?

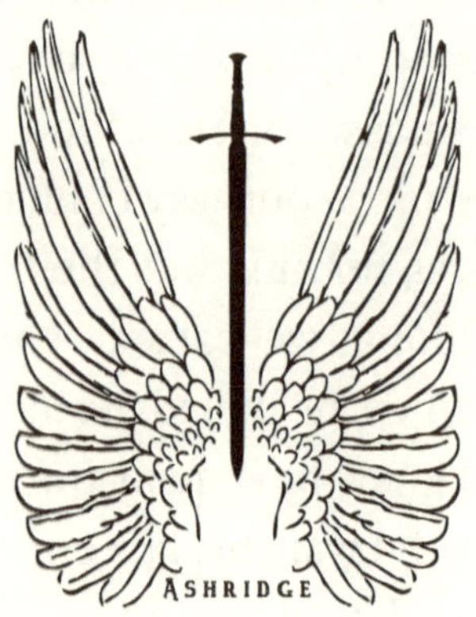

CHAPTER 27

JESSIKA

TODAY WE HAD TO hold "court." I abhorred it. Listening to people who were surprised that we treated them like they were worth something, listening to them try to sort out their own household affairs, bickering about their neighbor's hair being turned blue when they liked it better pink... it was exhausting.

I fought with the council long and hard to cancel it. The only concession was that it would be a three-day event instead of a full week. I was also able to get them to agree that anything received that could help those struggling would be donated, and there would be a limit to the number of beings allowed in the main hall. Aiden had required the four Vernadali to be stationed at the dais, and he would stand at my side.

"I want you sitting next to me in that chair," I grumbled.

He lifted my chin at that statement and just whispered, "Soon, Kotě. Soon." Then he kissed the ever-living Underworld out of me, making me completely forget about it.

Now, we were standing in front of someone who had concerns about the water coming down off the mountain or the lack of it, actually. "We are aware of the situation and are working with the Lady of Ancemore to redirect some of the water back toward Ashridge. We are also working on bringing in water and other supplies from other territories."

"Thank you, Grand Duchess." The couple bowed and moved to exit the room.

When the next family came in, they had a box they were carrying in between them. They approached and set it at the base of the dais. When I stepped forward to open it, Aiden stepped in front of me and put a hand on my shoulder, shaking his head.

"Vernadali Aiden, all boxes have been inspected before they enter the main hall."

"Grand Duchess, please allow me to open it."

I sighed, allowed it, and when he opened it, he searched the container and found but rows and rows of bottled perfumes. It was much the same for any container that was brought forth, and I wasn't sure if he was just being overprotective or what.

Of course, there was nothing in that present either, or anything else that I had received that day.

When we got back to our residence, I asked, "Why did you have to check every single one?"

"Jess, there have been attempts on your life and multiple security breaches. I won't take a chance on your life. Do you not remember what happened to your arm?"

"Is it taking a chance on my life when they are already checking the contents at the door?" I asked as we settled into bed and pointedly ignored the question about my arm. While he had healed it, it was sore, and the grip in my left hand wasn't as strong as it usually was.

He sighed. "Kotě."

"Don't, Aiden. I realize you are trying to protect me, and I realize it's your job, but I want our people to understand that I trust in them. I stood on the rise, watching my mother lie on that pyre, and said that I trust my people, that they are independent and strong. I feel like checking their gifts *three times* is excessive." Snuggling up into him, he wrapped his arm tight around me.

He was tense, and I could feel it not only in his arm around me, but also in the muscles of his stomach as I ran my fingers across them. I knew if I wanted to, I could change the subject by running a finger along his lower rib and straight down his happy trail, but I needed him to hear me on this.

"It isn't that I don't trust our people. I don't trust Kaletta not to use our people to get to you."

"There are already double-checks at the door. Tomorrow, there will only be the two at the door. You will trust in our guards to inspect anything that comes in." When he didn't answer me, I sat up on my elbow. "Take two of your

Vernadali and put them in their place if you are worried about our guard."

His gaze held mine, and he finally relented. "Fine. I don't like it, but I understand where you are coming from."

I snuggled back down into him, and his arm tightened around me again. My hand reached up to find the rounded steel at his neck, and I ran my fingers along it. His hand had circled around to do the same with mine, and I looked up at him.

"Are you mad I'm pushing back on this?"

"Mad? No. Irritated? Yes." He huffed out a breath. "I'm just... I don't know what would happen if you got hurt. I'm not sure I would survive if you died and there had been something that I could have done to prevent it. It's so much more than the Vernadali bond. You are my mate, my soul, my being. I was miserable when we were apart. Now that I have all of you... I can keep the Vernadali in me at bay, but the protective instinct as your mate and Dom... That is much harder to stifle."

"You have to sort that out. I won't let it go anymore. Clear?"

"Crystal." Then he kissed the top of my head and held me tight as I snuggled into that comfort and fell asleep.

ON THE LAST DAY, Aiden had done really well at hiding the twitches when I accepted any gifts to the royal family. I had once again announced that anything received would be sent to the shelters to help the less fortunate of our city.

I saw Aiden getting increasingly more twitchy as the day went on. It was in the little shoulder twitches and gripping of his own hands at the restraint of holding back. We were almost to the end of the day when a family of eight came in and tried to hand me a box. Aiden stepped forward and put his hand on my back, stopping me from proceeding.

"Vernadali Aiden?" I looked at him and he stepped back into his position.

The youngest of the family was standing there holding a small box wrapped in silver ribbon. I knelt down so that I was eye level with the little girl and smiled at her. Her eyes were big and wide as she looked at Aiden.

"Hey, sweetheart. How old are you?"

Her eyes met mine and red bloomed in her cheeks. Slowly, she held up three little fingers.

"My name is Jessika. What's yours?"

"Rebecca." Her little voice was so adorable. "Momma and Poppa wanted me to give you this." She held out the small box, and her father said, "I know you had announced that gifts would be going to the less fortunate, but... years ago, your mother had stopped by our home and just listened to the hardships our section of the city was having. When she returned here to the main buildings, she worked to make things better and initiated change. We were on the brink of having little Rebecca and didn't have enough to pay our rent. Our businesses are now thriving, and we have enough to feed and clothe our family. The whole city is doing better because your mother listened to her people.

We had planned on giving this to her as a thank you." His breath hitched, and I saw a tear fall down his cheek. When I looked at his wife, tears were streaming down her face.

"So, Grand Duchess, please accept this as a sign of our gratitude for everything your mother did for our city."

I looked at the little girl, took the little box, and opened it. Inside sat the most beautiful blue stone encircled in Ashridge peppered-diamonds. The broach was breathtaking. I knew tears were filling my eyes, and I looked at them, nodded, and said, "Thank you."

"Thank you, Grand Duchess." Then the entire family bowed and left the hall.

I barely paid attention to the next five that came in, but Noah was taking notes I could review later. For the last few who came forward with baskets of food or casks of wine, Aiden put his hands behind his back and literally pulled himself to stay in place. It was making me twitchy, and I looked at him with narrowed eyes. His jaw had just clenched, and his lips thinned as he stayed in place. I had just about had it. He had to get himself under control. I gripped the Claiming tight and tugged, watching as he jerked with the movement. He took a deep breath and relaxed.

We were finally to the last group of the night, and two tall men had a crate between them. I took a step forward, and Aiden did as well. I gave him an even look, pulled hard on the Claiming again, and saw the twitch in his chest, which meant he felt it.

There was a shifty look between the two men, and when I took another step, I turned and said quietly, "Vernadali Aiden, you may return to your station."

His gaze looked over the two men, who were indeed fidgeting, but he didn't move. "Grand Duchess, as your Vernadali, I should accompany you."

"You may be my Vernadali, but I am the Grand Duchess, and I believe I have given you an order." The words burned in my mouth, and I hated to say them. There was something wrong about it, and I didn't like it.

"Kotě," he whispered next to me, and my anger rose to the surface. This was not his Vernadali side. We had talked about this. Fuck, we had talked this to death. He knew exactly where I stood on this.

In a voice low enough that only he could hear, I met his gaze and said, "Vernadali Aiden, I require a *pear*. I expect one immediately. Is that understood?"

Aiden's eyes widened at the words, but his lips thinned, and then he took a deep breath. He held my gaze, and I swore there was a flicker of pain in his eyes before he turned to leave the room. Vernadali Keith came and wordlessly stepped into his place. I turned, walked the few steps to those before me, bent down, and opened the chest to find a pile of handwoven blankets.

"These are beautiful," I whispered.

"Thank you, Grand Duchess. Our sons have spent much of the last two months weaving these to provide to the royal house. We would be honored to have them given to those in need."

I nodded and stood. By the time I was back at the top of the dais, Aiden was standing there, and there was a small Manusian pear sitting on the seat. When I met his gaze, there was an apology there. I ran my hand along the Claiming and watched as his eyes closed and he took a long breath. My anger was still boiling at the surface, but he seemed to be repentant. It didn't mean we were not going to have words over this.

As the final group left, I stood at the dais with my back to Aiden. I willed myself to keep my composure and release some of the icy anger that was flowing through me. I had never safe-worded Aiden before; there had never been a reason to pull that card.

When the doors shut, I reached behind me, grabbed the pear, and sat down. Out of the corner of my eye, I saw Aiden move to my side. I leaned forward, resting my elbows on my knees, and rolled the pear between my hands, staring at the green skin as it passed back and forth over my hands. Yes, we were going to have words, but I wasn't sure I could stand to do it in our residence. No, it needed to be where the infraction occurred, not in the sanctity of our space. He had allowed our personal lives to affect our professional ones.

When I was fairly certain that all citizens were not in the main hall, and without lifting gaze from the pear, I commanded, "Everyone out. All guard, all Vernadali, everyone except for Vernadali Aiden."

Aiden stiffened beside me as I heard movement throughout the room. Doors opened, closed, and people left as I continued to stare at the leathery-skinned fruit rolling against my palms. When it was just Aiden and me, Aiden moved and knelt before me, head down.

"Grand Duchess."

My frustration grew, but then I huffed it out. "This isn't a Grand Duchess discussion, and you fucking know it, Aid."

I hadn't raised my head but saw his throat bob. "I know, Kotě."

Slowly, I raised my head and said, "Look at me, Aiden." He swallowed again and slowly raised his gaze to meet mine. I did everything I could to keep my voice even, but I knew that part of my fury leaked through. "I have *never* ever used my safe word with you. The fact I had to today bothers me more than anything. I thought that *if* I *ever* had to use it, it would be in our bedroom, not in the middle of the main hall in front of the people of Ashridge."

The shame that fell on his face broke my heart. As I sat there looking into his eyes, I knew it was hitting home. "Kotě."

Moving the pear into my left hand, I reached up with my right and rested it on his cheek. A single tear fell, and I swallowed. "Please don't ever make me safe-word like that again, Aid."

There was a question in his eyes, and while I wasn't letting him off the hook for his actions, I leaned forward and kissed him softly. When I pulled back, there was a shuddering breath that came from him.

"Let's go home."

He blinked, and there was hope in his eyes. Before I knew what was happening, he had me cradled in his arms and was carrying me to our residence.

CHAPTER 28

AIDEN

FOR DAYS, I WORKED on earning her trust again. She had told me repeatedly that I had lost none of her trust, but I didn't believe her. I had failed her as her Dom and mate. I had broken the lines of our agreement, and I had to make sure I would never cross that line again.

When she safe-worded in that hall, everything within me wanted me to fall to my knees before her. After she cleared the hall, I did just that. I was ashamed of myself. I wanted to show her she could have some space, to spend some time together where we were not holed up in either our residence, in a council chamber, or her office.

When I walked into said office, her head was held up in one of her hands as she scribbled across the document she was working on. I gently closed the door and leaned up against it, just watching her.

"I know you are there, Aiden."

"Is there something wrong with me watching my mate work?"

Her head lifted, and she rested it on a fist. She looked at me for a moment, waiting for me to say whatever I needed to. I just stared at her, taking her in.

"Whatever."

I chuckled and pushed off the door. I rounded the desk, and her leg was bouncing. Kneeling down next to her, I put my hand on her knee to stop it. "Kotě, what has you all worked up?"

She opened her mouth, but Noah walked in. "Grand Duchess, the numbers that are coming in abo—" He froze as he noticed me kneeling beside her. His cheeks flushed, and I smiled at him.

"All clothes are on, Noah. I was just checking on the Grand Duchess. Please continue."

He blinked a few times, looking between us, and then met Jess' gaze but didn't say anything until she lifted her eyebrows in question. "Sorry. I should learn to knock before coming in. Old habits."

Jess huffed a laugh. "It's fine, Noah. If Aiden was going to be doing anything inappropriate, I'm sure he would have locked the door."

The flirty amusement I was getting off her was for sure getting my mind into those inappropriate places. I pulled on the Claiming in response to her sensual playfulness. As Noah started spouting off numbers and stats about one of the cities closer to the ocean, she gripped ahold of the Claiming and pumped it like she did when she had my cock in her hands. I stood and groaned, and when Noah's eyes met mine, I shook my head. "Sorry, just sore from sparring practice this morning."

I tried to stand at attention as her Vernadali, but I purposely stood behind Jess to hide that my cock was quickly also at attention. Closing my eyes, I took a deep breath as she did it again and again during her conversation with Noah.

Her eyes met mine for a second in the mirror across the room while Noah looked down at his papers, and I tapped a single finger to my cheek. I felt her jump in excitement, and then heat pulsed through my core and settled exactly where I knew it would.

Again and again, she pumped on the Claiming, and I gripped the back of the chair hard when I felt that tingling at the base of my spine. Her eyes met mine again in the mirror, and I gave her a wide-eyed, two finger tap at my cheek. She stopped pumping but instead ran a single finger down that Claiming as she thanked Noah for the information and asked him to please lock the door behind him.

Once the door was shut and locked, she spun around in that chair and undid my pants as I tapped my chin. Once my pants were off my hips, she was on her knees, running her tongue up the length of me. As she swallowed me, though, my hands threaded through her hair, and I held her there for a long moment before pulling her back. She pumped me along the Claiming again, and I thrust into her mouth and down her throat, mirroring the movements.

"Fuck, Kotě, you already had me on the very edge. I'm not going to last much longer." I moaned and her chuckle was what undid me. She swallowed me twice more before I spilled myself down her throat. I twitched as she slowly licked me clean. Her eyes had met mine and held them the entire time. When she was satisfied with the job she had done, she carefully put me away and re-buckled my pants.

Putting my finger through the heart in her collar, I pulled her up toward me and kissed her softly, letting it linger. I could taste myself on her lips, and she leaned into me. There was a soft moan, and when I lifted her and sat her on the edge of her desk, looking down between us, I licked my lips.

"When I came in here, I had something else planned, but I can't complain." Moving her legs so that I was standing between them, I ran a finger up the middle of her and pressed against that bundle of nerves. She took a sharp inhale of breath, but I felt the pleasure that went through her at the touch. Slowly kissing along her jaw and down her neck, she stretched out for me and yet pressed her legs against mine.

There was a knock on the door and she groaned, leaning forward to rest her forehead on my chest. I chuckled, kissed the top of her head, and stepped around the desk as she jumped down and straightened the documents before sitting back down in her chair.

Opening the door, Braxten, her head of finance, stood there. "I'm sorry for the interruption, Vernadali Aiden."

"It's no problem, Braxten. You can come on in. I'll sit and wait for you to be done, then I'll be taking the Grand Duchess out into the city."

Her eyes popped up and met mine. The shock through the bond was strong. "What?"

"I'll be taking you for a walk out into the city. Now, Braxten has something to discuss with you."

Her eyes narrowed slightly, but she smiled toward Braxten and they went about their discussion. I sat down in the oversized grey chair and closed my eyes for a moment.

"Aid?" Her hand was rubbing across my thigh, and I blinked awake.

"Shit. Sorry, Kotě." I rubbed my face, blinked, and looked at her.

"Braxten just left. We looked over at you after about fifteen minutes and saw you out like a light. Figured we would let you sleep. I needed to look at those numbers anyway."

Leaning forward, I shook the last of the sleep cobwebs out and looked at her. "Do you want to head home, then?"

"I believe my mate promised me a walk in the city." She smiled brightly at me, and I smiled back.

"Did he?"

"He did."

"Well, we probably shouldn't make him a liar, then. He's already in enough trouble with her." I stood but didn't look at her as I took her hand, threading our fingers together.

"You aren't in any trouble." My eyes flicked to her, and I turned to head toward the door, only she reached over and made me face her. "I'm not mad at you, Aiden. Where did this come fro... You are still reeling over what happened in the main hall."

"I know I've apologized, but I failed you."

She took a long, slow, deep breath and let it out slowly. "You fucked up. However, we have moved on from that, or at least I have."

"But—"

"Aiden, stop. We discussed it, and I don't think you will do something like that anytime soon, if ever. I believe you learned your lesson. So, stop. I'm not holding it against you."

I swallowed hard and nodded.

"Good." She reached up on her tiptoes and kissed my cheek. "Now, a walk?"

I let a small smile cross my face and squeezed her hand quickly before opening the door and gesturing for her to step out of the room before him. "After you, Grand Duchess."

It took over an hour to get to the landing outside the main hall. It seemed everyone wanted to talk to Jess about something. I simply stood by, the ever-dutiful Vernadali keeping watch. It was dark now, and that hadn't factored into my plans. I wanted to do this during the day so that I could see the world around us better. The dark created cover, and cover meant there could be Kaletta soldiers lurking in the shadows.

Jess, however, tipped her head back and looked up at the night sky. The moons were bright, and the streetlights helped with visibility, but daytime would have been better.

"It's nice to be outside. I've taken a few walks out on the back end of the residence hall, but..." She let out a heavy sigh. "It will be nice to walk through the city at night. It's been a while. Ashridge City at night is so quiet. It's peaceful."

Pinching my lips together, I stayed next to her as she walked down the stairs. It was everything I could do not to wrap my arm around her and hold her as we strode through the city. Slowly, I took a deep breath and just reminded myself that soon. Soon we wouldn't have to hide our love, our mating, our dedication to each other.

We walked in easy silence, and I didn't fail to notice that she was walking as close as possible. I had pulled my hands behind me, allowing her just those couple of extra inches. If needed, I could wrap her up to protect her or get to my syths, but I still got to have her close.

As we circled around the main road toward the main gates, a shadow burst out, and I had Jess in my arms and my Charge encased around her in the next moment. Sharp heat met the small of my back, and I hissed against it.

Guards funneled out of the gate and gave chase, but I didn't move. Throwing my power out, another attacker jumped from behind a crate. Whirling around, I gave Jess one simple command by running my thumb along my jaw. *Behind me.* I had my syths out in the next microsecond and felt her at my back.

When I lunged for the man, I felt my syth slice down his arm as he raised it in defense. His other arm swung, and I attempted to bend out of the way, but pain lashed through my core. There was another stab of pain that hit just under my ribs on the left side this time, and I froze, staring into the face of my attacker. An evil smile warped on his face, and I felt nothing but worry and anguish rush through me. He pulled his syth out of my side, and then a rush of anger pounded through me so fiercely, I didn't know where it had come from. Then Jess was standing in front of me with the attacker's head in her purple-lined hands.

When she let go, I saw just the glint of a syth flying through the air. Lunging, I threw my Charge at her. We hit the ground, but the syth was lodged in my back near the shoulder.

I tried to get up, but my strength faltered.

"Jess, we've got to get you into the walls." I groaned. I felt her nod, and then she was helping me to my feet. Pain lanced down my legs and across my back, which caused a breathless hiss to come from me. "This is supposed to be the other way around. I'm supposed to have my arm around your waist, Kotě."

I felt her huff. "Well, considering you are bleeding all over the place and I'm not, I think it's safe to say you've done your job protecting me." I threw a wall up at our back and within moments, another syth hit it. "Faster, Aiden."

I pulled more of my power to my legs to propel me forward when a burst of power was thrown at me. I felt its sharpness against my Charge, but another jab was thrown out and hit my calf. The smell of burned flesh hit my nostrils as I looked up and saw the opening five feet ahead of us. Using my power, I pushed Jess toward it, almost launching her into the air. When she landed in the archway, her head turned and her eyes were wide.

"Guards!" Jess was yelling, or at least I thought that was what she was yelling, but I had turned and shot my power out to meet the attacker.

There was a hum in the air, and I caressed down the Claiming as I felt her rage and worry fill me. When the attacker lunged, he froze mid-step before he grabbed his head in his hands and screamed. Blood was oozing out of his eyes and nose. Turning, I vaguely saw Jess, hands out, focusing her power on him and vibrating him from the inside out. I reached for my syth, but it wasn't there, so instead, I pulled my power together to punch his head back. When he crumpled to the ground, he didn't get back up.

I turned back to face Jess, but the edges of my vision were darkening, and I heard her screaming for the guards again as I landed face-first in the dirt.

I BLINKED, AND SHE had both hands on my face. "Aiden, open your eyes. You have to stay with me. Come on."

MY EYELIDS SLOWLY ROSE and fell, and I felt like I was swaying on a hammock. The ground moved under me, and I felt Jess' power vibrate through me. I tried to get up, moaning in pain.

"Relax, Aiden," she said, and when her hand caressed down the Claiming, I put my head back down.

Chapter 29

Aiden

There was nothing but darkness and everything from my neck to my ass hurt like hell. I cracked my eyes open, and I saw long white hair spread out over a hunched body. My eyes were heavy and felt like sandpaper as I blinked. Opening my mouth, it was as dry as the deserts of Cinder. I croaked, "Kotě."

Her head popped right up, and she shouted over her shoulder, "Nikole!"

A physician was standing in the door a moment later. Jess turned back around, leaned over, and kissed my forehead.

"Jess, are you okay?" I swallowed to get some saliva to my throat. I saw the healing cut on her forehead and lifted my arm to touch it. Everything pulled, sending a sharp pain down my back and into my legs. She grabbed my hand to stop me.

"Don't move, Aid." She repositioned how she was sitting, and only then did I realize I was lying on my stomach. Closing my eyes, I took stock of where I hurt, only I didn't feel much. When my gaze met hers, I felt anger and worry flow through that bond. "Aid, don't ever scare me like that again."

"You are going to have to explain a bit," I muttered, but then her eyes flicked over the other side of me, and I turned my head to see the physician. Her hands hovered over my back, and I felt a slight tingling along my right hip to my spine. A moment later, that tingling turned to a deep sting, and I hissed.

"Please try not to move, Vernadali Aiden. We have to repair this in pieces." Her voice was a little raspy from the concentration.

"Repair in… pieces?" My voice hitched as she focused on a spot. The physician looked at Jess and pressed her lips together. "Physician. How much is my back fucked up? I can hardly feel anything."

"Vernadali Aiden…" She stopped what she was doing and said, "You had a wound to your shoulder, which is fine. You will be tender for a bit. Then there was the puncture under your left ribs that damaged your lung, and you will be on liquids for a week." Her eyes flicked to Jess again, and she swallowed hard.

"Just say it," I said through my teeth.

"We put a nerve-blocker in from about here down." She pressed a spot just above the small of my back. "You'll have full mobility tomorrow by the way you are pumping through things, but for now, you need to stay on your stomach while we continue to heal the wound. If we were in Nalrin, you'd already be in recovery, but we don't have that kind of technology here."

"You still haven't told me what happened."

"Aid…" Jess' voice was a whisper, but I didn't take my eyes off Jess.

"You probably have more of the Grand Duchess' and Captain Dakota's blood in you than your own right now. The cut was deep, and we are making repairs to the muscles again and again. We've already repaired your large intestine, so again, liquids for a bit. You were a lucky bastard, and they missed your kidney, but the muscles and nerves along your spine are difficult to repair."

She took a long breath and looked at Jess again. This time, Jess was the one to say, "Because you are you, they are fighting against your body trying to heal itself quicker than a normal Sangra. It's trying to heal improperly, so they have to come in every hour to do a little bit and let that heal, then move on… undo some of what your body is trying to correct."

"Which is why I have the nerve blocker."

"Yes, Vernadali Aiden."

My gaze met Jess' and held it as I asked, "How long am I down?"

I felt all of Jess' anxiety and worry at that statement. "Hopefully, we will be done with the repairs today. With the way you are healing, you should be able to get up by morning. Then you are going to have to take it easy until the muscles rebuild themselves and you're steady on your feet."

"How long?"

"Vernadali Aiden, it's hard to tell with you. Your Angels Blessed and Vernadali status really messes with the timeline. If you were a standard Sangra, I'd say at least a few weeks and you'd basically have to learn to walk again, but I don't know. You need to take it slow and steady for a while. Don't push yourself."

I dropped my head down, leaning my forehead on the mattress I was on. I lay there as the physician finished what she was doing. When she left, I moved my head to look at Jess.

"What's wrong?" I whispered and reached out to touch her cheek where a tear ran down.

"Please don't scare me like that again. I almost lost you, Aiden, and I already did that once. I don't think I can handle losing you again."

I bit the inside of my cheek because as much as I wanted to tell her that I would not put myself in that position again, I would do it every day if it kept her safe. She knew it, too. I was sure she could see it in my eyes as I stared at her. "It is literally my job."

"You also promised to always be here to love me and take care of all my needs." She reached up and touched my necklace, running her fingers along it.

I took a shuddering breath and closed my eyes. "I know, but I wouldn't be able to do that if I had allowed those assassins to hurt you. So again, I was doing my job." She had laid her head down close to mine this time. "I will do everything I can to keep you safe and free from harm. I take that promise seriously, Kotě, whether that be as your Vernadali, Dom, or mate. That is the one promise I plan on never breaking with you."

"But when you get hurt, I hurt. If you die, Aid..."

I gave her a small smile and rested a hand on her cheek. "I will wait at the gate until Auntie Clarice ushers you to me."

"I love you."

I caressed my hand down the Claiming, reveling in the way her eyes closed and a small smile sat on her lips. "I love you, too."

THE NEXT MORNING, LEMI, Vincent, and Gerald came in to talk to Jess. When they saw me sitting on the edge of the bed, they snapped to attention. "Vernadali Aiden."

Chuckling, I waved them off and just asked, "What can you tell us about the attackers?"

Jess had told me they caught two and then brought in the two bodies of the ones we had killed in the attack. Really, the only thing that she knew last night was that they were Kaletta soldiers and that Vernadali Dadan and Vernadali Keith were interrogating with Vincent watching.

"Not much more than what you can surmise. One said that they were to kill the Grand Duchess, but the other said that they were only supposed to scare her so that she would comply with the Grand Lord's demands." Lemi leaned back and rested his head on the wall. "I'm not sure why he thinks he can bully you into compliance."

"Killy died in confirmation of that," I muttered, but my eyes went to Jess, who was trying to hide the pain she felt at that statement. "Sorry, Grand Duchess."

Jess only shook her head and asked, "So what now?"

Everyone stared at the floor in silence for a long minute before Vincent asked, "Have you heard from Lord Jayden?"

"I haven't heard from him," Jess said, a little disconnected from herself. I couldn't help but reach over and push some of my calm through to her. She looked over at me and smiled. "Thank you."

Lemi smiled, but Vincent and Gerald looked between each other and back at us. "What did he do?"

"He can push calm into me, and it helps take the edge off."

They blinked.

"I inherited it from Vernadali CJ." I shrugged and slowly slid off the bed to stand. Jess was instantly in front of me, just in case my back gave out. The muscles in my back pulled, and it felt like I had gone ten rounds with Vernadali Kamil back up at the Curtails of the North. I groaned but tried to stretch some. I was tight, but not as tight as I thought I would have been. Groaning, I muttered, "Getting the strength up in my back again is going to be a huge pain in the ass."

Gerald asked, "Vernadali Aiden, how do you want to proceed with the Grand Duchess' protection?"

"I will still be with her, but I want either Vernadali Dadan or Vernadali Keith with us or standing guard outside our room for the next week. By then, hopefully, I won't have to be so careful with my movements. Vernadali Dadan can trade with Vernadali Rokol in protection of Duke Lemi." Both of them blinked and looked a little surprised. Vincent even went so far as to look at Lemi, who just nodded. "If you think for one moment I'll be leaving my Charge's side, you can think again. Remember that discussion we had in the council chamber where I said that if I were hurt, or if she were, that it would be near impossible for the other to leave?"

They nodded in understanding and said in unison, "Yes, Vernadali Aiden. We will let them know immediately."

Sighing, I looked at Jess and asked, "Can we go home? I've been lying on my stomach for two days, and I would really like my own bed again."

"I'll check with Physician Nikole and get you signed off." She narrowed her eyes at me for a moment and said, "But first, you need to sit back down." I slowly moved and sat in the chair that she had been occupying and raised an eyebrow. "Stubborn."

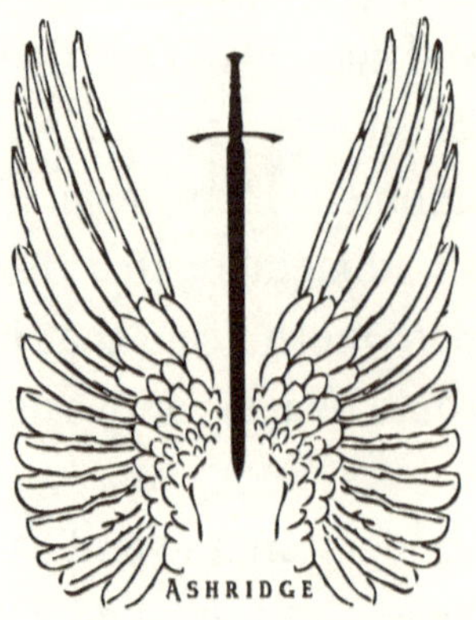

CHAPTER 30

JESSIKA

AIDEN HAD GOTTEN UP early every day for two and a half weeks, doing various exercises to get his strength back. It only took a couple days after his release from the physicians ward before he was walking around with hardly any wincing. Every once in a while, I would see him stumble a half-step, but then it would be like nothing happened. I gave him that, but I knew he wasn't in the shape he thought he was.

A couple days ago, he asked if I wanted to go on a run with him, and being too worried about his back hurting, I pushed him off. This morning, though, when he snuggled up and asked again, I was up and changed quicker than he could put together a coherent thought.

"I don't want to run through the city. Feel up for doing some trail running?" he asked carefully.

"Isn't that going to mess with your back, though?"

We were walking down the hall to the back end of the residences when we reached a small alcove. He pushed me into it, my heart instantly raced, and my eyes looked behind him as he backed me against the wall. His face filled my vision, and his finger slipped through the heart on my necklace.

"If fucking you into the bed last night didn't hurt it, a little trail running won't." He ran the scruff of his beard along my jaw, and I had to press my legs together and bite the inside of my lip to keep the moan at bay.

"Yes, sir."

He kissed me softly but quickly and pulled back a step before pulling me by my hand to the door out toward the back hills. We jogged down the stairs, and when he opened the gate, I saw a couple of the guards come running down the hall.

"Grand Duchess," a tall red-haired guard said. He looked at the door and then back at me with a questioning look on his face.

"I'm with Vernadali Aiden. No need for concern. We will return in a couple of hours," I said, lifting my chin.

"Yes, Grand Duchess."

We ran along the north wall to the trail that would take us into the forested area of the hills behind the city. For about twenty minutes, when we reached the river pool and waterfall. I stood there taking in long deep breaths as I stared at the water flowing and crashing down into the pool below. The air was clean and crisp until it was filled with nothing but Aiden.

"Aiden, you are ruining my zen."

He hadn't touched me yet, but then he ran a tongue along my neck and kissed just under my ear. My stomach coiled and tightened at the gesture. "Your zen, huh?"

I made a confirming noise as he placed his hands on my hips and pulled me close to him. Every hard inch of him pressed against my stomach, and I slowly opened my eyes to find his full of heat and lust. "Sir?"

"I have been watching you run in front of me, that ass swinging side to side, ponytail swaying with each bounce..." His breath hitched as his hands ran down my hips and gripped my thighs. "These powerful thick thighs of yours propelling you up the hill."

"You could have taken the lead," I whispered but kept my gaze on him.

He hummed, brushed the tip of his nose on mine, and said, "And miss the view on the way up here? Angels, no."

I bit my lip, waiting to see just how far he was going to go out here. We'd been so careful about where we were affectionate outside of our residence, and while I didn't think there would be anyone up here, I would not push anything. He was my Vernadali and my Dom. He would direct it. As my mate and Dom, he would give me the option of declining, but...

He cut my thoughts off with a kiss and lifted me so that I could wrap my legs around his waist. His tongue explored every inch of my mouth, and when I ground against him and whimpered, I felt him moving us.

He broke the kiss but kept his forehead to mine as he set me down, bent over, removed my shoes, toed his off, then picked me back up. A moment later, I was flying through the air and crashing into the pool of water below the waterfall. I popped up through the surface of the warm water, and he was standing there smirking and pinching his bottom lip between his teeth.

"What the Underworld was that for?" I scooped my hand and ran it across the surface, splashing him.

A mischievous smirk bloomed across his face as his head dipped lower, and he looked at me through his eyebrows. "Oh, my kotě is feisty."

My eyes widened, but unable to keep the snark at bay, I retorted, "You are the one who threw me into the pool, *sir*."

I felt the growl rumble along the Claiming and crossed my arms in defiance. I should run. I *wanted* to run but focused on planting my feet by gripping my toes in the sand. My mate was stalking me as he slowly came to meet me in the water, and my animalistic side purred at it. His finger lifted to rest below my chin, and slowly, he circled me in the water, once, twice. When he stood behind me again, his hands curled around the waistband of my running shorts and pulled them down. Because I was in a mood to be punished, I stuck my ass toward his face as he slid them down my legs, and I stepped out of them.

Ducking under the water, he bit my ass. I yipped, but there was a burst of pleasure that went through me. The water moved behind me, and a moment later, I felt his long, hard length slide between my legs. Moaning, I leaned back against him, resting my head on his shoulder as one of his hands held my hip in place and the other ran up my body, between my breasts, and gripped my neck.

I caressed down the Claiming, and his hips pushed against me, causing the head of him to rub against my clit. "Angels, sir. Please."

Aiden ran his lips up my neck, kissing and nipping along the way. When his teeth held my earlobe and he rubbed against me over and over again, my hips moved with him. "You've been doing such an amazing job, Kotě."

Then he took his hand off my hip and lifted my leg, thrusting into me in one deep stroke. He tightened his grip on my leg and throat just the slightest bit as he dragged his length out and pushed back into me slowly, almost painfully.

"Aiden." My voice was a plea.

"You've been handling everything with our kingdom beautifully." Out, in. "You stayed with me while I recovered." Out, in. "You waited on me nonstop while I healed. Do you have any idea how much of a turn-on that was?" Out, in, out, in. I felt myself tightening around him with each drag out. I didn't want him to leave me. "And then last night, you relinquished yourself to me again. You left the control at the door and gave it back to me." He tipped my head to the side as he kissed along my shoulder. "You are mine."

"Yes, sir." I moaned, just as he thrust hard into me.

"No one else will have you."

"Yes, sir. I am yours." I bit on my lip as he moved quicker against me, hitting that spot so expertly. His breathing was getting quicker, and when I gripped him along the Claiming and pumped him, he slammed deep within me and whimpered, his teeth gripping the spot where my shoulder met my neck. When I did it again, his whole body twitched before he pulled out of me, turned me around, and lifted me, instantly impaling me with his cock once more.

He walked backwards to where a small flat rock area was. It was just high enough that he was able to lean back, to lie down. "Ride me, Kotě."

I started out moving slowly against him while pumping him along the Claiming. His fingers were digging deep into my thighs as he watched me roll and move. His head tipped back, and I reveled in the sounds of pleasure that came from him.

Lifting myself, I moved faster and harder against him, bouncing up and down. His eyes trailed up and down my body as my tits bounced. I barely heard his, "Fuck yes," over the waterfall as I leaned back, resting my hands on his knees as I continued to bounce and ride him. His hand moved, and he pinched my clit. "Cum for me. Scream my name so the whole kingdom knows who you belong to."

I wasn't sure if it was him working my clit or the fact he wanted everyone to know I was his that spurred it, but my orgasm hit hard. My back bowed, my vision narrowed, and my head flung back as I screamed his name. His cock twitched as he lifted his hips and pounded into me. When his release hit, he echoed my name into the Black Mountains.

His hands pulled me forward, and I fell onto his chest. My breathing was ragged, and I couldn't force my eyes to open. His chest was rising and falling as he tried to catch his breath. I turned my head slightly to kiss his chest, and his arms pulled around me, holding me close.

"The whole kingdom, huh?" I whispered, tilting my head up to look at him when my breathing returned to normal.

"You insist on making me Duke, so yes. Let them know." Then he kissed my forehead with a smile on his lips.

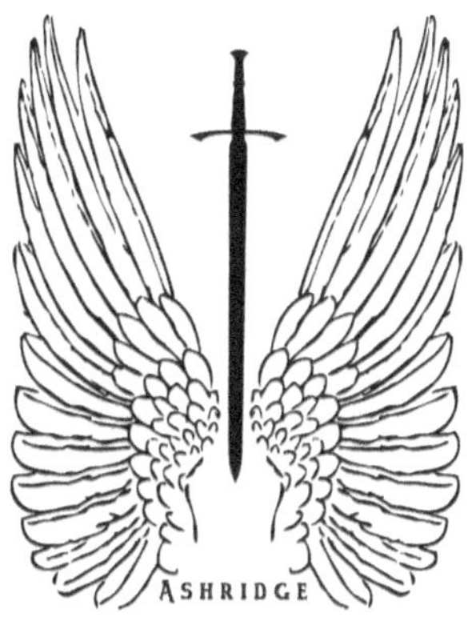

CHAPTER 31

JESSIKA

WE HAD BEEN SITTING in this council meeting for hours. Lunch was served, and here we were, still trying to sort out how to reroute the water back over the Black Mountains. When a knock on the door sounded, Vincent stood and answered it.

"Message for Vernadali Aiden, sir," the girl croaked, her cheeks flushing brightly. Vincent wasn't a hard man to look at and knew it. He was a bit of a ladies' man, and his wife enjoyed every minute.

Vincent took it and met Aiden halfway around the table. As Aiden opened it, he sent a feeling of calm through the Claiming, and I took a deep breath. I saw him blink twice before he turned to me and opened his mouth to say something, but stopped. He looked around the room and strode for me before bending down and whispering, "It's Owen and LJ. They are waiting on a LightCall from us in Silentport."

I nodded. "Excuse me, but I need to take care of this, and it cannot wait." I tried very hard to keep my face neutral and that of the regal Grand Duchess. While my council knew a lot, they didn't know anything that involved family. Aiden had mentioned that the twins were en route to Silentport, but I didn't expect them to be there yet.

We rushed down the hall to my office, and I asked, "Did they say why this was urgent?"

We were at my office door when he pushed it open, saying, "No. Just that they needed to speak immediately."

"Are they staying at the manor?" I asked as I placed my fingers on the touchpad and the door popped open.

"They are. I told them to stay there when I sent the last correspondence to them." Aiden pulled the door open and let me inside before closing it behind us.

"Good." As we sat down in the chairs, the LightCall turned on, and Owen, LJ, and another woman appeared on the screen. She was stunning. Long brown hair, apple cheekbones, eyes the color of shimmering silver, and her plump rosy-red lips were tight. That wasn't what really caught my eye though. It was the way Owen's arm was possessively around her the way Aiden's was often around me.

"Owen, LJ, ma'am," I said carefully.

"Grand Duchess," the girl said with a nod as Owen and LJ smiled with a, "Hey, Jess."

"Owen, care to introduce our guest?" Aiden's voice was one that was just him trying to be the Grand Duchess' Vernadali.

He swallowed, and when she looked up at him, he looked down at her and the tension released in his face. A wide smile spread across mine because whether he admitted it or not, what Aiden had said after the message we received weeks ago was true.

Owen shook his head when he saw our expressions. "Grand Duchess and Vernadali Aiden, this is Clarissa Mathewson."

"I'm sorry. What did you just fucking say?" Aiden said. Each word was laid thick with the shock that was flowing through both of us.

LJ started to laugh. "I told you that's how they would react."

"Mom and Dad are going to flip their fucking lid. You got married without the family present?" I asked, laughing, but when Clarissa's face filled with fear, I said, "First, welcome to the family, Clarissa. Second, I'm going to be peppering you with all the questions on how you landed Mr. Fuckboy here."

That broke through the fear on her face, and there was humor now in place of it. "Oh, trust me, LJ and I had a long discussion about Owen's history."

Owen's eyes narrowed at me, and I shrugged. "Hey, the girls now outnumber the boys, so..."

"Short story, please, Owen," Aiden said beside me. I felt the humor that went down the Claiming and smirked.

He sighed heavily. "We were in Frikland. I saw her, and I knew instantly. We were married two days ago."

Clarissa smacked him in the chest. He smiled down at her, rubbing the spot, and mocked hurt. "What? They wanted the short version. Am I wrong?"

She only rolled her eyes before expanding on his very short version. "He was at a bar, got into a fight defending me from some men who were trying to haze me. I had it under control, but he got all high and mighty about defending my honor or some shit. The three of us kicked some asses, and when he asked me to come with them, I felt like the Angels were pushing me to go. I trusted my gut, and within a couple of days, something just felt right about him. The last month and a half have been a whirlwind, but it's been fun and terrifying all the while. LJ looked at us while we were in Camilou two days ago and asked why we didn't just make it official. Owen looked at me, asked like a proper gentleman, and we married."

"Like a proper gentleman." I huffed a laugh.

Aiden looked at me, looked at Owen through the screen, and then to LJ, who nodded, saying, "That is the extended short story. Before you ask, yes, she knows about Maridel."

"My heart broke for LJ in that." Clarissa's eyes were sad, and I didn't miss the shadow that went across LJ's face. Maridel was a disaster. She lost the only person she had really let inside and who could calm that fire within her. Alex gave his life to make sure that the twins could get out. It had shattered her to her core when it happened.

Clarissa looked at me, though, and said, "I apologize, Grand Duchess, but one thing these two didn't tell me was that their Vernadali brother was involved with the new Grand Duchess of Ashridge. All of Kaletta believes you still to be betrothed to Lord Jayden."

My fingers lifted to the rounded steel at my neck, and I smiled. "For obvious reasons, it isn't knowledge that is allowed outside the family. As you are now part of this family, it will be expected that you keep a great number of secrets, this one included." She nodded in confirmation. "What also hasn't been publicized is the fact that for a long time, my mother, Lord Jayden, and I have been trying to get the agreement nullified. The Grand Lord, however, is not all that cooperative."

She was contemplative for a moment before she said, "That would explain the rise in military movement we have been seeing, and his move toward Silentport. When I asked Owen and LJ about it, they just looked at each other and kept their mouths shut. Owen told me there will be things he can't discuss with me, but..."

Owen leaned down and pressed a kiss to the top of her head and then looked at me. "Kaletta is a total shit show, Jess. The military along the ridge are moving quickly. We expect them here within a week.

"Looks like you missed the fires." Aiden's voice was knowing, and I tried to suppress the chuckle but failed.

"Yeah, it was the strangest thing. We seemed to just stay ahead of them." LJ's eyes were bright, and her voice thick with sarcasm.

I rolled my eyes, and then I thought of all the people who would be in jeopardy when the armies arrived. "What of my people in Silentport?"

"We've put out the word that people should pack up and leave. They already figured there was something happening with the influx of military arriving," Owen said, becoming the Nalrin Guard he was trained to be.

Clarissa blinked at the change in demeanor and then shook her head, whispering, "I hate when you do that."

"It's a requirement, Clarebear."

"Besides the point."

LJ took a deep breath. "I spoke to the Lady of Silentport, and she's already trying to get nonessential beings out. We will do what we can to save the city, Jess."

"My citizens are first and foremost, but the city does carry economic and support weight. As Grand Duchess, I am asking you to not allow the city to fall to Kaletta."

I felt Aiden stiffen slightly next to me, but LJ and Owen nodded. "Yes, Grand Duchess."

Clarissa looked at the twins and asked, "Can she command you?"

I heard the worry in her voice, and the twins looked at each other and nodded in unison. "Clarebear, not only is she Grand Duchess, but she is our sister. By being bound to Aiden, she is family, and it's what Mathewsons do. We protect each other."

I waited for her to look back at me, and when she did, I said, "I will use whatever resources I have to protect my people, but just as Owen said, Mathewsons protect each other. That means that should you ever need us, I will use my kingdom to protect you as well. It's the blessing and curse of being bound to Lady Megan and Vernadali CJ."

The twins and Aiden all nodded. They had grown up with it.

My eyes narrowed at Owen. "Please tell me you warned her about who your auntie and uncle are? Who your other brothers and sisters are?" Her eyes went wide at my statement. "Owen Mathew Mathewson. Please tell me you told the poor girl."

He winced when even LJ jerked her head, faded out purple hair swishing with the movement. "Owy! You didn't tell her about Auntie Clarice and Uncle Alexei or Reka and Karlo?"

"Clarice and Alexei?" I saw her brain working overtime, and then her eyes went wide. "No." She turned to Owen, who raised an eyebrow at her in the same way that Aiden did, and I couldn't help but chuckle.

"Your poor wife, Owen," Aiden said through the sputters of laughter he was trying to suppress.

"Just remember you love him," LJ said.

Her hands covered her face, as she muttered, "Are you seriously saying you call the Empress of Obsecuritan, the Gatekeeper of the Underworld, *Auntie Clarice?*"

"That is exactly what I'm saying," Owen said, smiling.

She turned back toward me and began, "Grand Duchess—"

"Look, I'll pull the same shit their parents did when we made this official. In public settings, titles are fine, but when it's family, it's family. In those times, I'm just Jess. Okay?"

"Yes, Jess. But I have a question." I lifted my eyebrows, waiting for it, and she asked, "Anyone else I should know about that he hasn't told me?" Owen groaned, and he tried to hide the wince in his face as he realized that I was indeed about to spill all of the family tree. She reached back and smacked his stomach again, and the ompf that came from him was really satisfying.

"There is Lady Megan, Vernadali CJ, their parents obviously. Empress Clarice and Grand Duke Alexei, their aunt and uncle and their kids. Janreka and Karlo are considered their brother and sister. Janreka is one of..." I swallowed before continuing. "...is my best friend. Then there is Uncle Mickey and a few other aunts and uncles, but the only other big one would be Popa."

"Popa?"

"Head Julian."

Her head fell back to rest on the chair. "Oh, Angels."

"It's been a whirlwind." He tried to be defensive and said, "Yeah, okay, so advising her of who she was binding herself to was pretty important. I did tell her about Mom and Dad though... She knew who LJ and I are and who Aiden is."

I looked at his brother, who was shaking his head. "Well, at least you covered the bare-bone basics."

"Are you okay, Clarissa? Feel like throwing him back into the pond yet?"

She looked over at Owen and smiled. "Nah. He's cute, and he makes me happy."

"You'll always be my first concern, Clarebear."

I saw the shadow in LJ's eyes again, but then I felt Aiden's finger on my chin, forcing me to look at him. I leaned forward and kissed him softly before turning back to the floating orb in front of us. I let out a heavy sigh.

"We will do everything we can to keep the city, Jess."

"Except for one thing, please," I said, and when they sat up straighter, I smiled. "Don't sacrifice yourselves. Don't burn or flood out. Understood?" They both blinked and nodded. I looked back at my new sister. "I'm sorry that you had to find Owen in the middle of what appears to be war. Unofficial, but a war nonetheless. Regardless, again, welcome to the family, Clarissa."

"Thank you. I look forward to meeting you both."

"After Silentport is secured, come to Ashridge City."

They all nodded, and then LJ reached over and clicked off the call.

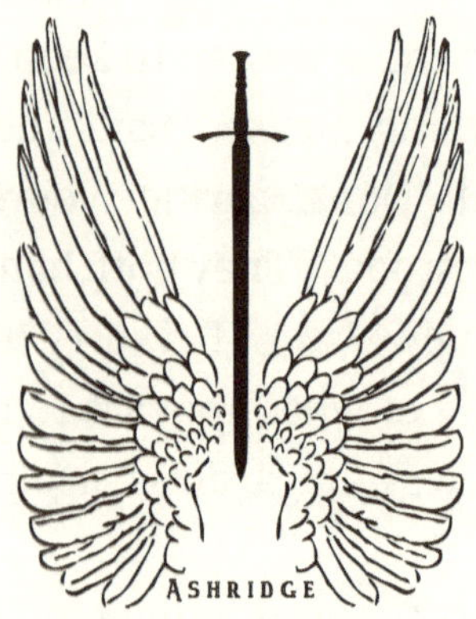

CHAPTER 32

JESSIKA

I LET OUT A long breath and leaned back in the chair, resting my head on the back. I rolled my head toward Aiden, who was staring at the wall on the other side, just shaking his head and blinking.

Reaching over, I took his hand and rubbed my thumb across it. "What are you thinking?"

"Owen... Mr. Party Boy. Mister, I'm never going to settle down... married that girl." He pointed to where she would have been on the LightCall. "We must protect her at all costs. She tamed Owen!" He laughed then, and I chuckled with him. "How did she break through all those commitment issues that he married her without thinking twice?"

"You know Megan and CJ are going to lose their shit when they find out, right?"

"I'm not sure if they are going to be happy that he found someone or pissed they weren't able to be there for the wedding. You know damn well that if we married without them present, we would be tortured only the way Mom can do."

"True. True. They may make them have another private ceremony, though."

"I'm sure that kind of privacy was what Owen wanted, though. He knows that when any of us marry, the dimension is going to want to be in attendance."

I looked at my fingers and thought about that, looking back to where the seal of Ashridge was on the wall. Everyone was going to be at my wedding, whether I wanted them to be or not. Aiden's knuckle and thumb pinched my chin and turned me to look at him. "What's wrong?"

I searched his face and then his eyes. "Aiden..." I swallowed. "When we are finally free to marry, I want a small private ceremony where we are legally bound."

His lips crashed onto mine, and when he pulled back, he said, "I want nothing more than to have a private ceremony where the world doesn't have to be watching, but you are Grand Duchess."

I nodded. "Still, once we get all the sign-offs, all the approvals, I want just our family there for the actual, real, binding marriage. We can go somewhere quiet where I can legally bind myself to you." I watched as his eyes filled with tears. "Then we can put on the show for everyone else, for the territories, make you my duke, and move forward with Ashridge."

"Nothing will make me happier than to legally bind myself to you and call you my wife, but you are my mate. That is the binding I treasure most." He ran his nose against mine before kissing it.

"Not the Vernadali bond?" I smirked, teasing him.

He chuckled. "Jess, having you as my Charge is just the Angels agreeing to us. I've told you before that I have known I would lay my life down for you and protect you until my dying breath since the day I first laid eyes on you. You are mine and I am yours. While, yes, having the Angels bind me to you as your Vernadali is a title I take incredible joy and pride in, nothing, and I mean nothing, holds a candle to being your mate. That is the title I will cherish forever."

"Well, just so we are clear, you will also be my husband and Duke of Ashridge."

"That's what you keep saying." He sat back and raked his hand through his hair. "Only I really don't know how that is possible. There are Vernadali..." His gaze returned to mine, and I didn't dare breathe for him to read the thoughts going through my head. His gaze flicked all over my face, looking for the answers to what I was keeping, and when he saw me just staring at him, his eyes went wide. "That is what all those messages between you and Dad have been?"

I didn't move. I didn't mean to let him know that was what I had been talking to him so much about. His eyes went wider, and I smiled. "Maaaybeee."

He picked me up and pressed me against the wall, kissing me like it was our last day in Nalsar. He pulled back just slightly, and he whispered, "I've been trying to figure that out since the messages in Avalan. How?"

"The law was dismissed after your parents were married, Aiden. There are things that have to be signed off on, and dimensional approvals because of my position, but the Vernadali laws aren't in our way. Kaletta is." I kissed him.

His voice was thick, and the heat swelling in his eyes made my stomach swim in all the right ways. "You are serious." I nodded. "I only have to wait for Kaletta to be out of our way and then I'll have you every way possible?"

"Aiden..."

"I said what I said. I know I have you in every way, but I want to legally call you my wife. We've covered that."

"Yes. Once this conflict with Kaletta is done, then yes, we have to have Popa sign off as the dimensional head, Empress Clarice sign off as the *neutral third party*, and Vernadali Samuel sign off for the Vernadali, then, yes, we can marry and make you Duke."

He kissed me quickly again, and I thought I felt his chest hitch. He rested his forehead on mine a moment before his head popped up. "Wait.

"Did you say that Empress Clarice has to sign off as a neutral third party?" His eyebrows were almost touching his hairline, they were so high.

I chuckled, and he set my feet down on the floor. "That is what I said. When they set up the procedure, they wanted to have someone who would have access to those that had been dispatched by the Vernadali, so if there were issues, that could be addressed. CJ rambled on a lot about it, but I just took it as Vernadali business. Popa has to sign off because well, head of dimension, and that makes sense. And then the head of the Vernadali."

"Yeah, yeah, yeah. I understand the process of it... Auntie Clarice as a neutral third party?" he repeated. I smiled at him, nodding. "Well, shit, guess no one thought it would ever be applied for with one of her kids or family members."

"CJ said the same thing. He thinks that when they put those processes in play, they didn't think your parents were going to have more kids after the elemental twins. They weren't Vernadali, so they didn't think it would be a thing. Then your parents had you and you tested as being Vernadali. CJ said there was talk about it briefly, but..." I shrugged.

"They just never thought that I would have you." His voice was full of awe, love, and devotion. I just held his gaze. "Is it wrong that I want to be a fly on the wall when they get that request just to see the reaction? I mean, auntie will sign it no problem. Popa will want to talk to me about it, but I suspect I'll have to go to the Curtails of the North to meet with Vernadali Samuel to get that sign off."

CHAPTER 33

JAYDEN

I WAS WANDERING THE halls and, for the first time, feeling completely safe and content. Ilris and I had been able to just *be* for almost four months. We hadn't had to hide, be careful about what we said, how we moved, anything. It'd been so unbelievably freeing.

Taking a sip of my tea, I pulled my sweater around me and sighed. It was quiet, too, which was such a blessing. Everywhere I'd ever had to go, my entire life, I had to be accompanied. Granted, one of them was Ilris and I loved the man with every ounce of my being, but having these quiet moments to myself was refreshing. Ilris was for sure my calm in the storm, but every once in a while, his breathing would annoy me. I huffed a laugh at that thought but then sobered. Killy. I swallowed. Angels, Killy. I still missed his presence like a phantom limb. While we may not have been intimate, I loved him deeply. He was as important to me as Jessika and Janreka.

Stepping outside onto one of the balconies that looked out over Obsecuritan, I walked to the railing and saw the garden workers tending to the grounds. It was still so strange to see most everything in black, grey, and white here. I was used to so much opulent color in Kaletta that Obsecuritan was still taking some getting used to, even all these months later.

Therth itself was still in the process of renovations. Once Empress Clarice had taken over and returned, she hated the borderline poverty that most of the people here lived in. She appointed all new governors and had a much stronger hand in how the city was run from what her father did. Well, at least that was what Erida told us. She had been keeping her distance, but I noticed that Witch Dorith had been buzzing around a bit more. When I asked Janreka what was going on, she said that there were some strange things going on in the witch colonies.

"Jade!" I turned to see Janreka coming down the hall. "I just checked your room and Ilris said you had gone for a walk."

"He's awake? He was out like a light when I snuck out." I smiled and shook my head, taking another sip of my tea. Spicy and smooth. I didn't know how the people of Obsecuritan had combined the herbs to create such a spicy, creamy beverage without additives, but it was delicious.

Looking back out at the grounds, I tilted my head to the side. "You never said how those strange patterns in the dirt were made."

She chuckled. "Uncle CJ calls it *The Magical Hissy Fit of Therth.*"

"What?"

"Apparently, during the war, Aunt Megan had a bit of a meltdown after they lost Aunt Lindy."

Nodding in understanding, I drained the rest of my tea and set the cup down on the ledge. Flattening my palms on the railing and watching them for a moment, Janreka came over and bumped her shoulder against me.

I breathed in the cool air and asked, "So, did you need something?"

She tensed beside me. "Yeah. Sorry. Mom needs to talk to you and Ilris. We got some disturbing info from Silentport about what your father—"

"He isn't my father anymore except for when I have to acknowledge him to claim my title," I ground out through my teeth.

"The Grand Lord is doing."

I took a deep breath, grabbed the cup off the ledge, and faced her. "Lead the way."

We stopped by the room, and I changed quickly. Ilris was ready and waiting. As I walked by, I kissed him quickly, and he smirked as he noticed Janreka in the doorway. "I'm not hiding from Janreka, Ilris."

"I know, Jade. I'm just not used to us being allowed to be so open." He let the left side of his lip lift. "It is going to make it harder to hide when we go home."

"Jayden has plans for that, Ilris," Janreka said carefully.

"He does, but it doesn't mean that our people will be receptive when the declarations are made." His voice was full of sadness and anxiety.

I finished strapping on my syth belt and took a deep breath. He wasn't wrong, and it was something I was really concerned about. Hell, Jessika and I had talked about it for hours. I knew it would not be a quick fix, which was why I wanted to get the laws and procedures changed to line up with Ashridge's before I turned Kaletta over to her.

When I stood up, Ilris was standing there and took my hands, running his thumbs across my knuckles. "What has you thinking so hard?"

I shook my head. "I'm fine. Just working through some things in my head."

"Lord Jayden," Clarice said as I walked into her office.

"Angels, what happened?" I groaned.

She huffed a laugh and shook her head. "Why do you think something has happened?"

"First, you summon me here by sending Janreka. Then you greet me with *Lord Jayden*? Now, *Empress Clarice*, what is going on?" I stood tall and crossed my arms, lifting an eyebrow at her.

Ilris and Janreka were trying not to laugh behind me, and then Clarice broke into a wide smile. "Yeah, okay, your... the Grand Lord is moving against Ashridge."

I blinked. I wasn't surprised, but before I freaked out, I wanted details. "Explain."

"Troops are on their way to Silentport. Mysterious fires are burning the forest along the ridge between Silentport and Kaletta, slowing them down, but he's sent a large force."

"Mysterious fires?" I lifted the left side of my mouth and huffed a laugh. "I'm assuming a certain family member we know may be responsible for that?"

She smiled at me but then became somber again. "Lord Jayden, he has sent thousands of troops to Silentport."

"Get me a Lark Messenger. We need to let Jessika know."

Janreka's voice was careful. "I've already let her know. I've been in contact with them. Well, with Aiden, at least. I'm trying to discuss things with him so if someone thought you were here, it wouldn't jeopardize your plan."

There was something more to the way she said that, and I swallowed but asked, "What else is going on, Janreka?"

She stared at me for a long moment before Ilris said, "We may be in hiding, Princess Janreka, but that doesn't mean Jayden isn't still Lord of Kaletta and privy to the information that affects him and those he cares about."

"Keep your syths sheathed, Ilris. I was going to answer him. I was just trying to figure out how to say it short and sweet. The short story is there have been a number of security breaches at the Ashridge main hall, some with ties to the witches."

"Which is why Witch Dorith has been running around like crazy," I said in realization.

Clarice nodded but continued, "They are closing in on answers there, but nothing is for sure. There are also issues with the supply chains between Silentport and Ashridge City." I nodded. I knew that. Jessika had been fighting that before I came down here. "There are also issues with getting water and the like from the Black Mountains. They are working with the Lady of Ancemore, who has water in abundance, because the Grand Lord has rerouted water to flow to the west side of the mountains."

She waited to say more and met each of our eyes. It was Janreka who tipped her head to the side and asked, "What is it, Mom?"

"I just received word that not only is there a large force heading to Silentport, but they have orders to take the city, not just disrupt or show a presence."

"That would cripple Ashridge. The city is too important to the supply chain in both economics and goods. It's the territory's main receiving port." My heart was beating so quickly that Ilris came over and placed his hand on my back in support. I looked over my shoulder and stared at him. I needed to help, but how? He tipped his head quickly as if to tell me to go. I narrowed my eyes at him, making sure he was saying what I thought, and he nodded.

I looked at Janreka, who I could see was making the same decision, and then back to Clarice before saying, "Get me to Silentport so I can help keep the city out of the hands of Kaletta."

Clarice and Janreka shared a long look before Clarice's lips thinned and she nodded. "I'll take you," Janreka said.

Clarice leveled an even look at her daughter. "Vernadali Natasha can't go, and she's going to be livid that this is the second time you are leaving her behind. Frankly, I'm only doing this because it's Jess. Vernadali Natasha is assigned to protect you, Reka."

Janreka sighed and tipped her head back, putting her hands on her hips. Her long microbraids that ended in a beautiful jade color swung against her butt. "I know. I can handle her, though."

"The point of a Vernadali is to have them watching your back when you are in a fight or to protect *you*, Suk'Natal."

"I understand that, Empress, but you must know that I can't stand by and let my friend's city fall. Not when I can do something to help."

I stood back and let them have their verbal spar because even though this was a mother worried about her daughter, titles were being used, and there was protocol to adhere to in politics. Unless your name and title were used, you kept your lips sealed the fuck shut.

After about five minutes of them going back and forth, Empress Clarice looked at her daughter and said, "May the Angels grant you wings."

Janreka nodded to her and whispered, "Thank you, Mom."

"Just promise you will be careful. I know Jess needs us, and I was not pushing back about that. We will always be there to help. If you need more help, just let the dead know, and I'll be there instantly."

Ilris and I looked at each other, confused, and when I opened my mouth, Clarice lifted a hand to stop me. "Gatekeeper secrets, Jayden."

"Yes, Empress," I affirmed, nodding my head once, and Janreka gave me a look that said she was sorry, but I understood. She took a deep breath through her nose, and I asked, "What?"

"I'm sorry, Ilris, but you can't go. Too much of a liability. You two will be too concerned with each other, and one of you will get hurt." When I looked at Ilris, he nodded to her.

"You are agreeing to stay here? You are my guard. You can be teleported with us. It's not the same as Vernadali Natasha. We have the darkness in our blood."

He took my hand, pulling me closer to him. "But she's not wrong, Jade. You will be too concerned about me to protect yourself. One of us would end up trying to protect the other and die. I have a bad feeling about this one. Silentport is..."

"Critical," I whispered as I nodded and leaned my forehead against his.

He nodded against mine before reaching up, placing his hand on my cheek, and kissing me softly. "Come back to me, Jade."

"Always." Then I deepened the kiss, feeding all my love for him into it. He opened for me and grasped my neck tight, holding me to him. I tipped my head to the side, letting my tongue explore every inch of his mouth. When we pulled away, we were breathing hard, but I sucked on his bottom lip in that way that did have that moan coming from him.

"I was about to ask if you wanted us to leave for a moment." Janreka chuckled.

Without removing my gaze from Ilris', I whispered, "Fuck off, Janreka."

"I'll leave the fucking to you two."

"Janreka!" Clarice admonished, and Ilris and I just laughed.

I gave him one more quick kiss before pulling back and asking, "So, Janreka, when do we leave?"

CHAPTER 34

JAYDEN

IT TOOK A COUPLE hours to get Vernadali Natasha to relent, but when Empress Clarice gave her an order, she balked but conceded. By then I was pacing my room.

"I'm sorry that took so long, Jayden," Janreka said, closing the door behind her. "Where do you think is the best place to land?"

"Jessika's manor. It's not far from the city center, and the staff there should be able to give us an idea of what they know."

"Alright, let's do this." She held her hand out, and I gave Ilris one more quick kiss as he once again reminded me he loved me.

As I took her hand, black smoke surrounded us, the ground fell out from under me, and then we were standing at the top landing of the Silentport Manor. Screaming, yelling, and the sound of rushing water was everywhere.

I looked down at the bottom of the stairs and saw LJ, Aiden's sister, pulling another woman into the house. I glanced at Janreka quickly and bounded down the stairs.

"LJ!"

"Jayden?" She looked up. "Reka?" Looking between us again as she used her power to shut the door, she looked down at the woman before us. She was cut from head to toe, the worst of which appeared to be her shoulder. The girl moaned, and LJ cooed, "Shhh. It's okay, Rissa. There is someone here who can mend you up."

She looked up at me, and I nodded.

It was Janreka who asked, "What's the state of things out there?"

"You mean, other than Kaletta killing everyone in town, including the Lord and Lady, their guards, and half their staff?" LJ spat the words, and I looked at Janreka as I started working at the woman's feet, healing whatever cuts I could along the way up her body.

"Yeah, other than that." I tried not to think of the ramifications of what she had just told me.

LJ sighed and said, "We were strategizing what to do when we got word they stormed the main hall and took to the city center, slaughtering everyone in their wake. We stepped outside, and Clarissa here threw a slicing incantation, but it somehow bounced back and hit her. Went right over Owy and I, though."

Janreka looked toward the door. "I'm assuming Owen is out there right now, and that's why I hear rushing water?"

She nodded but swallowed. "Clarissa is his wife, Reka. They married only a little over two weeks ago."

"His *what*?" Janreka and I said at the same time.

"His wife. Clarissa is a Mathewson. So, Jayden, I would appreciate it if you would calm your shock and save my sister here?"

"Owen's wife. Underworld's being. Who would have thought that Owen would ever agree to marry?" She shook her head. "So, she got hurt, and that is what has Owen out there and you in here?"

All of a sudden, there was a loud crash outside, and the windows next to the door shattered. Janreka threw up a wall, protecting us from the spray of glass flying through the foyer. I looked through the long window that lined the door and my eyes widened.

Owen was standing there with a giant orb of water encompassing four guards, slowly drowning them within the bubble. His arm flew out, and another joined them.

"I've never seen him like this. He's usually the one to keep me in control. I tried to reach him. He won't..." She looked back down at the brunette, tears in her eyes. "Jayden, make sure she makes it."

I ran my hand over her body, and there was a lot of superficial damage, so I said, "She will be fine. It's mostly just skin and soft tissue damage. Her organs are fine. Her heart is fine. I'll stay here and get her stable." Looking over my shoulder, I called down the hall, and the cook came around the corner. "Once I have her stable, I'll need you to keep an eye on her."

"Of course, Lord Jayden."

LJ ran out of the room, and I looked at Janreka. "Go get Owen back to sanity."

"I'm not leaving you alone. You are technically still Kaletta. They see you out there alone, and any citizens who are fighting back are going to tear you apart."

"Go out there, work with LJ, and bring Owen back to sanity. Then you can come back in. Seriously, this shouldn't take too long. She'll be out for a little bit, but I need to tend to these wounds. Some of them are pretty deep." I turned and ran my hand over the worst of them. She was bleeding all over the place, which made moving her difficult.

Fifteen minutes later, I had Clarissa on the couch and was working on the worst of her wounds—a large, deep gash on her left shoulder. Her eyes fluttered open as she muttered, "Owen?"

"No, Ms. Clarissa. He's outside. I'm sure he will be back for you soon, but you are hurt and need to stay still. I'm almost done, but I need you to not move."

She nodded, but I knew when her eyes had focused because they went wide as she burst out, "Lord Jayden."

"Surprise. Now seriously, hold still so I can get this cleaned up and stabilized. You were a bit of a mess."

"Yeah, one of my incantations was thrown back at us, and Owen and LJ pulled us mostly out of the way, but it was spelled against Kaletta. Since I'm Kaletta-born, it whipped over me but passed over them. I blacked out when I felt my arm slice open," she muttered with a groan.

I was looking at her arm, and I was surprised to see it was trying to heal already. "You heal pretty quick."

"Yeah, my mom was part Piklari. I didn't get any of the physical abilities, but I do heal quickly and rarely get sick." She looked down at her shoulder and hissed when I hovered over it, working on closing it up. "This will take a good week to be back to normal."

She lay there for a long moment before she asked, "What is your connection to the Mathewsons?"

"I've known and been friends with them for a very long time. You are as safe with me as you are Owen. I won't let Kaletta touch you." She smiled and looked at where I was working on her shoulder. "Okay, fair point."

"I do love him, Lord Jayden. I know that Owen and I..." She stopped and sucked in a hiss of breath through her teeth. "It's fast, and I know all about his commitment issues. I was shocked when he turned and asked me to marry him. Everyone knows that he's got a player's history, but he's a real softy inside."

"He is, but only his family knows that. You also don't have to justify your feelings for him to me. I'm much more faithful to the Mathewson family than I am to Kaletta, but that is a secret you will have to keep as a Mathewson now." Winking at her, I huffed a laugh as I put the finishing touches on her shoulder. "Stay here. Don't move from the couch. We will be back. I promise you."

She nodded, and when I got to the door, LJ opened it. "She's fine. Resting now. She's willing to stay here."

Behind her, Janreka had a hold of Owen with her power around his waist. There was nothing but fury in his body.

Only, when he saw me in the door, I saw it lessen. Janreka released him, and he ran past me to check on Clarissa. He had just reached her when I said, "She's fine, Owen. You're welcome, and hello to you too."

He gave me a gesture over his shoulder, cradled her head in his hands, and kissed his wife. Shaking my head in disbelief, I cursed. *Shit. Owen's married.* Can't wait to have that discussion with the family.

Screaming filtered down the streets, and while we gave Owen a moment to check on her, it was Janreka who finally said, "Owy, the city."

He nodded and kissed his wife one more time, whispering something to her. She lifted a hand and ran her thumb across his cheek and nodded.

"Janreka, Jayden. Thank you," he finally said when he was standing before us. "But I have a question."

"We are here to help," I said carefully.

"For Jess?"

"For Jessika. It's what family does." I reached over and put a hand on his shoulder and squeezed.

Nodding, he looked at each of us and then back to Clarissa. "Well, she asked that we not let the city fall to Kaletta. Since it has technically already done so by them killing the royal house..." He looked at us before saying, "Let's go get it back for her."

CHAPTER 35

JAYDEN

WATER AND FIRE SOARED down street after street. I wasn't sure how they kept it from tearing through the citizens. Somehow, it all just flowed over them and only incinerated or destroyed Kaletta soldiers. Clarissa had said something about spelling her power to only attack those of Kaletta. They must have learned that trick from her.

Any Kaletta soldiers who got out of their path, Janreka and I dispatched easily enough. The closer we got to the main hall, the more soldiers there were. While Owen and LJ worked on clearing the landing, three Kaletta soldiers burst out of an alley, syths up. Janreka tossed one back with her power with a flick of her wrists, but the other dodged the shot and whirled around, slicing down her leg as he rolled by. It was only a moment of distraction, but the other Kaletta soldier lunged for me, and I was able to get a wall up just in time to keep his syth from hitting my chest.

His power thrummed against the shield, and I tasted cinnamon in the air along with hearing the scream of Owen for LJ to watch her left. Water sprayed over me, and I dodged another syth, cursing Owen. I whirled, kicking the side of the soldier's knee, and as he went down, recognition hit as to who I was.

"Lord Jayden." His hands went up, but it was too late.

"There is no mercy for people killing innocents." Throwing my power into his chest, he collapsed, completely unmoving. Turning, I saw Janreka running her syth over another soldier's neck, blood spraying into the air. I turned my head away and moved so that I wasn't caught in its aerial splatter.

When we reached the twins, Owen was bent over as we disposed of those watching the front. "LJ, you owe me for this."

"Well, if you hadn't stayed up late with your wife last night and had actually gotten a good night's sleep, maybe you wouldn't be so tired." They laughed, and when a Kaletta soldier tried to sneak up on her, she huffed out a breath, and he fell to the ground.

"I have seen you on many a battlefield, LJ, but that shit still freaks me out," Janreka said, putting a hand on her shoulder. "Your temperature is rising, though. Be careful."

She gave a simple nod. Owen came over, closed his eyes, his hands wreathed in blue. LJ shivered but muttered, "Thanks."

We were running up the stairs and bursting through the doors a moment later. My power flung out with the others, but I pulled it back when I saw Owen had the captain encased in water, except for his head. LJ flung her arms out to the left, and everyone on that side fell to the floor as charcoal. At the same time, Janreka snapped the necks on every guard on the right, and there was a collective thud as they all hit the ground.

"Shit, remind me not to piss you guys off."

The ball that Owen had the captain encased in rose, and I placed my hand on his shoulder. He turned his head to face me, hand still out in a fist. "Just one moment—"

"Jayden, he led the forces that hurt Clarissa." His voice broke a little as he said it.

"She's healing. She is fine. You saw that yourself." His eyes were full of fear, but as he listened to me repeat the words, they settled. "Once I'm done, then you can kill him."

The captain laughed, and my gaze swung to his. "Shut up."

"Lord Jayden." The color drained from his face.

"Oh good, so you know who I am. That should make this easier." I shrugged but then said, "Did the Grand Lord command you to take the city?"

"Yes, sir."

"For what purpose?"

He was silent a moment too long, and I saw LJ's hand glowed red. The water bubbled, and I just said, "LJ..."

She huffed, and I saw a puff of smoke next to my shoulder but cocked my head to the side, looking at the captain. "I will repeat. For what purpose did the Grand Lord command you to take the city?"

"For supplies. Said that we need to take what is ours and stop giving it to people who go against the wishes of the Angels."

I sighed heavily through my nose. I had heard that speech so many times in my life that it did nothing but raise my blood pressure. The captain looked at me and said, "Have you been spending so much time here in Ashridge, you now have sympathy for *those* people?"

"*Those* people?" LJ said carefully.

"Those people who believe it's okay to be with—"

"People like me and Ilris, LJ," I interrupted.

The guard's eyes went wide. They bounced between all of us, but then they landed on mine again, and there was fear. True fear. When I lifted an eyebrow at him, I could see where he realized he wouldn't ever feel the ground under his feet again.

"Jayden..." Janreka was standing behind me and put a hand on my shoulder.

"LJ? Owen?"

"Yes, Lord Jayden?"

My voice became completely void of any emotion as I said, "Boil him alive."

I barely saw where Owen and LJ gave each other a quick, surprised look before they answered, "As you command, sir."

I crossed my arms and watched as the water boiled. His head went under water, his skin turned red, and steam raised from the top of his head. It took a few minutes, but before long, the water was rapidly boiling, and I watched as the life left the captain. I had to resist the urge to wave my fingers in a goodbye motion at him as he died.

Owen and LJ let him cook a minute longer than they needed to. "Just to make sure he's good and dead," LJ had said before I turned, and hot water coated the hall floor. Blood sizzled as it washed away.

"So, Princess Janreka, what do you think we should do first? Clean the hall or slay the rest of the Kaletta soldiers who are fucking with Silentport?"

Her hand was over her leg where the soldier had gotten her earlier, healing it. I took a step toward her, smacked her hand away, and took the time to make sure that the healing process wasn't locking in any infections. She hissed, but when I had it closed back up, she smiled. "Thank you."

Turning to LJ and Owen, I asked, "You two okay?"

"Yeah," Owen said at the same time as LJ said, "Peachy keen."

"Alright." I ran my hands through my hair. "Janreka, where do you want to start?"

"Me? Why are you asking me?"

LJ laughed. "Because you are the highest ranking official in the city, Princess."

Janreka reached over and smacked LJ upside the back of the head. Owen and I snorted our laughter.

CHAPTER 36

AIDEN

"Is it weird I miss Jayden?" Jess said as she washed the pots and pans from breakfast.

I huffed a laugh and reminded her, "It's been almost four months. You haven't gone this long without talking to him since you two became friends."

She reached up to put the pot on the top shelf, but was struggling. When she was on her tiptoes, jumping a little, I walked up behind her and took her hips to lift her. The pot slid into place easily, and as I lowered her back to her feet, she turned in my arms, hands on my shoulders. "I can't believe it might all work. I miss him, though."

"I know, Kotě." I leaned down and kissed her. She pulled back and rested her head on my chest, pulling me close, trying to hide the nervousness and fear. Jess knew she couldn't, but I couldn't blame her for trying. I had to give her that. Holding her close, I moved my thumb back and forth along her hip.

"I need to talk to Lemi later about what his duties are going to be for Ashridge." She was staring at the rounded steel at my neck and then said, "Kat's duties are in Cinder, for now. Since he abdicated the throne, technically, he is still Duke, but does he want that title? I'll retitle him if he wants." She was quiet for a moment. Her mind was bouncing around and she was just word vomiting, so I let her. "He may just need to be a figurehead. I don't know. He's... He's loyal, and he's my brother. I want him here, but he needs to be with Kat and the kids."

"We'll have him over for dinner tonight. Dakota, too." Her emotions were all over the place, and it took a few minutes of her in my arms before she settled down. I kissed the top of her head and asked, "You ready to do the gathering again today?"

She groaned, burying her head into my chest. She mumbled something that sounded like, "I don't wanna. I hate the damn thing. We don't need any of it. It's like holding an old-fashioned court. I don't mind listening to my people, really, I don't. What I hate is them bringing me presents. I don't want or need any of it. They need it. Besides, the last one was a disaster."

I chuckled and then lifted her head. "I promise to behave, and I already have everything all set up."

Her eyes narrowed at me, and I slid my hand up, wrapped it around her throat a moment, and waited for her to release some of the tension before I slipped my finger inside of the heart at her neck. "You got this. Then, when you are done, you will come back home, I will make dinner, and then I will have dessert."

"What? I don't get dessert?"

"If you are a good girl, then you can have it, but I'll have mine spread out wide on the table." Her eyes went wide, and I felt exactly what spots heated in her body. "Tonight, Kotě. Tonight."

Her breath hitched, and she closed her eyes, concentrating on behaving. "That is mean, Aiden. How am I supposed to concentrate for the rest of the day?"

"You'll figure it out."

Then my kitten looked at me through her eyelashes and pumped me against the Claiming. I tipped my head back and moaned. "Fuck."

Her chuckle rolled across the Claiming, too, and through my ears. "I'll behave if you do, sir."

Looking back down at her, she gave me the most innocent look she could muster. "Two, Kotě."

"Two?" She pulled back. "What did I do to earn a *one*?"

"Last night, when you ran your fingers through the cum dripping out of your delicious pussy as I came back with a towel to clean you up."

She blushed and looked off to the side, muttering, "I don't remember that."

Humming, I kissed her temple and turned her toward the door, smacking her ass. "Now get dressed to see your people."

EVERYTHING WAS GOING SMOOTHLY, and I had even been able to keep my protective streak mostly at bay today. I clenched my fists when I felt it rearing up and discretely touched the rounded steel at my throat. She was mine. She was safe. If I needed to get to her, she was no more than five feet from me at all times.

The main hall was packed today, but I had set up extra precautions just in case. Jess dismissed one family, and another stepped up to the dais. A young boy no older than five or six reached up with a small black box toward her, and I marveled at the smile she gave him. She bent down, talking with the young boy, when Gerald came bursting around the corner.

"Silentport!" She stood and immediately turned toward him as he strode for her. Taking a step toward the family that had just come up, I asked them to please step back while the Grand Duchess had a moment with her secretary of defense.

She stood before the throne as Gerald came and bowed before her. "I'm sorry to interrupt your time with the citizens, Grand Duchess, but I bring news of Silentport."

As I took my place next to Jess on the other side of the throne that would one day be mine if she had her way, she commanded, "Stand and speak, Gerald."

He looked quickly between us and said, "I just received word that Silentport was attacked late last night. The Lord and Lady of Silentport, along with all of their guards and most of their house, were executed in the city center."

"We have lost the city?" Jess' voice croaked with the thought as she practically fell back into her throne to sit, her hands lying flat in her lap on her black jeans. I felt the panic and fear that went through her, but her eyes stayed on Gerald. While she may have sat quickly on her throne, she still looked poised and collected.

I ran a hand down the Claiming, and I saw her take a deep breath. "My people?"

"Someone had given the city a heads-up and about half had left." He swallowed, and the fear and confusion in his eyes were an interesting combination with this man who had seen so much. "Roughly a third of the people still there were killed. Then fire and water rolled down the streets."

She blinked and looked at me. My heart was racing because we didn't want to assume, but it was clear that LJ and Owen had taken it to heart when she had asked them to protect the city.

"Fire and water. You are sure?"

"Yes, Grand Duchess. It was then followed by a wave that would direct it. There are reports that..." He looked at me, asking me if it were possible. I nodded, and his eyes widened. "There are reports that the Mathewson twins are in Silentport and have taken it back, with the help of Lord Jayden and Princess Janreka."

Relief flowed through both of us, and I wasn't sure if it was more Jess or me.

"Grand Duchess." Tears filled Gerald's eyes. "The twins are staying tight-lipped, but someone else was hurt badly in their party. They were adamant that we let you and Vernadali Aiden know that they will be okay."

Her worry deepened, and a hole in my chest opened for Owen if it was Clarissa. "You said Lord Jayden is there?"

"Yes, sir. I spoke to him personally. Asked where he has been, and he only said he had his reasons for leaving. I tried to find out when he would be returning to Ashridge, but he said nothing."

"Please set up a LightCall with Princess Janreka. *Only* Princess Janreka. I do not wish to speak to the twins, and I refuse to speak to Lord Jayden. This is territory business. Is that clear?" He nodded, and I turned to Vernadali Dadan, nodded, and she disappeared down the hall. "Gerald, do we have a number of dead yet?"

When Gerald paled, I held my breath. "The preliminary numbers sit at about one-hundred-twenty-thousand people killed by Kaletta forces in the last thirty-eight hours."

"That many in just one day?" I asked because Jess had gone very still, her gaze vacant, and I was getting nothing from her.

"Kaletta guards poisoned the water supply. It was all delivered through the main aquifer through the night. Nearly seventy-thousand were dead by morning."

"You said that Princess Janreka, Lord Jayden, Owen, and LJ took back the city?" I stepped forward and spoke softer, so it didn't carry through the halls.

"Yes, Vernadali Aiden. They did everything they could to save those they did, but the ruling house is gone. They even killed the children." A single tear fell down his cheek.

"Thank you."

Gerald stood, and I rested a hand on Jess' shoulder, waiting for her to dismiss the hall. When she didn't, I squeezed tightly, but she didn't move. She was just looking out over the main hall through the double-wide doors with a face of stone. There were no emotions coming from her, and I stood before her.

"Grand Duchess, look at me."

Nothing.

Pushing my Charge into the words, I repeated, "Grand Duchess, look at me."

Her stare slowly tracked to meet mine. Her eyes were full of despair, turmoil, and pain, but I felt none of it from her. She lifted a hand and put it to her throat. I nodded and winked.

"You need to get out of your seat and keep your eyes on me. Is that understood, Grand Duchess?"

She blinked, and I repeated myself again, throwing more of my Charge into the words. I heard the room clearing out; the guards maneuvered the citizens of Ashridge out of the main hall when Vernadali Dadan returned. "Princess Janreka awaits on the LightCall, Grand Duchess."

Jess blinked again.

"Did you hear Vernadali Dadan?" I pulled on the Claiming but also pushed my Charge into my words. She was disassociating, and I needed to get her to snap out of it. She needed to be the Grand Duchess.

Fuck! I knew that one day, it was going to have to be like this. She would have to pick her kingdom over processing her own feelings.

"Yes, Vernadali Aiden, I heard Vernadali Dadan. Janreka awaits me." Her voice was not quite deadpan, but there was little to no emotion in it.

"Kotě," I ran down the Claiming. I saw Vernadali Dadan narrow her eyes slightly, but at this point, I didn't care. She wasn't responding, and I didn't want to have to go full Vernadali on her.

Jess looked at me again, took a long breath through her nose with closed eyes, and let out the breath through her mouth. When she opened her eyes again, she was back.

"Janreka is waiting, Vernadali Aiden. Let's go talk to your sister."

I reached out, and she took my hand, squeezing it tight. When she stood next to me, she whispered, "Thank you."

When we passed Vernadali Dadan, she thanked her and asked that she have the council be assembled for an emergency session.

"Of course, Grand Duchess."

"Let them know I will be there as soon as I'm done talking to Princess Janreka and thanking her for taking back my city."

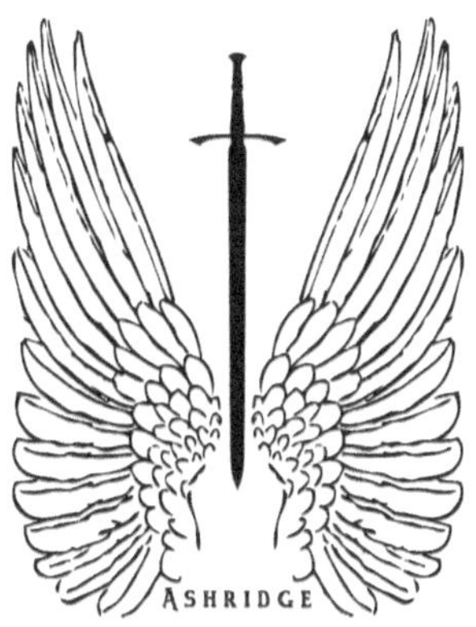

CHAPTER 37

JESSIKA

"JESS," JANREKA SAID ONCE the door was closed behind Aiden.

"Reka, is everyone okay?" Aiden's voice was tight, but my chest hurt, and I didn't know where to go from here.

"A bit beaten and bruised, but we are okay. Clarissa got hurt pretty bad, but *he's* been excellent and healed her up. She's apparently part Piklari, so she's healing quickly. Owy is, well, temperamental. I've never seen him like this." She looked off to the side. "He's always just been my overprotective brother. Jess, Aiden, he was off the rails. No hesitation in swirling those soldiers up and watching them drown. No remorse... I now see why people are so terrified of the twins. Underworld's being."

"We've seen them fight before, though, Janreka. We were in Maridel, for Angel's sake."

"Yeah, but it was LJ we had to keep under wraps. She practically burned the city down after what happened to Alex." She shook her head. "Rightfully so."

"Before you tell me what happened, thank you for saving Silentport," My voice was hollow in my own ears.

"I'm sorry we didn't get here sooner."

I opened my mouth to ask her why she was there, when Aiden beat me to it. "And just why are you there, Reka? I thought you and auntie were in Therth."

"Mom is. However, when we heard that Kaletta was overtaking the city, we knew we had to help." She looked off screen and shook her head before she said to someone, "Don't say the name. I'll explain later."

LJ came, stood next to Janreka, and said, "When *they* arrived, the three of us had just gone outside to put a stop to it. In the process, Clarissa's incantation was bounced back over top of us. Like Reka said, she's healing. Owen hasn't left her side."

"He's really fallen for her, huh?"

"Yeah, Aid, he has." There was a small smile on LJ's lips, and her eyes brightened. "If nothing else comes of this whole thing, I'm glad they found each other. I never thought I'd see him happy with someone."

We all nodded.

"I know you probably heard, but thank you. Just what are we looking at?"

"First, you are welcome. Second, what do you want us to do?"

Jess took a deep breath. "Well, I sort of need to know what I am looking at?"

"They slaughtered a lot of people. What Nalrin and Silentport Guard are left, we have instructed to get the streets cleaned up and gather the dead. We are working on getting some help from Greenvale to build pyres. There are also directives that citizens not return to Silentport until the Grand Duchess issues that order." Janreka's voice was sad, and a shadow crossed her face. "I talked to Mom. The dead are telling her that the Grand Lord is making his way to Ashridge City. They are gloating about it, in fact."

"Any other details?" Aiden asked, and she shook her head. "I'd feel better if the family were here. Is there anyone who can oversee the city?"

Janreka and LJ shared a look before Janreka said, "No. I'm getting on a call with Popa after this to discuss new coverage. I suspect Aunt Megan and Uncle CJ will end up here for a bit."

I sighed. "At least until he can find someone permanent."

"You mean until *you* can designate a new Lord or Lady of Silentport." Janreka raised an eyebrow.

Closing my eyes and leaning my head back on my chair, I breathed, "Right. One of the perks of being Grand Duchess." I heard three sets of chuckles around me. "Jerks."

"Yeah, and?" LJ chuckled. I opened my eyes and gave her an even look. She just smiled brightly at me.

"Seriously, Jess, we will talk to Popa and hold down the fort. We will get there as soon as *we* can." Janreka was careful with her words.

"You know the timeline we are on." Sighing, I looked to LJ and said, "Can you three come to Ashridge City?"

She blinked twice before nodding. "Of course, anything you want, Grand Duchess."

"That wasn't a request of the Grand Duchess. I was asking my sister-in-law if she was coming now or going to hang out and help her other sister." I got a little too snarky, and she lifted a finger, the tip glowing red with the heat of her power. I stuck my tongue out at her, Aiden chuckling next to me.

"Give us a couple of days to get some things smoothed out here. Make sure Kaletta doesn't come in with a second wave."

"Yeah, okay." Yeah, I was disappointed. After what happened there, I was concerned about Aiden's and my ability to keep Ashridge City. If Kaletta could take Silentport in one day, even with all the military I have here, would we be able to stave them off? Sure, they would have to get through the city walls, but it had been done before. What if Kaletta had bought some of my guards and they sabotaged their way through? What if they were to poison our water supply as well?

I leaned on the desk and ran my hands through my hair, completely forgetting that I had it half up in a braided bun. My rings got caught, and Aiden was instantly on his feet as I was cussing under my breath. "Stop."

I huffed, and he unhooked my hair and freed my rings from the tangles. My temper and frustration were riding a thin edge. At this point, I was just waiting for the other shoe to drop.

"Jess, you alright?" LJ said, worry lining her face.

I felt Aiden stiffen next to me as the flood of emotions came to the surface. "No, LJ, I'm not. In the last six months, the Grand Lord demands that we stop delaying the marriage to one of my best friends, Mom dies, then I'm on my way back home and Amala gets killed by my best friend's territory in what appeared to be an attempt to get to me, I get home, have to light that pyre, try to put back together my kingdom after all that, and then have the Grand Lord kill another one of my friends in an attempt to force my hand. Then the man I'm betrothed to vanishes." LJ opened her mouth to correct her, but Janreka put her hand on her arm to stop her, shaking her head, mouthing, "*Later.*" "Then the Grand Lord tries to take my port city to cripple my ability to take care of my people. So no... I'm not fucking okay, Lindy Jean."

I knew it was unfair to lash out at her, but Angels, it had been a trying time to say the least. I took a deep breath and Aiden flattened his hand against my back, pushing some of his calm into me. I whispered, "Thank you." I took another deep breath. "A week?"

"Maybe two. As soon as we can, Jess. I'm sorry I can't be more specific with the time frame, but—"

"You need to see how things go. You talk to Popa. I'm heading to a council meeting."

"Love you guys."

"You too. Stay safe, please."

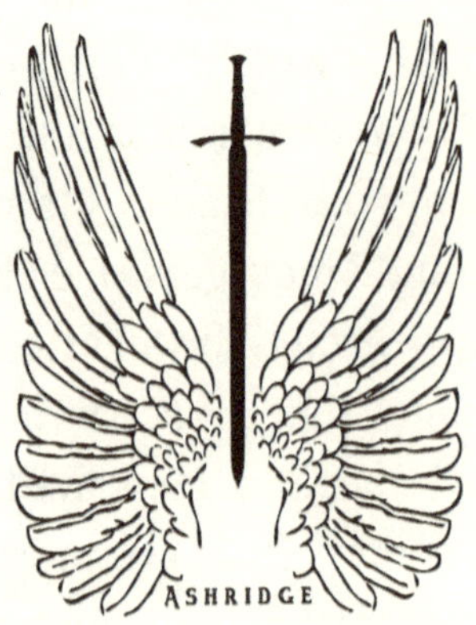

CHAPTER 38

JESSIKA

I WALKED INTO THE council room to see them all staring at me stone-faced. My boots thudded across the floor as I strode to my chair.

"This is an act of war. It needs to be declared, Grand Duchess," Braxten said. I knew his concern. A large portion of our financial district was stationed in Silentport.

Ignoring him, I held my head up. "I just spoke to Princess Janreka. She will be speaking to Head Julian, and we will then need to assign a new Lord or Lady to Silentport, someone we trust. I want nominations by the end of the week."

"Yes, Grand Duchess."

"There is a lot of cleanup happening, but yes, they were able to take back the city. While it is an act of war, I will not declare it yet."

Gerald and Vincent's gazes met across the table, and it was Vincent who swallowed and said, "No disrespect, Grand Duchess, but may I ask why?"

It was my time to swallow. I was doing the math in my head when Aiden said from beside me, "We can declare war in thirteen days. Not a day before."

"But Grand Duchess—" Declan sputtered from down the table.

"No." When he went to open his mouth, I cut him off, "No is a complete sentence *and* my final answer." I saw the fire in his eyes, and the rest of the council erupted into chaos.

Standing, I sent my power through the room, and everyone froze. "I have made my position clear."

"Why are you holding off? They have killed over a hundred thousand of our people and tried to take our city!"

"There are reasons for my decisions that extend beyond those privy to my council. Is that understood?"

Declan's lips thinned, his eyes still red with anger, but he gave a curt nod. "I've heard your position."

"I don't expect you to agree with it, Declan, but I *do* expect you to honor and follow it."

It was Noah who asked, "Now, how are we going to assist Princess Janreka in getting supplies and repairing Silentport?"

FOR TEN DAYS, WE worked on getting supplies rerouted to Silentport. We were walking into another one of those meetings when I opened the door, a messenger bursting by us, and Noah screaming at the others, "You just ruined months of work. Do you realize that?"

"You refuse to elaborate on that," Vincent ground the words through his teeth.

"I do because I am under the orders of the Grand Duchess."

My heart dropped, and Aiden's hand was on my back as we strode through the room, and I refused to sit. "And what did they just ruin, Noah?"

"You have refused to declare war on Kaletta."

Every muscle in my body froze as I said through my teeth, "As I stated, I will entertain the idea in three days."

Vincent swallowed, and his face hardened. "Kaletta took Roseward and Arrowhead yesterday."

"And no one cared to tell me?" I looked around the room.

"We received word an hour ago."

"Then I should have been informed fifty-nine minutes ago." Chins raised, and then there were hard looks by a majority of my council. My eyes went wide as I said slowly, "What. Did. You. Do?"

"We, the Council of Ashridge, in a majority vote, declared war on Kaletta."

"You *what*?" Aiden's Charge wrapped around me tight as my power encircled them, freezing them in place. I heard a couple of them groan, but I was past the point of caring. My most trusted, betrayed my directive.

"In an eight to one vote, ten minutes ago. We are officially at war with Kaletta," Vincent declared.

"I'm assuming the one who dissented was you, Noah." He nodded, and I was barely containing my rage. We almost hit the four-month mark. "Three fucking days. We needed three more fucking days."

I released my power, shattering the glasses on the table. I reined it in as quickly as I could because the fact was that I didn't have the luxury of killing them all. It would do nothing, and I would regret it later. "You all have betrayed my trust. There were reasons for the day limit."

"Noah said as much."

"And yet no one dared to listen to him?" Aiden was pure Vernadali. His eyes met each and every one of my council, who were trying to stand tall in their decision. "I realize that you all think you have done what was right for Ashridge, and while I can see how you came to that decision, I thought you had enough faith in your Grand Duchess to trust her judgment."

"Vernadali Aiden, they attacked Silentport and took it. If it had not been for Princess Janreka, your brother and sister, and Lord Jayden, who had up and left us, then it would have fallen completely to Kaletta."

"You are all well-informed of the Ashridge-Kaletta Territory Agreement, are you not?" They nodded their heads, and Aiden's voice dropped to a deadly level as he said, "And just how long has Lord Jayden been gone with zero contact with the Grand Duchess?"

It took a minute before Vincent paled, and Gerald uttered, "Fuck."

I threw my hands in the air and said, "Glad ya'll fucking caught up!"

I couldn't hold still. I started pacing. "Three fucking days. I needed three days to nullify the agreement."

Georgina whispered, just loud enough for us all to hear, "You've known where Lord Jayden and his guard were this entire time."

"No shit," I spat. "He's one of my best friends. You were all here when Noah was instructed to work with Lady Megan to find a way to get out of the agreement. How could you have been so short-sided as to think that we hadn't found something but had to keep it all under the table?"

"You should have told us," Vincent ground out, but there was shame in the tone as well.

"I am your Grand Duchess. My word should have been enough for you!" I screamed at each of them. "You should have told me an hour ago that two more of my cities fell, but no, you took it upon yourselves to undermine your Grand Duchess, your monarch. So here we are, back at the beginning, leaving only *impossibly dangerous* solutions to nullify the contract!" I looked at Aiden, my stomach falling out of my core and my voice cracking at the end.

His eyes told me everything I needed to know. He was scared shitless because he knew that I wouldn't marry Jayden, consummate that marriage, and wait for him to terminate it three months later. He trusted me and believed in us enough to know that I wouldn't put him through that. Then his eyes grew hard, and I felt the Charge in the word, even though he had obviously tried to hold it back. "No."

"Aiden…"

"No."

I took a deep breath. "Later. We will discuss it later."

"You fucking dumbasses," Noah muttered with his head in his hands. "You really have no idea what position you put her in."

"Because no one told us," Vincent growled.

"She is your Grand Duchess. You should trust her judgment!" Aiden's voice bellowed across the room, bouncing off the walls. A couple of my council finally had the decency to wince.

"Since you're all insistent that you know best, do allow this mere woman to explain a thing or two. Because we couldn't chance even the most innocent of slips, the plan had to be held so damn tight to the chest that there would literally be only eight people who could be at fault for it, most of whom are family," I spat.

"They have been in Therth," Charles said, sighing in realization. "But how did they get there and then to Silentport?"

Aiden slid his eyes toward the man and just said, "Gatekeeper secrets."

I stomped for the door, so angry and scared at what my only option was at this point that when I got to the threshold, I turned and said. "Again, since you seem to know how to run *my kingdom* better than I do, please, prepare for war. Then you can bring me, the Grand Duchess of Ashridge, up to date."

CHAPTER 39

AIDEN

I HAD RARELY SEEN her so mad, but the hurt and desperation running through her was really what had me on edge. When she slammed that door behind her, it had every guard in that hallway standing very, *very* still.

I followed her, but when she turned to head to our residence, I grabbed her hand and pulled her downstairs.

"Where are you going?"

I didn't say anything. My jaw was locked tight, and it was everything I could do not to storm upstairs and end them all. Instead, I focused on taking care of the Grand Duchess. I was her Vernadali, and I was going to focus on doing what I could right this minute.

When we entered the sparring ring, I dropped her hand and faced her. "Strip."

"Aiden."

"Leggings and bra. Let's go," I commanded, not letting my Charge flow through but stern enough she knew I was being her Vernadali at the moment. "Boots, too. Bare feet."

"Aiden."

"Now, Grand Duchess."

She did, and when she was standing before me, I handed her the bow staff. "Go."

"Why?"

"Because if you don't, you are likely to kill someone, and I think that Vincent and Gerald are high on that list. The fact you didn't while in that room has me in awe."

"I wanted to." She growled the words, and I could feel the hate and fury behind them. *You and me both, Kotě.*

"So, you are going to work out some of that rage and fury." I didn't let my gaze leave hers. Then I sent a jab of my power at her side, and she took a step back.

Rotating the staff in a figure eight and warming up her wrists, she flipped the staff across her shoulders and rolled her neck. I put my hand out and used my power to pull one of the ones on the rack to me. Her eyes were still on me, and once the bow was in my hand, she lunged toward my left, but I blocked it. Left, right, right, left. Each block had my hand stinging, and when she whirled to bring it toward my head, I ducked, swinging mine for her legs. She jumped, landing nimbly on her feet, before she continued her swing toward me. I bent fully forward and jabbed the end of my staff in her left side.

Stumbling back, she let out an ompf but came at me directly. Right, left, right, left. She kept hitting the stick closer and closer to my hands. The sting grew stronger with each hit.

"Ahh, that is such a move my mom does. You don't think I know how to handle it?" I said, twisting and hitting her beautiful ass with the staff.

There was a sigh that came from her that was somewhere between a groan and a moan, and I smiled. I felt the heat that spread through her and settled deep in her core. *Good. Distractions. Get that temper down,* Aiden.

When she tried to strike again, I repeated the motion, and it took four more before she lunged directly for me, saying in a voice that was much too heated, "Are we sparring or flirting?"

"That's up to you, Grand Duchess." I blocked the jab she gave me and flipped the staff up, bringing mine over her head and around her shoulders. I pulled her to me.

Her chest lifted in quick, short breaths as her grip on her staff loosened and it fell to the ground. She reached up on her toes like she was going to kiss me, but I flipped her over my back, turned, and caught her head as she fell to the ground. Gently, I set her down on the dirt ground. She was panting, and I leaned against the staff, watching her chest rise and fall.

"That was cheating." I raised an eyebrow. "I was trying to kiss you and you used it against me."

"Yeah, and?"

She huffed a chuckle and lay there, looking up at me. "Thank you."

I gave her a single nod. She did indeed feel calmer. More balanced. Then there was a wave of heat that hit me in my core, and I raised my eyebrows, looking down at her. "Jess?"

"You literally whooped my ass. You know what that does to me."

"I do, but that was just sparring. That wasn't funishments."

"I realize that, but any chance I can convince you to give me an attitude adjustment back in our residence?"

I took in my surroundings to consider who was nearby. "I don't know, Kotě. Is that something that you deserve?"

"I don't know if I *deserve* an attitude adjustment, but I would like one, please."

Looking down at her still lying on the dirt-covered sparring area, I couldn't deny her. "I can't do much of anything with you down there." Reaching down, she took my hand, and I pulled her up and close to me, kissing her quickly. "Come on. Let's get you home and cleaned up."

CHAPTER 40

AIDEN

I WANTED TO HAUL her over my shoulder and drag her back to bed, but there were appearances to uphold. As we passed the guard, my hand firmly in hers and her struggling to keep up, I knew every eye was on us.

"Vernadali Aiden!" she complained behind me.

"Move your feet." My voice was pure command, but not the one that everyone else saw. No, my voice had dropped half an octave into that tone that had her swimming inside. I felt that effect almost immediately.

When we finally got back to our room, I pulled her inside and immediately pushed her against the door. Running my hands up her sides, I realized she was still only in her bra and leggings. I chuckled as my arms caged her in, and I ran my lips along her neck.

"What's so funny, sir?"

"Just realized I hauled you halfway through the main buildings in only your bra and leggings."

I felt her breathing stop in surprise, but then her breath released with a whispered *fuck* as I sucked in the flesh where her shoulder and neck met.

Pulling back from her, I kissed her quickly before leading her to the bathroom and commanding, "Strip."

"What?"

"I swear, woman, if I have to repeat myself again today, the funishment you are going to get will be torturous." I eyed her in the mirror as I reached into the shower and turned it on. "You need to shower."

Jess looked at me up through her lashes as she peeled her leggings off. "What about my attitude adjustment?"

I yanked on the Claiming just as she released her leggings from her limbs, and she physically stumbled forward, where I caught her. "Only good girls get those. You've been a bit... temperamental today, Kotě." Then I bent down and whispered in her ear, "Now bend over the counter."

There was a hitch of breath before she turned. I unclasped her bra, and she let it fall to the ground. Her gaze met mine in the mirror, and when she paused, I lifted an eyebrow at her. "Why are you testing me so much today?"

Bent over the counter, she wiggled her ass toward me, and I growled low and deep. The sound echoed through the bathroom, and when she looked over her shoulder, she smiled. "It's been a while."

"Guess I need to fix that, but you, kitten... don't move."

She bit her tongue as I moved behind her, pressing myself against that beautiful ass of hers. Fuck, she was gorgeous. She hadn't taken the thong off, and I ran my hands over both her cheeks and pressed against her as I gripped her thighs. Her answering moan had my cock swelling against her.

I lifted my hand, brought it down hard on her right cheek then the left, reveling in the jolt and then melting of her body against me. I repeated it and then ran my hands over the slowly reddening skin.

Her gaze met mine, and I spread my fingers into a V. There was a short hesitation, but when my hand came down on her ass cheek again, she whimpered and followed the instruction. I tsked at her as my other hand landed on the other cheek.

"Damn, woman." I dropped to my knees before her and brought both hands down at the same time. "Now, you do not cum until I tell you to. Understood?"

"Yes, sir." Her answer was breathy, and I could tell by how she was trying to bring her legs back together that she wanted to have that friction between her legs.

Rubbing across the redness of her ass, kissing each cheek gently, I slipped my fingers through the center of her and purposefully avoided her clit. She whimpered again, and I chuckled. Slowly, I slid two fingers inside of her and brought my hand down on her left ass cheek again, just as I curled my fingers along her G-spot.

"Sir!" I felt her tighten around me and how hard she was trying to hold off the orgasm, but she hadn't earned that reward yet.

"Do. Not. Cum."

Her head dropped to her hands, and I felt her take long, hard, deep breaths, trying to control herself as I moved in and out of her. My hand lifted, and I landed on the reddest portion of her ass. Her whimper was music to my ears.

Removing my fingers for a moment, I couldn't resist running my tongue along her folds and tasting her. Her hips moved and stuck out farther, chasing the feeling of my tongue on her. When I reached her ass, my fingers returned to fucking her, but my tongue swirled around the puckered skin.

Her wetness coated my fingers, and I pulled out of her, spreading it along her swollen flesh. When my tongue snaked out again and flicked her clit, I pressed against the puckered skin, feeling her freeze and moan all at once.

My other hand raised and landed on her right cheek. "Do. Not. Fucking. Cum."

"Sir…" She whimpered, and I dove back into her, licking, sucking, and exploring every inch. She tasted like the sweetest thing in any dimension.

I slowed my ministrations, and when her breathing was not so ragged, I pulled away from her, bringing both of my hands down on her ass and running them down to her thick thighs, gripping them tight. "Fuck, I love these," I murmured against her skin.

Reluctantly, I pulled her thong off. The shower had long since turned the room to a sauna. As I stood, I kissed each one of her ass cheeks, now beautifully red. I ran my hand up her back, felt her bow against it, and wrapped my hand slowly and carefully around her neck, pulling her to stand back up against me.

I carefully ground against her, and I felt her pump along that Claiming. My head dipped to her neck and I gently bit it, growling.

Taking a deep breath, I muttered, "Let's get you in the shower." She turned to face me, and I let my hand trail around her neck so that I could thread my hands through her hair at the nape. I kissed her softly. "Shower. Now."

Before she got in, I double-checked to make sure it wasn't too hot and let her step in first. I grabbed the small cloth and lathered it up, going down her body, making sure to pay very special attention to certain areas I knew would drive her crazy.

When she reached down, wrapped her hand around me, and stroked, mimicking the movement against the Claiming, I couldn't hold back one second longer. I pushed her against the tiled wall and lifted her.

"Fuck," she whispered just before my mouth crashed onto hers and I lined myself up.

"You want this?"

"Yes."

"What exactly is it you want, Kotě?" I leaned my forehead against hers, trying not to tremble with the restraint to plunge into her.

"Sir, please fuck me." Her eyes were highly glazed over.

"I can't deny you." I slammed into her, and her head flew back against the tile, but she smiled and was taking long breaths. "Don't—"

"Don't cum. I know, but please. I'm not sure I can hold it off much longer, sir."

I nipped at her lip as I slowly pushed into her. Her moan rattled through me. Slowly, I dragged out of her before filling her in one quick stroke again. She was clenching around me, and I smiled. "Arms tight around my neck."

When she did, I kissed her hard. I didn't hesitate to give her what she wanted. I fucked her like a starved man, because damn if I wasn't one. She would always have me craving her, starving for her. I felt my balls tightening and that tingle at my spine. "Cum for me."

A few more strokes and she was screaming, milking my cock for everything I had. I couldn't hold back anymore, and with one final deep thrust, I succumbed to my release.

We stood there, the water spraying on my back, forehead to forehead, breathing heavily. She recovered before I did and tilted her head to kiss me softly. It was sweet and full of the love I knew she had for me, but that didn't stop her from saying, "I love you."

"I love you, too."

The feel of her chest pressing against mine was euphoric. I took a deep breath and slowly set her back down. I didn't let her go because she wasn't exactly steady on her feet. Slowly, I turned her around so she would be under the hot water, and she tilted her head back into the spray. Her long white hair fanned out under the water, and I couldn't help but run my fingers through it.

She hummed a content noise, and I reached for her shampoo. "Here, let me wash it." She moved back out from the water, and I went about caring for my girl. Once she was cleaned up, I quickly washed and stepped out of the shower.

After I had a towel wrapped around my waist, she stepped out, and I dried her off. Kissing her softly when I was done, I said, "Go to bed. I'll bring you dinner. It's been a shit day, and we can sort things out tomorrow."

She headed to the bedroom, and just as she was at the doorway, she turned and with too much emotion in her voice, that I felt through the bond, she said, "Thank you, Aiden."

"Always."

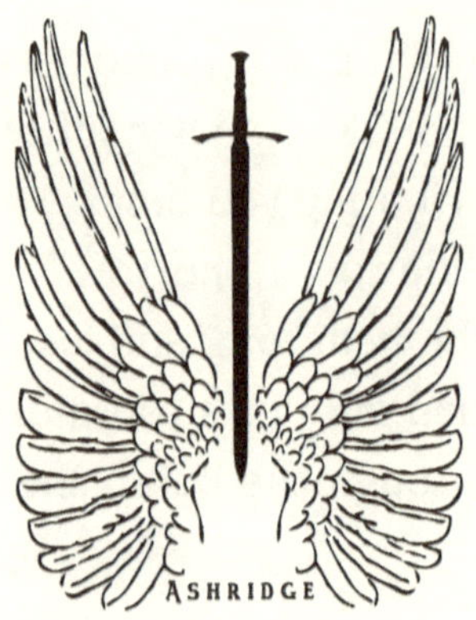

CHAPTER 41

JESSIKA

FOR FIVE DAYS, WE tracked the Kaletta army as it moved across the black sands. We had spent days strengthening the wards around the castle walls and moving the citizens who didn't want to fight into the protected areas of the city.

I was standing on the landing outside of the main hall when the sound of soldiers coming to a stop outside the walls flowed through the city. Aiden had said that when he was at the outer wall there appeared to be over twenty-thousand standing outside the gates.

"Aiden." He hummed an acknowledgement next to me. "Why are you not letting me just liquify the sands under their feet?" I couldn't keep the anger and fear for my kingdom out of my voice.

"Because you know they are just following orders from the asshole hiding within. You also want to have the pleasure of destroying him yourself."

I tipped my head to the side in agreement.

"And my council?" We had fought for hours this morning about whether I needed to leave the city, and I told them that while they may have no qualms about declaring war in my stead, I wasn't going to run from the face of it.

"In the chambers." He smirked at me. "Should you fall, they said, someone needs to run the kingdom."

"Pathetic."

"Doesn't matter. You won't fall. I swear it as your Vernadali and mate."

"And I swear, as your brother, I will not let the Grand Duchess of Ashridge fall," Lemi said, stepping beside Aiden.

Dakota stood just behind him, met my gaze, and smiled wickedly. "And fuck if I'm gonna let anyone take you down. I swore my being to Ashridge. More than that, you are family to me, Jess." My chest swelled with pride. "Besides, it's been awhile since I've gotten to throw hands with Kaletta."

Soldiers flowed down the streets of Ashridge City. My power itched to be let out.

"Jess," Aiden muttered, "You need to breathe or you are going to overheat. I can feel it through the bond. Don't burn yourself out."

I took a deep breath and tried to recenter myself. Slowly, I turned, leaned toward him, his forehead meeting mine, and said, "No matter what happens today, I love you, Aiden. You are my mate, my everything."

He shifted his head as if he were going to kiss me, but we both froze and pulled back, hearing a commotion outside. Then he was pulling me out of the main hall as a wave of blue-grey power shattered the doors. Before the dust settled, a streak of power burst through the room, incinerating the tapestries on the wall behind us. Whirling, I threw my power out but felt it catch in the air.

The Grand Lord of Kaletta had his hand up and fisted, with four other males mimicking his movements behind him. Releasing my power and seeing them all move in unison, I muttered, "Can't take me and my Vernadali on your own, so you need mimics?"

"Just trying to even the playing field." He looked at Aiden, Lemi, and Dakota before he shrugged. "They were volunteers."

"Well, you and your *volunteers* are not welcome in my home." I reached out and pulled them from the hall, tossing them over the edge of the landing and railing. Aiden was hauling me farther into the main hall, using his power to help seal the entrance behind the Grand Lord and his mimics.

"Reinforce the hall. Seal the entrance. No in or out," Aiden commanded, and the two Vernadali instantly went to work.

"Yes, Vernadali Aiden." Their voices were in such unison, I wondered just how much that had been drilled into them.

Vernadali Dadan and Vernadali Keith suddenly appeared from behind us to stand between us and the doorway, Lemi and Dakota forming that extra line between us and the approaching Grand Lord. There was a loud clang that rang through the hall, and the three of them chuckled. "Well, we know that the wards work to keep anyone else from coming in."

I took a deep breath as my anger flowed through me. My vision shifted to purple as Aiden sprinted forward and the Grand Lord moved toward me. One of his volunteers flew back into the barrier that was cast over the front entrance. Blood sprayed as his body was incinerated.

I splayed my hands out wide, attempting to hold the Grand Lord in place. I concentrated on his bones, but I couldn't get any further than that. Something was protecting him. Tilting my head, I concentrated on his blood, trying to heat him, and he let out a huff of smoke.

Aiden quickly dispatched the two men at the Grand Lord's back and turned to assist Lemi, Dakota, Vernadali Keith, and Vernadali Dadan at working through the throng of soldiers attempting to make their way into the main hall.

An evil smile pushed across the Grand Lord's face, his black hair faded away like sheer fabric in the wind at the tips, and there was a push against my power. He huffed out another breath of smoke as he flung my power back at me and hit me with a wave of his own, sending me soaring through the air, almost to the dais.

My back hit the ground and I lay there gasping for air. I felt footsteps come closer. "Pathetic."

I looked up at the Grand Lord and wheezed, "How?"

I needed to distract him long enough to get my air back and go on the offensive. My hands slid to my thighs, but my syths were gone. I didn't know where they landed, but as he leaned forward, I felt Aiden pull on the Claiming, and one landed in my hand.

I thrust upward, but he moved, and I caught his side. He pulled my syth with him as he stumbled back. I scrambled to my feet, seeing more and more Kaletta soldiers. Without taking my eyes off the Grand Lord, I threw my power at one of the guards that was sneaking up behind Aiden, and he froze for a moment before blood leaked from his ears and he fell to the ground.

I dispatched two more before the Grand Lord pulled my syth from his side. He threw a burst of power, and when I put up a shield between us, it pushed through like it wasn't there and hit my shoulder. Another one hit my hip, and then my stomach, causing me to bend over and groan.

Everything happened within moments, but it felt like hours. When my head lifted, Aiden's eyes met mine, as I saw the Grand Lord pull his power into a ball out of the corner of my eye.

I concentrated, trying to build what was left of my power into an impenetrable wall. Then, I said down the Claiming, "*I love you, Aiden.*"

His mouth moved, but as the Grand Lord's power hit my chest, I heard him scream down the Claiming, "*Kotě!*"

I flew back into the stairs to the dais and gasped at the shuddering of my heart. Searing hot pain was spreading across and through my chest. My vision faded, and the last thing I saw before everything went dark were hazel eyes ringed in bright purple.

CHAPTER 42

JAYDEN

As I stood there discussing rebuilding plans for Silentport with Janreka, we both jumped as a burst of black smoke formed a few feet from us. When we saw who was there, I shook my head. "Clarice, what are you doing here?"

"We have to get to Ashridge City. Now. It's Jess." Her eyes were full of so much fear and urgency that Janreka and I nodded.

Janreka stormed out of the room and I heard, "Janak!"

"Yes, Princess Janreka."

As Janreka gave Janak instructions for the running of Silentport, I watched Clarice pace back and forth. She only made three rounds when she said, "Reka, get your ass in here or Jayden and I are leaving without you."

Janreka jumped back into the room, grabbed her mom's hand, and we popped out of Silentport. As the world fell out beneath me, I saw Janreka's gaze meet mine. When the smoke cleared, I blinked, surprised that we landed in the middle of the Ashridge City main hall. Sounds of steel meeting steel, groans, and the smell of the tang of blood assaulted my senses.

Assessing just what we had stepped into, a flash of white caught my eye and horror filled me as my father gathered a black ball of power at his chest and threw it at Jessika. *How in the hell did he do that?*

Aiden moved like lightning and was at her side just as she fell to the ground. Clarice's arm swung out, dispatching the guards going after Aiden, and Janreka threw both hands out, sealing the room. No one was getting in or out.

Janreka ran toward the Grand Lord, but Clarice and I were heading for Jessika. As Janreka distracted the Grand Lord, we fell to our knees next to Jess. Her eyes faded closed, and Aiden let out a scream so horrifying it broke my own heart. Aiden pulled Jessika close, tears streaming down his face.

Clarice sat very, very still, but when I looked at her eyes, they had gone a little smoky in that way they did when she was talking to the dead. She shook her head and it cleared. "61."

Aiden's head popped up. "Auntie..."

I looked at Clarice. "Sixty-one seconds." She nodded, and I looked back at Aiden. "Has her heart stopped?"

Aiden's mouth opened and closed, but he shook his head. "Once it does. Start counting." His eyes flicked between the two of us.

"Once it does, Aiden. Count to sixty-one."

"No. She can't... I can't..." His power wrapped around her tight, then his focus went to her face and he was screaming. The sound was horrendous.

I felt the ball of emotion that worked its way up my throat. "Jess!"

I turned to see Lemi fighting his way to us, but I turned to Aiden, clapped my hand on his shoulder, fed my power through him, and said, "Count!"

His whole body shuddered a moment later as he said, "One."

Looking at Clarice, she nodded as her eyes glazed over with that smoky haze as she concentrated on what she needed to do.

"Two... Three..."

"Stay close, Jess. I'll bring you back at sixty-two," Clarice muttered. "Jayden, you have to stop him. The Grand Witch Bethezda fed him her power before she died..."

"Four..."

My father had turned and was facing off with Janreka as he gloated about how he was an unstoppable power.

"Five..." Aiden's voice was broken, and the tears were flowing as he held her close.

Clarice's voice was husky and thick as she said, "Janreka won't be able to stop him. He has to be permanently terminated."

A Kaletta guard was lying not far from where we were, and I saw his sword. Eyeing it, I looked back at Janreka. She was holding her side, blood leaking out, but still holding her own. Lemi was covered in blood, and his left arm was dangling. Dakota had taken position beside him, and they were working as a single unit. If the terror of what was occurring hadn't been a tangible thing, I could have admired the beauty of it.

"Eight..."

Standing and striding the few steps to the dead Kaletta guard, my footsteps echoed in the grand hall. The soft thud of my heel hitting the stone matched the aching beats of my heart. This was for Jess. For Ilris. For Aiden. For all of us. I picked up the dead soldier's sword, savoring the sound of the steel against the stone as it scraped along. Looking down at the blade, I didn't even care that it was already covered in blood. As my grip on the handle tightened, I pulled all my power into my muscles and fed it down the blade. Bits of blood shivered off the edges, and I forced myself to take a deep breath as I turned toward my father. It was going to take every ounce of strength and power I had to do what I needed to.

As I walked by Aiden and Clarice, I heard Aiden's broken, "Twenty." I stuttered a step, taking in Jessika's face, the burned whole in her top. Aiden's fingers fisted tight in her shirt as the tears continued to flow down his cheeks. His voice cracked again as he said, "Twenty-one."

When I was standing behind my father, Janreka's eyes lit up as they met mine, and I nodded. My father turned toward me, a small smile on his face.

"Oh look, it's the ultimate disappointment. And just where were you and that *guard* hiding." His eyes flicked to Clarice behind me, realization finally hitting. "Therth. You've been hiding with the Empress."

"Your rule of tyranny is over."

"Tyranny? I was trying to save Ashridge from the impurity that destroys what the Angels require of us." He continued to ramble on about the atrocities that were Ashridge's values as Janreka came to stand beside me and I heard Aiden croak, "Thirty."

How did we still have over half a minute to go? Come on Aiden, keep it together, and dammit, Clarice, you better bring her back.

My focus returned to the Grand Lord as he said, "When I learned of your and Ilris' affliction, I knew you would never produce a legitimate heir for Kaletta."

My heart stopped a beat as I stared at him, Janreka going impossibly still next to me. Anger and rage flowed through me as I hissed, "Say it."

Please, in the last moments of your pathetic existence, prove to me just what a piece of shit you are. Prove to me, once again, just how there is no saving you.

His eyes lit with satisfied amusement as he said, "She would have produced the purest of heirs for me."

Deadly calm settled within me as I felt Janreka's hand on my back.

This is for Killy. My hand tightened on the hilt of the sword.

For Jessika. My power flowed down the blade as my muscles tensed.

For every other Kaletta citizen you slaughtered just because of who they were. Then I raised my arm and pushed every ounce of what was left of myself into that swing as I cut my father's head off his shoulders.

His facial expression went from smug to confused to fear as the blade slid through muscle and sinew, only finding resistance for a moment at the spine before his eyes widened just slightly and the blade carried through.

The world tipped, slowed to the span of microseconds as I blinked, realizing that the sword shouldn't have slid that easy through his neck. Janreka's huff next to me as her hand released my back made me realize she had helped feed power through me into the blade.

A slow smile crossed my face as I stood there, panting as I watched the Grand Lord's head slowly slide off his shoulders and fall to the ground, blood spraying into the air and coating me and Janreka. Neither of us flinched as we watched what was left of the Grand Lord of Kaletta crumple to the ground.

Slowly, Kaletta soldiers registered that the Grand Lord had been dispatched, and my gaze slowly crossed the room as I saw them lay down their swords and kneel before the guards and Vernadali of Ashridge.

"Forty-four."

I heaved a heavy, deep breath, but then Janreka was there, holding my face in her hand, asking if I was okay.

My eyes met hers, and there was nothing I could say other than, "Will this minute ever end? "

We turned to where Jessika lay. Aiden stared at Clarice, counting.

Janreka whispered, "Come on, Jess, hold on."

"*Fifty*"

"Lay her down, Aid. I need to have access to her," she instructed, and he nodded.

"Fifty-eight... fifty-nine..."

"Jess—" Clarice said and placed her hands on either side of her head.

"Sixty-one... Sixty-two."

Clarice's hands went black as night as her forehead dipped down to Jessika's and she muttered incomprehensible words over and over again.

"Auntie, please." The heart-shattering agony in Aiden's voice was more than I could stand. Janreka took my hand, and we knelt next to Jessika's feet. Janreka reached out and put a hand on Aiden's shoulder.

"Kotě... please."

Moments later, Dakota and Lemi were next to us, the guard and Vernadali alike creating a barrier between us to give us privacy. Vaguely, I heard the murmurs of those in the hall praying to the Angels.

Jessika and Clarice were covered in a film of black haze as Clarice was still muttering that language. A heavy, rich power filled the air and I blinked. Turning to Janreka, I saw her eyes widen, and then she loosed a breath, her shoulders relaxing just slightly. That power swirled around us, and I realized that I had only felt it in one other place: the Gate to the Underworld.

I grabbed Janreka's hand. She squeezed it and smiled at Jessika. "That's it, Jess. Come on."

Focusing back on Jessika, the haze shifted and threads of purple started to flow through it as her body began to twitch.

CHAPTER 43

AIDEN

I WAS LOSING A grip on any speck of reality every moment she was gone. I was becoming nothing. Where the meaning for life once sat within me, there was nothingness. Where a will to survive once sat firmly next to the mating bond... it was all gone. A massive dark hole was swirling around in my chest, gobbling up anything that had previously had any meaning in my life.

The only thing I could concentrate on was keeping my eyes on Auntie Clarice and counting. There was something in the recesses of my memories that knew why this was important, but I couldn't find it.

That Vernadali bond was fading out, but I couldn't accept she was really gone. From the corner of my eye, I watched her name fade from my scroll the longer she was out. The disbelief was second to the shredding in my veins as our mating was pulled more and more taut, only to become tattered ribbons at the end.

"Aid..." Auntie Clarice said, but I heard her more in my head, than I saw her lips move. "Lay her down, Aiden. I need to have access to her."

I nodded. "Fifty-eight..." I laid her down, and it took everything in me to do it. "Fifty-nine..."

"Jess—" Auntie Clarice commanded and placed her hands on either side of her head.

"Sixty-one... Sixty-two." I ground out, my throat closing up.

Clarice's hands went black as night as her forehead dipped down to Jess' and she muttered incomprehensible words over and over again.

"Auntie, please," I begged. I had never begged Auntie Clarice for anything. "Kotě... please," I whispered.

In the distance of my mind, I recognized that there were guards and others circling us, protecting us from whatever else might come. Vaguely, I recognized that Jayden, Lemi, and Dakota had joined us.

"Come on, Kotě. Come back to me." I felt like I was screaming against the shredded remnants that was the Claiming, screaming as the wisps of the edges that barely clung to the stillness that was my soul.

Focusing back on Jessika, the haze shifted and threads of purple flowed through it as her body twitched.

Every nerve ending within me heated. Those wispy edges of the Claiming were glowing bright purple. My arm burned where her name scroll had been only a minute ago. "Kotě."

The world was purple. Everything was purple. Then there was a bright purple starburst just above auntie and I fixated on it. Where there had been grief and loss shredding everything within me, it was now burning with the warmth and surety of life. That starburst came and hovered before me, and I swore I felt her hand on my cheek. I closed my eyes at the feel of it but heard the sound of five voices in my head at once. *"Be well, Aiden Mathewson. Live with your mate."*

My eyes popped open, and the starburst dropped into Jess. I threw my head back as my body burst into white-hot starlight and went taut. I shrieked at the intense heat. Every fiber was as if someone had put a red-hot poker to it, the Claiming branding deeper into my soul before my entire body jerked as it snapped back into place between Jess and me. My arm burned like the fiery pits of the Underworld, and when the flames simmered to a constant set of embers, I bent over, resting my head on Jess' stomach, gasping for breath.

It moved slightly underneath me, and my head popped up. "Kotě?"

Jess' chest moved with her breathing, and Auntie Clarice sat back, smiling. Her dark skin was ashen, but there was a relieved sense of satisfaction on her face.

I pulled Jess into my arms and cradled her, tears once again flowing down my cheeks. She was still limp against me, but I felt her heartbeat. I felt the Claiming burn, and her name was once again in that scroll on my arm. She was alive.

I looked at Auntie Clarice and croaked, "Thank you."

Her cheeks were streaked with tears, but she smiled and nodded. I looked at Reka, Jayden, Lemi, and Dakota. Their faces mirrored hers, blood and tears streaming down their cheeks. Looking around the room, I saw guards with their back to us, creating a barrier. Only, between the legs of a few of them, I saw the Grand Lord of Kaletta's body crumpled on the ground with his head at his feet.

"Oh shit, who?"

"That would be me." Jayden smiled. "But we can talk about that after we get Jessika fully back."

Auntie Clarice's voice was hoarse and tired, but she said, "The Angel of Death didn't want to let her go. Said something about he allowed the Mathewsons to return once. I'll have to talk to your mother about that one. Jess, though, wanted to return. Said she wasn't technically a Mathewson and that you were becoming a Valenti. She's a fighter, Aiden, and she's yours. Give her time; she'll come back around."

"Damn straight, she's mine." The knot in my throat was painful to speak around, and as I focused on her breathing in my arms, I smiled. "She's everything."

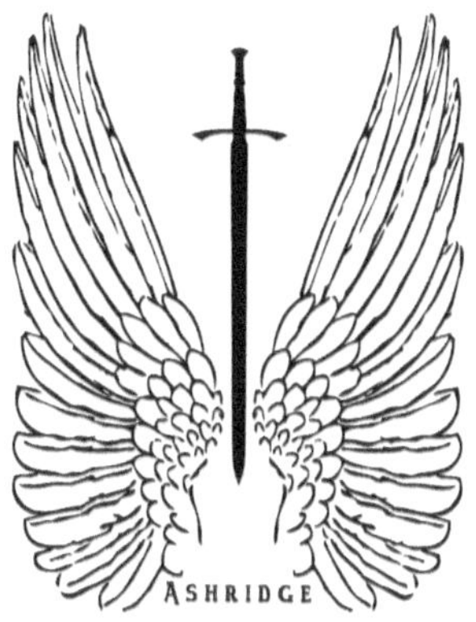

CHAPTER 44

JESSIKA

I WAS CONSCIOUS, BUT without being attached to my body. I felt the smoothness of the sheets and the soft curve of the mattress under me as Aiden laid me in our bed. He curled up behind me and held me, his fingers threaded with mine for hours. Holding me as close as he could manage, his breathing finally evened out and I let the darkness pull me under.

I heard him get up, get in the shower, and then get dressed. Felt his kiss on my lips, his whispers of love and dedication, his kiss on my forehead, a loving stroke along the Claiming, and a promise to return as soon as the meeting was done.

I heard Janreka telling me story after story of Jayden and Ilris' time in Therth. She told me that the twins would be here soon, and that she really liked Clarissa. Said she was a great match for Owen, and if I wanted to meet my new sister-in-law, then I needed to stop being a lazy ass and get up. I mentally laughed at that.

I heard Jayden come in with Ilris and thank me for everything I had done and remind me I had done more than my share. So, it was now time for me to get up and start enjoying my life with Aiden as Duke of Ashridge.

I heard Lemi and Dakota come in. Lemi read one of our favorite childhood books. Then Dakota got all mushy and told me how honored he was to serve under the Grand Duchess Jessika Valenti. Lemi, of course, told him he was a fucking sap, and I mentally laughed at their continual banter.

I heard Aiden come back, get something to eat, and talk to Jayden and Ilris before coming back into the bedroom. He told me about how his parents had freaked out about Clarissa and that they would be here within a couple of days. He then had the guts to lecture me on the finer points of not being a proper Grand Duchess to greet Lady Megan and Vernadali CJ if I didn't wake. Aiden laughed as he explained how he laid into the council and threatened them all with being replaced should they ever do something like that again. Then he told me how they had taken to calling him Vernadali Duke Aiden. I could hear the eye roll in his voice, and I wanted to smile.

Before long, he was snuggled up next to me again. I lay there listening and feeling him breathing. I felt myself reconnecting more and more with my body, and when he rolled over in his sleep and started whispering against my skin, I smiled... feeling my lips actually move.

I caressed down the Claiming, and Aiden jumped away. "Jess..."

I concentrated as hard as I could on opening my eyes and was met with the wide hazel eyes of my mate. I blinked, and Aiden's eyes filled with tears. "Oh, my Angels. You came back to me. Thank you." He kissed me hard and fast.

I pulled on my consciousness and pushed it fully back into my body. When I did, I felt us both twitch in conjunction with it. Lifting my hand to run my fingers through the hair on his face, which was longer than usual, I smiled at him. "Did you think I wouldn't?"

"Auntie Clarice... She... She said that you wanted to come back, that you two had to fight with the Angel of Death over it."

I blinked. "I don't remember that. I remember a lot of bright warmth. I remember your pain, your screaming. I felt it.... I hated it. I wanted to come back to make it all go away. I wanted to be with you. Then I saw your face, it smiled at me, and then I was falling back into my body."

"Jess..." His voice broke, and the pain in it hurt. I caressed down the Claiming again, and he let out a relieved sigh. "Never die on me again. I won't survive that kind of pain ever again."

"It wasn't necessarily the most enjoyable thing on my side, either." I curled my fingers through his beard again and felt him growl through the Claiming. I sighed. "The Claiming is still there. What about the Vernadali bond?"

He leaned down and kissed me softly. "Both were restored when you fell back into your body." Then he pulled back and showed me my name on the scroll on his forearm. "Watching your name fade from there shattered me. But feeling that Claiming shred apart as you... died..."

I blinked and felt the tears in my own eyes as his fell heavily down his cheeks. "Please. I can't go through that again. I swear that should your heart stop again, I will follow you. I can't live this life without you. The only thing that kept me going in those sixty-two seconds was Auntie Clarice reminding me to count. To wait until she could push you back to me."

"As I said, it's not in the plan. I hope to have a long, happy life with you." He pulled me into his lap as I sat up. I changed how I was sitting so that I was straddling him and sitting on his thighs. Wrapping my arms around his neck, I leaned forward, resting my forehead to his. He held me close. My muscles were weak, but I needed to be against him. "You are mine, Aiden Chatwell Mathewson. You are my Vernadali. You are my Duke. Most of all, you are my mate, and I won't live another moment without you."

Then he was kissing the fuck out of me.

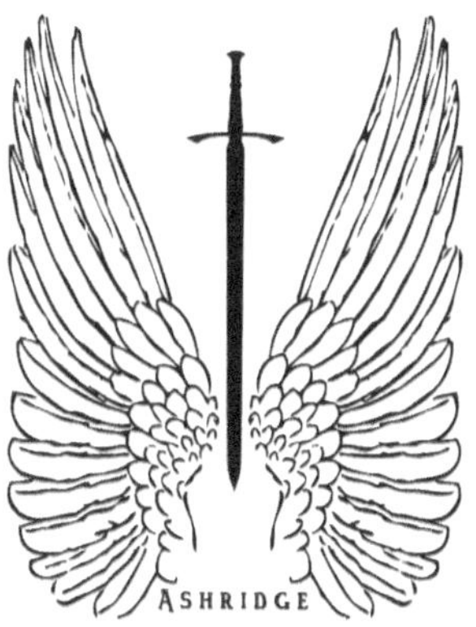

CHAPTER 45

JESSIKA

THE NEXT MORNING, AIDEN was cleaning up breakfast when a messenger was at the door and said that visitors had just arrived at the gate and would be in the main hall in a few minutes.

"Who is it?" Aiden asked.

"I was only told that they were special guests and that they are not a security threat to the Grand Duchess," the kid said as I walked up.

"And how do we know they are of no security threat?" I asked as Aiden's forearm muscle tensed under my palm.

"I was reassured by Princess Janreka, sir. She is the one who has asked that I advise you that guests are arriving."

His eyes were a little wide as his gaze flicked between the two of us.

"Thank you. Please let Princess Janreka know we will be there momentarily."

There was a quick nod as he ran down the hall.

Closing the door, Aiden turned and wrapped his arms around my waist, pressing his front to my back. He pressed his lips to my temple for a long moment before taking a deep breath and whispering in my ear, "Is it wrong that I was hoping we could just spend all day in here? You've not been conscious for a full day yet."

"Janreka...," I trailed off because he was kissing down my neck and then slowly licking that area where my neck and shoulder met, sucking the skin into his mouth. I moaned at the feel of his tongue as it circled the flesh.

"See that sound right there?" I hummed a response. "That sound is the one I want to hear coming from you all damn day. I want to spend the whole day pulling it from you in every way I know how."

"Sir..."

"Yes, my kotě?" He ran his tongue up my neck, sucking my earlobe into his mouth and flicking it with his tongue.

That wasn't what made me weak, though. It was how one of his hands had snaked around between us and was now cupping me. He gripped me, and my clit was already so sensitive that I couldn't help the whimper that came from me. "Fuck."

Aiden released me, and then I was pulled against him. His hands ran up the side of my body, and then he was cupping my face. His lips were a hair's breadth from mine as he whispered, "Later, I'm going to spend a long, long time making it up to you."

"Yes, sir." I breathed before his lips crashed onto mine in a demanding, passionate kiss that alone would have made me weak in the knees. It wasn't until my lungs were burning for air that he pulled back. His forehead rested on mine as he tried to catch his breath.

"Reka." His words were more of a reminder than anything else. "I love her, but her fucking timing."

Smiling, I said, "Let's get dressed."

Aiden's hands slid down my sides, and he laced his fingers through mine then squeezed before he let them go and scooped me up. "I'm perfectly capable of walking."

"You died on me. If you think I'm not going to baby you for a long while, think again."

He used his power to open the door to the bedroom and then sat me down on the edge of the bed. Aiden headed for the closet, and when I stood, his head whipped around, his eyes flicking to the bed. I sat back down and opened my mouth to complain, but there was a demanding pull on the Claiming, and I huffed, rolling my eyes.

He brought out a pair of black leggings, underwear, bra, my favorite black knee-high boots, silver top, and my black faux corset. Slowly and methodically, he undressed me, pulling my nightshirt over my head and kissing my shoulders, collarbone, and neck.

Kneeling before me, he slid on my underwear and kissed all the way up as he did, nibbling at my hip when I lifted slightly to allow them over my ass.

"Stand up." His voice was softly commanding, and my breath hitched at the sound of it. "Arms out."

Standing, he slid the straps of my bra over my arms, hooked the fabric under my boobs, and then circled around me to clasp it in place. As he straightened the fabric around my breasts, he paid special attention to my nipples, and I couldn't help but lean back into him. He chuckled as he kissed my shoulder and fixed the straps.

"You are so *not* playing fair, sir."

"Who said I would ever play fair?" He came to kneel before me, motioning for me to lift my leg so that he could slip my leggings on one leg, then the other. His hands were gentle as he pulled them up my legs. When they slipped over the curve of my ass, he released the elastic with a snap. An unintended moan crept up my throat.

Fuck. How has he made dressing me such a fucking turn on?

He gathered my shirt, slipping it over my head but capturing my lips in a soft, lingering kiss. He broke it with a deep inhale through his nose. When his eyes opened, there was nothing but heat and lust in them, and I bit my lip. His gaze caught on where my teeth pinched the flesh, and then he let the breath out slowly.

I let a smirk cross my face. "Is my Dom going to allow me to put my own boots on, or is he going to take over completely?"

He let out a small chuckle as he took a step back, dropped to one knee, reached out, and grabbed the boots. He put each on, slowly zipping them up the inside of my leg and then squeezing my inner thigh. "You will be lucky if I allow you to go to the bathroom alone for a while, Kotě."

"I'm fine. I'm capa—"

His focus snapped to mine, and I pinched my lips together. Standing, he pinched my chin between his knuckle and thumb. "Jess, you died. I had to sit there and fight every ounce of my being, both as your mate and your Vernadali, not to cast everything I know to bring you back." His voice hitched, and I saw the tears well in his eyes. "I had to sit there... *counting the seconds...* while I felt the Claiming shred away and become a tattered mess. I had to sit there and feel the agonizing burning of the Vernadali bond turn to embers. I had to sit there and watch your name vanish from my arm."

My eyes flicked to his forearm that I could just barely see from where he held me still. I reached up and gripped his forearm and ran my thumb over it. My name sat there bright as ever, but when his fingers tightened on my chin, I looked back up at him, a tear sliding down his cheek, and I swallowed.

"Jess, I had to sit there and trust that Auntie Clarice could convince the Angel of Death to release your soul and let you come back to me. I had to sit there and let you be dead for *sixty-two seconds* before she started bringing you back." His breathing hitched as if he were trying to swallow a sob. "So, as your Vernadali, I will trust you can wipe your ass without getting hurt, but... as your mate, you will be lucky if I ever let you go to the bathroom alone."

"I'm sorry." I was. "Jayden or I dying was an option, but it was going to be the last possible fully-planned-out one.

Nothing that happened in the main hall went the way it should have. None of us should have gotten hurt in a perfect scenario."

"That doesn't matter. Planned or not, the fact is, I almost lost you. Forever."

"I'm here, Aiden."

"I know, but please have patience with me. As your mate and Vernadali, I am going to be more overprotective. The dynamic is what it is, but considering recent events, you are just going to have to understand that."

I nodded, and he kissed me quickly before he scooped me back up and carried me out of the bedroom, down the hall, and to the door. I kicked, and he gripped tight.

"Seriously, Aiden, please, let me walk."

He sighed. "Fine, but you are always within arm's reach. Understood?"

"Okay." I had to give him that much. There was no way, as Grand Duchess, I was going to be carried out to the main hall.

CHAPTER 46

AIDEN

We were just about at the end of the hall where the double doors were when a streak of electricity bolted past the door and hit the wall. A moment later, there was a quick yip, and I looked at Jess.

"Looks like the family arrived." She was trying not to burst out laughing, but the chuckles sputtered out anyway.

"Sounds like the twins arrived and Mom is giving Owen a run for it about Clarissa."

Walking into the main hall, Jess bellowed, "Owen, you deserve it. You should have told your mother before she found out." Then she turned to my mom, finger pointed at her, saying, "And you, *Mom*, stop marking up my main hall. We have enough to clean up and repair in here without adding another magical explosion to the mix. That is your son. Be happy for him."

Everyone in that room froze. Mom raised an eyebrow at her, and when I looked around the room, Owen was standing in front of Clarissa, LJ's eyes were bugging out of her head, Auntie Clarice, Janreka, Jayden, and Ilris were smiling and trying not to laugh, while Mom and Dad were looking between each other and Jess.

"Did you just call me Mom?"

"Oh, don't think too hard on it." Jess rolled her eyes dramatically then asked, "Where is Lemi?"

"He's telling the council where to shove their demands." Dad's smile was spectacular. When Jess gave him a look, he said, "They seem to think they still have the right to dictate what happens here. To say Aiden and Lemi are telling them exactly where to shove things..."

"Mom, Dad, when did you get here?" I asked, pulling Jess closer to me and gripping her other side at the waist tight.

"The council meeting went long. CJ had to have a meeting with some assholes who think they are something more important than they are. We came in late last night. Then we got up and heard that the twins were arriving. It was time to have a discussion with my eldest son about his new woman."

"Wife. Mom, she is my wife." Owen sighed, tipping his head back to the ceiling.

"And mother to your grandchild," Clarissa said carefully.

Everyone. Every single one of us, including Owen, looked at her. "What?"

Clarissa looked up at Owen, put one hand on his chest, and took hold of his hand with the other, placing it on her belly. I saw his power flow over his hand, and he blinked.

"You're pregnant." She nodded, and then he was kissing her. He pulled back, his brows furrowed, and then his eyes went wide as he pushed more of his power into her and said, "Oh, Angels."

"What? Is there something wrong with the baby? I'm only a few weeks. I only found out yesterday morning in Shuset. I wasn't feeling well, and LJ suggested I go down to see the physician and he... told me."

Owen turned to LJ who just shrugged. Clarissa made Owen look back at her. "What's wrong?"

"I could be wrong, and I want to have a physician truly verify, but I feel two separate forces."

"Twins?" various people said around the room, and when I looked at Jess, she was smiling brightly.

I wasn't able to process what that could mean. Twins of an Angel Blessed elemental twin? I looked to Clarice, whose head was cocked to the side, and her eyes went wide.

"Clarice?" Jess whispered, grabbing my hand and squeezing.

"There are indeed two beings in there."

Mom's head whipped around. "How do you know? You didn't know when I was pregnant with the twins. Didn't feel them until we were almost back to Nalrin from Morana."

"I was months into being a Gatekeeper and still getting a grasp on my new powers. I've had a few years to grow into them, *Megan*." Auntie Clarice rolled her eyes and smiled.

Dad laughed, but then she turned back to Owen and Clarissa. "Congratulations, Owy and Rissa."

"Rissa?" Clarissa asked, but there was a hint of a smile on her face as Owen pulled her closer to his side.

"It's what they do. They give you nicknames or shorten your name."

"Well, thank you." Her cheeks reddened.

"Well, Underworld. What am I doing here, then?" Jayden scoffed playfully.

"Don't you even start, mister," Janreka said, whirling on him. "I tried to give you all kinds of nicknames over the years, and you have repeatedly told me to just call you Jayden. Jess and I tried to use Jade, but you said that was only allowed by Ilris, and we have fucking respected that."

Ilris chuckled next to Jayden and pulled him close, whispering something in his ear the rest of us didn't hear, making Jayden's cheeks flush brightly, and he just nodded his head quickly.

Janreka's gaze met mine and the wickedness in it had me chuckling.

Dad cleared his throat, and when I met his gaze, he smiled. "So, the Grand Lord is dead."

"He is. Jayden relieved him of his head and all coherent thought." Reka chuckled.

Dad looked over at Auntie Clarice, who nodded. "He's burning quite painfully for the shit he pulled in Kaletta."

"Well then, it is my pleasure to do this. I received an enchanted memo from the Curtails of the North yesterday before we left."

Jess smiled as she looked at Dad, and they seemed to have a whole silent conversation. Jess' voice trembled slightly, almost apprehensively, even though she tried to pull on her well-known sass. "Oh, is that so? And are there any official seals? Any official declarations?"

Dad shrugged. "It looked very similar to the one that I received from Empress Clarice as well."

Auntie Clarice chuckled next to him as my mind started spinning. I blinked and looked around the room. LJ, Owen, and Clarissa were just as confused as I was, but when I saw that auntie, Mom, and Jess were all looking at each other with amused smiles on their faces, I remembered what Jess had told me. "No... We haven't petitioned yet."

Then my father stood up straight, smiled at me, turned to Jess, and became that ever-powerful Vernadali. "Grand Duchess Jessika Petra Valenti."

My gaze was bouncing between Dad and Jess, and when Jess smirked, I blinked, realizing this was really happening. "Yes, Vernadali CJ?"

"I have messages and official declarations announcing your hand in marriage is free and clear from Head Julian of the Nalsar dimension."

"Thank you." She reached over and took my hand, holding it tight. I could feel the nerves in the small trembles of her grip, and I squeezed, pushing some of that calm through her.

"Vernadali Aiden Chatwell Mathewson, Rank A2, Vernadali to the Grand Duchess of Ashridge, Jessika Petra Valenti." Dad then turned to me.

"Yes, Vernadali CJ?" I tried to stand up straighter, but I was so floored that it was a struggle.

"I hereby bring forth the necessary declarations, orders, and clearances for you to marry your Charge. Signatures from Head Julian, Vernadali Samuel, and Empress Clarice are all contained and were verified by the dimensional heads last night." Dad smirked at me, but then a wide smile crossed his face and the official façade dropped. "That is, if she will have your sorry carcass."

He handed me the scroll, and my hands trembled slightly as I took it. Using my power to unbind it, I read the declaration.

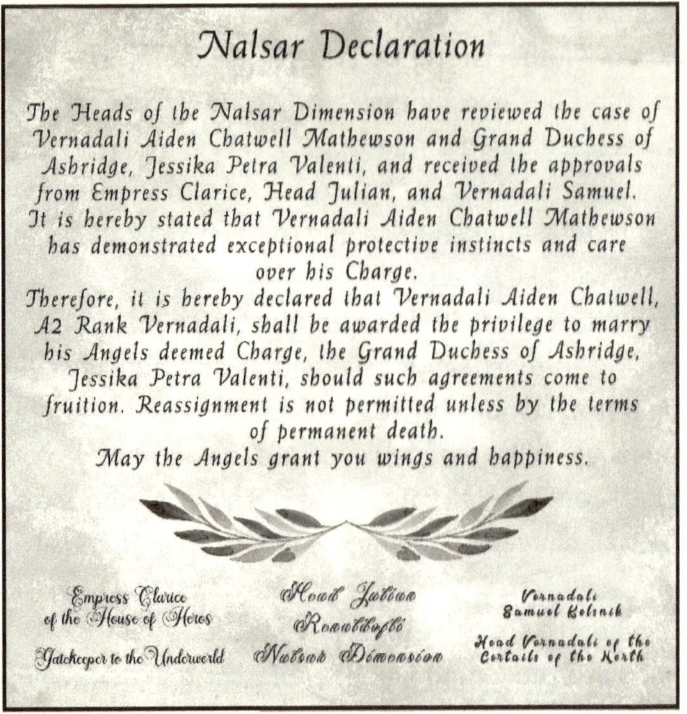

Nalsar Declaration

The Heads of the Nalsar Dimension have reviewed the case of Vernadali Aiden Chatwell Mathewson and Grand Duchess of Ashridge, Jessika Petra Valenti, and received the approvals from Empress Clarice, Head Julian, and Vernadali Samuel.
It is hereby stated that Vernadali Aiden Chatwell Mathewson has demonstrated exceptional protective instincts and care over his Charge.
Therefore, it is hereby declared that Vernadali Aiden Chatwell, A2 Rank Vernadali, shall be awarded the privilege to marry his Angels deemed Charge, the Grand Duchess of Ashridge, Jessika Petra Valenti, should such agreements come to fruition. Reassignment is not permitted unless by the terms of permanent death.
May the Angels grant you wings and happiness.

I read over it twice, Jess reading over my arm.

"Angels, it's real." Her shaking fingers trailed over the lettering. I dropped it, wrapped my arms around Jess, and swung her around in a circle before setting her down and kissing her hard. When I pulled back, her eyes were wide, but I commanded, "Don't you move. Dad, don't let her move an inch from this spot."

I ran for our residence and used my power to open every door between me and the bag that I had tucked away under my side of the bed. Reaching in, I grabbed the little black box and bolted back for where everyone was standing in the main hall.

"Aiden, what is going on?" Jess said, but then I was practically skidding to a stop before her. I kissed her hard again and dropped to one knee before her.

"Kotě, I know regardless of what you say, I am bound to you for life. You are my Angels deemed Charge, but most of all, you are my mate. I've said this a million times, but I have loved you and known I would die to protect you since the first day our eyes met. My heart has only ever belonged to you. Marry me."

"I can't believe I have to even answer this, but yes. I will happily marry you." My heart leapt for joy, and I thought it might burst as the room became slightly too blurry. She smirked at me and reached a hand down to run through the too long scruff of my beard. The amusement through the tears that had gathered in her eyes had me on a slight edge, though. "As you said, since you are already my Vernadali and my mate, I guess I can make you my husband and Duke, too."

"Whatever you want, Grand Duchess, I am here to serve you." I stood, taking the ring from the box and sliding it on her finger. I wasn't even sure that she had looked at it. When I saw it two months ago in one of the shops here in Ashridge, I bought it without a second thought. I knew it belonged on Jess' finger. The marquise black quartz looked like it had the night sky in it but was flanked on either side by two oval diamonds with an Ashridge peppered diamond between them. The accompanying second band was a row of clear round diamonds, alternating with oval Ashridge peppered diamonds that cradled the larger point of the marquise quartz. I would have held onto it for a hundred years, but to be able to give it to her now... Angels.

Her arms pulled me against her, and then she was kissing me, pushing her tongue to dance with mine, and I was lost in her touch. There was that pulling squeeze motion along the Claiming, and I pulled back, gasping. "Fuck, Kotě. Just wait until we are back in our room."

"Yes, sir." Then, with a smirk, she did it again, and I groaned.

"Eww," echoed beside us as LJ and Owen were shaking their heads.

It was Jess that turned to face them and stuck her tongue out. "It isn't like you have to watch."

"Grand Duchess—"

"I swear, Rissa, if you call me Grand Duchess one more time when it's just family, I will... Okay, so you get a pass for a few months while you are growing those nieces and nephews of mine, but..."

"Okay, okay." Rissa chuckled, putting her hands up in defeat. "Jess." She sighed. "Do you have any idea how weird that is going to be?"

Jess laughed as I wrapped my arms around her waist and stood behind her. "Not any stranger than when Mom and Dad, and not to mention Clarice, demand that you stop using titles."

Her eyes went wide. It was Reka who joined in, saying, "Oh yeah, Mom will have a total fit if you call her Empress Clarice. You can start with Clarice, like Jess has, but better get used to Auntie real quick like."

"The one I think that will be the hardest, though, will be Popa." LJ snickered when Rissa groaned.

"Right, Head Julian is also part of this family."

"Popa," everyone said in unison.

"Angels," she muttered, and Owen pulled her closer.

"So, it looks like there are two weddings that need to be planned."

"Two?" I looked at Mom. "The council will practically put ours together."

"Not completely, if I have any say about it," Jess muttered next to me, wrapping her arm tight around my waist.

Mom's gaze swung over to Owen and Rissa. "Well, since these two got married without the family..."

"Mom, we are already married, though." Owen groaned.

"Yes, but again, your family wasn't there."

"Owen, we warned you Mom would respond this way," I muttered. Glancing at Mom quickly, I kept an eye on where her electricity may shoot because I really didn't want to be zapped in the ass again.

"We got married in a paper signing so we didn't have to do the whole thing. I wanted it to be about Clarissa and me. We get married here, and it's going to be all about the Angel Blessed elemental twin Owen Mathewson and his parents. I don't want that for Clarissa."

"It doesn't have to be that way, Owy. Your family just wants to celebrate you being happy and finding Rissa. You've been unhappy for years, and we want to enjoy that with you."

His face was hard and stubborn until Rissa looked up at him. He turned to look at her, and his whole demeanor changed. Yeah, he would do anything for that girl. He was putty in her hands, and if she knew the power she wielded over him, may the dimension have mercy. "Owy, if there was a way to have just your family there, I would love to have a little ceremony. I know it wasn't feasible on the road and all, but I would like it. It's sort of been a dream of mine."

Owen's hands moved up her sides and cupped her face. "But was it your dream? Do you want this for you and us or because *Lady Megan* is asking?"

"I used to dream about having a little ceremony in a room filled with a bunch of people I didn't know. I felt raw power in that room, looking at those people." Her eyes closed, and she smiled, "I also remember the love and admiration. How I felt in the no-faced man's arms. I had no idea who he was, but..." Her eyes opened, and that smile widened and brightened. "I would like a ceremony for us, if you want one, but I won't make you do something because you feel obligated or want to do it just to make me happy at the expense of your happiness."

"Clarissa Mathewson." He kissed her quickly on the lips and muttered, just loud enough for the rest of us to hear, "I will do anything to keep that smile on your face."

Well, fuck. That boy was smooth.

"So, we can have a small wedding?" she asked, and he nodded, turning to our parents.

"Only if it is limited to the family. I don't know if Uncle Mickel, Aunt Kait, Uncle Logan, and Aunt Amber can make it, but if we can do it in the next couple of days with just the family and Popa officiates, okay."

Mom nodded, and when her eyes flicked to Auntie Clarice, they were filled with mischief. "I'll be back in a few hours." Then she was gone with only the wisps of black smoke in her wake.

"Where did Mom just poof off to?"

I tipped my head back and chuckled as LJ said, "To get the clan."

"Angels and Underworld being." Reka huffed.

Owen leaned his forehead on Rissa's and said, "What have we just agreed to?"

"Well, it looks like I need to take my new sister-in-law to the bridal store." Jess smiled at Rissa.

Oh, the fuck she was. "First, I need some alone time with you. You two can meet up after lunch."

Then I scooped Jess up into my arms and turned my back on my family to head to the bedroom. I was going to make sure my mate knew just how fucking happy I was about being her fiance.

"You have an hour, or Rissa and I are busting into the room!" Reka screamed behind us.

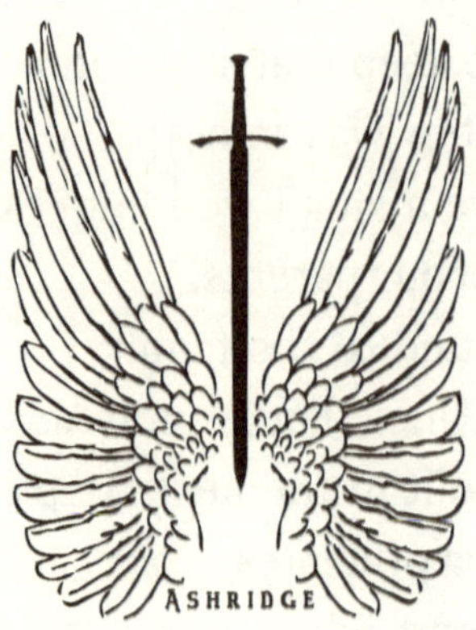

CHAPTER 47

JESSIKA

I HEARD JANREKA GIVE us the hour, which meant we had to be quick, and I couldn't do anything but chuckle. When Aiden got us to our room and threw me on the bed, he dipped his head, and I felt the growl that flowed down the Claiming.

Smirking, I jerked it the way I knew would have him instantly hard. I saw him falter a step as he moved toward me, and the corner of his mouth lifted. "Oh, you are so in for it."

I didn't how he did it, but after he had my boots off, my clothes were a tattered, shredded pile of cloth on the floor just moments later.

I reached up to take his shirt off, but he grabbed my wrist, and he kissed my palm, locking his eyes on me. "No. This is me showing you how much I love you and what you mean to me."

The glint in his eyes was enough that I swallowed at the same time I felt his other hand running along the inside of my thigh. He released my hand and spread his fingers into a V. Instantly, I spread my legs, then he was bent down, kissing down the inside of my thighs. When he reached the center of me, he carefully spread me wide and flicked his tongue over my clit.

"Fuck." I moaned, tilting my head back.

Aiden explored every inch of my exposed flesh, branding me with his tongue, his name permanently seared into me. When two of his fingers pushed inside of me, he latched onto my clit, sucking and nibbling on it. His fingers curled against my front wall and hit that spot, making my back arch.

Lifting his head, he flicked my clit again and repeated the motion over and over. I felt my stomach tightening, but he stopped.

"On your knees. Legs wide."

My eyes popped open. "What?"

He lifted an eyebrow, sitting back. "Do I have to repeat myself?"

Blinking at him a few times, I couldn't put what he said into action. "I mean, yes..."

"On your knees. Legs wide." He tapped one finger on his cheek, and I swallowed.

I did as he commanded but asked, "Why?"

"Don't you trust me?" he said, rolling onto his back and sliding beneath me.

"Sir?" My breath caught.

"Kotě, you are going to sit and ride my face until you can't hold yourself up. Is that understood?"

"Sir?" So rarely did he allow this kind of power shift.

"Is. That. Understood?" He tapped two on his cheek.

"Yes, sir. Until I can't hold myself up."

Nodding, he pulled me to him and went back to work. I tried to hold still, but I couldn't help the way my hips rode him. He lapped up every inch of me as I slid back and forth. The feel of his scruff brought a new sensation at this angle that I rarely got lying down.

My hands slowly trailed up the side of my body until they gripped my breasts. Aiden growled along the Claiming, and I mentally pumped him. There was a sharp nip at my clit in response, but I moaned loudly as heat flashed through my body. One of his hands lifted, and he smacked my ass as another wave of unadulterated pleasure flooded through me.

I bit my lower lip and continued that pumping motion while concentrating on the feel of him under me. His tongue snaked deep within me, but when he pushed me up so he could breathe, he ordered, "Bounce." His tongue was back at my entrance as I followed his orders.

"Sir," I breathed as I felt myself reaching that edge again. He smacked my ass over and over. When he felt me close, he wrapped his arms around my hips and pulled me down, latching onto my clit. Refusing to relent, I continued the motion along the Claiming, feeling his pleasured growl flow back across it. I ground against him, and I felt him half freeze for a moment, then there was a smack through the air again that sent me over the edge into my orgasm.

I fell forward and noticed a wet spot in his pants where my face fell. Chuckling, he kissed my inner thigh. "Roll over, Kotě."

I did, and I looked up at him with a sated smirk.

"That was three, and you will get that funishment later, only because I have no doubt that Reka will come barging in here in—" He looked at the clock and sighed. "—eight minutes to take you guys to the bridal shop."

"What did I do that caused a three?" I asked, intentionally giving him big doe eyes.

He waved to where that wet spot was now sitting at his dick. "I believe I said this was about you."

"It's not my fault you can't control yourself." I was trying to act all innocent, but he knew better.

"If you pumping and pleasuring me along the Claiming didn't earn your three, that certainly did." He bent down and kissed me.

"I love you, sir."

"I love you, too, Kotě." He kissed me quickly again and said, "I'll grab a towel and help you get cleaned up."

Nodding, I said, "I just need to catch my breath."

WE WERE WALKING INTO Whimsical in Lace, which had a beautiful, knee-length, white, long-sleeve lace dress hanging on a mannequin in the window. It had a solid skirt and a bodice with a sweetheart neckline, but with sheer lace to the collarbone and down the long sleeves.

"Grand Duchess!" the worker said, immediately dropping to one knee.

"You may rise," I said automatically, and Janreka and Rissa smiled. "While you will soon learn who stands with Princess Janreka and myself, you are hereby silenced from acknowledging publicly that any of us were here or the knowledge you will soon learn. Is that crystal clear?"

"Yes, Grand Duchess."

"We would like to try on the dress in the window for the Lady Clarissa," I said carefully.

"Lady?" Rissa said, blinking carefully.

Janreka laughed. "She is Grand Duchess. She can deem you whatever she wants. Not to mention, since you married Owen and he, well... He technically has a lord to his name. He just never uses it. LJ never uses her lady title either, does she?"

"Does Aiden have a lord title as well?"

Janreka chuckled. "Technically, yes, but since he is a Vernadali, that is a higher ranking... add on that he's the son of an Angels Blessed Vernadali… and yeah, titles get complicated."

"Which is why most of the Mathewsons hate using any of them."

I saw the ladies at the counter blink, then realization crossed their faces. The redhead closest to us curtsied and asked, "What size do you need, Lady Clarissa?"

A few minutes later, after the assistant talked to Rissa for a few moments, she led her to the back to get dressed.

"She is perfect for Owen, by the way," Janreka said next to me.

I smiled. "I'm glad Owen found someone. Perfect though, huh?"

"She challenges him and meets him step for step. LJ said that after just a few days of them being together, she knew Owen wasn't going to be looking at anyone else ever again."

I raised my eyebrows in surprise. "Really?"

"Apparently, they were at a bar outside of Klasdetine and women were hitting on him left and right. He completely ignored them, brushing them off. When Rissa asked about it, he just shrugged and pulled her closer to him." She was smiling brightly in the direction that Rissa was changing in.

"Owen? Are we talking about the same man?" I asked.

"I am." She looked at me and gave me a droll look. "You can't tell me you don't see that he looks at her just like Aiden looks at you."

I smiled because I had.

"I had a long talk with him one night when she had gone to bed early. She was exhausted, but I figured it was just because she had been so hurt. Now that we know about the babies, it was probably a combination of the two."

"Angels, that girl is lucky she didn't lose them. From what Jayden said, she was really beat up."

"She was." She took a deep breath. "Anyway, he said he knew she was the one within the first day of her being around. Apparently, after they got her out of that situation, they fought and fucked, fought and fucked. He said that she was the only one who could ever match his energy in both aspects. He wasn't going to let that woman go. So, when LJ gave them shit about just making it official, he knew she meant just to be together. Owen said there was half a thought of her not being at his side and it was a punch to the gut, so he asked her to marry him. She waited only a half moment before agreeing."

I smiled brightly and said softly, "He loves her."

Janreka smiled, and when Rissa walked out from behind the barrier and twirled with the biggest smile on her face, I knew we didn't have to look any further. "It's perfect. You look amazing in that dress, Rissa."

"It's the first one, though." She started playing with the soft lace layer on top with her fingers.

"Do you feel amazing in it? Do you like it?"

Rissa nodded.

"Send the bill to Georgina."

"What?" Rissa said, jerking her head in my direction. I smiled at her.

"Did you think I was going to let you pay for it? Hell, Mom is requiring you to get remarried to Owen. The least we can do is foot the bill." I rolled my eyes.

"But, Grand— But, Jess, I can't."

"You are a Mathewson. Get used to it. And when one of us tells you something is going to be the way it is, it really is a waste of your breath to fight it." Janreka chuckled next to me. "Welcome to the family."

She mocked some anger and raised a finger. "I may have to reconsider it now. Apparently, there is a whole lot that man of mine neglected to tell me about what exactly it means to be a Mathewson."

"It's not so bad, really." I shrugged. "It means you always have people at your back. It means that no matter what, you always have a support system."

"It doesn't hurt that you also have the Empress of the Underworld as your aunt, her daughter, the most powerful fire elemental in the dimension, and the Grand Duchess of Ashridge as your sisters." Janreka's voice was serious for a second as she added, "And I pity the idiot who fucks with our sister."

Rissa's eyes filled with tears. "Thank you." Then she flung her arms around us and held us tight. "I wish LJ had come with us, but I understand why she didn't. She told me all about what happened with Alex."

"When Alex died, she became a shell for a long time. It's really only been the last couple of years we've heard her laugh." Janreka's voice was sad, and there was a knot forming at the base of my throat again, so I cleared it and blinked the tears also threatening to form.

"I think Mom just got back, so the wedding could happen as early as tonight."

"You *think* your mom just got back?" Rissa asked carefully.

"Gatekeeper secrets, but basically, our power sources from the same place. I can feel its proximity." Janreka rolled her eyes.

Rissa blinked a few times, looking between us, and when her eyes held mine, I shrugged. "Gatekeeper secrets."

"Alright, let's go get me married to your brother... again." Then she was practically skipping off to the back room.

Yeah, they were going to be just fine. Meanwhile, Reka looked at me, asking, "Are you even going to look?"

"Am I going to have any say in what I wear?" My eyes crossed the room and landed on a particularly beautiful dress.

Reka noticed where my attention landed and walked over the dress hanging on the wall. "First, you are the Grand Duchess. Who is going to tell you what to wear to your own wedding? Second, this is beautiful, but you need a slit up your thigh, and we will have to add some of Ashridge's colors."

Standing next to her, I crossed my arms. I took a long breath through my nose before calling for the assistant that was helping us. I gave her some base information and asked them to provide a mock up with the changes that I wanted in three weeks.

"Of course, Grand Duchess." She was making notes and I could see her mind already spinning with ideas. "We will have it to you in three weeks."

She turned and headed for the counter just as Rissa came out, smiling brightly.

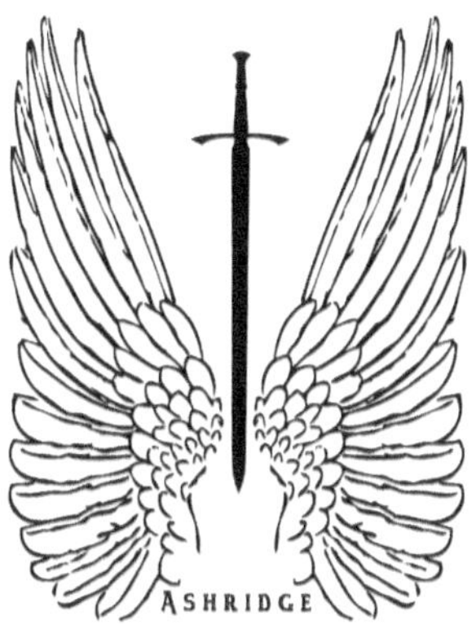

CHAPTER 48

JESSIKA

"HI, HONEY, I'M HOME!" I said, coming through the residence door. When I turned the corner into the living room, I came and sat down on Aiden's lap, giving him a kiss.

"Have fun?"

"We did." Turning to where Owen was sitting and pulling Rissa onto his lap, I said, "Owen, this poor girl needs a full brief of what it means to be a Mathewson. She actually thought she was going to have to pay for her own wedding dress."

I had tried to mock offense, but the rest of the family knew that I hadn't *really* meant it.

"You didn't?" Auntie Clarice muttered.

"What? It's our wedding. Of course, I would think I would have to pay for my own dress."

"Jess, you didn't pay for her dress, did you?" Owen asked.

"I did, and there is nothing you can do about it." When Owen narrowed his eyes at me, I lifted a finger. "Do I have to sic Mom on you?"

His eyes shifted to where she was sitting across from him. I could just see out of the corner of my eye how she lifted her eyebrows at him. I saw him wince and knew that she had given him a good mental tongue-lashing.

"First, she's your mom now, too, *sister*. Second, thank you for welcoming Clarissa into the family so easily." His eyes scanned the room and only then did I do the same. I had been so focused on returning to Aiden that I hadn't noticed the entire Mathewson clan was here. "Thank all of you for that."

I blinked and waved it off like it was nothing. "I, however, apparently owe everyone else an apology." I tried to stand, but Aiden had a tight grip on my hips. I turned, narrowed my eyes at him, and sighed. He could tell I was tired, and I really wanted a nap, but it wasn't going to be often we had the family here. I shifted in his lap and felt a groan along the Claiming and tried to hide the smirk.

"Since my betrothed here won't let me stand, I am sorry I didn't properly greet everyone. Welcome to Ashridge."

Uncle Logan bellowed with laughter. "Fuck that shit. Don't you dare get all regal."

"Loge," CJ said, and Logan just flipped him off.

I smiled and let all the sass come out. "Well, I know the travel isn't easy for an old man like you, Uncle Logan."

"Hey, Grammy and Pa traveled here until they were in their 90s. Amber and I are only in our 70s. Give us a bit of a break," Uncle Logan said.

"Never." I smiled at him and looked at Uncle Mickey. "Popa let you escape the confines of your office, huh?"

He ran his hand through the side of his beard and scratched his cheek but said, "I get to choose my assignments, and for some stupid reason, I chose this one, but yeah, it's one of the perks of having him be the grandfather to your nieces and nephews."

"I just don't understand. You aren't all Mathewson's by name though," Rissa mused. "And from what Owy said, Aunt Amber is a childhood friend of Mom and Dad?"

"The short version, Clairbear, is that Mom and Dad, as I told you, are from the Manusia. Mom accidentally teleported her and Dad here to Aunt Jean's house. Auntie Clarice was there along with Aunt Jean, Uncle Owen, and Aunt Lindy. Unfortunately, they died in the Keller War." Owen's voice tightened, and the sadness in the eyes of Auntie Clarice, Mom, and Dad was heartbreaking.

"I remember hearing about them in my studies," she muttered and looked to LJ, who just gave her a soft smile. She'd been really quiet since the decision for them to remarry was made. I didn't blame her. I couldn't imagine what she was feeling.

Janreka picked up where Owen left off, saying, "And when you fight in a war like that, you realize that the family you choose is more important than the one you were born in. Aunt Megan is proof of that."

I looked over to where Mom was and tears were in her eyes. "LJ and Owen are named after those aunts and that uncle."

Rissa looked at me and tilted her head to the side. "Noted."

A lot of heavy sat in the room so I asked, "Where are Popa, Jayden, and Ilris?"

Mom looked up at me and gave me a soft smile as she blinked the tears away. Even after all those years, it still hurt like hell. "They are meeting about Kaletta."

"Fuck." I looked at Aiden. "Why didn't you tell me? You know what he's planning to do."

Just then, the door opened, and the three of them came through it. I jumped out of Aiden's lap, somehow able to get his hands to release. I strode for the door and met them at where the entry hall opened up into the living room, hands on my hips.

"Jayden, I know you didn't just tell Julian your plans."

He raised an eyebrow at me and huffed a laugh. "I did, and he loves the idea. Thank you very much."

I glared at the little four-foot man standing there. Julian glared back at me and then smiled brightly. "I do, and it will take time, but it can be done." He scooted behind me, and I vaguely heard him introduce himself to Clarissa.

"Jessika, we are doing this. You know it's the best solution."

"It's *a* solution," I muttered, crossing my arms across my chest.

"We have time to sort this all out."

I pinched my lips together and stared him down for a long moment before Ilris wrapped his arms around Jayden's waist from behind and smiled as Jayden leaned back into his touch. "Not fair, Ilris."

"You aren't mad at Jade, Jessika. You are intimidated by the undertaking this is going to be." Then he kissed Jayden's cheek and said to the room, "By the way, the main council chamber is prepped and ready when you two are, Owen and Clarissa."

CHAPTER 49

AIDEN

WE SPENT A FEW more hours just exchanging stories, and then, finally, Janreka and Jess took Clarissa back to her and Owen's room to get ready. The decision had been made that the small ceremony would occur tonight, dinner would be in the main hall as a celebration, and then everyone could head home tomorrow.

Clarissa was beautiful, and I had to admit that even Owen cleaned up pretty well. As they sat at the head of the table for dinner, I couldn't help but notice how often Owen would lean over and tell her how beautiful she looked. The red in her cheeks gave her a beautiful glow, and I couldn't help but think about how Jess and I would share those same looks. Would gaze at each other with all the love and admiration and, ultimately, the respect the other deserved. Slowly, I stroked down the Claiming, looking at her with a small smile on my face. When I did, though, Jess did the *thing*, and I couldn't help but groan.

"What's wrong, Aiden?" Rissa asked.

Jess snorted, covering her mouth, and when I glared at her, she was trying desperately to keep from spitting water all over the place.

At this point, we had just about everyone looking at us.

"*Everything okay?*" Mom asked without saying a word.

"Everything is fine. Right, Jess?"

She finally forced herself to swallow her water and nodded. "Yeah, everything is fine."

"*You two aren't fooling me for one damn moment. What is going on?*" Mom pressed, and I felt Jess stiffen beside me.

Jess answered her by being non-direct-direct, "Mom, there are things we don't need to know about you and Dad's bedroom adventures. You don't need to know about ours."

There were a few snorts and a few murmurs of agreement around the table, and when I met Clarissa's gaze, I gave her an apologetic look. Smiling brightly, she chuckled. "Oh, I think I'm gonna like having you as a sister, Jess."

"My sister doesn't need to know about what we do in the bedroom, Clairbear." Owen's voice held a tone to it that I had used on Jess all too often. I groaned and felt when Jess recognized it as well. She tried to hide the chuckle, and I had to tug on the Claiming hard to get her to knock it off.

There was a nod from Mom, and the table resumed its individual conversations.

"I won't say anything to LJ because something tells me she doesn't want to know all about it, but who says you and I can't compare notes?" Jess whispered smoothly.

"Clairbear…"

I only saw the hand signal because I was sitting right next to her.

"It's okay, Owen. I'm sure the two of them have a lot more in common than you realize." My eyes flicked down to his hand, which was still resting on her leg in a *one*, tapping away.

He looked at me with wide eyes. I lifted the corner of my lip, and he let out a resigned sigh.

When I looked back at Clarissa, she was looking at Jess, smiling, with another blush to her cheeks.

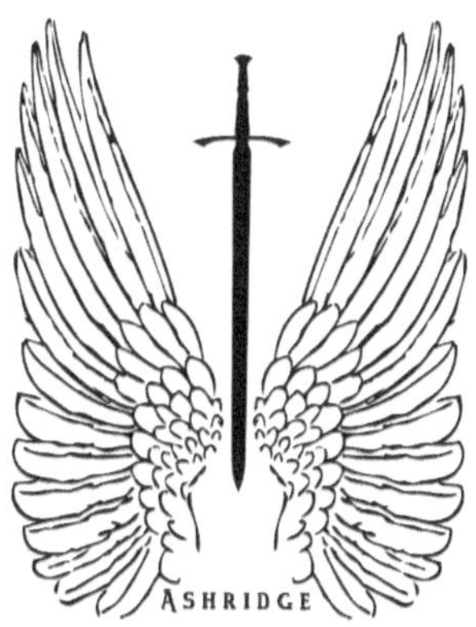

CHAPTER 50

JESSIKA

THREE MONTHS. IT HAD been three months since Aiden asked me to marry him and I told my council that the wedding needed to occur as soon as it could be properly set up. Now I was outside of the main hall, pacing, just like I had all those months ago for my coronation.

I tossed my hair back over my shoulder and took a deep breath. Janreka had pulled it half back and then attached royal-blue roses where it gathered, curling what hung loose so it cascaded down in gentle waves. So that my crown wouldn't distract from the back, I had chosen a simple small tiara with Ashridge peppered diamonds that fanned out, reminiscent of waves with small blue stones surrounding a heavily peppered diamond in the center. I cursed when the heel of the stilettos I was wearing caught on a small crack in the stone under my feet, causing me to step out of the stupid shoe. Kicking them off, the second one went flying into the main hall just as CJ opened the double doors. His hand flew up and caught it, and with a raised eyebrow, he asked, "Problem, Grand Duchess?"

"No." I huffed a laugh as he placed my shoe down on the ground next to the other, so that I could easily step back into them. They were simple white satin, with the stiletto heavily jeweled to match the ones in my dress.

"You look stunning," my future father-in-law said to me as he took my hand. The dress was a simple loose wraparound satin dress with spaghetti straps that had a heavily-jeweled underbodice with a sweetheart neckline, with a deep V, a long side slit down to the floor, and sparkling stones near my hip hanging to mid-thigh where I had strapped my mother's syth to my leg. If Mom couldn't be here in person, then I would proudly display her personal syth to have her here anyway I could.

Vernadali Keith was standing at the door, and CJ asked, "Ready to officially become a Mathewson?"

"Well, technically, he's becoming a Valenti." I smirked.

"Stupid technicalities." He chuckled, rolled his eyes, but then he turned and dropped to one knee, fist out.

"You may rise," I said loud enough that Vernadali Keith nodded to the orchestrators of this showboat event that I was making my way down the aisle in just a moment.

CJ's voice was loud and clear as he declared, "Grand Duchess, it is time."

I smiled brightly at him, reached up, and touched the rounded steel heart at my neck. "It *is* about damn time."

He raised his arm up, and I placed mine on top of his. He led me to the double open doors of the main hall, and when the vicar nodded, CJ and I took equal, measured steps toward Aiden. When I was halfway down the aisle, Aiden turned, and I felt the pride flow quick and fierce down the Claiming. I tugged on it, and he blinked to keep the tears at bay. By the time I reached him, one dropped heavy on his cheek.

"Thank you all for gathering here. Family, friends, diplomats, Ashridge Guard, and Vernadali," the vicar said loudly for everyone to hear. "Vernadali CJ, you may present the Grand Duchess to her betrothed."

CJ's voice rang out, "Vernadali Aiden Mathewson, may I present your betrothed."

Aiden's mouth opened, but then his throat bobbed as he took my hand and somehow found his voice to say, "Thank you, Vernadali CJ Mathewson. I accept her."

At those words, I felt the Claiming burn hot. When Aiden's eyes rimmed with purple, I smiled, knowing he felt it, too. There was more talking, but I couldn't focus on anything but the fact I was standing before Aiden, before all of Nalsar, and was finally able to marry him. He was my Vernadali, my mate, and now, finally, my husband.

AIDEN CHATWELL MATHEWSON, YOUR VOWS TO JESSICA PETRA ARE...

I TAKE YOU, JESSICA PETRA VALENTI, AS MY WIFE.

I PROMISE TO PROTECT YOU, TO ALWAYS PUT YOUR NEEDS BEFORE MY OWN.

I PROMISE TO LOVE, HONOR, RESPECT, CHERISH, AND BE WHATEVER YOU NEED.

I PROMISE TO ALWAYS ENCOURAGE YOU AND STAY WITH ONLY YOU UNTIL I VENTURE TO THE UNDERWORLD.

YOU ARE MY HEART, MY SOUL, MY CHARGE, BUT THE TITLE I CHERISH MOST OF ALL IS MY MATE.

YOU HAVE HAD MY HEART SINCE DAY ONE, SO IT IS EASY TO GIVE IT TO YOU.

I GIVE YOU MY HEART, FOREVER TO HOLD.

Jessika Petra Valenti, your vows to Aiden Chatwell are...

I TAKE YOU, AIDEN CHATWELL MATHEWSON, AS MY HUSBAND.

I PROMISE TO LOVE, HONOR, RESPECT, CHERISH, AND GIVE YOU WHAT PIECES OF ME I CAN.

AS GRAND DUCHESS, I SAY THE ASHRIDGE KINGDOM AND I ARE ONE IN THE SAME.

YOUR LOVE FOR ME IS LOVE FOR THE KINGDOM.

MY LOVE FOR YOU IS GIVEN FROM THE KINGDOM.

AS YOUR KOTĚ, YOUR MATE, MY LOVE FOR YOU IS NEVER-ENDING, NEVER WAVERING.

I PROMISE TO ALWAYS ENCOURAGE, LOVE, AND SUPPORT YOU.

I WILL ALWAYS BE YOURS.

I GIVE YOU MY HEART, FOREVER TO HOLD.

Then I reached up and placed my hand on the thin, silver heart at my throat, just as he did the same.

"Forever, Kotě," he whispered.

"Forever, Sir," I whispered back.

The vicar then asked the words that would change Aiden's status forever. "Do you, Grand Duchess Jessika Petra Valenti, wish to ascend your husband to the throne as Grand Duke?"

"By the power of the Kingdom of Ashridge, I command that Vernadali Aiden Mathewson be deemed Vernadali Grand Duke Aiden Chatwell Mathewson Valenti." My throat closed up because the purple in Aiden's eyes flashed brighter, the Claiming glowed, and Aiden's hand tightened in mine.

"Grand Duchess—"

"The Angels have deemed him my Vernadali. That will always be his first and foremost duty. He will, of course, have the Ashridge Kingdom in his view at all times. However, he is, at his core, a Vernadali. I will not take that from him."

My eyes met Aiden's again, and there were tears and pride in them.

"Is this true, Vernadali Aiden? Will you keep your duties as Grand Duke your priority in your daily life but always ensure the protection of the Grand Duchess?"

"It is as she said, and what the Grand Duchess wants, I will execute. I am at her command in all things relating to the Kingdom of Ashridge."

"Then it shall be done. I now present to you the Grand Duchess Jessika Petra Mathewson Valenti and Vernadali Grand Duke Aiden Chatwell Mathewson Valenti.

Chapter 51

Jayden

-3 YEARS LATER-

"We are almost there, Jayden," Ilris whispered in my ear.

"Yeah, we are." I leaned back in my chair in the office Jessika had provided for me in Ashridge City three years ago. It had given me the ability to not have to return to Kaletta. Sure, I had to go back often for short periods to handle business, but it wasn't home anymore. Soon, it wouldn't even be my territory.

Six months after I killed my father, Ilris and I wed in an intimate ceremony of just our friends and family here in Ashridge. It wasn't much bigger than Owen and Clarissa's, but it was all we needed. We wanted to share it with the people who had proven to be there for us. The Mathewson clan were many of those beings. Only, Jessika decided that in the announcement of our legal joining, I not only would be Grand Lord of Kaletta, but Ilris would be keeper and guardian of Kaletta.

For three years, we had been assimilating Kaletta's laws to be in line with Ashridge's. After thirteen months, questions arose about the multitude of laws being changed. It was then, I openly declared that Kaletta was being absorbed by the Ashridge Kingdom.

I was surprised at the agreement and lack of push back I had received from the council and people of Kaletta. Of course, there were those who were wholly against the law change regarding same sex marriage, but we had offered to assist in the relocation of their households to the sole territory in Savanora that still held those archaic laws. No one was forced to leave. As long as they didn't cause any problems, they could stay, but if they did, they would face the stiff punishments that had been put into place by my council.

Looking down at my desk, I signed one of the last documents I would as Grand Lord of Kaletta and put it in the formal file. In ten minutes, I would walk into the main hall to meet with Head Julian, Jessika, and our respective councils to sign the final documents.

Wailing came from the little room off to the side, and Ilris said, "I got her."

I sighed. "I just fed Annabella lunch not thirty minutes ago. Seriously thought she would nap until after the ceremony."

Standing, I went into the little playroom we had set up in the walk-in closet that was attached to the office. The toddler bed fit along the far wall but still gave her plenty of room to play. I didn't really need the room. We had the opportunity to adopt Annabella almost a year ago when her Mom died from a brain aneurysm. She had been one of the helpers here in the main halls of Ashridge, and Ilris and I had barely looked at each other before we both said we would adopt her. A month later, we were signing the papers and had a daughter.

Sitting up, she wiped at her big brown eyes and reached for Ilris. "Poppa."

"Hi, Angel. Why are we crying? Daddy said he put you down for your nap?"

She shook her head, her dark hair longer than either of us had expected and falling in cute little ringlet curls. At a year and three months old, she was the most adorable thing in the world. About the only thing we knew was that she was born to a woman in Kaletta, but the father's identity and race were unknown. We were told that she started teething at only three months, and those canines were sharp. We suspected she was at least part of one of the shifter races from the Krawkinal dimension, but we just hadn't gotten around to having her tested to verify anything. She was our sweet little Annabella. If she were a shifter, she wouldn't be any different from any other kid, except for the canines, until she was about eight or nine. Then she would likely start developing some of those emotional traits, and we would have to be on the lookout for any shifting starting.

Her big brown eyes swung to look at me in the doorway, and she reached her little hands out, opening and closing them quickly. Ilris huffed a laugh. "I'm always second to Daddy, aren't I, princess?"

"No, Poppa. I wuv Poppa."

"I know, princess." He kissed the top of her head, and she started giggling as he tickled her sides.

Laughing, I said, "Oh, sure, just rile her all up before you hand her off to me."

She practically jumped into my arms, and I hugged her tight. There was a knock on the door, and Ilris went to answer it. "We will be right there."

"Well, princess, since you are wide awake, can you promise to be good for a few minutes? Daddy and Poppa need to sign some very important paperwork with Popa Julian."

"Aungis and ugles, too?"

"Yes, some of them will be there, too." I was surprised at how quickly she was learning to talk. It just lent more credence to her having shifter blood. Those kids were wicked smart, aged quickly, and she was hitting the markers that other shifters were at this age. Not to mention the fact that she could already form sentences and communicate so well.

I set her down, and she latched onto my finger. She hated being carried and wanted to walk whenever possible. Ilris came over and took her other hand as we made our way out of the office. I turned back to look at it again and sighed. This was it. I wouldn't be leaving this office as Grand Lord ever again. I would return as just Lord and keeper of the localized territory of Kaletta.

"It's going to be okay, Jade," Ilris said quietly as we made our way to the main hall.

When we walked in, Owen was there wrangling Ailana, his two-and-a-half-year-old daughter, and his wife, Rissa, threw her hand out to pull their son, Beckett, from off of the throne, setting him down next to her. He narrowed his eyes at her and huffed. Rissa was pregnant again and would deliver at any moment. It was another girl, who they were going to name Jessika Megan Mathewson.

Jessika and Aiden were standing with Popa Julian, and when Annabella saw Julian, she tried to pull us over to him. She loved the man, and I couldn't thank him enough for all the help that he had been the last few years.

He saw us about the time we got halfway there. "Annabella," he shouted at her and bent down, opening his arms. She bolted for him without a second thought. Strong and sturdy, she'd been sure in her walking, but running, she still tripped on occasion. Ilris and I looked at each other, and I gulped. Ilris wrapped an arm around my waist, kissed my temple, and said, "Well, guess she's full-on running now."

Annabella landed in Julian's arms, and he picked her up, swinging her around in circles. High-pitched giggles filled the hall, and I looked to where Jessika and Aiden were standing. I raised an eyebrow at them, and they just shook their heads and smiled. I had asked if they were going to have kids, and they told us they would but wanted to get

Kaletta sorted before moving forward on any children. In the meantime, they loved being an aunt and uncle.

"Grammy!" Beckett screamed at the same time that Ailana hollered, "Pa!" I turned to see Megan and CJ walking through the door, catching the two toddlers and hugging them tight.

Jessika stood next to me now and muttered, "Well, that's everyone except for Auntie Clarice, but she got tied up and won't be able to make it. The plan is to go down to Therth in a couple months, though." Her eyes sparkled with mischief.

"What is it, Jessika?"

"Talk to Janreka lately?" I shook my head. "She's got a girlfriend. Pretty serious too from the looks of it. Been together for about a year."

"No way! A year?" I shook my head in disbelief. "I spoke to her about six months ago, and again just a month ago. Had a LightCall so she could even meet Annabella, and then have continued to talk to her many times since. She didn't mention a damn thing. That twerp. I'm so going to—"

"Do what, Jade?"

I smirked, and as I turned to face Janreka, I said, "Kick your ass for not telling me about your girl."

Janreka blushed, and then she glared at Jessika, who shrugged and uttered, "What? You should have told him. He is nothing but happy for you. Underworld's being."

"Yeah, yeah, yeah." She waved us both off and went to love on her nieces and nephews. When she reached Julian and Annabella, Annabella smiled brightly at her. It was the first time they had met in person, but in the arms of her Popa Julian, she was fearless.

They made their way back over to us, and Julian said, "We should get this done so we can eat. I'm starving."

Once the kids were settled and the documents lay before us, I swallowed. On either side of the table, our councils stood there. I looked down the line of Kaletta council members and saw no hesitation or resentment for what I was about to do. I took a long deep breath in through my nose as Julian said, "Grand Duchess. Grand Lord. It is my understanding that you wish to join your territories with the details so itemized on this document. If that is still your agreement, you simply need to sign and the Kaletta territory will become part of the Ashridge Kingdom."

"Are you sure about this, Jayden? I know it's what we've been working toward for three years, but once this signature is on there, it's done," Jessika asked one final time.

"Grand Duchess, I am at your command. The territory of Kaletta is yours." I took the pen from Julian's hand and signed the document, giving over the territory.

"Well, Underworld. I was really hoping that you would back out at the last second." Her gaze held mine as she signed the document.

Julian placed his seal beneath our signatures, making it official. Jess let out a heavy sigh and stood up straight, Aiden at her side. I felt Ilris' hand on the small of my back as Julian's hand waved in the air and clenched into a fist, and the document vanished from the table.

"Long live the Kingdom of Ashridge!" The sounds and voices echoed through the hall from our councils and our family.

I smiled at her. "Long live the Kingdom of Ashridge."

She scoffed. "You may rise and are dismissed." Once everyone left, she crossed her arms over her chest and asked, "Alright, Lord and keeper of the Territory of Kaletta, what do you want to do first?"

"Well, we should feed Julian. He said he was hungry."

Julian chuckled. "Don't have to be a jerk now."

Aiden's arm circled Jessika's waist, and he pulled her close to him, kissing her brow. I saw the weight that was etching itself on her face. She just doubled her responsibilities, and that was my doing.

"Jessika, you know I'm still here to help. I may not be your husband and Duke of Ashridge, thank the gods, but I'm not just giving ultimate control of the Kaletta territory to Ashridge and walking away."

Her gaze found mine, and she sighed as Ilris' hand sat on my back. His thumb moved against my spine and I took a deep breath.

"I know that, Jayden. It's just–"

"A lot," the three of us said in unison. Head Julian chuckled.

"The four of us will handle it." Ilris smiled at Jessika, and she gave him a warm one back.

Suddenly, there was a loud crash across the room, and our eyes found Beckett and Annabella looking at each other wide-eyed. They both turned to the four of us and shouted, "Didn't do it!"

Aiden's chuckle next to us made me smile. "Life won't be boring."

THE END

About the Author

Kimberly M. Ringer lives in Santa Cruz, California with her husband, little human, and two furballs, Wall-E (a Jack Russell mix) and Pippin (a Pomeranian Terrier mix). When she isn't writing, she is reading, playing with the dogs, playing video games or down at the beach. She's a bit geeky and nerdy, so sci-fi references and other things going on in the science world will often end up in her stories.

Contact Kimberly M. Ringer:
  www.kimberlymringer.com
  Instagram: @kimberlymringer

F a c e b o o k :
https://www.facebook.com/kimberlymringer

Sign up for my newsletter on my website and receive
freebies, coupon codes, and stay up to date on all things
Kimberly M. Ringer and K.M. Ringer
Newsletter Signup

Books Also By Kimberly M. Ringer

The Ashstrike Sanctorum Series

The Astral's Bonded

The Exorci's Touch

The Kismot's Undesirable (July 2023)
The Therugi's Shiver (October 2023)

The Five Angels Trilogy

The Five Angels

The Ash'bani

The Helena Crystal
A Five Angels Novel

Duchess' Crown

Duchess' Throne

Other Books

Ashes and Flame

Weekend Series by K.M. Ringer

Weekend with Rylie

Weekend with Malcom

www.ingramcontent.com/pod-product-compliance
Lightning Source LLC
Chambersburg PA
CBHW031300210726
48287CB00005B/1362